By K.M. Davidson

THE SIRIANS SERIES
Darkness Comes Again
Fate Demands Sacrifice
Death Raises Gods

THE ANDROMEDANS DUOLOGY
Sundered Heavens

Soul, Sun & Stars: A Sirians Series Novella
Balance Must Remain: A Sirians Series Prequel

THE
ANDROMEDANS
DUOLOGY

BOOK I

SUNDERED HEAVENS

K.M.
DAVIDSON

Cover Design by Selkkie Designs
Chapter Headings, Scene & Part Breaks Illustrated by Marta Riva
Edited by Hannah (April Editorial)
Proofread by Samantha (Radiant Editorial)

EXTRA INFORMATION

CONTENT WARNINGS

I am an advocate of mental health rep, which means *your* mental health is important to me. This book contains mature themes and content that may not be suitable for all readers. This includes on-page violence, graphic imagery, and emotional and physical abuse. There are also challenging topics discussed such as infertility, infant loss, and suicidal ideation. For a full list of trigger warnings, please visit **kmdavidson.com/trigger-warnings**.

SPOTIFY PLAYLIST

If you enjoy listening to the songs that inspired the book and played while I wrote, check it out below:

If you do not have a Spotify, you can find the list of songs at **kmdavidson.com/extras**.

The Andromedans Reference Guide
I was told this was a necessity, so here you go.

The Lyrans / Gods & Goddesses

Dola (doe-luh)
Goddess of Fate

Danica (dan-eh-kuh)
"The Morning Star", Goddess of
Nature & Energy of All Things

Rod (road)
God of Matter & Morality

Irena (eye-reen-uh)
Goddess of War & Peace

Valeria (vuh-lair-ee-uh)
Goddess of Healing & Disease

Morana (more-ah-nuh)
Goddess of Life & Death

Gallus (gael-es)
"The Evening Star", God of the
Aether & Stars

Nen (nehn)
God of the Sea

Zephyr (zef-fur)
God of the Hunt & Wild
Animals

Asteria (uh-stare-ee-uh)
"The Brightest Star", Goddess of
Sirians

The Andromedans / Demi-Gods

Sybil (si-bull)
Lemurian-House of Echidna,
Drakon

Garuda (guh-roo-duh)
Lemurian-House of Nemea, Gryp

Bodhi (bow-dee)
Enhanced Human

Endora (en-door-uh)
Sirian, Necromancy

Taranis Beaumont (tuh-ran-ehs)
Sirian, Lightning Manipulation

Caine (cayne)
Lemurian-House of Echidna,
Drakon

Marin (mare-in)
Lemurian-House of Argo, Ketea

~~Enki~~ (en-kee)
Former Enhanced Human

Dionne Basu (dee-own)
Sirian, Heat Manipulation

Phoebe Abbot (fee-bee)
Sirian, Gravitational Energy
Manipulation

The Andromedans Reference Guide

Other Characters of Note

Odo Hesper (oh-doe)
Head Elder of the Asterian Academy

Dustin Wesly-Abbot (duhs-tin)
King of Etherea, Phoebe's husband

Quintin "Quin" Carraphim (kwin-tin)
Crown Prince of Eldamain

Gavril "Gav" Farris (gahv-rill)
Lieutenant General, Piers's Partner

Savaric Basu (sahv-rick)
King of Riddling, Descendant of Dionne

Erika Hesper (air-eh-kuh)
Healer Elder of the Asterian Academy

Orwell "Wells" Carraphim (or-well)
Prince of Eldamain, The Spare Heir

Piers Carraphim (peerse)
Prince of Eldamain, Lieutenant General

Orvyn Carraphim (ore-vin)
King of Eldamain

~~Ruelle Carraphim~~ (roo-el)
Wells's Deceased Wife

Lemurian Houses

House of Echidna
Drakon (drah-kin) / dragon
Thirío (tih-ree-oh) / behemoth

House of Argo
Nereids (ne-reid) / mermaid
Ketea (keh-tay-uh) / sea monster

House of Nemea
Lycan (lie-kin) / werewolf
Gryp (grip) / gryphon
Hippgryph (hip-poe-grihff) / hippogriff

Sirians
Energy / kinetic energy manipulation
Aether / dark energy/matter manipulation

Places of Note

Eldamain - el-duh-main
Celestia - suh-less-tee-uh
Riddling - rid-dling
Allanis - uh-lahn-ihs

Pizi - pee-zee
Sylvan - sill-vin
Teslin - tess-lyn
Aveesh - uh-veesh

Etherea - eh-theer-ee-uh
Eonia - ee-own-ee-uh
Riddling - rid-dling
Thalassa - thuh-la-suh

MAP OF AVEESH

THE MAIN
CONTINENT

MANA

AGGELOS PALACE

SCORPIO PALACE
THE BLACK
LAKE
THE BLACK
AVALANCHES

HERIDY

THE RED
RAVEN

GHITA

CERELIA
ALLANIS

ORION'S
LAKE

ELDAMAIN

ARMITAGE
BADORA

SAROS

TESLIN
RIAN

LANGEN

ELVION

SAROS
TOWER

SADO

WEBSTONE
FORT

CANDOR

THE RAVEN'S
WOOD
SYLVAN

LOLIS

DEKALB

ETHEREA

ERYPHUS

CHIMBRIDGE

RIGEL'S KEEP

TO THE EASTERN
CONTINENTS

THE NORTHERN MOUNTAINS

KILGATE

CASTLE ASHE

ARGAN WOOD

CINDERTON

ASHLAND

ARGA

SOUTHERN WOODS

THE NORTHERN PIZI

THALASSA

GLANIA

OSIRIA

AKROTIRI

THE ASTERIAN ACADEMY

CELESTIA

KRISHNA CASTLE

RIDDLING

SITARA

YAMALOKA PRISON

KABAL

JAGAT

TEJA

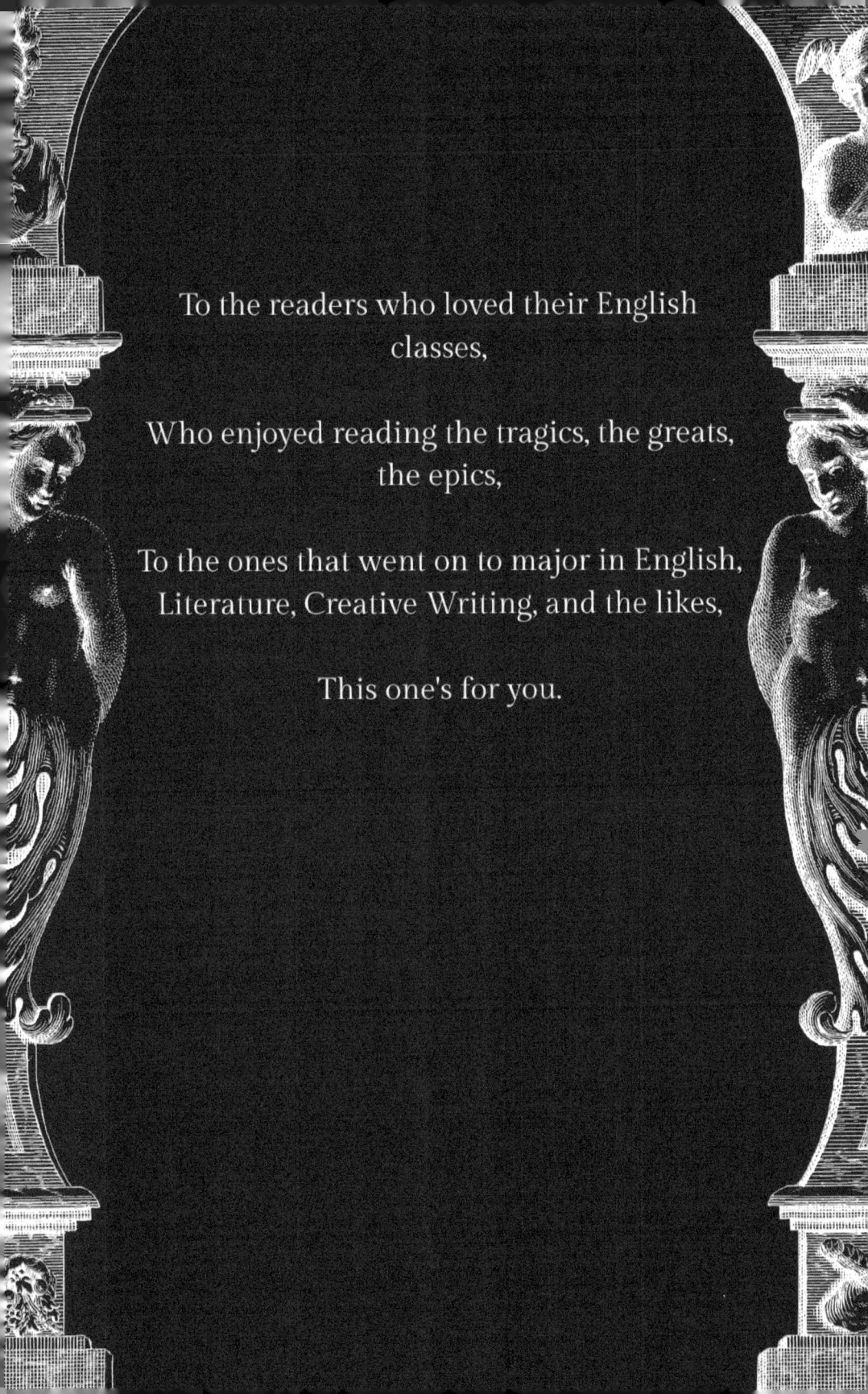

To the readers who loved their English
classes,

Who enjoyed reading the tragics, the greats,
the epics,

To the ones that went on to major in English,
Literature, Creative Writing, and the likes,

This one's for you.

PROLOGUE

THE NINE LYRANS & THE BRIGHTEST STAR

O nce upon a time, there lived a Realm beyond our known Universe where Beings of immense power could manipulate the laws from which we know. They utilized these powers to create or destroy worlds, ascend or topple others, or a combination of the four.

They were called the Lyrans, but to mortals such as us, we are far better off calling them Gods.

These Gods had two Paths they could follow: remain in their Realm to teach the following generations or voyage into the Universe to find their own world in which they could build, interfere, and rule.

Like their ancestors and fellow Gods before, one God and Goddess yearned to discover, to find meaning and purpose in their existence. We will call them the Morning and Evening Star.

They desired a world where its Beings needed guidance, a world that lived wildly in its early development.

But the Morning and Evening Star did not wish to venture alone. They knew it was dangerous to travel amongst the Universe on their own. Who knew how long it would take them to find the perfect world? It could take eons, and they risked succumbing to their powers like the Fractured.

So they gathered other Gods and Goddesses, those they felt a kinship to, who would benefit their mission and contribute to the new world they hoped to find.

They chose seven other Gods and Goddesses they trusted:

The *Goddess of Fate*, who could reach her mind into the very fabric of the Universe, conversing with the element from which her namesake came: Fate.

The *Goddess of Life and Death*, who could touch the stars and turn them into living, breathing Beings, who could also take the breath from those stars and do with them as she pleased: set them free, send them to another plane, or harbor them for herself.

The *God of Matter and Morality*, who could alter the terrain of any given planet to better sustain life, who could also create a form from matter the Goddess of Life and Death could place a star within.

The *God of the Sea*, who could manipulate not just the liquid of the land but the liquid of the body.

The *Goddess of War and Peace*, two cyclic but interdependent concepts for which she could manipulate the Beings of any Realm by infiltrating the mind.

The *Goddess of Healing and Disease*, who found herself in a similar dynamic as the Goddess of Life and Death with her ability to restore or deteriorate.

Lastly, the youngest of the Gods, the *God of Wild Animals*, who could morph into any animal that existed in the Realm to which they traveled.

And so, the Nine Lyrans set off to the Universe in search of a world ripe for the taking. They traveled through portals between worlds and Realms, searching for one that called to them—one which the Talons of Fate responded strongest to.

They did not know how much time passed; they did not bring a God or Goddess who spoke with such a force. When they finally stumbled into a quiet, small Realm with a strange pocket already existing within, the Talons of Fate illuminated, and the Goddess of Fate declared their

Path stopped here without further explanation.

The Nine claimed the pocket as their home, using their combined strengths to build abodes for conducting business and ruling the planet shared with this Realm. They discussed how they wanted to create and rule, determining who would be responsible for the various Beings.

The Gods and Goddesses found the world had humans such as you and me, Beings for which they previously heard stories amongst their fellow Lyrans. Humans seemed to appear across multiple Realms, simple creatures with no real power other than a steadfast will to survive.

This world also housed animals of varying degrees, some with soft, furred coats and others with scaled, slick skin. The God of Wild Animals was thrilled to have creatures already inhabiting this world, and he claimed them as his own.

The God of Matter and Morality was relieved humans already existed on this plane because it meant there was no need to create a new type of Being, and he could institute himself as their God.

So the Gods and Goddesses observed for some time, occasionally interfering with a shift in the land to help the mortals travel faster or protect them from different creatures. The Goddess of Life and Death helped the mortals produce faster, giving life to their offspring and granting their dead peace in the Heavens.

But the Nine were disappointed when the mortals continued to struggle against creatures and various diseases running rampant through their colonies. While the Goddess of Healing and Disease wanted to assist them, one thing plagued the Lyrans that limited her interference; one thing kept their powers in check.

Using too much of their gifts in a short period of time would Fracture them, their powers taking over their minds and forms.

So the Nine came together to find a way to assist the mortals and advance their existence without sacrificing their sanity.

The Morning and Evening Star smiled at one another, for they had planned this all along.

Now, friends, we have not discussed the powers the Morning and Evening Star could wield, for they were unimportant until we found ourselves in this part of the tale.

You see, the Morning Star was formally known as the *Goddess of Nature and Energy*. She had the ability to manipulate the Energy of the very molecules that constructed the fabric of the Universe.

The Evening Star was her counterpart, the *God of the Aether and Stars*. While the Morning Star manipulated the Energy within all things, the Evening Star manipulated the dark space between those molecules: Aether. What separated him from the Goddess of Life and Death was that while she could give stars life, he wielded the matter from which they produced their heat: starfire.

So when the time came for the Morning and Evening Star to present their secret scheme, they came forward with a solution to help the mortals that piqued the interest of the other Gods and Goddesses.

What if they created Beings that had powers like them?

At first, some were confused. While the Nine could reproduce with each other to birth more Lyrans, it was not a simple endeavor. Some thought it nearly impossible; it only occurred once every thousands of years.

The Morning and Evening Star proposed that the God of Matter and Morality construct the forms for the new Beings, and the Goddess of Life and Death could place stars within these forms. They would build their bodies like humans so current inhabitants would not be fearful of them. The difference would be their ability to withstand the powers granted to them.

When the Gods asked which powers they would inherit, it was a simple answer for the Morning and Evening Star.

Some would be granted the ability to wield the Energy, while others could wield the Aether—to help defend the humans effectively.

The Gods and Goddesses wondered if the Morning and Evening Star would be wary of these Beings. What if they were too powerful with the

4

same gifts as the two Lyrans?

But the Morning and Evening Star explained it would be but a drop in each Being compared to the magnitude they themselves wielded.

With much excitement, the Gods and Goddesses were in unanimous agreement. They created the new Beings and called them Sirians.

The humans, Sirians, and creatures cohabited this plane in a balanced, beautiful existence, so much so that it inspired the name the Nine gave their pocket world.

Eonia, or *balance* in the language of their home world.

And so the Nine began to play amongst their people. They fell in love with them, mated with them, and graced their Beings with their presence. They helped name the world—*Aveesh*—and created new languages to see how the Beings would interact.

But their Realm of balance would soon teeter. The Goddess of Healing and Disease had favored a human child, and when the girl was attacked by one of the creatures—a drakon—she pleaded with her lover, the Goddess of Life and Death. The two conspired together to save the girl, placing the dying child's soul into the very drakon that attacked her.

When this occurred, the child could then shift between forms—the mortal form or the drakon. The God of Wild Animals and the God of the Sea saw what had been done, and they became greedy.

They wanted *all* creatures to shift to mortal forms, but the Goddess of Life and Death warned them of the consequences. These creatures' souls would be merged with the stars she plucked from the sky. The only way she was able to do it previously was because the child and drakon had both been dying. After the drakon's soul transcended and before the girl's soul vanished, the Goddess of Life and Death grabbed and placed it into the drakon that had recently passed.

Although the creature met its demise by the hands of the Goddess of Healing and Disease, none had seen the act.

The two Gods were outraged and threatened the Goddess of Life and Death. They assured her that if she did not merge the souls, they would kill enough humans for her to place into these creatures.

So the Goddess of Life and Death relented, and the Lemurians were born from the first act of coercion amongst the Gods: Beings that shifted from creature to mortal forms.

Too soon after, though, the Morning Star became with child from mating with the Evening Star.

It was the first Lyran to be born in thousands of years, and the first they knew of outside their home Realm.

Envy, greed, and suppressed wrath plagued the other Gods and Goddesses. There were those who wanted Lyran children of their own and did not understand why they could not be granted this gift. Others desired a mate of their kind, both so they could attempt to create another Lyran child but also because they desired what the Morning and Evening Star always had. Then there were those who saw this for what it truly was...

A new Lyran with new powers, and new powers meant another to rule beside them.

Forthwith, the Nine became Ten.

And so, dear friends, it did not take much for a world built on balance to suddenly find itself divided, the Gods never unanimously voting on what should be done on the plane they ruled. They swayed and tottered from one side to the next, some voices louder than others, some more timid, but nonetheless, the balance was in jeopardy.

Until one day—an ordinary day—Fate doled out a prophecy to one of its messengers.

One that would officially sunder the Heavens in two.

PART I

"FOR SO I CREATED THEM
FREE, AND FREE THEY
MUST REMAIN."

JOHN MILTON, *PARADISE LOST*

CHAPTER 1

ASTERIA

Asteria walked a steady path through the garden, following the blooming hedges that reached her thighs. The sun beat down from above, warming her skin to a calming degree.

She clasped her hands behind her back, watching over the tip of her nose as Healers picked various herbs and plants from the ground, stacking them onto their wooden carts. With every snip, she caught a faint whiff of their earthy scents twisting through the air, melding with the natural citrus aroma of the island.

She continued her leisurely journey as she dragged her gaze back before her, startling in her steps, rocks skittering at her feet. She sighed, her breath heavy with irritation as her arms fell limp at her sides.

Asteria felt the Energy of the Sirian to her right before the woman timidly chirped, "My Lady?"

She slowly hauled her gaze to the woman with an arched eyebrow, pointing at the statue erected in the middle of the gardens, the pure white marble glistening in the sunlight.

"Do tell," Asteria began, cocking her head toward the statue, "what in the Heavens is this?"

The woman started, alarmed by Asteria's reaction to the *identical* statue of her. The woman sputtered as she explained, "My Lady... the Elders commissioned—well, it was commissioned by the request of... Are you offended, Lady Asteria?"

She bristled at that forsaken title, her neck tensing. She inhaled through her nose, offering a small, tight grin that caused the Healer to cringe. Asteria walked closer to the base of the statue. She stared warily at the stone version of herself, the figure modeled uncomfortably so.

The marble wrapped in what impressively resembled a thin cloth for a dress that hugged the frame, hair falling to the sculpted waist. One hand stretched to the sky, the other toward the right. Asteria followed where the head was positioned, a roguish grin quirked up at the corner of the statue's lips.

At least they managed to accurately represent her sentiment about the world.

"I wouldn't dare use *offended* as the term, Healer," Asteria grumbled. She twisted to face the woman, crossing her arms over her chest and cocking her hip. "I don't wish to be made an idol amongst you. Think of me as Headmistress rather than your Goddess, *please*. I feel as though every decade I must reiterate this concept when a new Council of Elders is elected."

"From my understanding, it was the students graduating this next term who requested the monument, my Lady," the Sirian woman explained, stepping closer to Asteria as she clung to her basket of herbs.

A quick sweep of her frantic Energy told Asteria this Healer was a new student. She couldn't fault her for her timidness or let the formality get under her skin.

"*Monument*," Asteria repeated slowly, her lip curling. The Healer's eyes pulsed wide.

"Yes, my Lady." The Healer *curtsied*, which only soured Asteria's mood further. "I wish I could be of further assistance on how this statue came to be, but I'm afraid that is the extent of my knowledge, my—"

Asteria interjected with an unintelligible sound, a cross between a hum and a croak. "That formal title is unnecessary with me, especially here at the Asterian Academy. You can simply call me Asteria."

"Yes, my—" Asteria leveled the woman with a finger, and the tension in both of their shoulders eased when the woman slapped a hand over her mouth.

Asteria caught the Healer's cheeks lifting and the light in her eye glistening. Even the Energy within her settled.

"Thank you." Asteria sighed, hitching one hand on her hip, the other dismissing the woman with a wave. "You can return to your chores. I will take this"—she directed her gaze back to the statue, her nostrils flaring—"up with Odo and Erika."

The Healer dipped her head instead of curtsying, twisting on her heel and scurrying toward the other Sirians gathered in a semi-circle around the cart they'd been collecting plants on.

Asteria glanced at the statue one last time, rolling her eyes before strutting toward the Elders' studies.

Her boots clicked against the beige cobblestone, echoing around her as she walked the deserted hallways since various meetings and classes were in session within the Academy.

It was enough that the school was named after her, which she didn't complain about too often. She was the one to establish an academy specifically for Sirians to hone their powers and utilize them in various forms.

Whether they followed a military, healing, or political path, every Sirian was granted free education and training by the most talented teachers and Elders this plane could offer, including herself. She even bargained with the royal families, requiring them to send their Sirian children—should they have any—to be trained with their peers.

All she asked was to be Headmistress, not their Goddess—even if she was *technically* that.

Being the youngest Goddess of the Lyrans by the Heavens knew how many millennia, Asteria never felt like she belonged with them. She connected more with the demi-gods and her demi-god siblings—the Andromedans—than she ever did the Lyrans. She was more at home on Aveesh than within Eonia.

Eonia was roughly the size of Celestia, an anomaly created by the Universe when this Realm was formed. It was beautiful and ethereal, merely a fraction of the size of Aveesh. The skies were a deep indigo, splattered with stars of white, red, and blue, swirls of red and gold hugging the edges of the Realm like clouds.

There was nothing *wrong* with Eonia, per se. Asteria just didn't like the majority of those who inhabited it. In the last century or so, she only visited when absolutely necessary.

While it angered her mother to no end, she could care less.

Aveesh was home, but especially Celestia and the Academy.

Asteria burst through Odo Hesper's study, startling both him and his wife, one of the Healer Elders, Erika.

"Good Heavens," Odo gasped, the thick black cloud swirling in his hand and black glow of the six-pointed star signaling his Sirian status on his forehead winking out of existence. "I thought something was wrong."

"Who would be barging into your study that you would blast from existence?" Asteria asked, tilting her head as she flicked her hand, a faint gold light emanating as the door softly clicked shut behind her.

"Odo and Isadore are in something of a feud at the moment." Erika sighed, and Asteria narrowed her eyes as her gaze bounced between the couple.

"A feud over what?" Asteria walked over to the open, arched window on the wall beside Odo's desk. It overlooked the entire southern side of the island, one of Asteria's favorite views from the Academy's grand stone structure.

There were few buildings on this side of the island, lush, tall grass extending toward the shore where it stopped at the edge of a pebbled beach. Trees with large, fanned branches and leaves scattered sporadically, twitching with the light breeze. Beyond that was a clear view of the crystal blue sea.

Odo's Aether swirled restlessly within him as he remained silent, apparently foregoing any elaboration. Asteria took the opportunity to shut her eyes against the thick, humid breeze that drew in the salt of the ocean.

"Oh, for Heaven's sake, Odo," Erika hissed, a light *thunk* echoing around them. Asteria looked over her shoulder. "They are in the midst of a prank war."

Asteria threw a dull expression Odo's way, pursing her lips. "Are you being serious?"

"I can neither confirm nor deny," was all the male said as he carefully lowered to his seat behind his desk.

Asteria pressed her lips together as she leaned against the metal railing on the window.

A prank war explained the caution he exuded as the frantic Aether continued swirling through his veins despite the lack of any real threat around them.

She knew lowering the required minimum age for the Elders would pose potential conflicts. Still, she didn't anticipate the males kicking up a silly war amongst themselves, playing games with one another.

Asteria supposed the situation could be far worse, like a serious rivalry. She would take the lighthearted fun over the thick, petty tension that hung over the last Council of Elders.

Which reminded her of why she came storming into Odo's office in the first place.

"Why was there an erotic statue of me placed in the gardens?" Asteria blurted, and Odo spat the tea he was sipping across the parchment littered on his desk.

She contained the smirk that ticked at the corner of her lips, mimicking the aforementioned statue.

"Erotic?" Erika frowned, her head jerking back. "But you are clothed…" She trailed off, dragging her gaze to her husband. "She *is* clothed, isn't she?"

"Of course she's clothed," Odo managed around his coughs, dabbing the parchment on his desk with a handkerchief. He turned his gaze up to Asteria, scowling. "What in the Heavens do you mean *erotic?*"

The way he spoke the word, rolling it around his mouth like a foreign language, almost had a full grin breaking Asteria's impassive exterior. It amazed her how tame the Beings of this plane had become over the last few hundred years.

She remembered the vulgarity they once interacted with from her childhood. It gradually evolved into more regality as the countries continued to build their trade and travel across the seas to one another. There were even *classes* amongst the people outside of royals, which Asteria was not exactly fond of. Some were forced to live on the streets with their children because of it.

"The fabric forms to every crevice, dip, and *nip* of my body." She emphasized that last word with a stiff swing of her arm over the front of her dress, particularly over her breasts. "I don't believe I own a single dress resembling the one the statue is donned with, and I hope to the Heavens my clothes don't reveal my—"

"For Heaven's sake, Asteria," Odo mumbled, rubbing his fingertips across his forehead around his Mark, which was already sun-kissed from the late summer sun's rays.

"It is symbolic of your etherealness," Erika stated as if it were as simple as the sky being blue. "It was not meant to be offensive."

"The state of my undress is not even my greatest concern." Asteria shook her head in disappointment, and Odo glared at her. "It's the fact that the statue even exists! I have repeatedly expressed my feelings about my treatment as a Goddess. I don't wish to be worshipped like my fellow Lyrans. The school bears my name, and that is enough for me. If there are to be statues of me scattered about the school, then it will not be long before the students are throwing themselves at my feet."

"Asteria," Odo began, rising from his chair and walking across the room to his wall of tomes stacked neatly on the shelves. He perused the spines as he spoke, "The statue is not meant to be an idol for the Sirians to worship. If that were the case, we would erect one within the temple atop the mountain."

Asteria suppressed a growl at the reminder of the ridiculous temple the other Lyrans *demanded* she force the Sirians to build. They each had a statue depicting their mortal forms, and the students provided offerings based on their specialty and descendancy of their home country.

Her mother chastised her for initially wanting to name the school the *Sirian* Academy. It made the most sense to Asteria that a school *for Sirians* would be called that. Her mother believed the Academy should be a shrine or temple for Asteria, and she wanted none of that. When she agreed to the name *Asterian Academy*, she was still forced to create a temple for the other Lyrans.

Even though *she* was supposed to be the Goddess of Sirians. The rest had their own passions.

Odo offered her an open tome, and she accepted with a scowl. Once it lay in her hand at arm's length, he tapped a page, then circled an image of a statue.

"Statues have been used on Aveesh to honor people who have contributed great things to this world," Odo explained, walking back to where his wife perched on the edge of his desk. He gently laid his hand on her shoulder before sitting in the chair again. "There is a statue for the First King at Aggelos Palace in Eldamain, busts of former kings and queens in the halls of many other kingdoms, favored patrons of your fellow Lyrans depicted in libraries and temples where they were prophets—"

"I am flattered," Asteria interrupted, although she paired the phrase with a pained grin. "Unfortunately, I *am* still a Goddess, and Sirians aren't ignorant despite my best efforts to appear a woman of the people. They will see it as a shrine to place offerings."

"It will be very clear there are to be no offerings left within the middle of the Healers' garden," Erika jumped in, shooting Odo a look Asteria couldn't see. "I won't have pointless, miscellaneous *trash*—"

"Darling." Odo chuckled tightly, his eyes darting to where Asteria sat poised on the railing with an amused, shocked grin propping her mouth open.

"Did you just refer to Lyran offerings as trash?" Asteria asked, jumping to the floor with a soft tap.

Erika's body locked up, and the Healer's Energy swirled anxiously, gathering in her chest.

While Asteria and Odo had known each other for over fifteen years, he married Erika after he graduated from the Academy, and Asteria hadn't seen him since then. She met Erika for the first time when they moved in a few months ago, before classes began this year, and she no longer had any doubts about the Healer.

Asteria walked up until she and Erika were face to face and patted the Healer's cheek. "By the Heavens, Erika, you and I will be the best of friends in no time."

Erika sat dumbfounded as Asteria dropped her hand to her side, offering a tight-lipped grin to Odo.

His shoulders deflated as he slumped back into the chair, shaking his head.

"Odo," Asteria chided, making her way toward one of the far walls of the study. "Don't act as though we aren't well acquainted. I don't care about the offense Erika has made toward the Lyrans."

"I'm more than aware that if there is an offense to be made, you will be the first to cast a stone."

Asteria twirled on her toes, hands clasped behind her back and head held high with an innocent smile plastered on her face.

Odo Hesper and the rest of the new Council were some of the youngest Sirians to ever be elected Elders. Nearly all of them were in their thirties, except for one of the Diplomatic Elders, Philomena, who was in her early forties.

Every Elder appointed to the Council was taught under Asteria, and her relationship with each of them varied. Most of the time, they maintained a professional student-teacher relationship with her, attending the lectures she chose to teach when inspiration struck.

Odo was always different, though. From the moment they met, when he first walked through the Academy doors, he pushed her boundaries in an irritatingly fascinating way. At first, Asteria thought he was interested in a romantic relationship, which she *refused* to pursue with anyone. She quickly realized that wasn't his intent in the slightest.

Odo wanted to push his powers and learn all he could about how the Beings of Aveesh worked and where the different variations of power originated. He chose to master all three paths offered to Sirians, and Asteria made it her personal mission to make him her apprentice because of it.

When a new Council was elected five years later, it was the first one she didn't feel prepared to help elect. It was her responsibility to nominate the Head Elder while the leaders and royals of the various kingdoms nominated a Healer, Warrior, and Diplomat to be considered for a role on the Council. All the student levels would vote, except those graduating, and Asteria and the Head Elder would make the final decisions.

That year, she was distant after Odo graduated. She poured all her effort into him as an individual, but he accepted a Healer role within another kingdom since he was far too young at the time to become an Elder of any designation.

So she was forced to choose a Head Elder who appeared qualified.

In the end, it was a ruse by another country, Allanis, to gain an advantage and place a Sirian in every role within the Council of Elders. They were all stuffy, and the second chairs within each designation were from a country Allanis had tensions with.

To restore the balance of the Council and maintain the neutrality of Celestia, Asteria amended the requirements to be an Elder. She lowered the minimum age of an Elder from fifty to thirty and declared a country could only have one representative on the Council beneath the Head Elder.

When it came time to elect a new Head Elder, she didn't hesitate to contact Odo because he was of age. He accepted immediately, and Asteria knew she would never regret putting him in that position of power.

Except for the fact that he was allowing statues of her to be drawn up on the grounds.

"If I see another statue, bust, or even a depiction of me within a tapestry hanging in the Great Hall"—Asteria spun her head over her shoulder as she gripped the door handle, allowing some of her blue starfire to flicker around the edge of her body—"I will set you on fire, Odo."

"Go find a Lyran to harass," Odo called to Asteria as she walked out the door and headed toward her own study just a few doors down.

She chuckled to herself as she flicked her hand to open the door, but the laughter died off when she realized Odo's words must have echoed through the Realm.

"Hello, wife," Rod, the God of Matter and Morality, greeted from where he lounged in Asteria's chair behind her desk, his large frame barely able to fit within the wooden seat.

Asteria snarled, blue flames twisting around her arms like snakes. "Get the fuck off my island."

CHAPTER 2

ASTERIA

"That's no way to greet your husband." Rod chuckled, offering Asteria a pout as she marched up to him, fists clenched at her sides.

"We are not—and never were—actually married, remember?" Asteria chided, gripping on his shoulder roughly and squeezing. He winced at the extra strength she put into it. "Lyrans don't get married, if I recall properly. Now, I will not repeat myself again. Get out of my chair and off my island."

With that, Asteria called forth her starfire, branding her handprint on Rod's mortal form. He lurched from the chair, hissing as he stared down at the imprint she left, his skin charred and flaking.

"That was uncalled for," Rod grumbled, flashing in and out of his god-form briefly to heal himself. Golden, gilded skin flickered before fading back to the sun-kissed mortal skin he wore.

The blemished mark was gone, not even a scar remaining.

Asteria shrugged as she curled a lip at her chair, brushing off the invisible residue she believed he left behind. "I warned you last time if you stepped foot in Celestia uninvited again, I would burn you."

"As much as I love your murderous side," Rod began, winking at her, "and I do love the venom you have inherited from your father, you can't go around threatening to burn people."

"I can do as I wish." She lifted her head as she lowered into her chair, arms floating to rest on either side of her. "You forget I am a Goddess, too." She leveled him with an annoyed glare. "Besides, I don't threaten people."

"You seem to play Goddess only when it's convenient for you." Rod shot her a slack expression, one dark brown brow raised. "I also just heard you threaten your Head Elder."

"Again, I don't threaten," she repeated through clenched teeth. She calmly sat back in her chair as a sly grin crawled up her face. "I make promises."

"Of course." Rod sighed, falling into one of the cushioned chairs by the fireplace.

Asteria simmered at her desk, blue light pulsing around her. "Why are you sitting, Rod? You're not welcome."

"It's been some time since you last visited Eonia, and I thought I would check on you." Rod shrugged with pursed lips as he made no sign of moving despite Asteria's heavy displeasure.

"It's not been that long." Asteria rolled her eyes, averting her gaze so she didn't have to look at him.

Despite everything he'd done—everything he'd put her through—it was a challenge at times not to be drawn to him.

Especially when it'd been over one hundred years since—

"It's been fifteen years, Asteria," Rod interrupted her thoughts, rising from the chair and heading to the liquor cabinet.

She side-eyed him, briefly admiring the flex of his back muscles beneath tanned skin as he opened and shut the cabinet. It wasn't her fault he refused to wear a shirt. "That long, huh?"

"Your mother sent me to check on you," Rod shot over his shoulder, keeping his eyes on the two glasses of whiskey he poured.

"And here I thought you were trying to gain my favor by checking on me because you simply cared." Asteria narrowed her eyes at Rod as he approached, a glass outstretched. "Wishful thinking, I suppose."

Asteria scooted to the edge of her chair. She leaned forward to grab the glass, but Rod pulled it back at the last second. Her balance thrown, she nearly crashed her face into his brawny abdomen.

She froze at the proximity, that warm, feathery scent wrapping around her. She shut her eyes, biting back the swell of memories overwhelming her.

Rod lowered to eye level, squatting before her as his mortal, honey eyes gazed into her bright blue ones. She kept her face expressionless, the tension crackling around them as he slowly lifted the glass between their faces.

Asteria quickly snatched it, throwing back the whole thing before placing the glass in his hand.

"If I told you I came because I cared," Rod said quietly and evenly, an amused yet pained smile gracing his squared face, "would it have improved our relationship in the slightest?"

Asteria squinted, perusing his face.

Despite being in his mortal form, she still glimpsed the god-form beneath, his golden glow squeezing through his pores and radiating around him like he brought his own sun wherever he went.

The God of Matter and Morality, beloved by humans, yet he couldn't pass for a human regardless of how hard he tried.

As far as Asteria was concerned, he had no real morals either, at least not when it came to love and respect.

"I guess we'll never know," Asteria answered, reclining until the top of the chair dug into her shoulders.

Rod hummed under his breath, the sound vibrating the room as he moved too fast for mortal eyes. He planted himself between Asteria's legs, hunching as he gripped her chin between his fingers. Her eyes flashed blue at the force, the six-pointed Mark on the middle of her forehead glowing.

"Do not tease me, Asteria," Rod groused, his voice echoing. "It is unkind."

She smacked his hand away and rose from the chair, her feet hovering half a foot above the ground so they were eye-to-eye again. "Who ever said I was kind?"

"You're kind to your Sirians," Rod challenged, narrowing those golden eyes. "Why can't you extend that same treatment to your fellow Lyrans?"

"Because the Sirians have always been kind to me," Asteria snapped, gracefully dropping her feet to the ground. She placed her hand in the middle of his firm chest, testing her self-control with the inviting heat radiating up her arm. She bore into him, adding, "Some of my *fellow Lyrans* have not been kind to me."

She shoved his chest, and he stumbled backward, clipping the edge of her desk with his thigh.

He glared at her as he righted himself and the desk, unfazed by what would have bruised a mortal. "When will you end my punishment for an act I committed nearly one hundred and twenty years ago?"

Asteria tilted her head, locking her gaze on Rod. "I told you the barest conditions that would have me even *considering* what we once had. It seems you can't manage that, which is precisely why I will continue to punish you for eternity."

"We all have needs, Asteria." Rod ran a hand through his hair—such a mortal move. "Whether human or Lyran, we naturally seek to fulfill those needs."

The way he uttered *needs* like a rich secret only they knew of made Asteria painfully aware of the ache growing between her legs the longer he stood shirtless before her.

An ache she refused to allow any other to satisfy for the last one hundred and twenty years.

"I seem to be managing just fine without seeking others to *fulfill my needs,*" she said mockingly, her hands creating quotations.

Rod raised an eyebrow in challenge, slowly stalking around the desk like a predator. She stepped backward until she hit the wall, but he closed the distance and caged her between his arms.

"I would beg to differ," Rod said, the words rumbling as he lowered his head toward her.

Asteria flung her head to the side, which was a mistake because it bore her neck to him. His soft lips brushed against her racing pulse, and a hand slipped up her hip, snaking around her waist. He yanked her flush against his body, and the sudden force ripped a gasp from her.

"Stars, I've missed that sound," Rod murmured against her throat, his breath tickling. She shivered, her stomach dipping. "Just a taste, Asteria, to remind you of what it was like."

Despite her body betraying her, Asteria knew everything about Rod was a mistake. If he genuinely wanted her back, he would stop fucking anything that turned its gaze to him.

"Rod," Asteria whispered, turning her head so her lips just brushed his cheek, her voice caressing his ear. "The next time you lay a hand on me without my permission, I will obliterate you with my starfire."

She used the Energy to shove him off her, sending him flying through the door on the other side of the room. The wood splintered into minuscule fragments as he landed in the hallway, the ground concaving beneath him.

"And fix this mess before you leave," she shouted before portaling to the opposite side of the Academy. When she landed within the plains of the northern tip of the island where all the housing was located, she snarled, "My fucking mother."

CHAPTER 3

PHOEBE

"**M**ommy!" a small voice shouted gleefully from the other end of the shadowed hallway.

Phoebe Abbott's attention instantly waned from the Royal Healer, Thorne, informing her of the illness plaguing one of the smaller villages in Etherea.

The small boy galloped across the sandstone slabs, his little boots clacking as his arms pumped beside him faster than his legs could keep up with. His wild, dark brown curls bounced with every step, sea-green eyes wide against his sandy skin.

Phoebe smiled broadly as she squatted, holding her arms wide as she ushered her son into her embrace.

"My baby," she cooed, clutching his head to her shoulder.

"Jeremiah!" his nursemaid shouted, holding her skirts as she rushed upon Phoebe and the boy. "Your Majesty, I apologize for the prince. He's been rather insufferable today, distracted by every small thing that passes by him. His decorum needs much work—"

"Oh, hush your fussing, Delilah." Phoebe chuckled tightly, rising with Jeremiah still secured in her arms. He wrapped his legs around her waist, his arms locked behind her neck. "He's just a boy."

"A boy that needs to be trained," Delilah chastised, frowning at where Jeremiah clung to Phoebe.

Her chest stirred, irritation tickling the back of her throat. "A boy"—Phoebe took a menacing step forward, staring down the tip of her nose at Delilah, whispering harshly—"who is just a boy."

"He requires discipline," Delilah snarled, throwing her hand at Jeremiah. "He no longer requires his mother's milk. There should be no reason why he clings to you like he's starving for your attention. To add to matters, he cries like an infant being burned when reprimanded for his misbehaviors. Try as I may to break in the boy, his weaknesses have latched onto him far longer than they ever did for his grandfather."

The old woman had worked with the Abbot family since Phoebe's Sirian father, Former King Drogo, was a small child. Delilah was supposed to be responsible for raising the next king, teaching him how to walk, talk, and act in preparation for his role.

Since Phoebe wasn't male, she never received Delilah's training. It wasn't deemed necessary. Drogo's Council wanted to wait until he produced a male heir.

Unfortunately for them, Drogo never produced a *proper* heir.

Not that he produced Phoebe either, but those were words only hushed behind gray limestone walls.

"Tell me, Delilah," Phoebe inquired, taking another step into the woman's space, forcing her to take one back. "Do you know what happens when you use fear to train a dog?"

Delilah's pride was greater than her common sense, and Phoebe knew how to use it to her advantage. She was one of those who stood against her when Drogo officially named Phoebe heir to the Etherean throne and called for a tournament to name the man who would win her hand.

Since her coronation a year ago, Phoebe tried tirelessly to get Dahlia to slip up so she could relieve her of her position or execute her for treason.

She needed a good reason to fire the woman, and if she could prove any potential harm being done to her son, the opportunity would arise.

Delilah started working with Jeremiah when he turned six last month. Phoebe was quite wary of the idea, but the Council insisted he go through Delilah's training. Apparently, they still anticipated her son ascending the throne over his older sister, Emmalina.

Since working with the nursemaid, Jeremiah's personality had changed. Phoebe watched as her bubbly, energetic son slowly began to fold within himself and flinch at any swift movements. As a mother, she just knew the hag was laying hands on him.

"No, Your Majesty," Delilah answered, clasping her hands before her as she held Phoebe's gaze. The corners of her eyes pinched with age, but the woman was far older than she appeared.

"Funny." Phoebe chuckled, a breathy sound. "I thought you reigned from the House of Nemea. Does your lot not have the lycan under its banner?"

"Correct," Delilah snapped. "But I am a feathered gryp shifter, Your Majesty, not a mutt."

"How unfortunate. Now, I must waste my breath on a lesson on mutts since you seem to look down upon other shifters in your own House." Phoebe turned to Thorne and forced a rough laugh. Thorne's eyes widened as he pressed his lips together. "Well, when you use fear and aggression to train a dog, it heightens anxiety, escalating the dog's aggression. You damage trust and never form a loyal bond. When a dog doesn't trust you, it suppresses anxiety, which ultimately leads to unpredictable outbursts.

"What I'm trying to say is they become *unstable*," Phoebe said, articulating the last word, relishing in the flinch from Delilah as spittle landed on her cheek. "From what I've witnessed over the last month, you seem to follow a similar training style for my son. Am I correct in that assumption?"

"Your son is a Sirian boy—"

"Am. I. Correct?" Phoebe interrupted, her power thrashing beneath her skin.

Delilah clenched her jaw, grinding it back and forth before answering. "Yes, *Your Majesty.*"

Delilah's confirmation of her methods was exactly what Phoebe needed.

"As I thought." Phoebe sighed, clicking her tongue as she lowered her son to the ground.

He desperately clung to her leg, hiding his face.

That angered Phoebe more. She let the Aether spring forward, a thick, dark cloud gathering in her hand, her veins turning black like vines crawling under her skin.

She inspected her power, toying with the Aether. It slithered between the gaps in her fingers. "You are relieved of your position, Delilah."

Thorne stiffened beside Phoebe, his entire body rigid as a low growl rumbled from Delilah.

"I beg your pardon," Delilah screeched, her hand flying to her chest. "You don't have the authority—"

"On the contrary," Phoebe whispered, the sound rolling around them like storm clouds threatening to wreak havoc. "I am *Queen* of Etherea. It's well within my authority to relieve staff of their positions, especially the role of a simple nursemaid, when they harm the royal family."

"The king will not have this," Delilah snarled, spit gathering at the corner of her mouth, fangs peeking out.

"I believe my husband, King Dustin, will agree wholeheartedly with this decision." Phoebe peeled her son off her leg, guiding him to Thorne. Jeremiah hesitated as he wrapped his small hand around the Healer's. "If you were referring to King Emeritus Drogo, I'm afraid there's nothing he can do since stepping down from his position last year."

"You will make this country *weak*," Delilah spat, stepping into Phoebe's space with a raised finger. "A queen should never be given authority, and you most certainly don't deserve the throne. Everyone here knows you are the bastard child—"

"I would choose your next words carefully." Phoebe's god-power thrummed in her veins, echoing the beat of her heart as it attempted to overtake the Aether.

"You taint the royal bloodline with human blood," Delilah continued, pointing a menacing finger at Jeremiah. "You will be the ruin of this country, and I swear to the Gods I will make it my life's mission to ensure your children never—"

A white glow flared from Phoebe, the six-pointed Mark on her forehead flashing a warm white as her eyes illuminated the same color.

Delilah's words morphed into a scream of shock as she levitated into the air, hovering a foot above the ground. The old woman spewed profanities and curses at Phoebe, attempting to shift into her gryp form, but Phoebe flipped her up and down to throw off her equilibrium.

"Take my son to the nearest room, Thorne," Phoebe demanded as she kept her gaze pinned on Delilah spinning in the air. "I have diplomatic matters to take care of."

"Yes, Your Majesty."

Phoebe vaguely registered the rushed steps of Thorne followed by the quieter ones of her son. She waited until a nearby door slammed shut before using her god-power to yank Delilah's body directly before her, keeping the woman suspended.

"You threatened the lives of my children *and* questioned my right to the throne," Phoebe whispered, her tone cold. Black strings bled into her veins beneath the glow as she called to the Aether, snaking it around Delilah's throat. Delilah's hands scratched at the dark tendrils, but they didn't falter. "I believe we call that treason within these walls."

"The god-power you wield is proof you are not the daughter of King Drogo," Delilah gasped around the rope of Aether constricting her airway. "The world knows, but they fear the wrath of the Gods should they question your heritage."

"They should not fear the wrath of the Gods." Phoebe tilted her head,

28

a predatory glint in her glowing eyes. "They should fear mine."

With that, Phoebe threw the woman against the limestone wall with a flick of her wrist, her body cracking from the force and crumpling to the ground. Knights of Etherea rounded the corner in a rush, stumbling into one another as they came to a halt before Delilah's lifeless body.

"You have five minutes to get this body out of here," Phoebe ordered, wiping her hands on her skirts and adjusting the crown atop her dark brown, curly hair. "My son is in one of these rooms, and I will keep him occupied for that precise amount of time. I would prefer he not see a dead body at the ripe age of six."

"What would you have us do with the body, Your Majesty?" one of the knights asked, muffled slightly by the helm covering his face.

"Whatever pleases you." Phoebe shrugged, walking away with the tops of her skirts pinched in her hands. She reached for the door handle where she believed Thorne and her son to be just before throwing her head over her shoulder.

She frowned at the two knights as they lifted the body. "For the love of the Gods, don't do anything inappropriate. Be discreet."

"Yes, Your Majesty," they responded in unison.

With that, Phoebe left them to deal with the mess.

"Thorne says I'm responsible for finding a new nursemaid for Jeremiah." Dustin poked his head into the bathing chamber where Phoebe lounged in the giant brass tub. She sank deeper into the water until her mouth was fully submerged. "What happened to Delilah?"

Phoebe dragged her eyes over the top of the water and up the side of the tub. Dustin hovered with his arms crossed over his lean chest, an eyebrow raised. She narrowed her eyes at him but didn't remove her mouth from the water.

Dustin was a human, but to Phoebe, he'd always been so much more than that. Something about him fascinated her the first time they met, which is why she fell in love with him so hard the moment she laid eyes on him at her marriage tournament.

Those beautiful, sea-green eyes stood stark against his fair skin and the pitch-black hair he always kept long past his shoulders. There was always a serious set to his jaw, but if you looked hard enough, an inner gleam winked at you from those vibrant eyes.

Which is why when Phoebe's husband reached into the tub, gripping her jaw and tilting her head up from the water, desire coiled deep in her stomach.

"What did you do to Delilah, my Queen?" he asked quietly, his eyes glittering with mischief.

Phoebe inhaled deeply, inflating her chest so her breasts bounced on the surface of the water. She relished in Dustin's gaze momentarily dropping.

"She threatened our family," Phoebe whispered, her Aether playfully curling around Dustin's wrist and journeying up his arm. "She committed treason, so I sought punishment."

"You may be queen, my moon." Dustin sighed, his eyelids fluttering as the Aether traveled down his torso. "Unfortunately, there is a process in place to examine such accusations. The Council may be displeased."

"Then they can be displeased with me," Phoebe hissed through her teeth, and Dustin tightened his grip on her jaw.

"You wouldn't want to displease them so much that they seek to remove you from the throne." Dustin brushed the tip of his nose against hers, and her desire turned molten between her thighs. She clenched them beneath the water, waves rippling on the surface. Dustin smirked, adding, "Isn't that right?"

"Of course," she mumbled around his grip, lowering her lids. "I'm sure I can always make a rather convincing argument to the Council on why they should *not* remove me. Something my biological father passed down to me—"

"Phoebe," Dustin drawled in warning, leveling her with a glare. "You preach ruling with positive reinforcement, establishing respect over fear. Such actions would not be following that principle."

Bitterness burned the back of her throat as she set her jaw in his grasp, sucking her tongue to the roof of her mouth.

Since King Emeritus Drogo stepped down from the throne last year, Phoebe was forced to deal with the men still in place from his original Council. They were haughty, self-righteous men who lead with fear and aggression, a practice Drogo and his ancestors used to rule for centuries.

Using that approach for hundreds of years made Etherea a country to be reckoned with, but times were changing. The world was inching out of its barbaric ways, considering healthier forms of establishing respect and reverence. As other leaders adopted new ways of ruling, citizens fled Etherea's borders to live beneath those rulers instead.

Trade and travel made relocating even easier these days.

Etherea needed to adapt to the changing world if it wanted to remain a powerhouse. Phoebe's biological father challenged her constantly with the way she thought. It led her to experiment with her dogs growing up, studying the difference between positive and negative reinforcement.

When positive reinforcement led to obedience, behavior, and trust between her and the hounds, she realized humans and Beings alike were no different. She would rather have consistent obedience and established trust with her citizens than fear and unpredictable outbursts.

The men on the Council disagreed with her approach, despite the improved relationship between the throne and the citizens of Etherea. Unfortunately, laws prohibited Phoebe from relieving the Council of their roles simply because she didn't like or agree with them. They had to be found guilty of treason or other heinous crimes, or they had to step down from their positions before she could replace them.

"Why waste my breath on men who will never respect me?" Phoebe ripped her head from Dustin's hand, gripping the sides of the tub to stand at full height. His eyes darkened as he drank in every last inch of her, his gaze holding at both the apex of her thighs and breasts longer than anywhere else. "Those who don't grant me a chance or the grace to attempt my methods of ruling will face the justice they deserve."

Dustin hummed, holding his hands palm-up in offering to Phoebe. She accepted, gripping his fingers as she lifted one foot after the other over the ledge of the tub. She carefully released his grip, extending a hand toward the towel warming over hot coals.

He cocked his head, scrunched his nose, and swiftly drew her naked body against him, hands roaming over her wet curves. A burning trail followed wherever he touched, her core swelling as heat coiled tightly in her stomach.

"You won't be needing that." Dustin bent his knees, gripping the curve of her ass and hauling her up against him. She yelped with glee as she wrapped her legs around his waist and plunged her hands into his long hair. "Why dry yourself when I plan to make you *dripping* wet?"

Phoebe giggled in anticipation as he threw her onto the bed and began stripping off his clothes layer by layer, and all her concerns washed away with the press of his lips to hers.

CHAPTER 4

MORANA

Morana extended her arms in front of her, flicking her wrists and opening the doors to the home of the Goddess of Nature and Energy. She marched through the foyer, hoping the echo of the double doors slamming behind her would summon Danica.

When minutes passed without greeting, Morana stood at the bottom of the grand glass staircase, projecting her voice throughout the polished foyer.

"Danica!" she shouted, adding a bit of sing-song effect. "Danica, you can't hide from me, so you might as well face me—"

A quiet clap like the sound of a tome shutting echoed behind her. Morana turned in time to see the glittering portal seal behind Danica. "Why must you shout?"

Morana breathed evenly, staring at Danica with the same bored expression she graced any and all with. "Apparently, the loud entrance I made wasn't enough, so I must raise my voice."

"Why?" Danica asked again, her voice even as she tilted her head and blinked. "That is what I'm asking. Why are you raising your voice at me?"

"We're going to play this game, are we?" Morana sighed, rubbing her fingers into her temple.

Danica curled her lip, tilting away from Morana. "Between you, Rod, and Asteria, the mortal ticks you've all acquired are rather irritating—"

"You know what's rather irritating?" Morana interrupted, relishing in the flash of anger behind Danica's eyes. "How often you place yourself in your daughter's business, particularly her romantic relationships and what she wishes to do with her time."

"*My* daughter," Danica repeated, clasping her hands behind her back. She paced in front of Morana, her feet silent on the marble floor. "That seems to be a key point in your sentence, considering I have quite the hunch you are about to come to *my* daughter's defense regarding something you think I have partaken in."

"You sent Rod to berate her about the time she's spent away from Eonia," Morana said, her face slack. "Don't play your petty games with me."

Danica stopped pacing, the glistening starlight reflecting off her hairless head. "Yes, that was my doing."

"Why in the Heavens did you send *him*?" Morana threw her hands out to the sides, her iridescent veins radiating beneath pale porcelain skin with her amplified annoyance. "For the last century, Asteria has spent every moment away from Eonia because of him, yet you send him to ask what's wrong? Why not go ask her yourself?"

"I prefer to make my presence scarce on Aveesh," Danica explained, slowly approaching Morana. "It makes my visitations all the more special for the Beings."

Morana suppressed the urge to roll her eyes, if only because she needed Danica to listen and not make another comment about the mortal traits she acquired.

"Then you should've asked *me* to talk to her." Morana glared at Danica, especially as she averted her gaze, inspecting the invisible dirt beneath her glowing nails. "You know she prefers me. Unless every other Lyran is dead, there's no reason to send Rod."

"I figured it would be an opportunity for them to talk." Danica resumed her pacing, aimlessly walking about her empty home. She dragged a finger across a glass table, frowning at it. "I thought maybe it would be an opportunity to rectify their relationship—"

"She threw him through a door."

Danica pursed her lips imperceptibly, her head snapping up as she narrowed her eyes at Morana. "Pity."

"Heavens, Danica," Morana groaned, shooting to the opposite side of the room directly in front of Danica. She snarled as wisps of gold Energy swirled around her. "Why do you insist on involving yourself in their business? You know Asteria is more like her father than you, which means she holds a relationship and bond more sacred."

"And you also mean more like *yourself* than me since she has sworn herself off any other romantic relations," Danica seethed before Morana, her jealousy and a twinge of resentment simmering behind her glowing gold eyes.

Danica despised that Asteria held a closer relationship with her father, Gallus. She particularly loathed that Asteria was closer to Morana.

While Danica no longer held a bond between two Lyrans sacred, Gallus and Morana always had. That influence rubbed off on Asteria, so when Rod betrayed Asteria, she broke off their relationship and decided to remain celibate and avoid romantic relations of any kind.

It was exactly what Morana did when Valeria cheated on her over five hundred years ago.

"Asteria is grown," Morana began, gripping Danica's forearm. "You have to let her make her own decisions, despite what you believe is best or what you want for her. You must consider what Asteria wants."

"I have let her make decisions. She decides to spend fifteen years on Aveesh without so much as a peek into Eonia." Danica ripped her arm from Morana's grasp, floating across the foyer toward a painting hanging on the wall. "Beyond that, she has spent most of her life on Aveesh, and the Beings don't truly see her as a Goddess."

"She doesn't want to be seen as a Goddess, Danica." Morana shook her head, holding her hands out in front of her. "What about that is so difficult for you to understand? Why do you insist on ignoring your daughter's wishes?"

"She was born a Lyran!" Danica's voice bounced off the glass walls surrounding them, the diamond chandelier overhead quivering. Her Energy flared around her, those tendrils of gold swirling faster. "She forgets she is the first-born Lyran we know of in thousands of years, even before we left our home world. She is not half Sirian like her brothers or sister. She is a full-blooded Goddess. A Lyran, not an Andromedan."

"You seem to be the only one who cares," Morana spoke quietly. Danica lit up, clearly hearing her loud and clear.

"That we can disagree on, *sister*." Danica chuckled darkly, straightening one of the paintings that teetered during her outburst. "Gallus may have given her all the freedom she could ever want, but we have always agreed Asteria should take her place as a Lyran amongst the Beings rather than one of them. She should act as a Goddess, not a demi-god or simple Sirian."

"The more you push her—" Morana winced as a high-pitched scream echoed in her head, tearing through her soul. In her peripheral, the iridescent veins covering her body from the strands of her white hair to her pale, bare feet flared and pulsed in tune with her heartbeat.

"Morana." She vaguely registered Danica rushing upon her, catching her in her arms just as Morana's knees buckled beneath her. The warmth of the Energy wrapped around her, clearing the initial shock from her mind. "Morana, what is it?"

"It's Sybil," Morana gasped around another scream, tears burning her eyes as she faintly made out the word *momma*. "Something is wrong."

"Let us go retrieve her," Danica said, gently grabbing Morana's face. Her glowing eyes slowly transformed into hazel irises and defined black pupils as Danica took on her mortal form. "Can you shift into your mortal form and portal?"

"I have to." Morana sighed as she embraced her mortal skin, the transformation like slipping on a layer of clothing.

Her usual porcelain skin deepened into a fair, pink hue, her luminescent veins retreating beneath. By the way Danica looked upon her, she knew her iridescent eyes had solidified to their pale blue with pupils and the dark brown markings had appeared on her neck, chest, and back.

With a nod, Morana followed the connection between her and Sybil as she portaled them to Aveesh. Her body felt like it was falling backward as Danica's home swirled in streaks of color around her, fading from a vibrant warmth to pitch black. A low hum grew louder, vibrating as the falling sensation intensified.

Just when the noise of portaling became irritating, nearly forcing Morana to itch at the mortal skin she wore, a *pop* slammed against her ears as if someone clapped their hands over her head just as they appeared within Sybil's home.

There was no screaming. Instead, hushed whimpers penetrated the eerie silence.

Sybil's living room was untouched, brick walls dimly lit by the fire crackling in the pit against the far wall. Vibrant crystals and gems dangled from the ceiling by hemp cords, blinking in the light sneaking from the window over the front door. A heavy herbal aroma wrapped around Morana, and she frowned until her eyes landed on her daughter.

She rushed to where Sybil crouched in the middle of the kitchen, her arms encasing her head. Morana knelt before her, slowly peeling her arms away.

"Momma," Sybil gasped, her head snapping up to meet her gaze. Tears glistened against her ebony skin, her chartreuse eyes bright and frantic. Her white hair was wild and untamed, lips bleeding from where her canines must have pierced them.

"What is it, my drakon?" Morana whispered, pulling her trembling daughter into her arms.

Sybil was over six hundred years old, but no matter how much she matured, Morana would always see the small orphan she and Valeria had saved.

Even if it cost her.

"Dola," Sybil cried into Morana's hair, her sharp claws digging into Morana's mortal skin, warmth leaking from where they drew blood. "Take me to Dola, Momma. I need to speak to Dola."

Morana peeled Sybil off her shoulder, brushing her hair away from where it clung to her damp cheeks. "You had a prophecy?"

A sob burst from Sybil as she buried herself in Morana's arms again. She looked past Sybil's curls, meeting Danica's eyes. Even she looked hesitant, maybe even frightened by Sybil's state.

Sybil inherited prophetic powers the moment Morana saved her. Over her lifetime, she delivered plenty of prophecies, but none had sent her into a fit like this.

None had left her trembling in their wake.

"I don't know why, but I must speak to Dola." Sybil hiccupped around a sob, fisting Morana's white hair in her grip. "Dola for now. No one else."

"Okay, my drakon," Morana soothed, rubbing circles around Sybil's back. "We'll take you to Eonia to see Dola."

Morana paced outside Dola's study, the arched mahogany doors looming over her.

Unless the Goddess of Fate wanted outsiders to hear what was happening within the beige marble walls of her study, they were warded against intruders. Because of the nature of prophecies and Fate, Morana was forbidden from joining the conversation between Sybil and Dola, but her anxiousness buzzed beneath her skin at leaving her daughter.

"How mortal of you," Danica chided from where she lounged on a chaise, glittering legs dangling off the edge.

She'd shifted back to her god-form the moment they portaled back to Eonia.

Morana, on the other hand, had not. She rarely donned her god-form around the mortals, especially her daughter. Each for their own reasons, Asteria and Valeria rarely existed in their god-forms, no matter who they were surrounded by.

As for the other Lyrans, most cared very little to be in their mortal forms unless they were visiting Aveesh for purely personal reasons and not as a display of power.

"Has it ever occurred to you because I am the Goddess of both Life and Death that I have more life within me than most of you?" Morana snapped, iridescence pulsing around her.

A single twitch at the corner of Danica's illuminated, gold eyes assured Morana she wasn't amused.

Unfortunately, Morana was serious.

The Lyrans were not born with their powers, not unless they descended from Lyrans mating like Asteria, Gallus, and Valeria had. The rest of them were granted their powers by a gateway on their home world before they aged beyond the limit. She always wondered exactly how deep the powers they were granted ran and if they had any influence over their personalities.

Morana couldn't answer her own question as she no longer remembered who she was before her powers.

"Morana," Dola interrupted, yanking Morana from her thoughts.

She jerked her head, relieved to find Dola in her mortal form. Even the Talons of Fate, the gray-white bones typically sticking out of Dola's back, were tucked away. Instead of mismatched orbs, Morana met her dark gray eyes, which held nothing.

Dola was the expert of masks. It was required since she could never intervene or mettle with Fate, including any subtle ticks or twitches.

"You should come, as well," Dola added, her gaze flicking to where Danica lounged. She peered up at the ceiling before drifting up and off the cushion.

Stepping into Dola's study, it fascinated Morana how each Lyran chose to decorate, much like how their powers connected to their personalities. In her own home, Morana chose a vibrant emerald marble to construct her palace from, accented with gold and vibrant stained glass murals.

Danica's home was all white and light gold, clean and spotless, drastically different from the home where she and Gallus had raised Asteria. That home now lay untouched across the river.

Technically, it belonged to Asteria, but she no longer lived there. Morana didn't believe Asteria had set foot in the residence since her and Rod's separation.

Dola's study reflected the rest of her home: warm and nostalgic. The marble was more beige than white with various wooden furniture throughout. The ceiling stretched two stories high, the walls adorned with elaborately carved columns, crown molding, and statues of figures she recognized from Aveesh's history thus far and even some she believed didn't exist yet.

The murals on the ceiling and wall opposite the door told the story of the Lyrans, those who ruled this Realm and the ones left behind.

"Morana," Sybil whispered from where she sat in front of the mahogany desk, peering over her shoulder.

She rarely called her Momma, so when she did, it worried her because it likely meant her daughter wasn't in control of her mind, trapped in Fate's grip. Since she was using her real name, it meant she was herself again.

To confirm it, her appearance had also returned to norm: her skin its typical hue, white hair braided down her back. She held a cup of tea and appeared more relaxed, but exhausted.

For the first time, the shadow of her daughter's six hundred years of life muted those green eyes.

Morana approached the back of Sybil's chair, resting a hand on it as she gave her a soft smile. Dola and Danica floated over to the desk, the latter gently relaxing into the chair beside Sybil as Dola took up the one opposite them.

"What can you tell us?" Danica asked, her gaze flickering between the two women. "If you can tell us anything at all."

Sybil's eyelids fluttered shut. She sipped the liquid in the cup, her hands trembling.

"I have glimpsed the prophecy Sybil shared with me as a Path for Aveesh before," Dola spoke in her monotone voice, her back stiff. Morana knew the Talons would be pulsing with bright white light if Dola was in her god-form. "We must tread lightly—*delicately*—with this prophecy. One wrong move and what Sybil has foretold will become the True Path."

"So it isn't true *yet*," Morana interjected, her gaze bouncing between her fellow Lyrans and Sybil. "It can be prevented."

"What Sybil saw was but one Path." Dola carefully closed her eyes, breathing in steadily and taking just as long to exhale. Her eyes sprung open, flaring momentarily before she continued in an even tone. "There are many Truths, but we only have the power to achieve one of them. This is the least favorable outcome."

"How unfavorable?" Danica's face remained stoic, but her Energy rippled around them.

Sybil clenched the teacup in her hand, her knuckles lighter than the rest of her dark skin.

"We must share this with our fellow Lyrans," Dola said, her eyes connecting with Morana's. "And when we do, we must approach them as one would approach a frightened drakon. Otherwise, we usher in the end of all who reside in this Realm."

CHAPTER 5

ASTERIA

Asteria stood beneath the doorframe of Odo's study as Isadore Dacre, one of the Diplomatic Elders, carefully placed a small vial between the cushion and back of the desk chair. He tilted his head back and forth, adjusting the angle as he studied the vial, nodding once before turning to face the entryway.

"All the Gods in the Heavens," Isadore gasped, his Energy pulsing gold around him.

Asteria blinked in silence, hands clasped before her, shoulders pressed back. She tilted her head, an eyebrow raised.

"Lady—I mean… Hello, Asteria," Isadore greeted, smiling tightly as he locked his arms behind his back. Asteria took two steps in, inspecting either side of the room to ensure there was no trap to walk into. "Erika informed me you may be aware of the *situation* between Odo and myself—"

"You mean the prank war?" Asteria asked, pacing around the bookcases lining Odo's study, pretending to inspect the titles. She shrugged. "It may have come up."

"I assure you, it's all innocent, and it will not disrupt classes. Nor will the students get involved." Isadore shifted on his feet. Asteria glanced at him in time for his eyes to shift to the chair.

"I truly couldn't care, Isadore." Asteria chuckled under her breath, smirking. "If there is someone who can outwit Odo, I would rather enjoy bearing witness. What is it you plan on doing with the vial you hid on his chair?"

Isadore pressed his lips into a fine line, his nostrils flaring as he inhaled. He rubbed a hand on the back of his neck before explaining, "When he sits in the chair, the vial will shatter on the floor. It will release the odor contained within, which is quite pungent. It also tends to incessantly cling to one's clothing and hair."

Asteria battled the grin slipping up her face, pressing her fingers to her lips as she dipped her head. She twisted to the bookcase beside her, smile cracking as she cleared her throat. "Very well. Will it affect any others in its presence?"

"No, ma'am," Isadore mumbled, and she threw her head over her shoulder to find him suppressing his own grin. He failed as he said, "It will stay by his desk."

"Well, you should hope Erika doesn't sit on his desk when the vial bursts—" Asteria bristled at the sound of Odo, Erika, and another's voice she did not recognize traveling down the hall. She knew Isadore couldn't hear them yet, so she extended her hand toward him. "Your adversary is making his way here as we speak. If you'd like, I can portal you somewhere else within the school so you don't spoil your game."

Isadore didn't hesitate.

He clamored toward her, his smooth hand slipping into Asteria's as she waved a portal open beside her. Smoky hues of red, gold, and orange swirled within, but beyond the veil was the courtyard.

Without another word, she winked at Isadore, tossing him through the portal. He yelped and disappeared with a soft clap just before Odo entered the room.

Asteria spun on her heel, grinning half-heartedly as she made eye contact with him. He and Erika stopped abruptly, frowning as a companion bumped into Odo's back with a grunt.

"Were you talking to someone?" Odo asked, squinting.

Asteria made a point to glance around the room, even looking at the small space between her and the bookcase before facing the three individuals and shrugging. "Possibly. I opened a portal."

Odo blinked twice, then sighed heavily before waving his hand over his shoulder at what Asteria now recognized was a male behind him. "I'm not sure if you two have properly met, but I suspect there's a possibility with you having attended the Academy and being a prince. If not, Wells, might I formally introduce you to the Goddess, Asteria. Asteria, this is Prince Orwell Carraphim of Eldamain."

"Odo," Asteria chastised for the introduction at the same time this Prince Orwell—or Wells—said, "I used to see you in passing when I attended the Academy, but we have yet to formally meet."

As Odo and Erika shuffled toward the desk, Asteria forgot all about the vial.

The male stood in the middle of the office, facing Asteria head-on. He was only a few inches taller than her, which was average for Sirian males. As a full-blooded Lyran, she was about six feet tall, but it never mattered to her.

Everything else about Orwell was made to lure her in, testing her resilience against men.

Hooded eyelids and thick lashes shadowed beautiful, lighter hazel eyes that were more of a beige when she tilted her head. Curly, dark brown hair brushed along his forehead and ears, a hint of stubble hugging his defined cheekbones and strong jawline.

Despite the darker, shadowed aspects of him, though, there were qualities that made him appear young and lively, like the freckles spread across his nose and cheek and the permanent smirk tugging at the edges of his rosy lips.

"Asteria," Erika said, jolting Asteria from her ogling. She fought the mortal blush threatening to heat her cheeks as the subtle smirk on the man's face grew to an annoyingly charming degree.

"My apologies," Asteria mumbled, her eyes widening at the hoarseness in her voice. She clenched her jaw and forced a tight-lipped grin. "I'm rather surprised we've yet to meet."

"Is it because this is a face you can't forget?" the prince said, his boldness startling.

Nonetheless, her stomach swirled in response.

"I have met with the Carraphims on numerous occasions since they've ruled Eldamain," Asteria explained, neither confirming nor denying his statement. "Most recently, I've met with King Orvyn, who I presume is your father, and I believe I recall Prince Piers?"

"That would be my older but not eldest brother," the prince corrected, placing his hand over his broad chest. "I am the youngest, and my eldest brother is Crown Prince Quintin."

Asteria hummed, lifting her head as she peered down her nose at him.

Unfortunately, he seemed to find that amusing. His eyes lit from within, though she could sense the Aether in him.

"And you do *not* prefer Lady Asteria, is that correct?" He took a single step closer.

For some reason, she found herself mirroring the movement, mimicking his stance with her hands clasped behind her back.

"The only demand I ever make of the Sirians is that you refer to me as Asteria," she said, challenging him with another step closer, which he countered. Her heart hammered in her chest, such a mortal reaction to a simple Sirian male. "You seem to not prefer Prince Orwell?"

"Gods, no." He chuckled as they continued to inch closer. She was locked onto him like their world around the sun. "You can call me Wells."

They were nearly toe-to-toe, just a foot of space between them. She found she enjoyed not having to crane her neck to look at him. It was nice to simply tick her head back to meet his eyes.

At this proximity, she noticed a dark blue ring around his irises.

Then, either Odo or Erika cleared their throat, and Asteria and Wells snapped their heads toward the desk simultaneously.

Odo raised an eyebrow in amusement, and Erika seemed utterly baffled.

Those two expressions were enough to pull Asteria out of the strange trance—and what appeared to be a challenge—between her and Wells. She twisted on her heel and headed for her favorite window to distance herself.

"Was there something you needed, Asteria?" Odo asked, resting his hips against the side of his desk as he crossed his arms over his chest. Erika and Wells sat at the two chairs before him.

Wells looked back at her as he lowered.

She shook her head with pursed lips, sitting at the tea table by the window and waving a hand at them dismissively. There was a beat of silence before the three of them dove into conversation. Asteria was stuck between gazing out the window and sneaking glances at the male who so thoroughly jostled her by barely saying a word.

She wasn't sure how Odo knew the youngest Eldamain prince. For the life of her, she couldn't remember where Odo was originally from before he came to Celestia nor where he worked as a Royal Healer before taking the Head Elder position. There was a chance Erika knew the prince, considering she was from Eldamain, and maybe there was a connection through her—

"Does she do that often?" Wells asked, a hint of humor in his tone.

Asteria snapped out of her thoughts, clenching her hands in her lap as her eyes blew wide. She was quite literally gawking at him while the three of them spoke.

"I apologize," Asteria said, clearing her throat as she turned her attention to Odo. "How is it you know one another?"

"Asteria." Odo chuckled under his breath. She narrowed her eyes at him and vaguely registered Wells observing her with that damn smirk. "Don't you recall I was the Royal Healer for Eldamain before you called on me to be Head Elder?"

Oh. Right.

Asteria pursed her lips momentarily, tilting her head. "I honestly hadn't given much thought to what you were doing before I asked you to lead the Academy."

A single hack of laughter burst from Wells's lips before he slammed his hand over his mouth. Asteria glared at him as he fought the grin on his face. "I should apologize now. That was rather unbecoming of me. I just find it fascinating you summoned him without a second thought."

"He was my apprentice," Asteria explained, unsure why she found the need to elaborate for this measly prince. "I assumed he would accept the position since there's no higher honor in this Realm than leading the future Sirians of this world."

"I meant no offense, I promise you," Wells managed around his quiet cackle. He leaned back in his seat as he gestured for Odo to continue.

Odo seemed interested in what was transpiring between Asteria and Wells, even if she desired otherwise. His gaze lingered on Wells before pulling his attention back to Asteria. "I'm also from Eldamain. My father was the Royal Healer before me, so I grew up alongside the Carraphims."

Asteria's gaze bounced between Erika and Wells. "So he has come here to..."

"Visit," Erika said with a sad sort of smile. "He's merely visiting us, seeing how we are settling in at the Academy and within our roles since classes have been in session for the last few weeks."

"You traveled from Eldamain to Celestia for a simple visit?" Asteria frowned because she found it odd that a prince would just hop onto a boat and journey to the middle of the sea to visit his friends on a whim.

While the Lyrans could portal to any place within this Realm with a mere snap of their fingers, all the other Beings had to use time-consuming forms of transportation like boats, horses, and carriages. Granted, various Lemurians shifted into creatures with four legs, fins, or wings that expedited their travels, but they still had journeys to take.

"Being a second spare doesn't require much of me," Wells explained with a shrug, his hands clasped on top of his lap where Asteria found her gaze lingering far too long. Her stomach heated at the inappropriate thought of what those hands and that lap would feel like. "My family summons me when I am needed for diplomatic matters, so I find myself journeying across the seas often, which includes visiting my friends."

Asteria held Wells's gaze as Odo slowly walked around the back of his desk.

That was when she remembered the vial.

She stiffened as he pulled out his chair to sit. "Odo—"

The vial fell before he took his seat, the glass shattering and silencing the room. A green fog lifted from the ground at his feet.

"Good Heavens, what is that *awful* odor?" Erika asked around her hand, lurching up from her chair and moving closer to the desk. Asteria sprung forward and grabbed Erika's arm to stop her.

"Godsdamnit," Odo snarled, covering his nose as he peeked at Asteria. "No offense."

"Quite warranted." She winced, hissing as the smell reached her. She buried her mouth and nose into the crook of her elbow, slowly backing toward the door. "While I would love to stay and chat, I have other places to be."

"Isadore," Odo grumbled as he stared at the floor. He suddenly flung his head to Asteria. "You knew—"

"I bid you farewell, Orwell." Asteria flashed him a smile, and the one he returned warmed her chest. She beckoned a portal and stepped into her office, her stomach pulling back to Odo's briefly before it closed behind her.

Asteria inhaled a steadying breath, silently thanking herself for opening the windows before she left earlier. The light, late summer breeze wasn't as humid as a few weeks ago, signaling the fast-approaching autumn. She floated across the expanse to a plush chair between the stone fireplace and open window overlooking the Healers' garden.

She was uneasy from the meeting with Wells. She'd lost all her decorum, pulled to him in a way she wasn't familiar with.

Asteria had found plenty of men attractive since she ended things with Rod, but she refused to entertain them. She didn't trust any with her heart, and if she could easily please herself, what did she need them for?

She found friendship with those like Odo, Sybil, and her siblings to occupy her time. She also had the entire Academy of students if she wished to take on any other apprentices in the future.

Something about Wells irked her in the worst and best ways possible. For the first time in a *long* time, she found herself daydreaming about what his smirk would feel like against her lips, her throat, her breasts. Strong hands roaming her body.

If his build was any indication of what lay beneath—

"Aster," a deep, distinctive voice broke through her thoughts.

She startled for the second time today, although there was no mistaking who was in her office.

"Father," Asteria gasped, scrambling out of her chair.

Gallus watched her with scrutiny as she flattened the dress she wore, gathering her wits.

Her father standing in her office was a sure way to sober her up.

Asteria resembled her father not just in her god-form but in her mortal form as well. Many spoke of how he was an attractive Being to Lyrans, humans, Sirians, and beyond. Whether in his mortal or god-form, he had a way of looking into a person and drawing them in, even if their instincts screamed at them to run.

Gallus was a man with such an immense gravity that nothing—not even light—could escape it.

Asteria's mother said he was hauntingly and unforgivably beautiful as a mortal. Straight raven-black hair—which Asteria inherited—hung to his shoulder blades, ice-blue eyes peering from beneath a heavy gaze. He towered over her by several inches, only an inch taller than Rod, his build lean.

"Your mother says you haven't been to Eonia in nearly two decades," Gallus said, floating slowly around the perimeter of her office.

She pinned her arms at her sides as she battled her adoration for him and the resentment that simmered underneath. She loved her father dearly, but his actions over the last thirty years planted a deep, cutting thorn in her chest.

"She must truly be put out if she sent you to retrieve me." Asteria pulled her arms over her chest, cocking her hip. "I thought you, of all people, would have laughed at such a request from her."

Gallus chuckled darkly, tugging one of the ancient tomes from her bookshelf. He aimlessly flipped through its pages but paused as he stumbled upon something amusing. His eyes flitted across the page, and Asteria couldn't suppress the smile on her face.

"Father," she said again, softer.

His attention returned to her, those eerie eyes shadowed. There was a strange, foreboding depth behind his mortal eyes reminiscent of his godly ones.

An endless black that swirled with blue and red light where his pupils should be.

"I'm afraid this summons has nothing to do with Danica," Gallus said, giving her a knowing look that sent chills up and down her arms. He slipped the tome back onto the shelf. "Dola has summoned all the Lyrans. Sybil received a prophecy."

CHAPTER 6

ASTERIA

Asteria preferred not to linger in Eonia any longer than necessary, but she particularly disliked the meeting hall.

The walls were made of a smooth, dark gray stone that alternated between green and blue hue depending on which way the stars moved across the swirling sky and where one sat within the room. They arched three stories above, shaping the entire room into a circle.

The third story had rounded windows constructed from gold glass like the domed ceiling above. Surrounding a pure, molten gold statue within the middle of the room were curved tables seating two different Lyrans, only a few feet of space between each one. They were made from the same stone as the entire structure, which had Asteria itching at her skin.

"If you continue to fidget in your seat, your mother will be inclined to comment," Gallus said beside Asteria, wrapping his hand around her arm. The contact prickled her senses now that they were in their god-forms, tightening her chest.

Asteria rarely spent time in this form. Her body was an endless silhouette that reflected the deep night sky like Gallus's, except for the blinding blue flames caressing every inch of her skin and hair. When she transformed, the starfire tried to reach out and consume everything in its path, a punishment for being confined beneath mortal skin.

"She comments, and I will set—"

Gallus silenced her with a glare, scrutinizing what she admitted was a childish response. She growled under her breath, twisting in her seat to face forward, hands clasped on the table before her.

"Thank you all for coming," Morana began, holding eye contact with everyone. She anticipated her aunt would give her a wink or smirk, but Morana looked exhausted. Her pale skin was gaunt, her usually vibrant hair dull, and the iridescent veins running over her entire body dim. "Sybil called out to me the other day when a prophecy overcame her—"

"Why does she call to *you*?" Valeria sneered from across the room. Asteria would've rolled her mortal eyes if she were in that form, but alas, she was in her god-form. Instead of pure blue irises, she had glowing blue sockets and no pupils. The effect would be lost. "I'm just as much her mother as you!"

Morana rubbed a hand across her forehead, her pearlescent sockets widening as she blew a breath between pursed lips. "I do not *know*, Valeria. Maybe you should take that up with her, but now is not the time—"

"It's because you feed her nonsense about me," Valeria snarled, slamming her hands onto the table.

Asteria flinched, and Zephyr, the God of Wild Animals, roused from where he'd fallen asleep a few tables over.

Out of all the god-forms, Valeria's was the most terrifying. While Gallus's god-form was a depthless, black silhouette, it was a familiar sight. Valeria, on the other hand, was clouded by red and black smoke, resembling the latter of her title rather than the former: the Goddess of Healing and Disease. It oozed from her in place of a glowing aura, her face shrouded by shadow. All you could make out was sunken cheeks and hollow, crimson eye sockets.

Asteria always pictured Valeria as an Arcfallen. They were ghoulish Beings from the Lyrans' home Realm. Zephyr had taken great joy in telling Asteria about them when she was child.

"I don't feed her anything," Morana groaned, throwing her arms out. The multitude of colors shot through her veins and emitted a soft glow. "Valeria, we can discuss this on our own time."

"Just because I slept with a mortal *one time*..." Valeria began to spew off her justification for the vendetta she believed Morana held against her. The rest of the Lyrans either tried to settle the two down or began side conversations.

Asteria snickered as Valeria flickered from her god-form to her mortal form, asking Morana if she would prefer to speak to her this way since she was more pleasing to look at.

"Are you amused?" a deep voice said from beside her.

Her smile instantly slipped into a scowl. She attempted to roll her eyes—it was a second nature with Rod she couldn't resist—as she looked up at the ceiling, then peered back down to where he sat at the table beside her.

"I was," she grumbled. "You've ruined it now."

Gallus chuckled under his breath, those formless shoulders bouncing as he shook his head. His gaze locked onto Danica gliding to the middle of the room with unbothered grace.

But Asteria knew her mother well.

"They've done it, now," Gallus said as he leaned into Asteria. His face was an eggshell tone stark against his silhouette, the only part of him resembling actual skin.

Asteria sighed heavily when Danica's hands thrust out on either side of her, throwing Valeria into her seat and shoving Morana to the opposite side of the room directly in front of Asteria.

"*Children*," Danica chided, her gaze bouncing lazily across everyone in the room. Her brow raised when she met Asteria's gaze but furrowed when she met Gallus's, golden sockets simmering.

"Thank you." Danica bowed before roaming back to the table she sat at with Dola.

In her place, Dola rose nimbly, even with the Talons of Fate clicking against the ground behind her. The stark, gray-white bones hung from her back, the engravings dull.

For now.

"While Sybil called to Morana, she couldn't relay the prophecy to her," Dola began, her voice gentle and even. Asteria's heart clenched with nostalgia, remembering the countless tales Dola would recite for her when she was a child. Her voice easily lulled her to sleep as she spoke of historical and future events—at least the ones she was allowed to know—instead of the horrors Zephyr whispered. "I spoke with Sybil, and Fate let her relay the entire prophecy to me. As we all may have expected, I can't relay all of it to you lot.

"What I can tell you is the prophecy has shown the downfall of Aveesh." A hush fell over the room, silence pulsing around Asteria. She bristled, blinking rapidly as her senses tickled. "Sybil foresaw the extinction of not just the Sirians and Lemurians, but the Andromedans and Lyrans, as well."

The silence transformed, and every Lyran began to shout.

CHAPTER 7

ASTERIA

Asteria pressed her back against the chair, her palms flat on the stone as the chorus of voices echoed menacingly throughout the room. Everyone lost their emotions to their powers, various colors flaring to life with each Lyran's screech and caw.

"Stars above…" Asteria was grateful her father sat silently beside her with an air of complete indifference.

She was suspicious of him, though. Gallus was prone to arguments and took every opportunity to debate. He also balanced it with how knowledgeable he was, so she chalked it up to him thinking critically before exploding with emotion like the others.

Morana tried to calm everyone down alongside Dola by reeling the conversation back to them. Too many voices and too much power radiated throughout the room for anyone else to notice their efforts.

"Maybe you should do something," Asteria said, side-eyeing Gallus. "You have the brightest power."

"And yet you are my Brightest Star." He winked at her, the depths of his eye disappearing briefly. There was even the curve of a smirk at the corner of his lips.

"Right." Asteria suppressed her sly grin. "I appreciate the sentiment, Father. Alas, you wield blue *and* red starfire. I simply wield the blue."

The endless swirl of his eyes narrowed as he stood from his chair, leveling a finger at her. "There is nothing simple about the blue starfire, Aster."

Asteria watched with wonder as Gallus levitated a story above them, streaks of red and blue swirling around him like a whirlpool of fire. Her blue starfire pulled to its likeness as he expertly wielded the flames. Every Lyran except her shielded their eyes from the intensity of Gallus's heat and flare.

The room descended into uneasy silence, opening the floor for Dola to speak again. She dipped her head in acknowledgment toward Gallus, and he lowered back down in his seat as she spoke. "Thank you, Gallus. Now, please, I beg of you all… One question at a time. I will answer as best as Fate allows."

Nen and Irena stood from their seats simultaneously, glaring at each other from opposite sides of the room. Asteria curled her lip at the sinister grin crawling up Nen's face as Irena relented and sat.

As the Goddess of War and Peace, it was only in Irena's nature to let the loudest speak first. Asteria found it disgusting when the other Lyrans abused that instinct, especially Nen, the God of the Sea.

"How?" Nen asked, his voice low and menacing. "How do they—do *we*—become extinct?"

"I can't answer that directly," Dola said evenly, adding a nonchalant shrug. "Many Paths."

Asteria scoffed at the same time as Zephyr. She met his gaze from where he sat beside Nen, and he winked at her with a wiggle of his brows.

She nearly gagged.

"What were the exact words—" Valeria blurted, but Morana immediately interrupted her with, "Do not be daft, Valeria. If Sybil couldn't tell us the prophecy, it doesn't mean Dola can relay the exact words on her behalf."

"Please," Irena drawled, shooting an unamused glare between the two women. "One battle at a time."

"Maybe we should try rephrasing the question," Zephyr jumped in, resting his forearms on the table. He tilted his head, and Asteria wondered if the elaborate horns curling from beneath his blond hair ever toppled him. "What leads to… the Lemurians' extinction, for example?"

"Many Paths," Dola answered again.

"What leads to the Andromedans' extinction?" Zephyr tilted his head the other way.

"I beg of you, don't do this," Asteria muttered under her breath, suppressing the urge to run her hands through her hair. Considering the strands were living blue flames in this form, it wouldn't accomplish any relief.

"How about *you* ask a question?" Zephyr narrowed his eye sockets, which were just that—empty, soulless pits.

Asteria's power pulsed around her as she sneered at the Lyran.

Gallus asked a question instead. "Why is Sybil not here, Dola?"

"If she couldn't tell her mother anything, she isn't going to tell you," Asteria said, throwing her father a snide grin.

Gallus ignored the attitude, not even sparing her a glance.

"You all need to understand I only called you here today as a warning," Dola began, holding her hands out in front of her. "The prophecy Sybil witnessed is but one Path. This is one I, too, foresaw before Sybil when I conversed with Fate. Again, it was just one of many Paths.

"If Sybil has seen this Path, though, our Fate is narrowing in on it. Moves have been or are being made that influence this Path. Something has occurred or is on the precipice of occurring to make this a possibility."

"So it is yet to be the True Path?" Asteria asked, her shoulders relaxing. "We could still journey down a different Path?"

"These are questions I can answer." Dola smiled softly at Asteria. "Yes, child. It is one of many Paths, but as of now, it is not the True Path."

The room was quiet, but unease still buzzed in the air. Asteria frowned as she studied the various faces of her fellow Lyrans, a strange, thick tension weaving its way around them.

Something didn't feel right.

Asteria shifted in her seat.

"Can you repeat what you said about extinction?" Nen asked Dola as he peered at Zephyr.

Asteria scowled. *Who let them sit at the same table?*

Nen and Zephyr were two sides of a coin if one side was the leader and one the follower. They complimented each other efficiently, arguably an even pair as one claimed to be the God of creatures on land and the other the God of creatures within the sea.

Unfortunately, they never used their balance for good. Instead, they caused problems and riled up the Beings of Aveesh. Sometimes Gallus instigated the two, but he never fully participated in their antics, which only seemed to agitate Nen further.

"Sybil foresaw the extinction of not just the Sirians and Lemurians, but the Andromedans and Lyrans as well," Dola repeated, blinking her milky white and honeycombed eye sockets at Nen.

Asteria sat at attention as the Talons of Fate pulsed once with a warm white light. A foreboding dread pushed its way through Asteria's blue flames.

"It's curious, isn't it?" Zephyr held his hand up between him and Nen, a mischievous tick at the corners of his lips. "The humans aren't mentioned in this prophecy."

A deafening silence descended over the room. Asteria cautiously peeked at Rod.

He was too still. His pure aura hugged his body like liquid gold but no longer swirled. He clenched his jaw, eyes churning. She suppressed the instinctive urge to console him.

Just as Zephyr claimed all the Lemurians from the House of Echidna and Nemea as his people and Nen claimed those from the House of Argo, the humans belonged to Rod. They answered to and worshiped him, so naturally he favored them over the other Beings of Aveesh.

His fierce protection for the mortals and short temper would only encourage Zephyr and Nen. It used to be Asteria's responsibility to calm Rod and help keep his temper in check, but that was long ago.

She didn't belong to him anymore.

"You say there's a possibility something has occurred to start the journey down this Path," Nen began, rising from his seat. Asteria tracked him, water floating from his cerulean skin and evaporating in the air. "What if it has to do with the humans?"

"I would tread carefully, Nen," Rod droned, his gold aura churning like molten fire.

"They've been rather greedy," Valeria mused, and Morana whipped her head at her with dismay.

"Did you forget our daughter was once human?" Morana raised her eyebrows at Valeria in challenge, but she just sneered at her former lover.

"It could be that." Nen scratched between his pointed ear and gills on his neck, pursing his lips over sharpened teeth. "Their greed could lead to them thirsting for more power. They could turn those with gifts against one another—Lemurian against Lemurian, Sirian against Sirian."

He twisted his head to Asteria with a sly smirk, his milky blue sockets narrowed. Asteria's starfire flashed in warning as she raised her middle finger at him.

"I propose another possibility," Nen continued, hovering a few feet above the ground as he circled the statue in the middle of the hall. "The humans have purely mortal blood. Lemurians, Sirians, and Andromedans have god-touched blood. We aren't sure what happens to their blood when Beings mate with those who can't meet their strength. Mating a Sirian or Lemurian with a human may lead to powers vanishing in the future, ultimately inciting the extinction of all these powerful Beings."

Asteria recoiled with a snarl, gawking at Nen. "You can't be serious."

When her gaze swept over the other Lyrans, she was appalled to find some of them considering this possibility. Even her mother seemed to absorb the information. It was a brief moment of doubt—gone in a blink—but it had still been there.

As she beheld Dola, though, the cold dread that toyed with her after Nen and Zephyr first spoke dug its claws into her. An odd expression passed over Dola's face that incited a manic energy around the Goddess of Fate.

"Don't be an imbecile, Nen!" Rod roared, slamming his hands on the table, a crack skittering across the stone. "That is absurd and completely immoral and unfounded from a Lyran. You know damn well that's not how this works. Look at how our home was—"

"We don't know *precisely* how these powers work." Nen smiled around his words, which had Asteria simmering. She sunk back against her chair, jaw set, but she adopted an air of indifference since the men were now in a pissing match. "This Realm is not like home. When we mate with any Beings, whether human or Lemurian, they surely don't come out all-powerful like if we were to mate with each other. They certainly don't come out like those from home.

"Compare Endora and Asteria. One is the product of a Lyran and Sirian, the other the product of two Lyrans."

"You can't possibly compare the Brightest Star and Goddess of Sirians to an Andromedan," Gallus interjected, throwing a menacing grin at Nen.

"Precisely my point," Nen relented through clenched teeth. "We can't even compare the Lemurian and Sirian reigning Andromedans to the human Andromedans. Right, Rod? Bodhi and Enki surely have or had a sort of invincibility like the other Andromedans, but that was all. Nothing more. They inherited no true powers from you, and that's not an insult to your participation—"

"An insult to the humans is an insult to me, regardless of if they're my descendants or not." Rod stood to full height without hovering above the ground. Asteria realized he'd been hovering the entire time Nen spoke about two of Rod's children, one of which was the product of him cheating on her.

Rod suddenly snapped an imploring gaze to her, and she sighed heavily.

While the humans metaphorically belonged to Rod, most of the Lyrans still respected them as living organisms. The Lyrans acknowledged Asteria as the Goddess of Sirians, so in their minds, the Sirians belonged to her.

Except she didn't treat any of the Beings differently from one another. In fact, before she was born, her parents created the Sirians so they could protect the humans. If anything, Asteria had a soft spot for them because of it.

A fondness for the humans was the only thing Asteria and Rod had in common.

"I can speak for the Sirians and educate you all," Asteria said, straightening her back. "Your assumption is wrong. That's not how the Energy nor Aether works. Sirian offspring—regardless of whether they procreate with a fellow Sirian, Lemurian, or human—will either inherit the power or they won't. The Sirian blood determines their power levels and strength, as well as their grit and inherent desire to master it.

"I can't speak for your pets and how their powers work." Asteria turned her gaze on Zephyr, baring her teeth in a tight grin.

Zephyr set his jaw, staring at Asteria as a deep purple smoke slowly drifted around him. "Don't speak about things which you don't know, Little Lyran. Maybe that mouth is better suited for sucking Rod's—"

"Finish that sentence, Zephyr," Gallus's voice penetrated the air as his black form flashed red and blue. "I dare you."

Asteria snickered as she reclined, inspecting where her nails would be in her mortal form while Zephyr calmed beneath her father's heated gaze. Over the tips of her illuminated fingers, Asteria caught Dola hunching in on herself as her eyes and the Talons flared.

"I only meant to warn," Dola whispered, and Morana and Danica rushed to her side. She ran her fingers through her white strands, yanking on them. Asteria's body locked up. "This is still not final. This could change, but no one is listening."

Danica reached Dola first, soothing her with soft words that even Asteria couldn't hear. Her heart cracked for Dola as she ripped strands from her head, pleading with Danica. Morana just caressed Dola's shoulder, avoiding the blazing Talons.

Asteria only witnessed Dola's episodes a handful of times. The problem was they were becoming far more frequent, which could only mean she was teetering on the brink of Madness.

The state of this meeting may have very well pushed her over the ledge.

"Regardless of where this goes, the humans seem to be a point of contention," Gallus suddenly said, and Asteria stiffened beside him. "Why don't we just get rid of them?"

Asteria's flames stilled at the same time Rod lunged for her father.

CHAPTER 8

PHOEBE

Phoebe walked into the darkened foyer, peering from beneath her hooded cloak. Purple lace hung from the ceiling, separated by wooden beams supporting the sharp arches. Sconces barely lit walls adorned with rugs from floor to ceiling, surely a safety hazard where fire was concerned.

"You come on royal business, yet you still sneak into my abode with trepidation and concern." A lanky form slunk from an open door deep within the extended hallway, arms tucked into the billowing sleeves of her dress. Her voice projected across the expanse, wrapping around Phoebe. "And here I believed the Queen of Etherea didn't care for the opinions of simpletons."

"Don't test me, Endora," Phoebe chided, taking slow, cautious steps toward her fellow Andromedan in the middle of the dim hallway. "You know I don't see my kingdom that way. Human, Sirian, Lemurian... I care for them all and their perception of me is important."

"I don't speak of your civilians." Endora chuckled, stunning Phoebe as she didn't think the woman ever smiled. "I speak of the slime that crowds your Council."

"You know there is nothing I can do about the Council." Phoebe flicked her hood back, pulling her brown hair from beneath the seams.

"You know there are people who can do"—Endora took a single step forward, the glow from a nearby sconce casting light upon her porcelain skin, the Mark on her forehead pure white—"*something*."

It was Phoebe's turn to chuckle darkly, shaking her head slowly. "Let's solve the matters at hand before we raise arms against the Council."

Endora hummed, removing her bony hand from her sleeve to extend it toward the door she came from. Phoebe dipped her head and filed into what could be considered Endora's private study, but even that word felt too mortal for the workings done within these walls.

While still dim, the hearth on the far wall cast a bright glow across the small room. It made the elements of this space far more discernible than the entrance to Endora's home.

A stained barrel filled with black stones sat in the middle of the room, a thin, green-hued smoke wafting from within. Plants and vines hung from beams, climbing down the walls and stretching across stocked shelves, not a window to be seen. Copper bowls dangled from the ceiling filled with Heavens only knew what and glass jars were scattered haphazardly across the slate countertops.

The door locked behind her.

Phoebe's attention drew back to Endora, now illuminated by the fire. She was only an inch or so taller than Phoebe, but everything else about her contrasted the Queen of Etherea.

Ghostly pale skin stretched over her thin, sickly frame, the hollows of her cheeks sunken. Her full, blood-red lips complimented the slight blush of her cheeks. Black, monolidded eyes only served to accent her sharp cheekbones and pointed chin. Her long hair was pulled up, a few inches of white-gray coloring fading into a black bun coiled on top of her head. Phoebe knew when it was free, Endora's hair fell to her knees.

"Do you have anything to report on the illness appearing within humans?" Phoebe asked, side-stepping for Endora to glide through her study.

She stood before a counter beside the fire, her hand hovering over the items scattered there as though searching for something. "The Obsidian Decay."

Phoebe clenched her jaw, nostrils flaring as she breathed in to quell the buzzing of her power. "It's already been given a name?"

Endora peeked at Phoebe over her shoulder with a sneer, dark mischief dancing in the depths of her eyes.

Chills broke out across Phoebe's skin.

"I didn't want this to spread to a point that it needed a name, Endora," Phoebe chastised, stepping further into the room and closer to the barrel. "What else do you know about it?"

"The infection appears to spread by contact through a wound, maybe even ingested," Endora began, summoning the Aether to wrap around a glass jar on the top shelf, carefully lowering it to her. Once it rested between her fingertips, she twisted on her tiptoes to face Phoebe. "It reaches all vital organs and hardens them like an obsidian stone."

"And how long does it take for this to occur?" Phoebe accepted the outstretched jar from Endora.

Within the jar were large cuts of black stone. Upon further inspection, she realized they were the organs Endora referred to.

Phoebe thrust it back to her, scowling. "For the love of the Gods, Endora."

Endora frowned at the jar as she took it, aimlessly placing it on the counter. "It's impossible to tell. The only way I could determine the harvesting window would be to infect an individual and observe them as they die."

Phoebe clasped her hands behind her. Her boots echoed as she walked toward a wall of small vials, keeping her back to Endora.

"I suppose there is *one* other way," Endora continued, and Phoebe heard her coyness. "I could raise the human victim you provided back from the dead—"

Phoebe interrupted Endora with a raised hand, her god-power forcing the Andromedan's mouth shut with a *clack*. "You will not disturb the dead."

Not only was the mere idea of raising her dead citizens abhorrent and entirely disrespectful, but the last thing Phoebe needed was for the Lyrans to get involved in how she ruled her kingdom. Permitting Endora to use her forbidden power of necromancy would surely summon them.

While Phoebe was a child the last time Endora was rumored to have used that particular gift, she knew the tale well.

Like Phoebe, Endora was a Sirian Andromedan: half Sirian and half Lyran. While Phoebe's god-power manifested as gravitational manipulation, Endora's was necromancy.

Roughly thirty years ago, Endora simply got bored—according to other Andromedans—and raised all the dead in a cemetery to see what would happen. Their zombified bodies roamed a nearby town, spreading various forms of diseases.

Morana forced Endora's mother, Valeria, to clean up the mess, which angered her to no end. So much so that she forbade Endora from using her necromancy for the foreseeable future.

"Would you accept anonymous donations for test subjects?" Phoebe tilted her head as she twirled on her heel, arching an eyebrow.

Endora's face was entirely void of emotion, just as eerie as the hollow laugh she released. "A *live* human donation?"

Phoebe shrugged, pursing her lips. "My prisons appear to be rather full at the moment. I need to dispose of some criminals. What better way to atone for their sins than as test subjects for the study of a deadly disease infecting their communities?"

A harrowing smile crept up the woman's cheeks. She reached for a loose parchment and quill and began scribbling instructions for Phoebe. "This is my contact for donations. You'll need to organize how, when, and where the subjects are delivered. I have no problems performing whatever tests necessary."

Endora slunk around the barrel, folding the parchment numerous times before handing it to Phoebe, pinched between two fingers. When Phoebe reached for it, Endora snatched it back and leveled her with a look, adding, "The moment you have another ill individual, I need them here *before* they're dead. I need to harvest the infection before it hardens their organs and veins."

"That is *your* job to be tracing the infected." Phoebe snatched the paper, tucking it into the pocket within her cloak. She pointed a menacing finger at Endora. "You won't harm them while they are alive, do you understand?"

"I'll just need some of their blood," Endora explained, waving Phoebe's comment away. "They'll be taken care of, *Your Majesty*. I'll even ensure they receive the best medicinal treatments so they don't feel the pain the other poor bastards experienced before death claimed them."

With Endora's back turned, Phoebe rolled her eyes at the blasé manner in which Andromedans like Endora spoke—not just about the Lyrans, but about the Beings they sometimes deemed beneath them. The only ones to earn that disdain were the humans since every other Being of Aveesh was had been touched by the Lyrans in some way.

The Sirians were originally molded after humans but were able to withstand the power imbued in them.

Danica, the Goddess of Nature and the Energy, granted some the gift of Energy, which half of the Universe was made of. It presented itself as a gold, glowing power, allowing the Sirian who wielded it to generate and manipulate Energy stored within objects.

Gallus, God of the Aether and Stars, granted others the gift of the Aether, the element the rest of the Universe was composed of. Phoebe and Endora both inherited the Aether, which manifested as black matter. Where the Energy charged and brightened, the Aether morphed into a solid form, defying the natural laws of this world.

Then there were the Lemurians.

Their history was a little more complicated.

They hadn't been around nearly as long as Sirians, only the last six hundred years. Phoebe wasn't entirely sure how much time separated the inception of the Sirians and Lemurians. Sybil—Morana and Valeria's adopted daughter—was the first Lemurian. She was also considered an Andromedan, for all intents and purposes.

After Morana imbued the soul of a dying child within one of the mythological Beings that roamed this world—a drakon—it granted Sybil the ability to shift between her mortal and animal form.

The moment Zephyr learned what had been done, he wanted all mythological Beings to shift. Morana was forced to combine more creatures with mortal souls. They were separated into three Houses: Echidna, Nemea, and Argo. Any reptilian shifters were part of the House of Echidna, the marine ones part of the House of Argo, and the feathered and furred shifters part of the House of Nemea.

After Nen had a child, Brigid, with a ketea shifter and Rod had a son, Garuda, with a gryp shifter, each became the founder of their respective houses: Argo and Nemea. Sybil took responsibility for the House of Echidna.

As for Lyrans and Andromedans, which Phoebe and Endora were the latter, it was just another term Aveesh used to distinguish Gods and demi-gods. While most humans, Lemurians, and Sirians referred to the Lyrans as *Gods* and *Goddesses*, Andromedans still referred to their parents as Lyrans.

The relationships were fragile.

"By the way," Endora said, hitching her elbow against her hip and twirling a quill between her fingers, "how have you been feeling after the *medicine* I gave you?"

Phoebe's body tensed, her hand instinctively resting over her stomach. "I'm well. I only experienced the loss of my powers for half the day. There were no further complications after that."

"Any long-term, negative effects on your god-power?" Endora raised an eyebrow before twisting around and scribbling on an ink-stained parchment. "Has your Andromedan healing, strength, or stamina been affected in any way?"

Phoebe sighed, rolling her shoulders. "My powers are still as strong as ever, both the god-power and the Aether. I haven't had the opportunity to test—" Endora swiped the quill across Phoebe's forearm hard enough to break skin. "*Fuck,* Endora!"

Phoebe clutched her hand to her chest, gawking at the cut. Endora yanked Phoebe's hand forward to observe it in the light, rotating her arm back and forth. Phoebe hissed as the skin strained against the raw tenderness.

Endora squinted, flourishing the quill back and forth. "Let's see how that heals by the time you leave. Now, have you had the chance to speak to Sybil about your future? Can she see you aging?"

"I refuse to speak to Sybil about this," Phoebe grumbled, rubbing her temples. "She's far too close to the Lyrans. I fear she'll say something about what we've done here—"

"Are you more afraid that she will tell Gallus or Asteria?" Endora glared at Phoebe, judgment written across her face.

Phoebe simmered, if only because it struck true. She flicked her finger, and the quill went clamoring to the floor.

Endora deadpanned with obvious annoyance.

Phoebe was promised to her mother after King Drogo failed to produce an heir. He begged Gallus to grant him a Sirian child, so Gallus bedded Phoebe's mother, former Queen Petra. Even with his required absence and refusal to publicly acknowledge her as his daughter, Phoebe cared too much about his opinion of her.

However, Gallus being her biological father made Asteria her half-sister, and *that* relationship was just as fickle as Phoebe's relationship with any of the Andromedans, including Endora.

While Asteria was a Lyran, she spent more of her time with the Sirians, her Andromedan half-brothers, and Sybil, who she acknowledged as a sister more than Phoebe.

"Send someone else who can shine insight on my immortality or lack thereof," Phoebe demanded, shaking the swelling anger from her head. Endora watched her with intrigue, a small smile at the corner of her lips. "I'll get you your test subjects."

As she reached for the doorknob, Endora cleared her throat. Phoebe inhaled to quell her dwindling patience, then glanced over her shoulder.

Endora tipped her head towards Phoebe's arm wrapped around the handle. "Your wound?"

Phoebe frowned, looking down at the skin peeking out from her cloak.

Sure enough, standing stark and angry against her skin was the scratch Endora marred her with.

Being an Andromedan, Phoebe had inherited enhanced abilities like stamina, strength, and healing that went beyond the Aether and her god-power. It also meant she would have a seemingly immortal lifespan like any of the other Andromedans on this plane. Endora was roughly over five hundred and sixty, Sybil was well over six hundred, and Dionne—Asteria's other half-sibling—was two hundred years old.

Immortality was a problem for an Andromedan who didn't care about any of those qualities and was married to a mortal male.

Two weeks ago before Phoebe took the elixir, the wound would've healed within minutes. The elixir she tasked Endora with creating may have worked like they wanted if the wound still looked fresh.

There was a chance Phoebe was no longer immortal.

CHAPTER 9

MORANA

M orana shook herself out of her stunned daze as Asteria's blue flames flashed. Rod bounced off the shield she conjured around herself and Gallus.

Despite protecting her father, Asteria's blue-tinged face held restrained horror in the parting of her mouth and frantic flames.

"What in the *Heavens* is wrong with you?" Rod screamed, fists clenched at his side. "Are you telling me you agree with him?"

"Absolutely not!" Asteria shouted back, dropping her shield and stepping toe-to-toe with Rod. "If you think I would ever agree to his sick joke, then you truly never knew me."

"Getting rid of the humans would empower not only the Lemurians but your people as well, Aster," Gallus added, lounging back in his chair.

"Father!" Asteria whirled on Gallus, towering over him. "You must be joking. You can't commit genocide against an entire race of Beings."

"Why not?" Valeria chided, crossing her bony arms over her chest. Morana stared at her with disgust and dread. "They are fragile Beings compared to the Sirians and Lemurians. They have shortened lifespans."

"The Sirians have the same lifespans as mortal humans, you oaf," Asteria spat at Valeria. She collapsed into her chair and shot Gallus a sidelong look, but he simply shrugged.

"Do not insult your elders, Asteria. It is unbecoming of a young Lyran." Nen toyed with the water droplets around him. Morana wanted to lunge across the space and suck the soul clean out his body. "Gallus proposes a compelling idea. It's been some time since the humans sat on a throne, yet Etherea now has one as their king. This moment could be empowering for the humans, encouraging them to rise against the Lemurians and Sirians if they should ever see them as a threat."

"Fascinating you speak of anarchy against the Lemurians and Sirians for a perceived threat when you suggest a ruse against the humans," Danica interjected, stepping away from Dola with a predatory tilt of her head. "What sort of threat would humans see the Lemurians and Sirians as? They still rule every other throne on Aveesh."

"The more power the humans have, the more they'll want to guard that power for themselves." Nen met Danica's advancement with a step forward.

Morana went on the defense as she tucked Dola behind her, who was still muttering to herself and pulling at her hair.

"You speak in hypocritical loops," Asteria interjected, waving a hand in the air with blue flames dancing above her. "The Beings of Aveesh already behave this way. By trying to withhold any semblance of power from the humans, are you not hoarding power for the Lemurians and Sirians? The single human king is not even the figurehead of that kingdom. That role belongs to its queen, who you forget is Sirian."

"And Andromedan," Morana muttered to herself, which earned her a menacing glare from Asteria, Gallus, and Danica. *Lest anyone remember Gallus reproduced said queen.*

"The difference here is a prophecy speaks of the extinction of Lemurians and Sirians, not the humans," Zephyr countered, propping his elbows on the table and interlocking his fingers. "I thought you'd be more defensive of *your* subjects, Goddess of *Sirians*."

"I'm not plagued by hubris," Asteria said, her gaze bouncing to all those suggesting human genocide—including her father. "You forget how Fate operates. It doesn't behave under the constraints of your ambitions. Dola said this is but *one* Path, not the *True* Path. This means there is ample time to decide which to take.

"Your arguments could very well lead to our destruction, causing a war amongst ourselves. There's also a chance that what you say is true, although I highly doubt it. Regardless, we are helpless to Fate and what shall unfold, so we might as well go about our days."

"And just live with the knowledge that all we've worked for will crumble into extinction?" Valeria's voice rose to a pitch that could shatter glass. Morana recoiled as it grated along her skin. "I will not sit idle to such a Fate."

"You don't know for certain if that is your Fate," Morana said, shaking her head. "That's what Asteria means. We also don't know the time in which this extinction could occur. We're aware tales from home speak of worlds dying and evolving. This extinction could very well be a natural way of life."

"It may be for Lemurians and Sirians, but it is not the Lyrans' way," Nen snarled, his eyes flashing. "We don't die with them. We leave for a new world, or we go home."

"Heavens above," Asteria grumbled, folding her arms over her chest. Morana glared at her, setting her lips in a firm line. This wasn't the time for Asteria to display an attitude. "You're all so fearful of death when she stands in the room with you."

"Morana may be the Goddess of Life and Death, but she is not death itself." Valeria curled her lip at Asteria, gesturing across the room toward Morana. She pinched her nose, breathing through the headache forming behind her eyes. "What would you know of death? You're still young for a Lyran. To be frank, you don't know much of what you speak—"

"Then why am I here?" Asteria slammed her hands on the table as she

74

rose again. She pointed at Rod, Dola, Danica, and Morana, as she spoke, "You lot are determined to force my involvement in these discussions, yet the rest of them"—Asteria drew her damning finger to the other Lyrans, avoiding her father—"do not even acknowledge me as an equal. You must face the fact that I'm not one of you. Not where it matters. I might as well be an Andromedan!"

"You can't be an Andromedan, Aster," Gallus said gently, like he was consoling a child. "Your power is far too strong, and you're entirely immortal. Andromedans eventually die with age, whether that be hundreds or a few thousand years. Unless someone were to kill you purposefully, you'll live to see many worlds die and be reborn. Besides, it would take far more for you to be killed compared to an Andromedan."

Asteria simmered as she lowered in her seat, starfire waving erratically around her form. Morana tried to catch her blazing eyes, but Asteria averted them, her head downcast at a point on the table.

"This can't be," Dola mumbled behind Morana. She glanced behind her to find Dola crouched on the ground, her white braids a wild mess upon her head. Instead of her usual cool brown skin, it paled to a gray hue. "This can't be. Too many Paths, too many outcomes, so many deaths. Secrets, illness, betrayals, endangerment, wars, genocide—"

"Hush, Dola," Morana cooed, lowering to her knees beside her. She gently brushed loose coils from Dola's face, cupping her cheeks. "Many Paths is still good. That means there have been no final decisions, right?"

Dola searched Morana's face for answers. She morphed into her mortal form, and Dola relaxed at the sight of it.

"What are five things you see, Dola?" Morana asked, her thumbs resting on Dola's cheekbones.

Dola blinked rapidly, the fluorescent light within her honeycombed eye dimming. "Blue eyes, white hair, gold statue, brown markings, stone floor."

Morana smiled softly, gripping Dola's hand and guiding it to her chest. "What are four things you feel?"

"Cool ground," Dola began, her other hand dragging along the floor, "your heartbeat, the Talons, warm skin."

"What are three things you hear in this room?" Morana gestured around them, but the tension in Dola's body was already subsiding.

"A clock, familiar voices, the crackle of fire."

"Two things you smell?" Morana repositioned her hands at Dola's elbows. She carefully lifted Dola from her crouch and offered her arm to lean on.

"The tomes." A smile twitched at the corner of Dola's lips. "Death."

"I am rather close to you, aren't I?" Morana smiled, coaxing a soft hum from Dola. "Last one, and this may be difficult. One thing you can taste—"

"Blood." Dola blinked once, then gently pried herself from Morana's embrace. "I wish to rest."

"Now that we've coached Dola off the edge of Madness once again—"

But Zephyr didn't get to continue.

Asteria shot a streak of Energy at him, and he soared across the room.

Morana gawked at Asteria with wide eyes, but she simply shrugged. "I, for one, no longer wish to hear him speak."

"You ignorant *bitch*!" Zephyr yelled as he stalked back toward Asteria.

Those three words incited complete chaos.

Gallus and Danica simultaneously rose from where they were seated. Danica swirled her hands, creating a fizzling ball of Energy. Tendrils of Aether flowed from Gallus's outstretched arms, red and blue starfire unfurling from his shoulders. Morana glanced between Asteria sitting smugly in her seat and Irena silent on the other side, a bushy eyebrow raised with boredom.

"*Irena.*" Morana grabbed the attention of the Goddess of War and Peace who turned her jaguar head to Morana with her other eyebrow raised. "Are we about to let war ensue, or will you enact peace to prevent such a thing?"

Morana flinched as a *rip* echoed through the room. Zephyr was now a drakon, his large form taking up most of the empty space in the middle of the hall. He bellowed, snarling at Danica and Gallus.

Morana glared at Irena. "These three will level Eonia if you do nothing."

Irena sighed heavily as if she were a mother being bothered to parent her children. She levitated from her chair to the same height as the three enraged Lyrans. The muscles beneath her tan skin rippled, veins glowing faintly as she arched a hand across her body, fingers splayed wide.

All at once, Danica, Gallus, and Zephyr ceased movement, the usual glow of their eyes fading to a dull white as Irena forced them into a trance. She snapped her finger at Zephyr's still body, commanding, "Shift back."

In a blink, he morphed into his god-form without a twitch of acknowledgment. Irena positioned her hand parallel to the ground and slowly lowered herself, each Lyran following suit.

When their feet touched the ground, Irena clapped once.

Danica, Gallus, and Zephyr's eyes returned to normal. They looked at each other in a strange daze, inspecting themselves. They must have collectively registered what happened because they simultaneously whirled on Irena, their powers simmering.

She simply held up a finger as she walked around her table toward Dola and Morana.

"Arguing in loops will cause nothing but agitation," Irena began, her voice even as she inclined her head. She slipped her hand into Dola's. "You have resorted to insults and belittlement, which means you will no longer conduct a civil argument amongst one another.

"I agree more conversations need to be had. Until you all can do so in a behaved, *productive* manner, I see no use in prolonging this meeting any further." Irena gently pulled Dola into her embrace, dipping her head at Morana. "If you'll excuse me, I must bring Dola to her abode to rest. I don't know about all of you, but I prefer to not see our Goddess of Fate fall to Madness."

With her final words, Irena portaled her and Dola out of the hall, leaving the rest of the Lyrans in a congested stillness that settled uncomfortably over Morana's shoulders. Still in her mortal form, she fidgeted with her hands.

After exchanging a heated glance with all present, Asteria vanished from sight, and the others followed suit, leaving Morana, Rod, and Danica alone.

The whispers of Life and Death bristled quietly underneath Morana's skin. She turned to Danica with a frown, shaking her head. "This doesn't feel right."

"No," Danica whispered, her eyes trained on where Asteria had been seated beside Gallus with something Morana couldn't decipher. "It doesn't."

CHAPTER 10

MORANA

"S ummon her again!" Danica shouted, twirling on her heel, power flaring around her.

Morana sighed as she sunk into the chair at Rod's residence in Eonia, embracing the warmth radiating from the golden hearth. His entire palace was gilded gold, and while the flames within were comforting, the rest of the structure unnerved Morana.

Rod was so infatuated with himself, he needed a reminder around his home that his god-form was glistening gold.

"I told you she wouldn't respond if we hosted this meeting here," Rod explained, bracing an arm against the wall and pressing his fingers to his temple. "We should've hosted this at Morana's."

"She should not be so... so..." Danica stared at nothing, her Energy flashing as the word came to her. "Petulant."

Morana refused to listen to Danica poisonously remark on her daughter. "For Heaven's sake, Danica. She won't come to our summons. It has nothing to do with how she may or may not feel about you and Rod."

"Don't coalesce my relationship with my daughter to her relationship with this buffoon," Danica chastised, sweeping her hand in Rod's general direction. He glared at her through narrowed eyes, a muscle ticking in his jaw. "You believe you know her so well. What is her reasoning for not answering our summons after such a meeting if not to be an irritant?"

"Asteria defends all Beings of this world with equal fervor," Morana explained, attempting to keep her expression neutral. She shouldn't have to explain to Danica the character of her own daughter. "It was evident within that meeting what she believes regarding Fate. She won't answer a summons because she believes any Lyrans taking action to prevent the Path will ultimately ensure said Path occurs."

"You believe she will stand neutral?" Rod frowned to hide his hurt.

Morana had half the nerve to toss him across the room for it. He deserved any pain Asteria dealt him, and he should be thankful Asteria defended the humans at all.

"Until her father sways her to his side." Danica scoffed, standing before the hearth. "We will need to get to her before he does—"

"Did you not see Asteria's face when Gallus proposed the massacre of humans?" Morana slowly rose from her chair. "Asteria may love her father, but she is also intelligent, despite what you and the other Lyrans may assume of her. As I said, she will not be easily swayed to either side."

"And if Asteria is anything"—Rod paused with a snort, riffling through his liquor cabinet—"it's *strong-willed*."

"You mean stubborn," Danica muttered. Morana wheeled and leveled a finger at her. "Don't point that at me. It's the truth! We can't inflate her pitfalls by labeling them with kind adjectives. She isn't here, Rod, so there's no need to glorify her."

"I gave up trying to adulate Asteria decades ago." Rod shook his head as he poured dark liquid into his glass.

"Since we're all in agreement that Asteria won't be joining this discussion, we should move forward without her," Morana said, beckoning Rod to hand her the glass.

He glared before lifting it into the air and carefully sending it to her outstretched hand. "I agree. I want to start by saying I don't feel good about how that meeting ended. You both know Nen and Zephyr—they will not gather for another joint meeting to further discuss matters."

Danica and Morana hummed in agreement. Morana tossed back a mouthful of the burning liquid, shutting her eyes against it. She silently blessed the Heavens for the humans who created this enticing liquid.

"Nen and Zephyr with their Lemurians have the strongest influence over us outside of Asteria and her Sirians," Rod explained, shaking his head grimly. "They'll start whispering nonsense to the royals who worship them first. The greatest way to enact a feat such as enslaving humans would be to start with a country's highest level of authority."

"Nen and Zephyr are not wise enough to think so strategically," Danica countered, sitting in a chair near Rod. "They'll start with absolute chaos before even considering the royals."

"Not if Gallus is truly on their side." Rod wagged a finger at Danica, sipping his liquor as he stepped toward the middle of the room. "Gallus is the intelligent and strategic one. Asteria wants to believe he was kidding when he suggested genocide, but Gallus can be insensitive and just as bored with practical matters as Asteria. He is quick to scheme, and would start a war simply because he wanted something to entertain him."

"That's correct," Danica mused wistfully.

Morana threw back the rest of her liquor.

The weaknesses between the Lyrans were what would truly hurtle this world into chaos.

Gallus was Danica's weakness while Asteria was his. Asteria also happened to be Rod's weakness alongside the humans.

Nen and Zephyr were perfectly aware of these facts, which made the two more dangerous than anyone gave them credit for.

Danica and Gallus being on opposite sides of the discord—not even considering Rod—with Asteria in the middle put everyone in a precarious position.

"Regardless of how Nen and Zephyr incite their agenda, we must be cautious about how we proceed," Morana interjected, placing her glass on the coffee table by Danica's feet. "If we attempt to gather allies on our end in a way that looks like we're preparing for war, the others will retaliate and claim defense. We must first speak with the kingdoms we know will stand with us, and do so in a quiet, cautious manner."

"Play their game, then?" Rod mulled over the idea, swirling his glass. "If we're not *allying* with the kingdoms we have sway over, what are we doing with them?"

"Warning them," Morana said, shrugging. "Preparing them. We urge them to act on diplomatic matters rather than military. Encourage them not to instill policies that would harm humans despite what their sister countries may do."

"When does our involvement turn from advisors to warlords?" Rod narrowed his eyes, setting his empty glass aside.

"When we realize it needs to." Morana sat in the chair beside Danica, peering at her from the corners of her eyes.

Danica was ensnared by the dancing flames in the hearth. "For more reasons than one, this is why we need Asteria. She can assist with discussions amongst the royals since she knows them better than us. They see her yearly for the Patronage Gala when it comes time for them to meet the senior class of Sirian Warriors and Healers."

"Until then, we keep a keen eye on the movements of Nen, Zephyr, Valeria, and Gallus." Rod sat across from Danica and Morana, leaning his forearms against his gilded legs. "This must stay between the royals. We can't interfere with any citizens of these countries."

"How do you figure?" Danica lifted her gaze to Rod, tilting her head.

"If we approach the Beings, this will cause a divide amongst them rather than the kingdoms," Rod explained, splaying his hands. Morana watched him intently, following his train of thought. "While Asteria is the Goddess of Sirians, you are still responsible for those who have inherited the Energy, Danica, just as Gallus is responsible for those wielding the Aether."

"Light and Dark," Morana muttered breathlessly, but Rod heard, nodding in agreement.

"If we start a divide amongst the Sirians, not only will we ensure we have lost Asteria's support, but it will isolate the Lemurians to Zephyr's side." Rod sighed, shaking his head as he reclined in his chair. "The humans will be helpless in a war like that. They don't have the means to fight against half the Sirians and all Lemurians. They would have to watch the Beings battle each other. If we successfully defend the humans, they will forever fear the Sirians who wield the Aether and the Lemurians."

"A Path to extinction," Morana whispered, her face slack. "This is why Dola panicked. The meeting opened up more Paths to extinction just as it opened more Paths to redemption."

"We need to act fast," Rod said, lurching from his seat. He flew to the desk in the corner of the room, grabbing a feather from an empty inkwell and yanking out a piece of parchment from a drawer. "I will speak with my son. As founder of the House of Nemea, those who reign still may hold loyalty to Garuda higher than Zephyr."

"The same could be said of Echidna," Danica added, gazing at Morana.

She shook her head. "Echidna is unruly—they always have been. Sybil never led them the way Garuda and Brigid involved themselves with their people. She was simply a matron for them. One could argue Echidna and Nemea may even feel obligated to Valeria with their use of potions to heal."

"Who are the countries with Nemea or Echidna on the throne?" Danica asked Rod, frowning. "I can't recall."

"Presently, Allanis and Sylvan." Rod continued to scribble as he spoke, "The Rotherhams of Allanis are drakons, and the Mariandes of Sylvan are lycan."

"I thought it was the other way around." Danica pursed her lips, an eyebrow hitching.

"It was, but that was over a century ago," Rod explained, but Morana cleared her throat.

"It doesn't change the fact that one country is Nemea and one is Echidna." Morana glared at Danica, who only mimicked the expression. "There are still two countries with the House of Argo on their thrones."

"Well, one country is Thalassa," Rod said, folding his parchment with a shake of his head. "That is Nen's country. They'll do whatever he asks of them."

"The other being Teslin?" Danica guessed, and Morana simply nodded. "I know my sons still have Sirians on their thrones in Riddling and The Northern Pizi. We all clearly know who rules Etherea. Does Eldamain still have Sirians?"

Again, Morana nodded. "That's four Sirian countries, not including Celestia."

"Again, even more reason Asteria needs to be on our side," Danica repeated, her voice rising with agitation. "Tell me again why allowing Asteria to throw her tantrum—"

"Asteria will not be answering you or me," Rod interrupted, his voice thundering throughout the room. Danica relented, her power dimming. "We need to approach her cautiously. Until then, we do what we can without her."

"My sons will listen to their mother," Danica said nonchalantly, waving her hand. "We'll easily secure The Northern Pizi and Riddling with or without Asteria. It would be beneficial if we had her, though. Her relationship is stronger than mine since she communicates with them frequently."

Morana deadpanned as she stared at Danica, contemplating how the woman was so clueless about her actions and their consequences. She complained about her children, but she didn't try to know them.

"Which leaves Eldamain, Etherea, and Celestia," Rod whispered, locking eyes with Morana. "Sybil has quite a deep-rooted relationship with Eldamain, doesn't she?"

"She does," Morana confirmed, narrowing her eyes. "Although I don't know what her involvement can be considering it's her prophecy we toy with."

"If she can speak with Eldamain, she must," Danica griped, her eyes blinding gold orbs.

"Eldamain can be easily convinced." The parchment in Rod's hand vanished. Morana knew the enchantment well. The quill Rod wrote with was made from Garuda's feather, so he would receive the letter and be permitted to read it. "The Carraphims are fair rulers and always have been. They value human lives and would go to war to defend them."

"The Head Elder of Celestia also held the position of Royal Healer within Eldamain for ten years," Morana explained carefully, grasping all the patience she had left for Danica and ignoring Rod bristling in the corner.

"So, we may need Asteria for Celestia, Etherea, *and* Eldamain." Danica toyed with the Energy in her hand, glowing ringlets coiling around her fingers. "Celestia worships her, whether she wants them to or not, and Phoebe is her sister."

"Phoebe may not be as difficult as you anticipate despite Gallus being her father." Rod pointed a finger at Danica. She snarled, her lip curling. "She married a human male. For Heaven's sake, she rigged her marriage games so the man could win."

"She may respond positively to Asteria compared to the rest of us," Morana agreed, drumming her fingers on the chair. "Gallus may try to offer Phoebe immunity for her husband and his family, though."

If they could sway the countries they set out to ally with, it would put them at an advantage against the agenda of the others. They could possibly exploit the partnership with Celestia, forcing them to call forth all Sirians to rally for the cause of the humans.

If that happened, Gallus, Zephyr, Nen, and Valeria would surely stand down. It would allow them to stop a war before it started, keeping the discord amongst high-ranking Sirians, Lemurians, Andromedans, and

Lyrans.

"This all rests on Asteria," Danica said softly, one eye squinting as she gazed at her empty hand.

"Should we expect Dola and Irena to keep themselves out of the conflict?" Rod asked, gaze bouncing between Danica and Morana.

"Dola must stay as far away from this as possible," Morana whispered. "I fear this ordeal has started an unfortunate…"

She couldn't bring herself to say it.

What Zephyr spoke of—talking Dola down from Madness—was accurate. This was too close a call. Dola couldn't be involved if they wished to preserve her sanity.

"Irena will only involve herself when we are teetering on the brink of war or peace," Danica explained, but Morana snorted.

"The only reason she involved herself between you three during the meeting was because I urged her to." Morana sank into her chair, flicking her wrist. "She will remain neutral at all costs and prefer to protect Dola."

"I am more than comfortable with her doing so." Rod gazed out the window overlooking Eonia, their homes spread across the small expanse of their pocket Realm. "We have our tasks, then?"

Morana and Danica nodded in agreement, both lost in their minds.

They were flirting with Fate. Morana wondered if Asteria had the right idea not jumping to conclusions, and what they were about to do would hurl them into a war the world would never recover from.

CHAPTER 11

SYBIL

S ybil perched at the wooden dining table of her home in Eldamain. Heat rose from the cracked tea cup before her, a thread of steam swirling into the herbs drying from the ceiling.

It had been days since the dreaded vision, but the images still plagued her both in waking and sleep. They lessened every day, but Sybil worried she would never again wake from sleep without the strange smoky, vinegar taste lingering in her mouth—

The drakon within her perked up at a shift in the air, the voice within sending her a warning while her primal instincts went on defense.

There were only two who would dare portal into her home uninvited. Luckily, she didn't mind the company of either.

"Morana," Sybil greeted, dropping a mint leaf into her tea without looking up. "Did the Lyrans meet?"

Feet shuffled along the wooden floor, which meant Morana was in her mortal form. She confirmed it when she slid into the seat across from Sybil, pale blue eyes regarding her and white-blond hair pulled back in two braids on either side of her head.

"We did," Morana confirmed with a nod, folding her hands on the table. "Asteria was there. It was her first time in Eonia in nearly two decades. Although, Danica and Rod received no answer to their burning questions."

"Your lot meddles in far more matters than they should," Sybil said, glaring up at her. Her attention briefly held on the intricate, dark brown markings standing out against her mother's fair skin. "Why do *you* not ask her whether or not she is involved with the Head Elder? At least you can relay it to them so they leave her alone."

Morana shut her eyes briefly, inhaling slowly. "*I* don't want to meddle in Asteria's business. Besides, if she wishes to speak to me, I know she will. I don't believe she is involved with him, though, which is why I don't ask.

"Danica also has far deeper ambitions to get Asteria to spend more time in Eonia. She could care less who Asteria entertains herself with. It's Rod who will throw a jealous fit."

"Well, I can confirm she is not in a relationship with him, if that gives you any satisfaction in knowing her better than her mother and former lover." Sybil smirked at the thought of Asteria dragging all the Lyrans around in her games.

Asteria was the closest thing Sybil had to a sister or true, lifelong friend.

Being a strong prophetess made it challenging to maintain friendships. The world just wanted to know what lay before them. Asteria never treated her that way, purposely avoiding conversations that would lead to a prophecy and limit her words.

While Sybil technically had her sister, Endora, they were not blood-related. Neither were she and Asteria, but at least they grew up together. There were less than thirty years separating her and Asteria, while there was fifty years between her and Endora. Not to mention the circumstances around Endora's birth put quite a strain on Sybil and her mothers.

"Sybil…" Morana's tone had Sybil stilling.

She slowly dragged her gaze over the rim of her teacup with a frown.

Morana looked haunted. As the Goddess of Life and Death, that meant something terrible happened. "The meeting didn't go as anticipated."

"What do you mean?" Sybil asked, straightening her back as she hitched forward. "Dola was to relay the message—"

"Oh, she did," Morana assured, holding a hand up. "As you can imagine, the Lyrans had questions, which Dola attempted to answer."

"What is the problem, then?" Sybil narrowed her eyes, the drakon shuddering in her chest as a low rumble hummed from within.

Morana glared at her in warning before continuing, "The prophecy didn't mention humans."

Sybil blinked at Morana, searching her face as she reluctantly recalled the entire vision.

Her prophecies rarely had words. They were mostly images coupled with a strange sensation that stopped her from saying too much or forced her to say more.

Morana was right, though. She didn't see the end of the humans.

"Correct." Sybil tilted her head. "Why does that matter?"

"Nen caught that," Morana explained, a muscle ticking in her jaw. "He capitalized on it. We're concerned he and a few other Lyrans will do something drastic to cause war and bring chaos upon the humans. To add to matters, Dola is a mess. I've never seen her this inconsolable, and I fear she is on the brink of Madness."

"Dola?" Sybil's eyes flared wide, her body chilling. "The Madness?"

Dola taught Sybil about the Madness when she learned how to hone her prophetic abilities. The Madness specifically plagued any Lyrans who gazed into the Universe to converse with Fate, Time, or Destiny. Those who aged into the stars were lucky to do so before Madness took over. If they were not so lucky, and they succumbed to it…

Well, it was a Fate far worse than death. While Lyrans who Fractured found their powers taking hold of their forms, Lyrans who suffered from

Madness were stuck in their minds in a constant time loop of prophecies, futures, pasts, and possibilities without being able to discern reality.

It led to difficulty concentrating and reasoning, and problems with misusing words or forgetting familiar objects and people. There were sudden mood swings, to the extent Dola had seen personalities change entirely from where the Lyrans came.

Dola couldn't be sure if Sybil would ever fall to Madness since she was the equivalent of an Andromedan, but she educated her just in case.

"We are concerned she is in the beginning stages." Morana reclined in her seat, running a hand through the loose strands on top of her head. "She's resting for now. We're refraining from asking about any Paths."

Sybil knew why her mother had come now. She waited, tapping a finger against her teacup.

"I know you can only answer certain things, but I hope this question is the right one." Morana reached across the table, laying her hand on Sybil's. "Does the Path you foretold still hold strong?"

The feeling within guided her, and when it nodded, she answered, "The Path still rings true, but it is still not the True Path."

Morana sighed, leaning back again. There was a heaviness around her that Sybil wasn't used to seeing unless Valeria was involved.

"Morana," Sybil drawled, her heart dropping to her stomach as the drakon peeked from behind her eyes. "What happened?"

Morana averted her gaze, crossing her arms over her chest. She wrapped her hands tightly around her biceps. "Some of the Lyrans proposed humans would be the reason behind the other Beings' extinction. They thought it would be best to either rid them of this world or restrict their liberties."

"That is utterly absurd." Sybil snorted, mimicking Morana's position. She peered at her from the corners of her eyes, and Sybil blanched. "No. You can't... Who was it?"

"Rod, Danica, Dola, and myself attempted to defend the humans. We don't think it worked." Morana eyed Sybil knowingly, her expression also heavy with pity.

"Valeria," Sybil grumbled, fire burning at the back of her throat. She swallowed the smokey air, her heart stuttering when she asked, "Asteria?"

"I will say, Asteria argued with Nen for a moment, but ultimately, she and Irena took the same stance of neutrality." Morana perched an elbow on the edge of the table, rubbing her temple. "I know Irena will forever remain indifferent due to her powers, but I fear Asteria will be pulled in two different directions. Her mother and father stand on opposite sides of this discussion. While Asteria does love Gallus, she seemed perturbed by his argument.

"At the same time, Danica is one of her least favorite people next to Rod. I wouldn't be surprised with her surly attitude as of late that she would stay neutral purely out of spite." Morana leveled a look at her. Sybil rolled her eyes. "You know what I'm asking of you."

"You wish to use my relationship with Asteria to sway her to the right side," Sybil answered, a slight monotone to her voice as her prophesying snuck through. She didn't need Fate to tell her what her mother was asking. "If it is any consolation, I don't think Asteria would remain neutral if the Lyrans began to harm the humans."

"Regardless, I believe you will have more leeway with Asteria than I will in this situation despite my relationship with her." Morana stood from her chair and began pacing in Sybil's living area. "Asteria will be a massive advantage for more than one reason. Yes, she is the most powerful Lyran with not only the Energy and the Aether, but also blue starfire. She's also Goddess of the Sirians. Despite her vehemency to dismiss the title amongst her people, they still look up to her and take her word to heart."

"You want to utilize the Sirians to protect the humans?" Sybil tracked Morana's movements, frowning at the frantic energy radiating off her. Her god-form peeked out from beneath her mortal skin as it thinned with her emotions.

"The Sirians were originally created for that purpose." Morana stopped pacing, facing Sybil. "I'm not sure how some Lemurians will react if this were to become a larger ordeal than it needs to be. Many find themselves loyal to Zephyr as *their* God."

"Others find loyalty to the parents of the Andromedans who established their House." Sybil waved her hand over her body. She was the one who established the House of Echidna. "Garuda is Rod's son. I'm your daughter—"

"Some still recognize Valeria as your mother, too," Morana said softly. Sybil deadpanned. "We can't forget that Nen runs the entire island of Thalassa. The majority of Lemurians from the House of Argo worship him with their dying breath."

"What do you suppose I can do to sway Asteria that you can't?" Sybil rose from her chair to step before her mother, studying her face. "Will you not approach royal thrones in the hopes of winning countries? Ask them not to instill harsh rules and protect their humans?"

"That's how we hope to approach this," Morana said, clasping her hands. "It'll be better to approach royals rather than Beings to avoid dividing a war based on the different powers. Danica's sons have sway over Riddling and The Northern Pizi, considering Taranis is still their king. I hoped you could sway Eldamain to our side since you have a long-standing relationship with them. I'm sure it would mean even more to them if Asteria was part of it, as well."

"The Head Elder of the Academy is close with the Carraphim princes," Sybil pondered aloud, pinching her lips as she shrugged. "If they speak with him, they may be able to help Celestia choose, which would force Asteria's hand. With both of her brothers joining their mother's side—"

"We also think having Asteria would convince Phoebe to join us over Gallus," Morana added, and a harsh laugh burst from Sybil. She clapped a hand over her mouth as Morana frowned with a curled lip. "You find that humorous?"

"Let us focus on getting Celestia and Asteria on the defensive side first," Sybil managed around a chuckle. "Morana… She and Phoebe do *not* have a formidable relationship. From my understanding, it's practically nonexistent."

Morana clenched her jaw, veins illuminating beneath her skin in tune with what Sybil knew was her mother's heartbeat. Sybil sighed, reaching between them and gently gripping her arm.

"Sybil…" Morana shook her, rolling her lips together. "If word travels to any of the other Lyrans, this could ultimately push them to make a rash decision. I fear for this world if we don't prepare our chosen allies to come together to protect it. Is this a true crossroad, or will either decision lead to the same Path?"

Sybil gasped as her vision shifted, her mind twisting as it showed her the outcome of their decisions.

Stone clicked into place, blue power spearing through the sky and into the Heavens. A golden veil wrapped around the Realm, shimmering around Aveesh, Eonia, and an endless pit of darkness. Sealed off from each other and the Universe, Gods mourned their children.

Sybil opened her mouth to answer, but no words came out. She searched for any words that Fate allowed her to give, but it refused to let her confirm or deny with a single syllable or movement.

"I can't answer," Sybil finally said, her shoulders deflating. Morana gripped them, embracing her.

Sybil stiffened, but she let Morana have this small moment, even if the embrace offered her no comfort.

"I'm sorry," Morana whispered against Sybil's hair, stroking it down her back. "I don't mean to put you in a difficult position. I just worry we aren't doing the right thing and that this will lead to ruin regardless."

"The Heavens are divided, Mother," Sybil muttered, muffled by Morana's shoulder. "They have been, and it was only a matter of time."

This truth came from no prophecy. It was simply a statement of fact.

The moment Morana saved Sybil when she was a mortal child—all because of Valeria's pleading—the balance amongst the Lyrans changed.

K.M. DAVIDSON

They realized Rod and Morana were not the only two who could create life, and that Danica and Gallus were not the only ones able to pass powers to humans. They could all create, one way or another.

While it sounded like a lovely concept, Nen and Zephyr were greedy. They believed they were owed Morana's gift of life to imbue whatever they wanted with souls.

With Enki being the first human Andromedan and Sybil being both a type of Andromedan and first Lemurian, the Lyrans continued to experiment and mate with those on Aveesh, steering away from each other.

A world with so many imbalances of power caused conflict between the Beings and Lyrans. Betrayals of loyalty, commitment, and love ensued.

Sybil and Asteria watched it all unfold before them from young ages. Asteria resisted recognizing herself as a Lyran because of it, but Rod nearly won her over in embracing her goddesshood.

Until he betrayed her, too.

CHAPTER 12

SYBIL

S ybil laced her fingers behind her back, steadily placing one foot before the other as she paced the enclosure where she was to meet King Orvyn and Crown Prince Quintin Carraphim. Her eyes trailed along the wall beside her, skimming over tapestries until she reached the five-pane stained glass window.

The bottom half of the windows was clear, peering out into the forest behind the castle where leaves changed the backdrop, shades of burnt orange mingling with deep green hues to signal fall approaching. The top half was a mosaic of colors woven between its intricate frame, sunlight casting a glow against the polished, gray stone wall.

"The glass is more vibrant in the winter," a voice interrupted, and Sybil spun on her heel. King Orvyn stood in the room with his eldest son beside him, smiling. "The trees are coated with white snow, so it creates a blank scenery for the colors to reflect against."

"Who do you think gave your ancestors the idea to commission this window?" Sybil smiled softly, dropping into a curtsy. "It's good to see you, Your Majesty."

"Please." King Orvyn scoffed, his arms spread wide as he rounded the deep maroon chairs in the middle of the room. "It's just the three of us, Sybil. Let's drop the formalities."

"If that's the case"—she paused, smirking as he stopped before her—"you are aging far more beautifully than your father."

A boisterous laugh burst from Orvyn as he drew her into a tight embrace, briskly rubbing her back as she chuckled. "You flatter me, Sybil. A man who's been made a grandfather four times over appreciates the sentiment."

Sybil pulled back at arm's length, tilting her head.

He *was* aging rather gracefully despite being a man in his late fifties. While his hair was already graying, it was still full and long, curling at his ears much like his sons' hair. He even had a full mustache to match his beard, and still felt relatively firm despite no longer fighting alongside his men.

"Do our informalities still hold here, Prince?" Sybil teased as she turned to Quin, raising an eyebrow. He rolled his eyes and took her hand, placing a delicate kiss against her knuckles as he dipped his head. "Your wife complained about the last ball, I presume?"

"Are you inquiring if she expressed concern that I stayed up into outrageous hours of the night with my delinquent brothers and their friends, accompanied by a stunning immortal?" He pondered his own question before Sybil waved him off with a scowl.

Orvyn chuckled as he gestured for them to sit. "While it's always a pleasure to have your presence within our home, Sybil, I fear that your urgency sparked concern between myself and my sons."

"Unfortunately, what I bring you today should be of great concern." Sybil sat in the chair across from the two Carraphim men, adjusting the skirt of her black dress and shaking out her sleeves. "The Lyrans appear to be on the brink of war, and both sides are gathering allies."

All the humor winked from Orvyn and Quin's faces at the revelation. Sybil didn't beat around the bush, bringing them both up to speed—from the moment she received her prophecy to her mother asking her to speak with Eldamain on the Lyrans' behalf.

When she finished her tale, Quin nearly paced a hole behind the chair he previously occupied while Orvyn dug his fingers into his temples.

"You believe a battle is inevitable?" Orvyn asked, turning his gaze on his son. "What are your thoughts, Quin?"

"What the other Gods are proposing is genocide," Quin snapped, the Aether swirling at his fingertips. When he turned his gaze on Sybil, his eyes and Mark were entirely black. "If they don't eliminate an entire race, they seek to enslave them against their will and limit their freedoms just to control them. It's barbaric. We must stand against it."

"I'm glad you think so," Orvyn said, nodding absentmindedly. Sybil felt no relief, though, if only because she never had any concerns to begin with. Eldamain would always take up arms to defend those in need. "Lady Danica is positive Riddling and The Northern Pizi will come to their aid?"

"Of course," Sybil assured, shrugging. "King Taranis is her son—from what I understand, they don't have such a hostile relationship that he would join a different side than her just for spite. While Dionne may no longer sit on the throne, his descendants do, and Riddling still turns to him when they need counseling. It's every other country they are unsure of. I feel you may have further insight into who may join in the humans' defense."

Orvyn's sigh heightened Sybil's nerves. She waited impatiently for his response.

He lifted his tired gaze to Quin, an eyebrow raised in silent question.

Quin stopped pacing, returning to the chair before Sybil. He rubbed his hands on his thighs before speaking, "I'm sure you know already that Thalassa will side with Lord Nen. While we all worship the Gods, they follow him blindly. I would wager Teslin will also blindly follow Lord Nen since the Seymours reign from the House of Argo."

"What of Allanis and Sylvan?" Sybil asked, searching Quin's face. He pressed his lips together, giving her a sidelong look. "Oh, come now.

The Rotherhams are from the House of Echidna. May I remind you, *my* House?"

"How is your relationship with King Rotherham?" Quin pursed his lips as Sybil sunk further into the chair. "That's what I presumed. You've been detached from some of your fellow Lemurians for far too long, Sybil. I fear your other mother, Lady Valeria, may have stepped in. If she hasn't, Lord Zephyr has. He definitely influences Sylvan."

"I thought Garuda's influence would be heavier than Zephyr with Sylvan. I also thought you were allied with Sylvan and Allanis." Her gaze bounced from Orvyn to Quin.

It appeared Orvyn was allowing his heir to take the lead.

"They're closer with one another than they are with us," Quin admitted. "Alas, there may be something we can do. An improved treaty with either or both countries may assist in matters."

"Which leaves Etherea," Sybil uttered quietly, maintaining eye contact with Quin, his green hazel eyes studying her.

"Queen Phoebe has only been on the throne for the last year since King Drogo abdicated," he explained, tapping a finger against the arm of his chair. "She's silent with all the former allies King Drogo maintained and has yet to form any new relationships. From my understanding, she doesn't correspond with Sylvan. My intel believes she attempts to undermine her father's Council every chance she gets."

Sybil withheld an expression that would add incredulity to the declaration of King Drogo being Phoebe's father. Everyone on this plane knew Phoebe was a Sirian Andromedan, which meant King Drogo couldn't possibly be her father.

Just as she and Morana had discussed, Gallus was Phoebe's true father. The world may want to avoid the matter, but it was necessary to acknowledge the truth for this conversation.

"Let's not be reserved in our speech," Sybil said quietly, swiping a hand between them. "We all know King Drogo is not Phoebe's father. Even if her relationships with Drogo's former allies are nonexistent, she yearns for Gallus's approval. Do they have the healthiest father–daughter relationship? No, but neither does Asteria, yet both women hold love for him."

"There is another matter to consider, though." Quin sat forward, clasping his hands between his outstretched legs. He peered up at Sybil through thick lashes. "King Dustin."

"Phoebe's husband?" Sybil scrunched her face, curling her nose. "What of the man?"

"Do you forget Dustin is human?" A sly grin curved up Quin's cheek, and Orvyn admired his son from where he silently observed.

This dynamic between Quin and Orvyn had occurred for generations of Carraphims before. Kings would let the next in line to the throne gradually take over political matters before stepping down entirely. If Orvyn was allowing Quin to lead this conversation, they planned for the crown prince to become King of Eldamain soon.

Sybil came back to the conversation at hand with hope in her chest. "If Gallus openly supports this war against humans, there's no way she will stand beside her father."

"I highly anticipate Lord Gallus offering Queen Phoebe protection if she stays out of the war entirely," Orvyn said, shrugging.

"Danica believes Gallus will try to get Phoebe on his side and Asteria would join to spite her," Sybil added, shaking her head. "I can't speak for Phoebe, but Asteria would never do that. While Gallus seemed to be an instigator of sorts during the meeting, according to Morana, he was not the Lyran to introduce the idea initially. It was Nen and Zephyr leading the charge against the humans.

"I do agree Gallus will try to sway Phoebe and Asteria, but rather to stand neutral."

"And what *is* Asteria's stance on this?" Quin narrowed his eyes at Sybil, tilting his head. "Being a Sirian family with close ties to the Academy and Celestia, I must inquire. You have yet to mention her."

Sybil sighed heavily because she was waiting for this to come up.

All Sirians looked to Asteria. They admired her and sometimes worshipped her from afar, if only to avoid her wrath for such idolization. The fact she required Sirians not to address her as a Goddess only fueled their love for her. She was the only Lyran outside of Nen who spent considerable time amongst her people, conversing with and guiding them. Even Rod had withdrawn over the last few centuries, but his love for humans was still strong.

"When Rod, Danica, and Morana spoke after the meeting, Asteria refused their summons," Sybil began, picking at a loose thread on the chair. "Her silence doesn't mean her support is not with the humans. I believe Asteria is under the impression that forming alliances without proof the other Lyrans have acted against the humans will insight the Path we are trying to avoid. She will join the cause when she knows the humans are in true danger."

"Is there anything we can do to help persuade her to consider it further?" Quin asked, frowning. "I've met Asteria. I know she can be rather—"

"Crass and difficult?" Orvyn chortled as he stared out the window over Sybil's shoulder, lost in thought. "You try to make that woman do something she has no desire to do—or before she wants to do it—and you will find yourself threatened by starfire."

"You speak as if you know this personally, Father," Quin surmised, twisting his head to Orvyn.

Sybil held back her grin because Orvyn *was* speaking from experience.

The Carraphim family was one of the oldest reigning royalties. They'd ruled Eldamain for as long as Sybil could remember, which also meant as long as Asteria had been alive. Being a long line of Sirian royals, Sybil believed Asteria held a tender spot for Eldamain because of it.

Asteria may not want to acknowledge her goddesshood, but she did love the Sirians.

"Asteria tends to give Sirians more grace than others, unless you push her limits." Sybil threw her gaze at Orvyn, who waved her away. "While I appreciate the offer, I fear it may be best if as few people talk to Asteria about this as possible. She already ignored the calls of Morana, and I'm sure Gallus has either spoken to her or plans to. As I said, Asteria will need to be *moved* to join."

Orvyn and Quin shared a look that had Sybil stiffening in her chair. Orvyn tilted his head encouragingly.

"I'm warning both of you," Sybil snapped not unkindly, pointing a finger at them. "You may think you know what can persuade Asteria, but I assure you I have yet to meet anyone who is her match."

"I'm willing to test that." Quin shrugged nonchalantly, settling further into the chair and folding his hands over his stomach. "She'll join us once something happens, so why not try and move her sooner?"

Sybil pressed her lips together, nostrils flaring. "Quin... *No one* can get underneath Asteria's skin enough to make her do something she doesn't want to do."

"I would venture, Sybil"—Quin paused, winking—"she hasn't yet met Wells."

CHAPTER 13

ASTERIA

A steria portaled directly into the Carraphim's formal dining room, the snap of it closing behind her succeeded by two females yelping.

"Lady Asteria!" Queen Maribel Carraphim cried, one hand flat against her chest as the other clasped her husband's at the head of the table. "Welcome to our home?"

Asteria had been to the Aggelos Palace plenty of times over the last few centuries. A majority of her visits took place in this grand dining hall or the ballroom located somewhere near the front of the castle.

The dining room was dimly lit by a plethora of sconces along the beige walls, alternating purple and gold tapestries decorated with the Carraphim family crest. A larger chandelier with far too many candles hung above the extended table, casting a warm glow over its occupants.

Asteria inclined her head to scan the table where the entire Carraphim family seemed to be gathered. She narrowed her eyes at every single one as she inched closer, hands clasped behind her back.

She stumbled in her stride when she locked eyes with enticing beige ones.

Wells lifted his glass, an eyebrow raised and a smirk playing at the corner of his lips.

"No Lady Asteria, Maribel. Just Asteria." She smiled tightly at the queen. "You should know that by now. Although, you attended the Academy over three decades ago, so I suppose I can let it pass without too much fuss."

Wells choked on his mead, sputtering into his glass. His oldest brother, Quintin, leveled him with a glare from where he sat a few seats down. Asteria almost found amusement in that until she noticed the only remaining chair at the table was directly across from Wells.

She narrowed her eyes.

They wanted something from her.

"Please join us, Asteria," Orvyn called from the head of the table, waving a hand at her. "It's been quite some time since you visited Eldamain, so let us dine for the evening. There may be some reintroductions required, possibly some new ones."

"Thank you, I suppose." Asteria lowered to her seat, sensing Wells staring at her from across the table. She paused just before plopping down, squinting at him. "I didn't expect to see the second spare so soon after you graced the Academy with your presence last month."

"You two have met?" Quintin blurted, his voice climbing a notch higher. Asteria and Wells both hauled their gazes to him, and she glowered. "When?"

"I visited Odo and Erika at the start of the academic cycle before journeying home," Wells explained, and Asteria jerked her gaze back to him.

He shrugged, pursing his full lips, and it reminded Asteria of her thoughts regarding those lips.

She reached for her wine glass and took two heavy gulps of the clove and honey-based mead. Wells caught her out of the corner of his eye, gaze flickering to where her glass sat on the table then to her lips, causing her stomach to tighten.

"We've apparently always crossed paths but never truly met," Asteria jumped in, if only to give her something to do instead of ogling the prince in front of his loved ones. "It was a brief meeting, just in passing. Nothing quite worth noting."

"Oh no?" Wells chided, resting his elbow on the table as he fixed his chin into the palm of his hand. He batted those thick lashes at Asteria. "Are you certain?"

Her nostrils flared as she inhaled sharply, irritation bubbling in the middle of her chest. *Who does he think he is?*

"Brother," Quintin grumbled under his breath. "Save it—"

"Well, I'm glad you're familiar with my sons," Orvyn interrupted, gesturing to the side of the table where Quintin and Wells sat. To the right of Wells was their other brother, Piers, who dipped his head in acknowledgment when her gaze passed him. Between Wells and Quintin was a familiar female. "Let me introduce you to Quintin's wife, Princess Joan."

"It is a pleasure to meet you, Lad—Asteria." The princess caught herself before Asteria could level her with a glare. "I attended the Academy at the same time as Prince Orwell."

"I apologize for not remembering you from your time there." Asteria frowned, concerned as to why she couldn't remember this class of Sirians as vividly as others. Many royals appeared to have been there at the same time. "I believe I attended your wedding, but we didn't get the opportunity to speak."

"No need to apologize." Princess Joan smiled kindly, shaking her head. "There are thousands of Sirians who attend the Academy. I know you only get the opportunity to interact with a small group of them. I believe the Diplomatic teachings are not particularly your favorite to grace either."

"Not often, no." Asteria nodded at an attendant as they refilled her glass. "I fear I don't have much knowledge to lend in that area of the Academy." Asteria paused to sip her mead before reaching out, feeling the room for the Aether and Energy. "I know many of the Carraphims wield the Aether, but I detect the Energy as well. There are too many Sirians for me to determine which of you wield the Energy versus the Aether. Which do you, Princess?"

"I wield the Energy, as does Prince Piers." Joan extended her arm in front of Wells to gesture to the other Carraphim prince. Wells frowned at tje arm in front of him as though it were a foreign object, and Asteria was surprised to find herself suppressing a grin. "We're still not sure which of the two powers our children will inherit."

"How many children do you have?" Asteria inquired, her interest peaking. While the topic of children for herself was sensitive, she enjoyed them nonetheless.

"Four," Quintin answered, his hand wrapping over his wife's. "Our eldest is eight, so he may develop his powers within the next few years."

"Well, you two have certainly been busy." Asteria chuckled under her breath as she raised her glass to her lips.

By the reactions around the table, she realized she'd said it louder than intended.

Joan's mouth went slack, and Quintin's jaw tightened, as did his grip over his wife's hand.

Wells, on the other hand, spewed a stream of mead across the table.

Asteria's own eyes blew wide as Wells tried to reestablish decorum, attendants attempting to assist by patting down the tablecloth.

"Is there a problem with your mouth today, *brother*?" Quintin grumbled, leaning over his wife to glare at Wells.

"Sybil tried to warn you, and yet you refused to believe her," a man beside Piers said, his lavender eyes dancing with glee. He tipped his glass in Asteria's direction, scales peeking out from beneath his collar. "It seems you have caught Wells quite off his game."

Wells leveled a stern look at the foreign man and snatched a fresh napkin out from the attendant's hand. Asteria's lip flattened into a thin line, and she glowered at Quintin and Orvyn.

"Why would Sybil feel the need to warn you about me?" Asteria asked, her voice lethal.

Every individual at the table stiffened at the tone. Even the attendants stopped bustling.

Asteria's power hummed as every other sound in the room tapered into silence, awaiting her move.

Quintin cleared his throat, which Asteria found amusing. What better way to test how well his Elders taught him diplomacy than facing off with the Goddess of Sirians?

Asteria mimicked Well's move from earlier, balancing her elbow on the table as her hand cradled her chin. She felt said man's grin radiating from across the table, but she kept her attention trained on the Crown Prince of Eldamain.

"Sybil informed us about the meeting that transpired between the Lyrans. Morana, Danica, and Rod have requested our assistance in defending the humans, should the time come," Quintin explained, then threw back his glass.

Asteria straightened and clasped her hands in her lap, staring at him with a blank face despite the annoyance prickling the back of her neck.

"As one of the kingdoms with Sirians on the throne, but also one that only maintains loyalty to the Goddess of Sirians"—Asteria opened her mouth to protest, but Quintin held up a hand and continued—"we wanted to speak with you about whether you would be joining our side."

"The decisions I make on my own shouldn't influence yours as a leader of your country," Asteria countered, a small scoff falling from her lips. "For the sake of this conversation, I'll acknowledge my status as a Goddess. I've never given the impression that, as *your* Goddess, you should blindly follow the things I say and do. I've always given you the free will to make choices, and I won't change that now over some Path that is just that. *One* Path.

"I don't know how much Sybil explained to you about what is occurring. I also don't believe you understand how Fate works. Your lot tends to get Fate and Destiny confused." Asteria leaned forward in her seat. All eyes latched onto her, absorbing every word. "The trajectory of our world has many possibilities that not even a single prophetess can comprehend, whether or not she is an Andromedan. The only one who has the power to comprehend them all is Dola. This Path Sybil saw is not the True Path, which is an inevitable outcome. We still have the chance to journey down another. I have yet to see a decision made that makes the Path Sybil foresaw any more absolute than whatever the alternatives may be."

"You dare speak of my power as if you know it intimately," a voice penetrated the room, startling Asteria. She snapped her head toward the entryway where Sybil stood like a Goddess herself. "I don't flaunt about with royal families speaking on your power, now do I?"

The corner of Asteria's lip twitched at the sight of one of her favorite people in the world. She reached for her glass and tipped it in Sybil's direction. "I'm glad you joined us, Sybil, as this dinner seems to be your doing."

Sybil leveled Asteria with a glare before scowling at the two Carraphim men sitting near the head of the table, anger simmering in her chartreuse eyes. Her vertically slitted pupils thinned, and Asteria wondered for a moment if Sybil would transform into a full drakon in this very dining room.

"I told you to leave it alone, Quin," Sybil grumbled menacingly, borderline growling.

"Sybil, dear…" Orvyn pinched the bridge of his nose as he sighed. "Please join us."

"No need. You"—Sybil pointed at Asteria—"come with me for a moment, *please*."

"Everyone is so polite here. I do appreciate it." Asteria sneered at Wells, who was watching the whole ordeal in silent fascination. "Excuse me while I deal with my *sister*."

Asteria followed Sybil out of the room, allowing the drakon to grab her arm and haul her into the nearest room. Sybil slammed the door shut, locking them in a broom closet.

"Are we going to kiss, Sybil?" Asteria chided, smirking. "I know we aren't technically sisters—not even blood-related in the slightest—but I will have you know—"

"Why haven't you answered the Lyrans' summons?" Sybil interrupted through clenched teeth. "And you know which ones I am referring to."

"I'm not going to repeat what I said, Sybil, but I meant every word." Asteria took a step toward her, not that there was anywhere else she could go. "I also don't appreciate being ambushed."

"This was not an ambush of *my* doing." Sybil rubbed the side of her face, shaking her head. "I specifically told them to leave this to me, and I told Morana I would speak with you separately. Alas, the Carraphims did what they do best. They took it upon themselves to help the less fortunate."

"You call humans needing assistance against possible injustice simply *less fortunate*?" Asteria raised an eyebrow in challenge.

A sinister grin appeared on Sybil's face, exposing her sharpened canines.

"I thought you didn't believe they needed assistance yet," Sybil challenged, crossing her arms. Asteria rolled her eyes, but Sybil continued, "I saw this meeting with you and the Carraphims happening and knew I had to intervene. I raced here to intercept things before they got out of hand.

"You have to know the prophecy hasn't changed," Sybil explained, grabbing Asteria's hands in hers. "I know you don't believe it means anything, but it means *something* if the Path swings to extinction while you still choose neutrality. Have you considered what it could mean if you at least took a stance, Azzy?"

"Don't *Azzy* me." Asteria yanked her hands from Sybil's, narrowing her gaze as her power flared beneath her skin. "You know the other Lyrans are just waiting for an opportunity. I'm considering how choosing a side might anger my father, coaxing him to choose the wrong side. I believe he can be convinced to stay out of it, then Nen and Zephyr will lose interest in whatever game they think they're playing."

"How do you know the Lyrans haven't done anything yet?" Sybil asked, raising her eyebrows. Asteria stayed silent because, in theory, she didn't know. Like the rest of them, she was gauging everything off each Lyran's attitude. "This prophecy sprung upon me so quickly—so *strongly*—because something must have happened *before* the Lyran meeting. It isn't the True Path, but it's a severe one only growing stronger."

Asteria considered this, especially since Fate was allowing Sybil to discuss this much with her and in detail she never experienced from Sybil before. Fate was fickle, which is why Asteria preferred to avoid prophecies, especially when Dola and Sybil were concerned.

The less Asteria knew, the better. She wouldn't drive herself mad by questioning every single move.

And she wasn't about to start.

"The fact remains it is still not the *True* Path, Sybil," Asteria said softly, searching her face. "My father—"

"*Gallus will lead*," Sybil suddenly blurted, her voice taking on a steady tone. Asteria stiffened, horror washing over her as Sybil's eyes shifted from their drakon trait to a cloudy mist that reminded her of Dola's milky white pupil. "*They will rise with Gallus. Ascension. Endless dusk.*"

Sybil fell into Asteria's arms with a gasp, eyes rolling to the back of her head as her eyelids fluttered. Asteria held her against her chest, soothing Sybil with hushes. She scrunched her face, fighting whatever vision she was receiving.

Asteria had never witnessed a prophecy from Sybil in the six hundred years of their existence, and there was a brief moment where she wondered if Fate was attempting to force her hand.

"I refuse to claim a side right now," she whispered as she helped Sybil upright, brushing back her white hair. "But I'll consider what the Carraphims have to say and how they expect to work with the other

Lyrans. I can act as a mediator for now only because they recognize me as their Goddess. I don't want to leave them entirely helpless. Let me speak to my father and try to understand where his mind is."

Sybil nodded, exhaustion evident in her dull gaze. Asteria cupped her cheek, forcing her to meet her gaze.

"I can't believe my father would lead such an attack on this world." Asteria shook her head, and when Sybil opened her mouth, she leveled her with a flash of her eyes. "I'll do my part, though, to be safe."

"Thank you," Sybil whispered, sighing as she leaned into Asteria's embrace. "If you can trust anyone, Azzy, you know it's me."

"I know, Bee," she said with the love she felt for the Andromedan. "Always you and I, right?"

When Sybil nodded with a grim smile, Asteria pulled her into a quick hug before they left the closet.

Horror and dread left behind a chill that clawed at Asteria's god-form.

CHAPTER 14

ASTERIA

Asteria sat in a warm study, mahogany wood lining the walls and ceilings in slats and giant beams. She drummed her fingers on the deep emerald, cushioned chair, one leg crossed over the other as she lounged back.

Her gaze bounced between the Carraphim brothers, lingering longer on Wells each time, if only because he kept observing her with a knowing smirk that set her on edge.

"Would you stop taunting her?" the non-Carraphim male from dinner said to Wells, standing behind the prince as he lightly slapped the side of his cheek. "You forget she's a Goddess—one with quite an attitude I've heard."

"You scold him for taunting me, yet utter I have an attitude right before me?" Asteria raised an eyebrow, her head lolling to the side. "That seems rather foolish."

The male's lavender eyes glistened with amusement, the pastel hue stark against his deep bronze skin. "Excuse my manners, darling, but I believe you have only supported my case."

"What did you just call me?" Asteria leaned forward in the chair,

111

squinting as her flames simmered under her skin.

"Could we please begin before something terrible occurs?" Piers called out to no one in particular as he slouched in his chair, rubbing a hand against his forehead.

The unknown male patted Wells's shoulder before taking a protective stance behind Piers.

"Indeed," Quintin said, perched on the edge of the desk. He toyed with a glass between his legs. "Asteria, what would you prefer to be considered in this scenario?"

Asteria frowned at him. "What do you mean by that?"

He sighed heavily, raising his hazel eyes to meet hers.

The Carraphim brothers shared minor similarities across the three—tanned skin, wavy brown hair, firm builds. Quintin and Piers looked far more similar, sharing greener hazel eyes while Wells's had a sandier tone.

"I know you vehemently oppose being treated like a Goddess," Quintin began, maintaining eye contact. Asteria dipped her head, holding her tongue. "So what is the role you wish to play within these endeavors we are tasked with? Do you wish to be an advisor, ambassador, General—"

"I'm simply a resource," Asteria interrupted, swiping her hand. "As I've expressed to Sybil, I don't wish to choose a side until I see undeniable proof the Lyrans have started their expedition against the humans."

"Sybil said Lady Danica and Lord Gallus may be on opposite sides," Piers said, twisting a ring around his finger. It was identical to the ones Quintin and Wells's wore. "Would this further prevent you from choosing a side, even with undeniable proof?"

"I owe no loyalty to either parent," Asteria explained, her brow pressing deeper into a frown. "I'm just as protective of humans as you all claim to be. Where do you think your country acquired the mentality if not from what my school has taught you?"

Piers dipped his head, apparently appeased with the answer.

"So what is it Rod plans to do?" Asteria folded her hands in her lap, avoiding all their gazes. She didn't need them catching her distaste for the Lyran. "I don't doubt he's the one behind the strategy you'll take moving forward, or at least the basis of."

"It's rather what he does *not* plan to do." Quintin pushed off the desk and walked around to settle behind it. He braced his hands on the cluttered surface. "We're to make no military movements, and we can't coral our troops beyond their normal training. Our Gods have advised us to meet with other kingdoms in the hopes of persuading them against instilling harsh laws that may harm humans. We must be discreet and not make our campaigning obvious."

Our Gods? Asteria recoiled imperceptibly.

"How do you suppose you'll do that?" Asteria followed where Quintin looked between his brothers and the unknown male. "Do you plan on appearing in every kingdom and kindly asking them not to do anything moronic?"

"Our sister countries along our borders are supposed to be our allies," Quintin continued, gesturing to the map on the wall behind him. Asteria's stomach twisted uncomfortably at the reminder of Allanis and Sylvan. "Unfortunately, they both have Lemurians on the thrones. The first step is to gauge whether or not Lord Zephyr has spoken with them and fueled their minds with nonsense. If that has yet to occur, we hope Garuda has spoken to the Mariandes after receiving the letter Rod sent. We also hope Sybil can persuade the Rotherhams."

"That doesn't answer my question." Asteria released a frustrated breath.

Wells shook his head, snorting quietly before sipping his drink. She clenched her jaw to keep from snapping.

"I'll propose marriage treaties with my children as a show of good faith." Quintin shuffled the parchments on his desk, avoiding his brothers' heated gazes. "Allanis and Sylvan's heirs are all spoken for, but both countries have a human Lord ruling a village, and they both have children around the ages of my two middle ones. Therefore, any harm done to their human citizens will be a direct insult to our marriage contracts. It would grant us the opening to incite war."

Asteria pursed her lips, contemplating. "You believe your army is capable of battling both countries should they break a simple marriage treaty?"

"That's where you and Wells come in," Piers said, pointing a finger at her and his younger brother.

Asteria swung her head to Wells, who winked at her over the brim of his glass. Her fingers dug into the arm of the chair, cool tendrils of the Aether coiling around her arms.

"I promise, darling, he's not all that bad." The male behind Piers snickered under his breath.

She narrowed her eyes at him and flicked a finger, his glass tipping from the force of the Energy and spilling down the front of his tunic. He swore under his breath, glancing down.

When he looked back up at her, she was already paying more mind to Piers.

"You were saying?" she asked, voice dripping with bitter honey.

Piers sighed heavily before continuing, "We need to form new alliances, and we need your help to do so."

"Why would you need..." Asteria's face went slack from her confusion as she considered what countries she could possibly help acquire. "You wish for me to involve my brothers?"

"Something tells me they'll already be involved by the time you and Wells venture to their kingdoms." Quintin methodically tapped a finger on the desk. "From our understanding, Lady Danica plans to speak with them."

"Then why do you need me?" Asteria narrowed her eyes as she swept them across the men. "More importantly, what does a second spare have anything to do with this?"

"I find I have far too much time on my hands." Wells winked, repeating what he'd said in Celestia. He set his empty glass on a side table. "Besides, my responsibility as the *second spare* and Prince Envoy is to negotiate alliances and meet with fellow diplomats."

Asteria hummed, pressing her lips together.

"We need you because time is of the essence," Quintin added, leveling Asteria with a pleading look. "You can portal to these kingdoms in the time it takes us to walk into the hall. Danica, Rod, and Morana want to ensure their activity on Aveesh is minimal to avoid inciting the other Gods, and your presence on Aveesh is permanent. With Dionne, King Taranis, and Queen Phoebe being your siblings, it wouldn't be out of character for you to visit them."

Asteria stiffened at the mention of her half-sister, face tightening. "You didn't mention Phoebe."

"He just did," Wells grumbled, and Asteria shut her eyes to quell her power.

The Carraphims were on course to being set aflame.

"Queen Phoebe is an important asset and strong potential ally," Quintin said, leveling his brother with a glare. "Her husband is mortal, as is his family."

"My relationship with Phoebe is quite different from my brothers," Asteria muttered, the burn of guilt settling in the back of her throat. Most days she avoided thinking about it entirely. "We don't speak."

Wells studied her, tilting his head as though he were trying to read her emotions. She swallowed at the scrutiny she found, nervousness fluttering in her chest.

"We will save Phoebe for when the situation leans toward a grimmer outcome," Quintin assured, clearly sensing the unease radiating from her. "Should the world turn to war, though, we'll need her just as we will need Celestia."

Asteria's patience shattered.

She lurched from her seat and advanced on Quintin, hips digging into the opposite side of his desk as she reached across and yanked him onto the surface by his collar. The other men shuffled behind her, but with a snap of her fingers, a quivering shield separated them.

She brought Quintin closer until there was but an inch of space between their noses. Her skin glowed blue beneath her fair tone as she battled the anger and defensiveness boiling inside her. By the absolute terror on Quintin's face, her eyes must have shifted to blue sockets.

"You do not *need*," Asteria insisted in an ethereal voice, raising her other hand beside their faces. Blue flames danced at her fingertips. "You *want*. Between yourselves, Riddling, The Northern Pizi, and Etherea, you have more than enough to battle Allanis and Sylvan. You do not *need* Celestia."

"And should Thalassa and Teslin join?" Wells's voice cut through her fury.

She shoved Quintin back into his seat as she whirled on Wells.

Her shield dropped, and she stalked toward him on mortal feet, her head tilted predatorily. The Aether danced around him, his irises and the Mark on his forehead black to match.

"Nen appears to be leading this cause, so we must assume there will be no hope in swaying either country from his agenda," Piers said as she stopped before Wells. "We *will* need Celestia should this turn into a war of our world."

"If I'm to be your resource, you must be forthcoming." Asteria sneered at Piers before turning her attention back to Wells. She narrowed her eyes at him, closing the distance between them. The blue flames returned to her palm. "I'm not above setting charming males on fire."

Delight gleamed in Wells's eyes as the Aether faded. The glow of her flames lit up the blue ring around his eyes, only partially shadowed by heavy lids. "So I've heard."

Irritation simmered beneath her skin, but she managed a coy grin as she added, "You're not excused simply because you're a prince."

"I should hope not." Wells leaned into her. She tried to angle away, but his breath caressed her ear as he whispered, "I would prefer you did."

She jumped back, the flames and light under her skin snuffing out as she curled her lip at him.

"Does that mean we'll have your help then?" Quintin interjected, his voice quivering.

Asteria took satisfaction in leveling the Crown Prince of Eldamain. It was during these moments she enjoyed being their Goddess despite her resistance. She may not want the worship, but she indulged in the power to send them to their knees.

"I will portal the *Prince Envoy* to the kingdoms he needs to speak with," Asteria agreed, brushing off the front of her gown. It took all her willpower not to comment on Wells's snort. "I don't foresee you needing my assistance to sway my brothers, and I can't promise I'll be of much help when it comes to Phoebe or Celestia."

Piers opened his mouth, but she pointed a finger at him without looking.

"As I said, my relationship with Phoebe is not tumultuous—simply nonexistent. Celestia may fall under the Academy, but I grant them the freedom to make their own decisions. You'll need to speak with my Head Elder."

The unknown male snorted, crossing his arms over his chest. "That won't be a challenge, then. It's Odo Hesper."

"For Heaven's sake, who are you?" Asteria turned on Piers and the male, her arms splayed "What is your role in all of this?"

Wells chuckled, a dark sound that rolled across Asteria's skin and caused heat to pool in her stomach.

"Gavril," the man replied with a tight-lipped grin. "Childhood friend of Prince Orwell Carraphim and lover of this strapping lad." Gavril clasped his hands over Piers's shoulders, causing the prince to startle with a quiet swear. "I also happen to be one of the Lieutenant Generals of the Eldamain army."

"Pleasure." Asteria returned the tight-lipped grin, squinting at Quintin from the corner of her eye. "Is that all you require of me?"

"For now." He sighed, leaning farther back in his chair. He glared at Asteria. "How do we reach you when we need you?"

"Use your Aether," she said, opening a portal behind her. "Summon it and call my name."

With that parting gift—the knowledge of a trick few people knew—she vanished through a portal.

CHAPTER 15

ASTERIA

Asteria appeared in Eonia for the second time in fifteen years, much to her declination.

A chandelier hung above the wide staircase, lit by red starfire that cast an ominous glow against the graphite marble of the grand home. Asteria sighed as she stepped toward the first set of stairs leading to a landing with two stained glass windows stacked atop one another. They were blood red, opaque enough she could glimpse the stars of the Heavens twinkling outside.

She shut her eyes and felt through the Aether, but stopped short when the melody of a piano echoed through the vacant home.

She knew where he was.

Asteria preferred the mortal act of walking, especially since she didn't frequent Eonia often. It gave her the opportunity to admire her father's home, one of many each Lyran constructed for themselves, her favorite being her childhood home.

Well, used to be.

She inherited it when Gallus and Danica first separated after the first affair, roughly two hundred years ago. They gifted her the residence and each built their own in Eonia. Asteria and Rod moved out of his gaudy, auric residence and into her old home, but they only lasted fifty years before he cheated on her.

The house was cursed.

Asteria journeyed through the west wing of the second floor, lamps on the wall alternating between red and blue flames, guiding her to the atrium where the swell of music traveled from. She stepped into the open doorway and leaned against the dark wooden frame.

The stars in the night sky lit the room enough to cast a luminescent glow directly on the white piano in the center. What appeared to be black, dead trees perched between the male sitting at the bench and the windows behind him, but Asteria knew better. The trees weren't dead but rather embalmed by the Aether she and her father shared.

Gallus paid Asteria no mind as she listened to his painful ode, the notes echoing through the room in dips and waves. She folded her arms as she watched him sway with his song, slightly intrigued to find him in his mortal form. His long black hair barely brushed the keys his lengthy fingers flitted across.

He was the epitome of haunting grace.

"You're only playing the minor keys," Asteria said as she finally stepped into the room, hands clasped before her. Gallus didn't stop entirely, but steered the song into a final decrescendo.

"The minor keys weave a delicate tension," Gallus explained, his fingers hovering above them, twitching as if it took great effort to stop playing. "They stir dissonance that lingers with a bittersweet beauty."

Asteria hummed, and Gallus peered at her from the corner of his eyes with a perfectly shaped eyebrow raised. She returned the facial expression, adding a tilt to her head.

Her father slid to the edge of the bench, patting the space next to him.

She moved quickly, taking her usual spot beside him. She let her fingers rest on the cool ivory keys, lingering momentarily before playing her own tune, something deeper and languid. An occasional black key slipped in just before moving to the next cadence.

"Tension and dissonance," Asteria spoke softly over the sound, glancing at Gallus, who studied her intently. "Is that what you wish to invoke amongst the Lyrans?"

Gallus remained silent, and her chest tightened from his lack of emotion or response. She averted her gaze and focused on finishing her song, battling the emotions raging within.

Her father was a complicated man, but she thought she knew him rather well. Danica was always distant and detached from Asteria, while her father was an active participant in every memory. He taught her how to understand the languages of Aveesh, how to play various instruments, and how to adjust between god-form and mortal form. He instructed her on wielding the Aether and blue starfire she inherited from him, honing her into a fierce Lyran.

When she wanted to be.

Where Danica wanted her to embrace goddesshood, Gallus encouraged her to think for herself and decide what *she* wanted, not what others wanted of her. He never pushed her toward an outcome or particular choice, even if there was one he favored.

After Danica had an affair with a Sirian male from Riddling two hundred years ago, there was a slight shift in Gallus. He gradually became more argumentative and intolerant.

Still, nothing changed between him and Asteria. He was the same devoted father.

Gallus was the one who consoled her when Rod cheated on her with the human woman, letting her stay with him at his private abode while she healed. They spoke at length about commitment, and Gallus said Lyrans like Danica and Rod thought themselves greater than the rest for their powers and what they could accomplish.

That was why they felt they could commit such acts without any concern for the consequences, so long as it provided them the thrill they searched for in their monotonous existence.

Gallus secluded himself even further after Danica had another child with a different Sirian male eighty years ago. He became reserved, retreating within his home. He still met with Asteria and allowed her in, but the spark she used to love was missing.

So, when Gallus impregnated the married Queen of Etherea thirty-five years ago, leading to the birth of her sister Phoebe, Asteria felt betrayed. She thought they were in this together, avoiding romantic relationships with the Beings of Aveesh like Morana, Dola, and Irena.

Since then, there was a constant tension in their relationship.

"You're angry with me," Gallus finally said when her song ended, the remnants of music fading into the corners of the room.

"Of course I'm angry with you." Asteria angled herself toward him, placing her hand over his. "Why did you say the things you did in the meeting? Why is Sybil having visions of you leading the charge into a war against the other Lyrans?"

Once again, Gallus only stared at Asteria, flipping his hand beneath hers. He raised it between them and encased his other over it. He rubbed his thumb across their same-hued skin. "This doesn't concern you, Aster."

"It does, Father," she drawled, ripping her hand from his and rising from the bench. She slammed the cover down over the keys, leaning against it. "You said I can't be an Andromedan or simply Sirian—I am a Lyran. If you're serious about what you said in that meeting, that means you wish to harm humans and wage war against the Lyrans who may stand against you. In turn, I would be required to stand against you."

"I would never force you to choose between your mother and me," he explained, cocking his head.

"It's not about you and Mother." Asteria scoffed, rolling her mortal eyes. "I care for all Beings of this world, including humans. I don't have quarrels with them. I didn't think you had any either, but alas"—she waved her hand up and down his body—"here we are."

Gallus chuckled, the sound rumbling through the room like thunder. He slowly rose from the bench, hovering above the ground and floating to the window overlooking Eonia. He kept his back to her, but she caught the wistfulness of his profile as he spoke.

"Dola spoke of the extinction of Lyrans, Andromedans, Lemurians, and Sirians." With the final Being, he gave Asteria a knowing look. She narrowed her eyes at him and clenched her teeth. "The omittance of humans was not accidental. It means this world is headed to a state where humans can thrive without these Beings. I don't fear death, but I don't wish to see all that we've worked to create vanish from the Universe.

"You care for your Sirians more than the humans. I know you do." Gallus spun around, tilting his head back to peer down at Asteria over the tip of his nose. "If you were given the choice between Sirians and humans, which would you save, my Brightest Star?"

"Neither." She walked around the bench and approached her father, crossing her arms. "I would let time do as it must. I would let them live out their existence as the Universe intended, and I would be there with them through it all."

"Good." Gallus grinned, tapping her on the nose. She swatted him away, growling. "I'll admit my approach was rather unsavory in the meeting, but I don't intend to inflict genocide on the humans. There must always be balance in a world to maintain survival. So, *that* is my goal."

"You wish to counter Fate by maintaining balance?" Asteria curled her lip. "You believe there's an imbalance?"

"Humans upset the natural balance of what we intended this world to be." Gallus turned back to the window, gazing out across Eonia. "When we journeyed to this world, the humans were primitive. They could hardly create fire to keep themselves warm, fighting to stay alive with the roaming beasts. Rod did what he could to help them by changing the land to diminish the beastly population. We thought it would give the humans an advantage, but they still struggled.

"So, Danica and I created the Sirians," he continued with a nostalgic tinge to his voice. "We empowered them against the beasts. The balance between human, Sirian, and beast was beautiful. When Zephyr requested the Lemurians' creation, the balance was serene."

Gallus frowned, a pained expression rather than one of anger or frustration. He battled an inner struggle, and Asteria waited patiently for him to continue.

"The humans must remain in their place," Gallus said, and she blanched. "The world will not sustain itself if humans outnumber other Beings. They must be suppressed to protect the Realm."

"What are you going to do, Father?" Asteria squeezed between him and the window.

He towered over her at this proximity, his icy eyes baring into her. "You know I would never force you to choose, but I must implore you to stay out of this."

"How am I to stay out of a war that breaks out amongst this world?" Asteria shook her head, jabbing a finger into his chest. "Nen and Zephyr will involve the Lemurians, and the Sirians will get involved. If any of my people fight, I can't be idle."

"Leave Nen and Zephyr to me," Gallus insisted, stepping away from her and pacing before the piano. "I don't wish to start a war, despite what your mother, Rod, and Morana may believe. Change doesn't happen with outbursts and actions driven by rage. Change requires precision and subtle"—he paused, considering—"adjustments."

"What sort of *adjustments*?" Asteria managed through clenched teeth. She curled her hands into fists, taming the power humming beneath her skin.

"You ask me what you should do, Aster." Gallus's cheeks pinched into a smirk, responding to the power they shared awakening within her. "Again, let us do our work. You may be six hundred and forty-seven, but that is still young compared to the other Lyrans. Where we come from, we were taught to wield our powers for the sole purpose of ruling other worlds and Realms. You were born here in Eonia, which is why you have such an affinity for its Beings."

"One would argue that makes me more than capable of deciding what is best for them," Asteria challenged, inclining her head. "You came to this Realm from another—you lot are but their old Gods. I was born in this Realm with them, so maybe I'm their true Goddess."

"You can't be their Goddess only when it suits you, my Brightest Star." Gallus turned to her with a pitying expression. A mix of embarrassment, guilt, and irritation burned the back of her throat. "It's all or nothing."

With a final glare, Asteria opened a portal behind her, maintaining eye contact with Gallus until she stepped backward, and the veil blurred him. When she was on the opposite side, surrounded by the familiarity of her room in Celestia, she waved it closed and stood as still as her statue in the Healer garden.

Asteria envisioned that discussion going quite differently. That was the most Gallus had spoken with an air of enlightenment in nearly a century.

Let us do our work.

She didn't believe Gallus would obliterate the humans with a snap of his fingers, but she also knew he wouldn't leave them unharmed.

She had no idea what he had planned for Aveesh.

Suddenly, letting him seclude himself away for almost two centuries seemed like a dangerous thing to have allowed him to do. Either he was considering this imbalance he claimed existed on Aveesh the entire time, or the Lyran had grown bored.

Asteria only hoped it was the former, because the latter made him far more dangerous.

CHAPTER 16

SYBIL

Every fall, just before the season turned cold, the Asterian Academy held the Patronage Gala where every kingdom gathered in Celestia to meet the senior Sirian class. Each kingdom sent a representative, ranging from the kings and queens themselves to appointed ambassadors with whom they trusted most.

During the gala, these representatives would mingle with students slated to graduate as Healers and Warriors in an effort to form connections and lay eyes on any seniors the kingdom would like to hire into their court or country.

It was a lovely affair, complete with music, decadent food and drinks, romantic lighting, ensembles to rival any royal ball, and a merriment that only Asteria and her Elders seemed capable of achieving.

Sybil had not attended one in *centuries,* but she couldn't forget the joy and excitement that radiated through the grand ballroom of the Asterian Academy during the gala.

This year's was not jovial.

There was a strange, thick tension in the air despite Sybil having only just walked into the ballroom.

Everything looked as it should, towering columns adorned with small glowing orbs resembling fireflies in the night and three impressive chandeliers bouncing light from the ceiling in such a way that cast a dramatic shadow over the bodies.

But it wasn't something Sybil could see. It was the air—an aura pulsing ominously in the background of the music. If she hadn't received her vision of the end of their world as they knew it nor been debriefed on the Lyrans meeting, she still would have been able to sense something was amiss.

"Sybil," Asteria called, and she turned in time to see the Lyran scurry from the side of the room. "What in the Heavens are you doing here? Not that I'm displeased to see you. You just never come."

"I anticipated you being startled by my arrival." Sybil took Asteria's hands in hers, carefully dragging her toward the nearest column while taking a moment to admire the dress she wore.

At times, it irrationally angered Sybil that Asteria denied her goddesshood, but never enough to tell her as much. It was only because Asteria *was* a Goddess in every way that mattered—including looking the part.

Asteria's dress was such a deep blue it was nearly black, similar to the hue of her hair. It was embroidered with pearls across the top and down the layers of skirts in the shape of various constellations. The bodice hugged her perfectly, giving her curves where she normally had none. The sleeves curtained her arms down to her wrists, the cut mimicking the way in which the skirts were layered.

Sybil peered around both sides of the column to ensure there was no one suspect present before explaining, "I saw a vision of the gala."

Asteria blanched, her eyes widening with a flash of glowing blue behind their mortal hue. "What do you mean?"

"Nen and Zephyr are going to be here." Sybil pinched Asteria's wrist when her lips disappeared into a thin line.

"Why?" Asteria clenched her teeth, breathing sharp through her nose.

"The Lyrans never come to this."

"I know they don't." Sybil nodded slowly, keeping her enhanced senses open. "That's why I came. I couldn't tell why they were in attendance, but I wanted to be present in case you needed backup."

Asteria's shoulders relaxed some, but she still held tension at the corners of her eyes and lips. "I suppose it's great that Dionne is representing Riddling, and Lumir is here for The Northern Pizi."

Sybil nearly asked who Lumir was, but then she remembered he was Asteria's nephew, the eldest son of her brother, Taranis. "Having those of us with god-powers and a drakon should be enough if either of them tries to pull something. Between the various forms of fire and a lightning wielder, I'm sure it's enough to scare them without forcing any Sirians into action."

"I'm going to speak with Dionne and Lumir now to let them know you're here and what you've said." Asteria whipped her head over her shoulder, eyes searching the crowd in the middle of the ballroom before a flash of recognition glistened in her bright blue eyes. She squeezed Sybil's hands without looking at her before adding, "Thank you for coming, Bee."

Without another word, Asteria grabbed her skirts and strolled to where Sybil spotted Dionne and Lumir speaking with a Sirian, determination driving her at an alarming speed.

She sighed as she shook her head, wiping her damp palms against the skirt of her own ball gown.

The drakon in Sybil's chest perked up at the sensation of someone approaching just before a familiar voice calmed the spark of anxiousness.

"I'm shocked to see you at the gala, Syb," Wells said not unkindly, but with a warm tone that brought a small smile to her face. She twisted in time for him to clasp her hand between both of his, a rather familiar male standing a few feet back. "What brings you here?"

Sybil's gaze bounced between Wells and the man as she chewed her inner lip with a shrug. "I've been meaning to support Asteria more at these endeavors. I also wanted to speak with the Rotherhams. I've realized it's been quite some time since I paid a visit, and what better way to meet with them than while they are searching for their next Healers and Warriors?"

Something wary flickered across Well's normally playful features before he gestured to the man giving her an unimpressed once-over. "It seems Fate has guided you clearly once again, friend. Let me introduce you to Prince Edward Rotherham, heir to the Allanis throne."

That's why he's familiar. Sybil extended a hand, which Prince Edward politely accepted, even if his gaze was guarded. "It's a pleasure to formally meet you. I wondered why you appeared familiar. You look very similar to your father."

"A compliment I get quite often," he agreed with a jerk of his head. He blinked those beady, sapphire blue eyes at her, the vertical slits indicative of drakon heritage. "I will say, I'm curious as to why you want to make my family's reacquaintance when you have done nothing to be an influence for our country. Not compared to how influential you've been for Eldamain despite them being a long line of Sirians."

Wells covered his gasp with a cough, sipping his champagne as he averted his gaze. Prince Edward side-eyed him dryly before waiting for Sybil's response.

She fought the urge to curl her lip and snarl at him, if only because she truly did want to see where the Rotherhams stood and how much persuasion she would have over them as the founder of their House. "I can acknowledge my absence from the House of Echidna. When you live hundreds of years, time doesn't quite operate at quite the same pace it does for mortals, and it's easier to lose track of."

"I suppose that's one way to put it." Prince Edward sighed as he glanced over his shoulder momentarily. "Well, perhaps we can speak later. I must excuse myself as I'm here to scope out this senior class on my father's behalf. There are a few I've been eyeing that appear unbothered at the moment."

"I appreciated the conversation, Prince Orwell." Prince Edward dipped his head respectfully at Wells, except there was a reservation in the gesture. "You give our family much to think about. I'll pass what you have said along to my father."

Wells returned the bow of his head as a way of goodbye, watching for a long, silent moment as Prince Edward walked into the crowd before downing the rest of his champagne. He turned to Sybil with a tick in his jaw.

"I take it negotiations aren't going as well as you hoped?" Sybil offered a pained grin with a shrug.

Wells hummed, the sound turning into a dark chuckle as he shook his head. "You can say that. It wasn't that I anticipated these negotiations to be easy, but I will say it feels as though both the Rotherhams and Mariandes are purposely battling us."

"In what ways?" Sybil tilted her head, blinking.

"This was the first time in the last month since we all spoke that I've actually been able to gain an audience with a member of either family," Wells explained, holding out his elbow to Sybil. She happily accepted, looping her hand into the crook and resting the other against his arm. He slowly guided them along the edge of the room beside the columns, leaning into her as he spoke. "If it weren't for the Patronage Gala, I'm concerned I would never have gotten an audience. It only supports our hypothesis that Lord Zephyr has spoken to both families already."

"That has been a concern of mine since the very beginning of this," Sybil whispered, dropping her gaze to the ground.

"And you, Syb?" Wells tapped his elbow against her side, raising an eyebrow at her as she met his gaze. "Why are you *really* here?"

She pursed her lips with a huff, rolling her eyes. "Funny you speak of Zephyr, since it's because I had a vision of him and Nen being here that I've come."

Wells stiffened, halting their stroll. His gaze latched onto something in the middle of the room that brought a gleam to his eye Sybil hadn't seen in years. "You've spoken to Asteria about this?"

"I have…" Sybil drawled, narrowing her eyes. "Why?"

He chuckled, the sound rather dark and sultry to be coming from him. "So that's what has her wound up."

Sybil startled, but she followed his line of sight to find him watching Asteria as she spoke quietly to Dionne and Lumir with tension in her shoulders, her jaw clenched. When Sybil dragged her attention back to Wells, she was awed to still find him looking at Asteria with something all too familiar.

Like he longed for her to look at him.

"What are your intentions with Asteria, Wells?" Sybil asked quietly, and he snapped his head to her. "I thought I saw something odd at dinner before I pulled Asteria away, and now this just confirms it."

He shrugged, tilting his head with it. "I'm intrigued."

"It seems you're intrigued enough to enjoy getting a rouse from her is what I've heard," Sybil admitted, removing her hand from his arm to cross her own over her chest. "Why do you enjoy rousing her?"

"Because from what *I* have heard, I'm the only one who can." Wells shoved his hands into his pockets and leaned into Sybil. "Speaking of which, if you'll excuse me, I'm going to do just that."

"*Orwell Carraphim,*" Sybil muttered, lunging for him, but it was too late. The little fox swerved from her grasp and slid between two Sirians, disappearing into the crowd toward Asteria.

CHAPTER 17

ASTERIA

"There was far too much tension in this room for something to not be amiss," Lumir said in his thick Pizian accent, shaking his head. "I'm not surprised to hear they'll come. I agree with Dionne—I don't think they'll do anything drastic."

Asteria's hand settled against the column of her throat where the neckline of her dress curved, quelling her powers that threatened to rise to the surface. She watched Dionne casually walk across the ballroom with annoyance.

If neither he nor Lumir found it cumbersome that Nen and Zephyr may be appearing at the gala, Danica most likely had not spoken to either of her brothers about the Lyrans meeting.

"Nen may have reason with Thalassa, but he hasn't come previously," Asteria repeated, hoping to spark at least some concern in her nephew since Dionne wanted to hear none of it. "Zephyr doesn't have a single reason to be here."

Lumir chuckled under his breath, patting Asteria on the shoulder, and she whipped her head at him with a quiet snarl.

Despite Taranis being over eighty years of age, his eldest son was in his mid-twenties, appearing a few years younger than Asteria looked. He was far too much like his father for her liking.

One Taranis Beaumont in the world was enough for her.

"If I summon either of you, you will come," Asteria said, shoving him away gently but with enough force to coax an unintentional, playful grin onto her nephew's face. "Until then, go away."

The grin stayed on Lumir's cheeks as he bowed and turned on his heel toward the opposite direction in which Dionne had gone. Asteria inhaled slowly as her left eye twitched.

"And here I was thinking I'd be able to catch up with Prince Lumir," said a voice that elicited far too much warmth within her. She stiffened, slowly turning to face Wells. "The last time I was in The Northern Pizi, we got into a fair amount of mischief."

When Asteria completed her rotation, she held strong as she came face-to-face with him because he was breathtaking.

His brown curls were perfectly coiled on his head in such a way that kept them from his face. His charcoal gray slacks and black silk shirt hugged his body in incredible ways that hinted at what lay beneath. The top two buttons were undone, peeking at the bare chest beneath she knew had to be muscled. Draped over his left shoulder and across his body was a black silk cape embroidered with gold designs—

Constellations.

The same constellations Asteria had chosen for her dress.

For some foreign reason, her traitorous heart fluttered at that realization, but she refused to acknowledge any of it.

The likely unintentional matching outfit or the fluttering.

"I'm sorry to disappoint with my solo company then," Asteria said with an air of nonchalance, narrowing her eyes and clasping her hands in front of her to avoid caressing the silk cape. "It appears you will have to settle."

"Oh, darling," Wells murmured, the sound rumbling low despite the crescendo of music echoing amidst the chatter of the room. He stepped closer into her space, and she leaned away. "There is nothing about you that settles me."

She gasped at his featherlight touch on her wrist, simultaneously tensing and melting into the contact. Her mouth opened and closed multiple times, his smirk climbing into a wider grin with each click.

Asteria sighed heavily, nostrils flaring before gaining her wits. "There are so many things I have to say, none of them kind."

"I doubt that since it appears you're at a loss for words." Wells dipped his head closer, enough that his breath whisked across her cheek, the scent of winter mead wrapping around her. "Although, I've found that being bullied by powerful, beautiful women tends to get me—"

"Interesting to find you two in the middle of the ballroom on a night such as this," Odo said, drawing Asteria and Wells's attention to him.

He sauntered up beside them, and Asteria sent a silent thanks to the Heavens for interrupting what surely would have been a conversation she wasn't ready to handle.

Not because she couldn't counter him—she was sure she could come up with *something*—but because he hadn't quite finished his sentence and Asteria already knew where he was taking it.

And now she was picturing what *that* would look like.

"My dear friend," Wells said, arms wide as he accepted Odo's embrace. "I fear I simply can't spend the rest of our lives separated for months at a time. Your presence is truly missed amongst the halls of Aggelos Palace."

"Is that why you're here tonight?" Odo grinned as he jabbed his elbow into Wells. "Searching for my replacement?"

"That, as well as a few other political matters with some of the other kingdoms…" Wells trailed off with a frown as he made eye contact with Asteria, who glared at him with an imperceptible shake of her head.

She refused to get Celestia involved in anything going on with the Lyrans and the damned prophecy, especially Odo and the other Elders.

Not until she was absolutely certain there was something dangerous going on worth noting.

"A busy man as always," Odo said, cupping his hand over his shoulder. "I hope you'll stay an extra day at the Academy. Erika would love it if you joined us for dinner tomorrow night once the rest of the royal guests leave."

Wells winked at Asteria with the corner of his lip turned up as he answered Odo, "I would be more than happy to—"

The moment Asteria dreaded arrived as she vaguely registered the clap of a portal shutting beneath the music.

She whirled around in the direction she heard it and instantly connected with Nen's teal blue, mortal eyes from across the room. The ghost of an eerie grin graced his lips, his deep-set eyes glittering with a roguery that prickled the back of her neck.

"Is that Lord Nen and Lord Zephyr?" Odo asked, his voice higher than usual with surprise. "What in the Heavens are they doing here?"

"Don't make a scene," Asteria ordered with her hand up, foregoing Zephyr and watching Nen as the two men split in opposite directions. "I want to simply observe what they are doing here first."

"Why not ask them?" Wells asked, but she shot him a glare over her shoulder.

"I don't speak with them unless it's absolutely necessary," Asteria explained as she lowered her hand, returning her attention to Nen.

He was no longer watching Asteria, but she knew he could feel her trailing him. His stark white hair, similar to Morana's, flowed down his back in tight waves that appeared damp. He wore tailored indigo slacks and a white shirt, complete with a long vest that reflected the glow of the room like a pearl.

Asteria clenched her jaw when he embraced Crown Prince Vasalis Seymour of Teslin and two Sirians the prince had been speaking with. She perused the room for Zephyr, spotting him just as Prince Edward Rotherham and Queen Catalina from Syvlan bowed to him.

"Have you seen the representative of Thalassa yet?" Asteria asked Odo without looking at him.

He saddled up beside her, his gaze bouncing between Nen and Zephyr on either side of the room. "Now that you mention it…"

"Fuck." Asteria sighed heavily, rolling her head on her neck. She gathered her skirts and started to make her way toward Nen and Prince Vasalis.

She was nearly there when she felt the presence of another behind her.

Asteria stopped suddenly, which only sent the firm body ramming into her. She stumbled slightly, but the individual gripped her waist in both of their hands before she pitched forward entirely.

Her heartbeat picked up at the sound of Wells's voice. "I suppose I should get used to this level of proximity if you're to portal me in the future."

She was frozen in place. It had been far too long since any male held her in such a suggestively intimate fashion.

While his chest wasn't touching her back, he was close enough she felt the heat radiating from him, especially where he still firmly gripped her waist. His thumbs and fingers pressed into her back, digging into muscle just below her ribs.

Asteria was quite certain she wasn't even breathing.

"Where are we headed?" Wells asked quietly, although there was a hoarseness to his voice she was unfamiliar with.

"We"—Asteria finally stepped out of his embrace, turning to stare at him—"aren't going anywhere. I'll be going to greet Nen, and you'll go back to Odo."

"I have political matters that involve Prince Vasalis, so I'll be joining you." Wells flicked his hand in the vicinity of Nen and said prince peering at the two of them. "Lead the way, ma'am."

"Do *not* call me that." Asteria continued toward the Lyran and Lemurian, glancing at Wells beside her. "In fact, don't call me darling, either."

"Noted." He nodded firmly, his face set in determination. "I'll have to come up with a better nickname, then." Asteria opened her mouth to protest, but a charming grin spread across Wells's face as he held out his hand. "Lord Nen! What a pleasure to meet you face-to-face."

Nen frowned at Wells, nearly curling his lip as his gaze bounced from his outstretched hand to his face. Asteria had the overwhelming urge to step between the two men, catching her off-guard from the protectiveness.

Then again, she would feel that way with any mortal or Sirian directly interacting with Nen.

"Pleasure," Nen said under his breath, awkwardly accepting the handshake. When he redirected his attention to Asteria, though, a sly grin worked its way up his cheeks as he scanned her from head to toe. "Little Lyran. It's good to see you again, especially in a more *neutral, welcoming* setting."

"Is that so?" Asteria narrowed her eyes, crossing her arms over her chest. "I can't say the same, unfortunately. Your presence at the Academy does not feel *neutral*."

"Come now," Nen drawled, slinging his arm over her shoulder. The gesture was comical if only because Nen was as tall as Gallus, towering over Asteria, but he was also extremely muscular like Rod. He tugged her into his chest, nearly pulling her into a headlock. "That's no way to treat a guest, particularly a representative of Thalassa."

"Prince Vasalis," Wells interrupted the exchange, his eyes still on Asteria, "I'd love to catch up. It's been far too long since I traveled to Teslin. Come get a drink with me?"

Prince Vasalis mumbled a reluctant agreement, and Wells paused with a hand on the prince's shoulder, raising an eyebrow at Asteria in question.

She nodded once, jerking her head gently toward the table of drinks.

Without another glance, Wells directed the prince to the table at the same time Nen dragged Asteria toward the middle of the ballroom where a few patrons had started a waltz.

"Dance with me, Little Lyran," Nen commanded, no question to it.

Asteria obliged if only to avoid making a scene in front of the Sirians. She managed to wiggle out from his embrace before facing him at the very outskirts of the dancing group. They bowed to one another as was custom, then she reluctantly let him take her hand in one of his larger ones, his other rather respectfully holding her shoulder.

"I have to say, I'm quite startled you're here," Asteria began, keeping her voice low enough that only the two of them could hear. "Considering the terms we left on after the meeting, the last thing I expected was for you to attend this year's gala… You know, your first gala *ever*."

Nen chuckled, the sound like a growl. "Just as you've been involved with your Sirians more frequently over the last fifteen years, I too have been spending more time with my people."

"So they thought it fit to send a God to speak with the senior Sirians?" Asteria met his gaze, having to crane her neck rather far back due to their proximity. She squinted up at him. "It seems a rather mundane task for a Lyran such as you."

Nen shrugged, searching the room over the top of her head. "I consider it an honor they entrust me with such an endeavor. It speaks wonders to their faith and trust in what I do and say…" The predatorial, painstaking drag of his head to meet her gaze sent chills down Asteria's spine, especially when he cocked and raised an eyebrow. "Does it not?"

Asteria swallowed against the burn at the back of her throat, suppressing the urge to fling him across the room. She always hated the ways in which some of the Lyrans spoke—like they required any who listened to solve the riddle of their speech. She didn't understand why they couldn't just speak outright.

Clearly Nen was being coy on purpose with some hidden agenda, blatantly hinting at such, and not outright revealing.

"If that's how you view it." Asteria averted his stare, trying to find Zephyr once again as they spun around. "What is Zephyr's reasoning for being here, then?"

"Are you assuming I note all that Zephyr chooses to do?" Despite not looking at him, she heard the smile in his voice, slimy and slick.

"I would think so." Asteria fluctuated her voice dramatically as she sneered at him. "Well, with how far you have your cock shoved up Zephyr's ass, I would assume you must go everywhere together—"

In a blink, Nen portaled them out of the ballroom to a darkened hallway somewhere within the Academy.

One minute, Asteria was in his arms. The next, she was pinned against a stone wall with Nen's hand wrapped around her throat, angling her head up to him.

"That mouth, Asteria," Nen growled, bringing his nose to hers.

She set her jaw, holding her power at bay. She was more than capable of taking on Nen should she wish, but part of her was more curious to learn his true motivations in being here. That meant letting him think he was overpowering her.

Men tended to run their mouths when they thought they were winning.

"Daddy isn't here to save you this time," Nen hissed, his mortal eyes morphing to their milky blue sockets. "Neither are Mommy or Rod. What are you going to do now that your guardians are not near?"

"They are not my guardians." Asteria curled her lip, adding a bit of a fight against his grip for fun. "Is this why you're truly here? To get me alone? I thought you and Zephyr were too hungry when you looked at me lately—"

"The way the others have treated you like a diamond has gone to your head." Nen chuckled low, shaking his head as he pulled back a few inches. "I don't know how Rod still desires you. Too much fight for me. I prefer a woman who will lay herself at my feet without coercion."

"Something tells me that's not entirely true." Asteria smiled, tilting her chin higher to look at him. "Maybe you prefer when men like Zephyr lay themselves—"

Asteria swore under her breath when Nen cracked her head against the stone wall, a brief flare of pain lighting up her vision. While it did no true damage with her enhanced strength and healing, it didn't make it hurt any less.

"You will learn respect eventually, Asteria." Nen released her and pushed away, hovering a few inches off the ground. "I speak the truth in my reasoning for coming here. I'm here on behalf of Thalassa and as an advisor to Teslin, just as Zephyr is here as an advisor to Allanis and Sylvan.

"It appears those four kingdoms are looking to bolster their Sirian Warrior population." The smile Nen flashed her could have charmed any Lemurian from the House of Argo, but it only chilled Asteria to the bone. "I told them they can never have too many talented Sirians wielding the Aether and Energy. You never know how the balance may tilt, and you want to be ready when it does."

Nen winked before portaling away, leaving Asteria alone in the hallway. She exhaled in frustration as she slumped against the wall, staring up at the stars peeking through columns and shining down into the empty courtyard.

Asteria may hate the riddles, but she'd lived with them for the last six hundred and forty-seven years. Nen and Zephyr used to school her on them as a child, so she was particularly versed in the way those two spoke.

The riddle Nen left her with tasted like a warning, and the talk of balance sounded far too much like Gallus.

CHAPTER 18

PHOEBE

Phoebe entered the Council meeting chamber, the men's chatter assaulting her senses. She abruptly stopped in the doorway, blinking at the sight before her.

All five Councilmen were in various states of disarray or outrage, red-faced as they argued back and forth. Edric Hawthorne's round belly nearly rested on the granite table as if his skin couldn't hold it up any longer while he pointed an accusatory finger at Gareth Montclair across the table. The latter remained in his seat, but his wrinkled face scrunched into deeper lines as he snarled at Edric.

Lucius Ashford and Noel Windmere appeared to be gyrating at one another as their voices carried the loudest, their willowy frames ready to snap in half at any moment. The final Councilman, Ronan Blackwell, may very well have been drunk.

Phoebe exchanged a glance with Thorne, who gave her a wary expression.

With an exasperated sigh, Phoebe scooped her hands into the air, and the table levitated. The edge knocked against Edric's gut, forcing him back into his chair with stifled swears, and Ronan startled. The silence and shock from the two men drew the attention of Lucius and Noel.

With a smirk, Phoebe set the table back down with a resonating thud. "Gentlemen. Let's speak civilly rather than as if we're a band of barbarians. I hope to quell any concerns you are arguing over."

The men grumbled, echoing one another, as Phoebe took her place at the head of the table. Thorne sauntered up beside her and stood stiffly diagonal from Phoebe's chair. She offered the male a sympathetic smile.

Since Thorne wasn't actually part of the Council, he could only stand like attendants would behind the member they accompanied. In this case, it was Phoebe he came with—not that the other Councilmen were granted the liberty to bring guests to an urgent Council meeting.

She longed for the day these men revealed their treachery or keeled over so she could replace them. Thorne happened to be one of the people she would appoint to her Council.

"You all have requested an urgent meeting," Phoebe began, exchanging glances with each male, all Sirian. "Why have I been called to these chambers at such an absurd hour?"

"Your Majesty," Lucius began, adjusting the buttons on his tunic, "it's come to our attention that a strange illness is spreading amongst the humans. Even more concerning, we've caught wind that it's not just isolated to one city, but several cities across the entire continent."

Phoebe schooled her face into neutrality, but her chest burned as the darkened walls of the room closed in.

She knew the illness Lucius spoke of was the Obsidian Decay, but she hadn't known it had spread beyond Etherea.

Granted, she hadn't held a single meeting with any of Etherea's allies since she ascended the throne, which could be why she was unaware of any goings on within those kingdoms. Regardless, the reminder that no other country reached out conjured the sting of isolation.

"I'm aware of the Obsidian Decay," Phoebe admitted, brushing invisible crumbs from the table.

The men began to shout again, but she held up a hand, hoping they would speak one at a time. *Like children.*

"My Queen," Edric sputtered, as if it pained him to utter it. Phoebe shot him a glare. "Why was the Council not informed of this?"

"If I were to inform you of every illness that passes through this country, we would never leave these chambers." Phoebe reclined back against the chair, shrugging. "Luckily, I was able to intercept this particular illness."

"You shrug as though it means nothing to you," Noel interjected, and Phoebe knew he purposely left out her title. The Aether twirled around her ankles beneath the table as her lips thinned. "Do you not care that an illness strikes the humans you care so deeply for?"

"I care deeply for *all* my citizens, *Sir* Noel," Phoebe chided, sneering at him. "It would do you well to remember my title, which is customary to use when referring to me. You have many to choose from, so it shouldn't be a problem to utter one. Go ahead, give it a try."

The room fell into uneasy silence, but Phoebe thrived in discomfort. It was where she stood out against friend or foe, giving her ample opportunity to be seen.

The other men shifted in their seats as she held Noel's dark gaze, an eyebrow raised in challenge.

"Of course, Your *Majesty*," Noel finally relented through clenched teeth.

She thought she heard Thorne let out a breath of relief behind her.

"As I was saying," Phoebe said, shooting Noel a malicious smirk, "I care for all my citizens, whether they are human, Sirian, or Lemurian. I care deeply about the humans being affected. One would argue I care more than the five of you combined, which is why I have the best Healers working on this."

"How could you question our love for our kingdom, my Queen?" Edric's round cheeks flushed deep pink, veins popping at his temples.

This man has to be dying soon. Phoebe held her tongue about the man's health, but she answered his possibly rhetorical question. "You all learned of the Obsidian Decay, but have you come to this meeting with a solution?"

Again, the men fell silent, exchanging hopeful glances until they realized none of them had an idea to propose to Phoebe.

"Fascinating." She rolled her eyes and leaned against the table, crossing her arms. "You see, the moment I found out about the illness, I went to work trying to find a cure. I have Healers conducting tests and studying victims who have been so graciously donated by their families—families I have spoken with directly.

"So again, I sit here and wonder, do you love your people"—Phoebe slammed her fist on the table, white light flashing before a crack coursed straight down the middle—"or do you love the status and sovereignty your positions give you?"

Phoebe reclined in her chair again, listening to the men grumble various forms of *for the people*, even if the words were lies on their tongues. She released a breath of disbelief and frustration, rubbing her fingers against her temples.

"Did you know the Obsidian Decay is also appearing in other countries, Your Majesty?" Ronan managed to utter the words clearly.

"That may be news to me." She ran a finger up and down the deep fissure directly in front of her, clenching her jaw. "Which countries?"

"Sado in Teslin and Lolis in Sylvan," Edric answered, the other men already arguing under their breaths.

"I find it astonishing you didn't know about the spread of this *Decay* with official royals and diplomats gathering at the Patronage Gala," Gareth grumbled, squinting at Phoebe. "Did you not send someone to the Academy to scope out future Sirians to hire?"

Phoebe waved a hand at them, averting her gaze. She refused to admit she hadn't sent anyone.

"Your Majesty, I plead with you to speak to our allies." Edric gently tapped his hands on the table, side-eyeing her. "Do we even know where loyalties lie anymore? It's unlike the Mariandes and Seymours to be silent for an entire year. Was there an exchange we are not aware of that caused this distance?"

Phoebe cut her gaze to Edric, holding her tongue.

She wasn't shocked they immediately blamed her for the silence of their former allies. She was more than positive that, if she were a male, they wouldn't blame her for an unknown exchange.

"I'm not sure why the allies I inherited haven't spoken with me," Phoebe explained calmly, breathing through her anger. "I've been wary of proceeding with any alliances from the previous kingship, if I'm to be frank. Those alliances were formed long ago and haven't been revisited in over a century. I question whether they benefit from our partnership far more than we do in trade and exchange. It needs further consideration.

"Alas, it would be worth a letter to inquire about the state of the Obsidian Decay within their borders." Phoebe relented only to appease the men and follow up her suggestion to end their alliances with a more positive statement. "I will see to it."

"If you wish to form a new alliance, Your Majesty, might we suggest speaking with Eldamain?" Ronan added, avoiding her gaze. "They are a powerful country, and Crown Prince Quintin has four children. From my understanding, only his eldest is spoken for. He has two daughters around Prince Jeremiah's age."

Phoebe narrowed her eyes, tilting her head.

"I also heard the Goddess of Sirians graced them with her presence for dinner a few months back, my Queen," Gareth added, peering at her with a knowing look. "Lady Asteria hasn't met so intimately with Sirian royalty in quite some time."

Phoebe remained silent because she had nothing good to say. Her jealousy toward her half-sister couldn't be displayed nor justified in front of these Councilmen. Declaring that Asteria should be visiting Phoebe—her sister—would only be admitting aloud she was not the daughter of King Drogo.

"I agree speaking with Eldamain would be beneficial for more than one reason, Your Majesty," Noel said, a smirk hiding beneath his air of inquisition. "Especially if you were to offer a marriage contract in exchange for an alliance. It could possibly rectify the tension with Eldamain after you interfered in your marriage games."

Phoebe curled her lip at that, studying the men. "What do my marriage games have to do with Eldamain?"

"If you recall, Your Majesty, Crown Prince Quintin competed for your hand." Noel leaned back in his chair, folding his hands across his stomach. "I believe it was the archery competition where King Dustin went head-to-head with the Carraphim prince—the archery contest *you* rigged for him to win."

Phoebe inhaled slowly, trying to keep the deep hum of her power under the surface.

She couldn't recall all who competed in her marriage games. In the end, she only had eyes for Dustin, and she focused all her attention and energy on helping him win.

That and stealing heated moments around the castle between competitions, dinners, and celebrations.

Phoebe adjusted her dress at the memories and reminded herself the sooner she ended this meeting, the quicker she could return to the love of her life in bed.

"I assure you, Councilmen, I'm working tirelessly on rectifying this illness," she explained, offering them a strained smile. "We hope to come up with a cure for the Decay soon. Once that is accomplished, I will review the former alliances with Teslin and Sylvan. We could possibly kill two birds with one stone by rectifying our alliance with Sylvan and establishing one with Eldamain. From my understanding, they always had a rather strong alliance being neighboring countries."

She rose abruptly from her chair, dipping her head as Thorne pulled it out from behind her.

"Your Majesty—" Edric protested, but she was done here.

"Enough, gentlemen." Phoebe swiped her hand in a line, holding her back straight. "It's late, and I wish to go to bed. I have a long day of visiting the human communities tomorrow to assure them they're not alone during this dark time. I bid you all goodnight."

She didn't wait to see the men bow their heads. Instead, she squeezed out the door and headed straight for her room without even a second glance to see if Thorne stayed behind.

Phoebe took the time alone to settle her irritation. She was vexed that the Councilmen gained the upper hand by knowing the illness had spread to other countries. It was agitating and slightly embarrassing that they knew of the dinner between Asteria and Eldamain.

There was also a deep, bitter hurt from Asteria meeting *anyone* outside of Celestia who wasn't her.

While the relationship between them was nearly nonexistent, Phoebe thought just maybe Asteria would attempt to remedy the rift between them—considering it was *her* fault.

By the time Phoebe shut her bedroom door, she'd already removed her crown from her head. She set it on the dresser before yanking out the braids that held it up. Peeling the kirtle of her dress, she shut her eyes as the layer slipped off.

"Here I was thinking you would need me to help you," Dustin whispered against the back of her neck. Her skin prickled at his proximity, burning where he snaked his arm around the front of her waist. He slipped the strap of her gown off her shoulder, placing a featherlight kiss in its place. "It seems you've done half the work for me."

Phoebe moaned softly as he moved his lips closer to her neck, instinctively arching against him.

He pulled her flush to his body, dragging his lips up the column of her throat, and her head lolled back. "How was your meeting, my moon?"

She stiffened but instantly relaxed again as his teeth grazed the sensitive skin behind her ear.

"Terrible," was all she managed. She gasped when he roughly spun her around to face him.

Dustin gripped her chin between his thumb and forefinger, raising her gaze to his. "How terrible?" He leaned forward until their lips brushed, and her core heated.

Phoebe slowly tugged at the strings of his slacks, smirking when they slipped from his waist with the final loop. She slid her hands up his bare torso and chest, wrapping her arms around his neck. "I wish to forget it."

"Then let me service the queen." He delicately pressed his lips to hers, and she sighed as all thoughts left her body.

After spending her entire life thrown to the side, forgotten until absolutely necessary, Dustin was the first person who ever showed interest in Phoebe because of who she was, not her status.

Every other male who'd enlisted in her marriage games was either Sirian or Lemurian, but Dustin was the only mortal. When she first met him, she was intrigued as to why and told him as much when she spoke with him for the first time.

He was from Chimbridge in Etherea, and he remembered when she once visited the town bringing food and supplies to the mortals without homes. He had no ambitions to be king, but he desired a wife who was compassionate yet still had a fiery edge. When he told Phoebe that's what he saw in her, she was helpless to resist him.

As she moved her lips in tune with his, emotion swelled in her chest at how different their love was from when they were younger and how they both had evolved. Despite his mortality, he was her anchor, grounding her when the politics and madness of her powerful world threatened to test her control.

That emotion turned molten when he swept his tongue into her mouth at the same time he tightened his grip on her waist. He pulled away only to hoist her onto the edge of the dresser.

"Dee," she whispered, morphing into a moan as he kissed her collarbone and bunched her dress. The cool air kissed her heated core. "We have a bed—"

"Respectfully, Your Majesty…" He rubbed his fingers through her slick heat, inching her closer to the edge of the wood with his other hand on her lower back. She groaned as he slipped a finger inside her. "We are fucking on this dresser."

She yanked his mouth back to hers, and he consumed her. His palms gently urged her legs wider, anticipation heightening her senses. He lined himself up, and she cried out as he thrust in, hitting a glorious angle. She clung to his hair as he rocked into her with quick movements, the dresser echoing their rhythm, mingling with their moans of pleasure.

Her limbs felt lighter with each shift of his hips as she teemed with ecstasy, teetering on the ledge and tightening around him. She tugged on his hair, pleading, "Dee, please."

"Such beautiful manners," he whispered against her, one of his hands making its way back to the apex of her thighs. He circled his thumb around her clit. "Is this what you want?"

"Yes," she groaned, arching her back as he hit that spot within her that made her—

She cried out his name as she fell over the edge of release, her legs quivering, walls throbbing as he wrung every last ounce of pleasure from her. His own release quickly followed, his movements slowing as he braced his hands on either side of her.

"You are just"—Phoebe paused as she caught her breath, Dustin peeking up at her through dark lashes—"very good at that."

He laughed as he slipped from her, helping her back down to the floor. He tucked her hair behind her ears, his hands framing her face. "Well, thank you, my moon. It's always my pleasure."

Phoebe snorted, shoving him out of the way as she headed to the washroom to clean up. "I'm certain it was."

She squealed in delight when he came up behind her, scooping her into his arms. They fell into one another again in the bathroom, all concerns about illnesses, arranged marriages, and sisters vanishing from Phoebe's mind.

CHAPTER 19

ASTERIA

Asteria hid within the shadows of the stadium pillars, observing the progression of the newest class of Warriors as they practiced outside in the early winter chill.

While she wore a light cloak to keep her warm, Celestia's winter never brought snow. During the day, it wasn't even cold enough to see one's breath.

"There you are," Odo shouted as he marched past the group of Warriors, waving his hand above his head. "You don't need to hide, Asteria."

The Warriors turned simultaneously, their eyes glazing with excitement and awe as they finally narrowed in on where she leaned. Asteria sighed heavily, dropping the Aether and stepping into the faint sunlight peeking through the heavy cast of clouds.

"Odo," Asteria drawled, curling her lip. She directed her attention back to the Warriors, waving them away. "Go back to your training. Don't even think about making some grand gesture to impress me. You'll only embarrass yourselves."

Some of the students snickered, jabbing each other with their elbows as they diverted their focus back to Conrad and Serena, the Warrior Elders training them.

"What's so important that you felt the need to reveal my hiding place?" Asteria sauntered up to Odo, meeting him across the lawn. He gestured for her to follow toward the Academy's main building. "You do realize I can't watch them train from there anymore. You've ruined my fun indefinitely."

"You could very well watch them like a normal person instead of lurking in the shadows." Odo gave her a sidelong look, peering over his spectacles.

Asteria gasped in disbelief, her gaze bouncing from Odo to the Warriors. "I was not *lurking*."

Odo laughed once, throwing his head back to the sky. He offered Asteria the crook of his arm, which she glared at momentarily before cautiously slipping her hand into it.

"I won't ask again, Odo," she chastised, squinting.

A smile crept up his cheeks, his eyes alight with mischief. "A little bird told me a certain individual had dinner with the Carraphims a few months ago and failed to tell me."

Asteria stumbled in her stride, her grip tightening over Odo's arm. She stared at him wide-eyed, ready to ask how he could possibly know, until her face went slack. "Which one told you?"

"I believe you have a fair chance at guessing correctly," he offered, the smile still on his face.

"Prince Orwell." She refused to use his familiar name to maintain a professional distance. The prince kept her on her toes, and not in an exciting way.

Don't lie to yourself, Asteria.

Odo nodded, studying her as though he knew her inner turmoil at the mere thought of Wells. "Don't think I didn't notice the strange tension between you two—"

"I'm assisting the Carraphim princes in a few royal endeavors," she interrupted, diverting the conversation. She still wanted to avoid the mention of Lyrans fighting and a potential threat to human lives. The Academy didn't need to worry until she knew with *absolute* certainty there was something to worry about. "I'll help Prince Orwell travel to speak with my brothers."

"Fascinating," Odo muttered, narrowing his eyes. "Why would the Carraphims need to speak with Dionne and Taranis?"

Asteria pursed her lips and shrugged. "That's their business, not mine. Besides, it's been some time since I visited either. They're due for a visit from their loving sister."

Odo snorted at that, and Asteria rolled her eyes. "Well, I wish you the best of luck, dear friend. Wells will keep you entertained, I assure you of that."

"I admit I don't know much about this generation of Carraphims," she said, gauging Odo's reaction. He maintained his composure. "I knew *of* Prince Quintin and Prince Piers—I went to the former's wedding—but was unaware of Prince Orwell. Tell me about them all. Do you believe they are good men?"

Odo frowned at her incredulously. "Do you believe I'd associate myself with them if they were not?"

Asteria shrugged again, staying silent.

Odo sighed, shaking his head. "My father was the Royal Healer during King Orvyn's father's reign and Orvyn's until I came of age. I spent much of my time by his side within the castle walls, learning all I could so I wouldn't have to take the Healer route."

"So *that's* why you were already so skilled as a Healer."

It's what intrigued Asteria about Odo the moment he stepped foot onto Celestia in his eighteenth year. Not only was he persistent in forming a bond with her, but he willingly chose the Diplomat route.

It confused her as to why he wanted to befriend her because she typically avoided that section of the Academy. She quickly learned he already mastered the basic Healer tests, and he wanted her to instruct him as a Warrior whilst attending his Diplomat classes.

When Odo graduated four years later, he was one of the few Sirians to master all three designations, hence why Asteria appointed him Head Elder this last year.

"Wells and I have been friends since childhood, but I grew closer to Piers and Quin during my time as their Royal Healer," he continued, straightening his shoulders. "Quin is passionate about being a good, fair ruler. He tries to maintain balance between being a good patron, monarch, and philanthropist. Subsequently, he knows how to make hard decisions when needed, but he'll work to find a solution before that's required.

"Piers is guarded for some reason." Odo squinted as they neared the Academy, considering his words. "He'll keep his distance and survey you from afar. That man is obsessed with patterns and puzzles. It's like he can't help himself. Once you get past those fortified walls, though, he has quite a soft heart."

"And Wells?" Asteria pushed. She had to admit, at least to herself, he was who she was more interested in. He seemed starkly different from his brothers, and it appeared both of his brothers knew it. "What's his story?"

A sort of melancholy passed over Odo's face before he spoke. "So it's Wells now?"

"Fuck the Heavens," Asteria hissed, shutting her eyes as Odo laughed, clutching his stomach.

"You know, dear," Odo began, his laughter subsiding, "there's nothing wrong with admitting your intrigue. He's a rather interesting and complex individual."

"Odo," Asteria warned, her nails digging into his arm.

He patted her hand, attempting to loosen her grip. "Wells is the youngest of three boys. He was wild and unpredictable when we were young, testing the limits and boundaries of his mere existence. He was always running into my father's study with new injuries he needed him to heal or mask before King Orvyn discovered them.

"When he came to the Academy, though, he learned discipline through the Warrior route." Odo's eyes turned sad as he continued. "It seemed his personality worked well with negotiations, so his father and Quin utilized him when they needed someone with wit. It allowed him to live a rather free life, coming when called, but he mostly traveled around other countries. That was until he met Ruelle."

Asteria's eyebrows rose high at that.

The three times she encountered Wells, she considered him to be flirtatious with her. She pondered whether his personality was just naturally coy, a tactic to win people over so they would do what he wanted. After she lost her temper in Quintin's study, he used his charm to calm her down and get her to—ultimately—agree to help them.

Maybe she *had* been played.

"He's married?" Asteria asked nonchalantly, keeping her voice even.

"*Was* married." Asteria snapped her head to Odo, who spoke quietly now. "Ruelle was Erika's younger sister. She and Wells met at our wedding and hit it off immediately. A few short years later, they married."

"You speak of her in the past tense," Asteria said softly, rubbing her hand against Odo's arm.

Odo pressed his lips together, fighting strong emotions as he nodded slowly. "It was two years ago, now. Ruelle and Erika were with child at the same time. She went into labor a few months too early, alone at home, and lost far too much blood by the time she was found. Both Ruelle and the child were lost."

Asteria sighed, her heart aching. "I'm sorry for both of your losses."

"That's where Elle's name comes from," Odo explained, referring to his and Erika's two-year-old daughter. "We named her after Ruelle."

Asteria smiled softly, patting her friend's arm.

"But Wells was absent after that, rightfully so," Odo added, straightening his back. "To be truthful, he hasn't been quite the same since. There's this spark of joy missing from him that had been there since childhood. He's frequented home more often these last few months, and

I suspect he'll be home indefinitely if he has a task that puts you two in cahoots."

"That's not—we're simply… You know…" Asteria sputtered before gathering herself. Odo smiled the entire time. "We're not in *cahoots*. This is at the request of Prince Quintin. I have simply offered to be a resource."

"Of course." Odo pursed his lips, shrugging as they passed beneath an archway. He stepped away from her and slid his hands into his pockets. "Colleagues, then? Allies?"

Asteria clenched her jaw, standing still. "I wouldn't refer to it as either."

"Only those who are familiar with him call him Wells." Odo dared to wink at her before stepping backward. "A penny for your thoughts—"

"Did you come across campus just to find out where I stood with Wells?" she shouted as he backed away, a sly smirk on his face. "If you say *anything* to him—"

"Ah, yes." Odo turned on his heel, lifting his hand to her as he threw it over his shoulder. "You'll set me ablaze if I tell him you're referring to him in a friendly manner. I value my life, Asteria, but I guarantee he's already caught your slip-ups."

Students filed out of classrooms, Odo disappearing amongst the masses as he walked away from her. She stood frozen amidst her Sirians, mouth propped open in shock.

Asteria was beginning to remember why she hated men.

CHAPTER 20

SYBIL

The drakon flew low over the mountain peaks as she neared her destination. The cool air caressed her wings as she tucked them closer into her body to angle her toward her trajectory. The wind rushing past was a comforting sound, calling to the solitary compulsion within her.

The small village grew as she neared. Plumes of smoke faded into the sky from short chimneys, the air mixed with aromas of charred wood, wheat, and vegetables. The most pungent smells, though, were rosemary, lavender, myrrh, and frankincense, all masked on top of the underlying stench of sharp decay.

The drakon veered right, aiming for the small plot of land to the home for which she was required to meet the foreign lord who summoned her. Before dropping to the ground, she threw her chest and long neck back, stretching out her hind legs.

Her feet hit the ground with a deafening thud that shook the nearby home, her front claws following suit. Her primal instinct recoiled at the thought of shifting back to her mortal form, yearning to stay in this preferred beastly body.

The mortal soul within urged her to transition. She lifted her wings, flexing the muscles one final time before they vanished within. Every last cell tightened and shrunk, the pressure within her body compressing—

Sybil slammed back into her mortal form, stumbling briefly as she regained her balance on two mortal feet without the weight of wings on her back. She shook her shoulders at the sensation of phantom limbs, rolling her neck to center her mind. She reeled in the impulse to immediately be on defense and snarl at the first person who approached.

"We hardly get enough drakons in this part of Allanis," a deep, gravelly voice called across the overgrown lawn.

Sybil slowly turned on her heel, fighting the war between her mortal and drakon sides. She met the gentle eyes of a rather large male who approached her as if she were a frightened animal.

"I'm surprised considering the Rotherhams reign from the House of Echidna," she said with a forced smile. "Do they not visit in their Lemurian forms?"

The man sighed heavily, shaking his head with a tight-lipped grin. "Afraid not. They don't grace us with their presence often, which is why I called for your assistance in this matter. You are the closest expert, and your name came with highly admired endorsements."

Sybil frowned at that as she walked up to the male, but two figures lurking by the home's entryway caught her attention. She would recognize the shorter one anywhere. "I see you also called on Prince Piers Carraphim and Sir Gavril Faris?"

"Indeed." The man glanced warily over his shoulder, gesturing for Sybil to follow him. "Where are my manners? I know I summoned you by parchment, but I suppose it would do well to introduce myself." He held out his hand as they walked, which Sybil dutifully accepted. "Lord Caius Farran of Ghita, madame."

"Pleasure," she muttered, slipping her hand behind her back. "Fortunately, I'm sure you're well aware of who I am, thanks to my entrance."

"Renowned Lemurian and Andromedan, Sybil." He smirked, side-eyeing her. Her grin slipped free as he continued, "Founder of the House of Echidna, Prophetess, and the Green Drakon."

"Very impressive." She chuckled, lowering her head in appreciation. "These days, it seems most people only find it convenient to address me as one title over another. You can simply call me Sybil in conversation."

Piers and Gavril stood at attention as she and Lord Caius approached, a playful grin twitching at the corner of Gavril's lips. Sybil narrowed her eyes at him.

She tolerated very few in her life. She could easily list those she allowed close to her, most of which included the Carraphim family for the last few hundred years.

Before Sybil was attacked by the drakon when she was young, she was born and raised in Eldamain. After Morana merged her soul with the drakon, though, she spent her childhood and adolescence in Eonia alongside Asteria.

When Asteria began venturing to Aveesh, the only throne that initially had Sirians was Eldamain. It just so happened she brought Sybil to meet with the old Carraphim family all those centuries ago and something about that family just called to her.

Maybe it was Fate or their family oozing with generosity, but since that momentous day, Sybil always had a soft spot for the family, including this generation of princes.

Gavril, though, was *not* a Carraphim and reigned from the House of Argo. She never liked the water folk, especially because they were typically infatuated with Nen, who she despised. Thankfully, Gavril didn't seem to enjoy the Lyran to which his people worshipped.

Still, he was a persistent fuck who Sybil found more irksome than anything else.

Alas, Piers loved him quite deeply, so Sybil always mustered the last dredges of her patience when Gavril was around.

But only for Piers.

"I'm not quite used to seeing you for professional matters, Sybil," Piers said, bowing slightly. "Then again, we haven't seen each other nearly as frequently over the last few years as we once did."

"I wish our meetings as of late weren't so..." Sybil and Piers exchanged a knowing look as Lord Caius cleared his throat.

"Let's journey inside," the lord insisted, ushering them toward the back door. "I'll lead you to the Healer's quarters."

Sybil, Piers, and Gavril glanced at one another curiously, but they followed after Lord Caius as he explained why he'd asked for them to come.

"Prince Quintin recently sent an invitation to dine with your family in celebration of our son's eighth birthday," he began, seemingly directing his tone toward Piers, "but I had to politely decline due to the state of Ghita. It wouldn't be wise to journey for luxury dining with a royal family while my townspeople suffer."

Lord Caius threw them a grim smile. "When I told your brother as much, he offered to send you, Prince Piers, to check in and see if there was anything Eldamain could do to assist. I told him I was unsure if anything could be done from a royal expenditure, seeing as this seems to be some infection, but that you were more than welcome to come."

Lord Caius stopped before an arched wooden door, sighing as he looked at Sybil. "At the mention of an infection, Prince Quintin said he had a connection to you and suggested your assistance in the matter since you are one of the eldest Andromedans. So, here we are today."

"You said an infection?" Gavril asked, tilting his head, gills flaring. "What sort of infection?"

"We've never seen anything like this," Lord Caius said quietly, leaning closer to the three. "What makes matters worse is that it only appears to be isolated with humans. No Lemurians or Sirians who live here have been affected. It's something you must see for yourselves. I can't go in because I fear I've exposed myself too frequently, and I don't want to..."

Piers laid a firm hand on Lord Caius's shoulder, offering him a grim smile. "Don't be ashamed for fearing mortality. We all fear death. The first man to tell you he does not is a deceiver."

Lord Caius nodded firmly. He met each of their eyes before knocking gently against the door. Almost instantly, it pried open, and a Sirian female peeked out from the small opening. She frowned at Sybil, Piers, and Gavril, but upon seeing Lord Caius, she relaxed.

"My Lord," she greeted, bowing as she fully opened the door. "Am I to assume this is the Carraphim prince and his Green Drakon?"

"I am not his," Sybil corrected quickly beneath her breath. Out of her peripheral, she swore Piers flinched.

"Please show them the most recent victim, Susane," the Lord said quietly. He laid his hand against Sybil's shoulder blade. "Don't feel obligated to help, Sybil. Any light you can shed on this illness for Susane is greatly appreciated."

"Your Highness," Susane said to Piers, curtseying deep before swinging her hand behind her into the room. "If you all would come this way."

Sybil snuck one final glance at Lord Caius, her senses heightening when she caught a whiff of fear radiating from him and Susane. Whatever this illness was, it was something a Sirian Healer had yet to crack, and that seemed to frighten them both.

It surely set Sybil on edge.

She and Piers approached the stone table side-by-side in the middle of the room, surrounded by walls of dressings, herbs, and other marked elixirs. Gavril peered at them as he perused the various tools and shelves in the room.

Atop the table was a sheet covering the silhouette of a human splattered with what could've been dried blood, the stains nearly black.

"I must warn you, it's an unsettling sight," Susane began, gripping the edge of the sheet with a trembling hand. Sybil unintentionally scooted closer to Piers, their arms brushing at the proximity. He glanced at her from the corner of his eye. "There's nothing I can say to prepare—"

Shouts of protest from the hall interrupted Susane.

Gavril immediately drew his sword while Piers conjured the Energy, standing protectively before Susane and Sybil. The door burst open, and an all too familiar figure stood smugly in the entryway as Lord Caius sputtered behind her.

"Endora," Sybil said, narrowing her eyes at her estranged sister. "Curious that you've traveled from Etherea to…" Sybil raised an eyebrow. "Why *are* you here?"

"I've been making my way around the various kingdoms in answer to an illness similar to one plaguing Etherea," Endora explained, stepping into the room. She glared at Piers and Gavril, who cautiously lowered their swords. "No need for violence, gentlemen. I'm simply here on behalf of the Queen of Etherea to confirm or deny if the Obsidian Decay has spread this far north."

"The Obsidian Decay?" Piers exchanged a speculative glance with Sybil, but she shrugged her shoulders. It was nothing she'd heard of before.

"If we may, then," Susane said, sighing in exasperation. She carefully peeled back the cover, and she was correct.

Nothing could've prepared Sybil for what she saw.

What she'd thought was dried blood *was* blood, but it appeared black because this victim's blood *was* black. Their veins stood out against their graying corpse, slightly risen beneath the skin like inky vines. The stench was sharp like vinegar, which was strange for a rotting corpse. Even more odd was it reminded her of the aftertaste in her mouth after waking from nightmares of her vision.

Sybil backed into Piers's chest, who steadied her with a hand on her shoulder, swallowing.

"What in the fucking Gods?" Gavril mumbled, hesitantly peering at Sybil. "Have you seen anything like this before?"

"Never in my six hundred years of existence have I seen anything like this," she whispered, shaking her head slowly.

"That's not all," Susane said, retrieving a jar from the countertop. She handed it to Sybil and directed her attention to Endora. "I see why your people call it the Obsidian Decay, then. This is what you are experiencing in Etherea, correct?"

Endora appeared unfazed by what she saw, which confirmed this illness wasn't just plaguing Ghita.

Sybil held the jar at arm's length, lifting it to the light. At first, she thought they were large black stones. Upon further examination, her stomach dropped in horror as a heart and liver took shape.

"These are their organs?" Sybil asked, her voice quiet with shock. "I don't understand…"

"What we have discovered in Etherea is that the victim is infected with this illness through ingestion or an open wound," Endora explained, her face impassive as though she'd been reciting this repeatedly. "I've recently experimented with the illness to discover the incubation period is almost a full day. Once the individual is infected, the illness spreads through their bloodstream to their organs. It solidifies them into hard stones, much like—"

"Obsidian," Piers finished for her, his gaze bouncing from the body to the jar to Endora. "You seem to be well-informed on this illness. Why has Etherea not shared their findings with the rest of the continent?"

"We were unsure just how far it had spread." Endora shrugged, waving toward the body. "Why create mass hysteria if it's isolated to humans and a single country?"

"I'd venture because you haven't shared your findings, you don't know how to treat it." Sybil narrowed her gaze at Endora as she handed the jar back to Susane. "Am I correct?"

Endora pressed her lips together, tilting her head. "Of course, sister. If there were a treatment, the Queen of Etherea would've shared our findings and the cure to prevent or treat the Decay."

At the mention of the queen, Sybil's vision wavered, and her knees trembled. *Heavens, please.*

She vaguely registered Piers catching her against him, whispering her name as fingers pinched her chin. Her vision clouded as the voice took over, showing her what it longed for her to see.

Endora thrashed, suspended in the air, as the Aether swirled wildly around her. Endora's chest cracked open, blood bursting as jagged bones revealed a beating heart—

Sybil gasped as she came to, jerking in Piers's arms. He cupped her cheek, her head resting in his lap as he searched her face.

"What did you see?" Endora snapped, shoving Piers's head away and clouding Sybil's vision.

Sybil shook her head in confusion but couldn't utter a single word. She opened and closed her mouth in an effort to explain what happened, but ultimately, Fate denied her.

She finally sighed, relenting. "I can't speak it."

"Useless," Endora snarled, stepping away to allow Gavril in.

He offered his outstretched hands to Sybil, an eyebrow raised. She nodded, slipping her hands into his, and he launched her upright. She laid a hand against his arm to steady herself.

"I suggest you get rid of the body," Endora explained to Susane as she made her way to the door. "We can assure you the Etherean throne has plenty of resources investigating this illness, and we are further along in our studies than you could possibly catch up to."

"I hope you haven't raised the dead to inquire how they came across this illness, Endora," Sybil warned, rubbing her neck. "Mother would be furious, as would the rest of the Lyrans."

Endora offered a tight-lipped grin as she squinted at Sybil, sneering. "I appreciate the reminder, *sister*."

With that, Endora exited the room, slamming the door behind her.

Sybil found it rather suspicious that Queen Phoebe wouldn't say something about this to the other kingdoms. If her sister traveled this far just to confirm or deny this was the Obsidian Decay, more villages on this continent were undoubtedly experiencing the illness. The moment it left Etherea, each country should've been alerted.

Which meant Etherea or Endora—or both—were hiding something.

"Don't touch the body!" Sybil blurted, her hand outstretched toward where Susane was covering it with the sheet. "I haven't concluded *my* studies."

"But Endora—"

"*There's another who can give answers to this,*" Sybil said, but her voice came out monotone, which meant Fate was the one planting the thought in her mind. Sybil turned to Piers, who raised his eyebrows. "Call Asteria."

Piers jerked his head back as if Sybil had slapped him. "I beg your pardon?"

"Sirians can summon Asteria." Sybil gestured at Piers's forehead, where his Mark stood against his sun-kissed skin. "So, summon her."

"I don't have the Aether," Piers drawled. "Asteria said to use the Aether, which only my brothers have."

Sybil sighed, rolling her eyes. "Asteria wields both. Do as she instructed, but use the Energy instead."

Piers eyed Sybil suspiciously, but he did what he was told and formed a ball of Energy in his hand, closing his eyes.

Gavril leaned into Sybil, studying her face. "How could Asteria be of use?"

"I'm not sure," Sybil admitted quietly, meeting those lavender eyes. "But Fate believes she knows."

CHAPTER 21

SYBIL

Asteria appeared in the Healer's quarters almost instantaneously.

Sybil suppressed her smile as Asteria stiffened, elbows bent at her waist, slowly turning around as though something might appear and attack her.

Her eyes met Piers, Gavril, and then Sybil's, arms falling to her sides with a slack expression.

Susane immediately dropped to her knee, and Sybil braced. "Lady Asteria—"

"No!" Asteria blurted, leveling a finger at her. She lurched toward the Healer and helped her rise to her feet. "None of that, now."

Susane muttered her apologies as she looked at Sybil with pleading eyes. Asteria followed her gaze, scowling when she found Piers and Gavril again as if she'd forgotten they were all there.

"Why did you summon me to—" Asteria paused, peering at Susane from the corner of her eyes.

"Allanis, my…" Susane trailed off when Asteria's frown deepened. "Allanis. Ghita, specifically."

"Are you mad?" Asteria cried, throwing her arms out toward Piers.

"Do you know how strange it will seem that I'm in Allanis? It won't send the right message."

Piers held up his hands in surrender, pointing a finger at Sybil. "She made me do it."

Sybil scoffed in disbelief, glaring at Piers. "Don't use me as your scapegoat!"

"Why are *you* here?" Asteria asked her, pursing her lips and throwing a hand at Sybil. She scoffed, then threw her hands up in exasperation. "In fact, why are any of you here?"

"There's a perfectly good explanation," Sybil began, stepping toward Asteria. She gripped her elbow, dragging her toward the corpse. "We were beckoned by Lord Caius to investigate a strange illness spreading amongst the humans. We got here, and Susane"—Sybil waved a hand toward the Healer—"showed us the body of a recent victim. Suspiciously, though, Endora appeared shortly after."

"Endora?" Asteria startled, her swirling, pure blue eyes crinkling. "Why in the Heavens was she here?"

Sybil shot Asteria an incredulous look. "She said Etherea was experiencing a similar illness, and she wanted to confirm it was the same one."

"She traveled all the way from Etherea?" Asteria curled her lip, shaking her head. "That's a rather odd thing to do."

"My thoughts precisely," Sybil continued, gesturing at the table. "I don't know why, but Fate believed you would be of assistance in identifying this illness.

"Endora called it the Obsidian Decay. She didn't say how long it's been in Etherea, but it appears to have been enough time for her to conduct *studies*. She believes they're far more advanced than what Susane can accomplish with my help, and that she would share her findings."

"I doubt that," Asteria muttered. She stepped to the edge of the table, tilting her head.

"These are the organs," Susane interjected, thrusting the damned glass jar at Asteria.

She recoiled with a grimace, but then her face fell, and her body went rigid beside Sybil. She searched Asteria's face as the Lyran snatched the jar from the Healer, twisting it in different ways. Those eyes twinkled like stars appearing in the night sky.

"You called me?" Asteria said, looking at Piers. He nodded, then she directed her gaze to Susane. "And you're a Healer, so you can't wield the Aether."

When Susane shook her head in confirmation, the light within Asteria's eyes dimmed.

"This can't be right," Asteria whispered, handing the jar back to Susane with downcast eyes. "Did you take a sample of the blood before it solidified by chance?"

"I was able to remove some before this patient passed." She scurried toward a cabinet, carefully placing the jar on the ledge.

"What do you think it is?" Sybil asked, leaning into Asteria as they stared at the victim.

Asteria swallowed audibly, opening and shutting her mouth a few times before finally whispering, "I fear I know what it is, and I pray to the Heavens above that I'm wrong."

Susane returned with a small vial that looked like black ink, handing it over the corpse. Asteria took it and uncorked the top. Holding the vial before her, she hovered a hand above the opening, her face tight in concentration.

The ink-like substance crawled out of the vial, splashing against Asteria's palm, and Sybil gasped. Even Gavril swore under his breath, and Piers inched closer to Sybil, his chest brushing her back.

"What in the Gods—" Piers stopped short, and Sybil felt him wince. "Apologies, Asteria. What the fuck?"

"It's the Aether," Asteria explained, recoiling as she wiped her hand on the sheet covering the corpse. "Someone has used it for nefarious purposes."

Sybil braced her arm against Piers, wrapping a hand around his wrist behind her as her vision wobbled. He flipped his hand to clasp hers, steadying her yet again, his other hand firm on her waist.

The touch seared through her gown, her stomach fluttering.

"What do you mean?" he asked Asteria. Sybil peeked over her shoulder at him, tightening her grip since her vision had yet to clear entirely from the fog of another oncoming vision.

"Nothing is confusing about what I've said." Asteria stepped back from the corpse, the blue glow of her god-form peeking from beneath her skin. "The Aether is being used as a contagion."

Sybil knew their Path teetered on the edge, the image in her mind bouncing from the prophecy she saw to another with Beings coexisting, then to another with Lemurians falling ill and chaining up humans.

Endora made it seem like the Obsidian Decay had been in Etherea for quite some time, possibly before the meeting with the Lyrans. If that was true, Sybil knew without a doubt the prophecy was a product of this illness.

Sybil met Asteria's gaze, horror washing over her. "I told you the prophecy was because of something already in motion."

"I'll need one of you to explain what's going on," Gavril interrupted, swiping his hand in the space between them. Sybil and Piers stepped away from each other while Susane stood to the side, a hand pressed gently to her lips. "What do you mean something already set in motion?"

"The war you were concerned about has already begun," Asteria said, vocalizing Sybil's thoughts. "I fear it began long before the Lyrans met. Sybil hypothesized her vision emerged because someone already committed an act that would lead to the extinction of the various Beings. This is evidence she may be correct."

"You believe this is the Gods' doing?" Piers asked, his breath brushing Sybil's neck.

"It's either the Lyrans, or Sirians doing the bidding on the Lyrans' behalf," Sybil elaborated, her eyes on Asteria's gaunt face. "Because if the

Lyrans have not recruited Sirians to their cause, only one Lyran is capable of wielding the Aether in such a way."

A blank mask covered Asteria's face.

Sybil knew she was warring with the thought of Gallus being behind this. Her heart hurt for her sister and best friend. Asteria was all too familiar with betrayal between her mother, Rod, and her father—and the latter just committed another.

"Either Gallus is using the Aether to infect humans, or he has taught Sirians loyal to him and the cause to do it for him." Asteria clenched her fists at her sides, inhaling slowly. "Regardless, Gallus is involved. By infecting the humans first, the Lyrans are trying to make them the enemy. Gallus will probably start spreading the illness amongst the Sirians or Lemurians next."

"Lemurians can contract this?" Gavril asked, taking a step away from the corpse.

Sybil instinctively stepped back as well, but she forgot Piers was still behind her. Her back pressed against his chest, her ass brushing his hips. She held her breath as his lips barely skimmed her ear.

"I'm beginning to think you're trying to torture me," Piers whispered, barely audible as Asteria spoke. Sybil almost whimpered at the brush of his finger along the back of her arm.

"The only way you can get this illness is if a Sirian wielding the Aether infects you directly," Asteria explained, shaking her head. "Aether can't act as an illness naturally. It's forced into this state, which means it has to be forced into the body."

"Endora said her studies have shown it's contracted through ingestion or wounds," Susane said, fidgeting with her hands.

"If that's Endora's conclusion, she's lying."

Sybil wasn't shocked or offended by Asteria's declaration. Endora was known for her deception and manipulation. If Phoebe had Endora researching this illness, it was because Endora did a favor for Phoebe. She likely manipulated the situation in a way that allowed her complete control over the investigation.

Sybil also wouldn't be surprised if Endora had a hand in starting the infection, considering the Andromedan wielded the Aether alongside her necromancy.

"The masses would blame humans for the start of the infection, targeting them for onslaughts." Piers caught onto Asteria's train of thought, his voice quiet. "That's a rather slow process to eliminate the entire human race."

"Gallus doesn't wish to exterminate humans completely," Asteria muttered, and Sybil narrowed her eyes. "He wishes to restore balance amongst the Beings of Aveesh. He said to do so would require a slow trickle rather than a grand stunt."

Sybil sighed heavily with one slow blink. "You spoke to Gallus?"

"Of course I spoke to Gallus," Asteria bit out through clenched teeth. She took a deep breath, calmer. "I had to."

She should've known Asteria was serious about speaking to her father. Sybil offered Asteria a small smile, but Asteria must not have appreciated the scrutiny, adjusting her dress and hair.

"I think it may be too late for treaties," Piers interrupted, stepping out from behind Sybil and between her and Gavril.

Sybil thought of the lord's words on the lawn about the royal family of Allanis. "Lord Caius insinuated the Rotherhams are detached from Ghita, quite possibly the situation. Do you think Zephyr has spoken to them already?"

"For more reasons than one, yes." Asteria shut her eyes for a moment before nodding. "I don't doubt he's also spoken to Sylvan."

"And if Zephyr has talked, Nen has, too." Gavril swore under his breath.

"Trust me…" Asteria stared off toward a point in the room before directing wide eyes at Piers. "Nen definitely has."

"You and Wells need to get on it, then." Piers pointed his finger at Asteria. "We need to rally who we can."

Asteria leveled a glare at Piers and held a hand up that faintly glowed blue. "Let me speak with Morana, Rod, and Danica. I'll warn them of what we've found. The other Lyrans still haven't made any military moves, so we can't respond with force until they do. What we can do is find out what heavily human-populated cities are infected and start distributing a cure."

"Do you know how to cure this?" Sybil asked, scanning Asteria's face.

She nodded slowly, her shoulders relaxing some. "I think there's a way. I'll consult with Danica to confirm, but I'm mostly certain."

Asteria cast her gaze to Susane, who looked utterly terrified. She carefully stepped toward the Healer, holding out her hands. Susane accepted and leaned into the embrace.

"I'll come back with the cure," Asteria assured, looking ever the benevolent Goddess she insisted she wasn't. "I believe it'll require your Energy. Gather any other Sirians with the Energy you trust to assist in administering the cure, understand?"

"Yes, my Lady." Susane curtsied as Asteria released her hands. Sybil knew Asteria was lost in her own mind when she didn't correct the Healer for the designation.

"Will you bring students from the school?" Gavril asked, searching Asteria's face. "I feel as though they'd be incredibly helpful in this situation."

"We leave the Academy out of this," she said roughly, eyes flashing blue. "There will be plenty of Healers on the Main Continent within each country to assist. Until then, let me take you back to Eldamain."

Asteria walked back to where Sybil stood with Piers and Gavril. She waved her hand at the empty space, a portal quivering open. A room visualized, blurred on the other side as if underwater.

Sybil motioned for the men to follow, stepping through the veil. She steadied herself once through, shivering at the strange tingle that spread over her body and the pressure in her sternum as she entered the room.

Glancing around, it was the receiving room in Aggelos Palace.

Gavril and Piers stumbled after her, the former ramming into her back. She whirled on him with a finger in his face, snarling.

"Don't get snippy with me," Gavril grumbled, rolling his neck. "I've never portaled before, and I'm not sure I want to do so again."

"It wasn't too bad considering that trip to Ghita took us days, and here it only took seconds with the portal," Piers said as Asteria stepped through. "I think the moment of uncomfortability is worth the time saved."

Asteria shut the portal, directing her attention to Piers. "Don't go far. I may need your help since you wield the Energy. Make sure Wells is ready to travel."

"Does this mean you're officially on our side?" Sybil searched Asteria's face, heart fluttering in her chest.

Asteria didn't give anything away, neither confirming nor denying. Sybil knew she may not be ready to face the truth of what they'd discovered and what she was about to do.

By curing the humans, Asteria would be putting a stop to the work Gallus was trying to do.

She'd be standing directly against him.

CHAPTER 22

MORANA

Morana walked through the barren hallway, following the trail of sconces glowing with the Energy.

It'd been at least a century since she'd entered this house. After Rod had the affair with that human woman, Asteria refused to live here. Instead, she spent most of her time at Morana's residence or Gallus's if she wasn't on Aveesh.

After Gallus impregnated the Sirian queen, Asteria only went to Morana's home.

"I didn't take you for such a casual drinker, my little spitfire," Morana said as she entered the living room.

Asteria sat sideways in the armchair in front of the empty hearth, her legs draped over the arm and a glass of clear liquid perched between her fingertips.

"The events of the last month have led me down a different path," Asteria explained, inspecting the glass as though she didn't realize it was there. "I have now visited Eonia thrice, two of which have been unpleasant. Because I have to meet with Mother and that piece of shit—"

"Asteria!" Morana chastised, morphing into a laugh as she floated to the chair beside her. "You're lucky he hasn't arrived."

"I would gladly call him that to his face." Asteria stared at Morana with a straight face. She gestured to it. "See? Serious."

Morana chuckled under her breath, snatching the glass from Asteria's hand. She glared at her as Morana tipped back a sip. "This is water."

Asteria snatched it back, cradling it to her chest. "I'm appalled you think so little of me to assume I've resorted to drinking to relieve my stress like you lot." Morana deadpanned. "Besides, I simply chose to fill this glass with water only because it'll piss off Rod."

"Because it's in a glass intended for brandy?" Morana grinned, shaking her head. "He'll be sour over that?"

"It's Rod, Moe." Asteria returned the smile, but it was mischievous. "Of course he will be."

Morana laughed again, patting Asteria's glowing knee on the armrest. "I'm proud you've chosen to meet in your god-form."

"To keep Mother from arguing with me," Asteria explained, resting a hand on Morana's, her blue highlighting the same-hued veins running through Morana's skin. "You're the only good thing about this place."

"I appreciate the affection." Morana relaxed into the chair, shutting her eyes at the warm familiarity of just her and Asteria together without the chatter of the other Lyrans. "I miss you being around, but I understand your desire to spend more time on Aveesh."

"It appears my presence will be needed even more now than ever." Asteria shot Morana a side-long look, raising an eyebrow. "I'm afraid I have some rather... unfortunate news to share."

"Well, let's wait for the other two."

As if her words summoned them, Danica and Rod snapped into existence in the living room, both blinking in shock at Asteria in her god-form.

"If you're here like this, I fear what you have to say," Rod said first, studying her. Morana wanted to tackle him to the ground when evident lust flashed across his gilded face. "To what do we owe the pleasure?"

"Fate," Asteria said, her glowing blue sockets blinking. "I have news about the other Lyrans."

Morana sat up in her chair, her back straightening. "What is it?"

Asteria sighed heavily, swirling the water in her glass. Sure enough, just as she'd assumed, Rod latched onto the movement. He frowned at it, an as realization crept in, he clenched his jaw.

Morana huffed a single breath.

"To start, Nen and Zephyr were at the Patronage Gala last month," Asteria explained, and Morana couldn't help the curl of her lip. Asteria caught it out of the corner of her eye, and she just nodded once. "Nen and I might have had a small altercation."

"What sort of altercation?" Rod snapped, his fists clenching and unclenching at his sides.

Morana tilted her head at that, narrowing her eyes as Asteria appeared to relax despite the dismissive wave of her hand at Rod.

"Nothing I can't handle." Asteria tipped the glass, studying its contents. "Besides, the altercation was purposeful on my part. I wanted to see what he would say because Heavens know men love to run their mouths."

Rod's gilded eyes dimmed as his lids twitched at the blatant insult. Morana snorted, though, because it was entirely true.

"What did he say, Asteria?" Danica asked, her impatience tightening the edges of her glowing eyes.

"He all but hinted that he and the others were planning war, and that he and Zephyr were there to help their chosen countries scope out the Warrior class."

Tension filled the room, thickening the air. Morana's gaze bounced from Danica to Rod, the former scowling at her daughter.

"Why did you wait a month to tell us?" Danica snapped, a flash of gold briefly illuminating the room.

"I wanted to assess the situation further," Asteria explained, adjusting her position to sit properly in the chair. She shook her head, the blue flames of her hair flickering in and out with the movement. "I wanted to wait until I was absolutely certain they would harm the mortals."

Danica and Rod both deadpanned, but Morana knew immediately what Asteria was getting at. "What have they done?"

"There's an illness spreading amongst the humans." The entire room stiffened at the declaration, and Morana's heart broke at the crack in Asteria's voice when she added, "It's a tampered form of the Aether. I believe it's a product of Gallus or Sirians instructed by Gallus."

Morana tried to read Asteria's face, but it was difficult in her god-form. The endless black and blue swirl of night within her silhouette left very few features defined, which meant no muscle ticks or skin wrinkles to detect emotion. All she had to feed from was the hue by which Asteria glowed.

It was dim.

"This is only with humans?" Danica stood by the large window, looking out toward where Gallus's residence sat ominously against the starry night, the deep red stone like a beacon on the horizon. "How did you come to learn of this?"

"Sybil was responding to a summons from the Lord of Ghita," Asteria explained, glancing at Morana. "She had a run-in with Endora."

"Endora?" Morana whipped her head to Asteria. "What in the Heavens would she be doing in Allanis?"

Asteria looked at Rod, who appeared as if ready to burst into a golden flame. "Endora said Etherea has been studying this illness amongst other things that didn't sit well with Sybil. It appears Phoebe tasked Endora with looking into the illness—whether Phoebe knows it or not, Endora is hiding something from her."

"Could Phoebe not feel the tarnished Aether?" Rod asked, his gaze bouncing from Asteria to Danica.

"Asteria is the only one who can sense the Aether or Energy within a Sirian because of her inherited Lyran abilities," Danica explained, shaking her head. "Just as I can feel the Energy within a Sirian and Gallus can feel the Aether."

"So you truly are the only one who could catch Gallus or his henchmen doing this." Rod sighed, crossing his arms over his chest as he leaned against the fireplace. When Asteria's gaze flickered to his flexed muscles, Morana wanted to roll her eyes. Alas, she was in her god-form. "Gallus wasn't kidding when he suggested mass genocide of the humans."

"Why not just kill them all quickly?" Morana scoffed, throwing her arms up. "Why this game?"

"He doesn't want the humans wiped from this plane," Asteria said, leaning forward in her seat. "He wishes to correct a balance he believes is tipping toward this extinction the prophecy spoke of. He just wants to create an enemy of the humans through this illness so that the other Beings enforce restrictions and limitations on them, keeping them *in check*."

Rod curled his lip while Asteria recoiled in disgust at her own words—which sounded exactly like something Gallus would say.

Danica beat Morana to it. "So you've spoken with your father?"

Asteria waved her question away. "Please. That isn't why I've come."

Danica opened her mouth to protest, the Energy flaring around her, but Morana didn't have the patience to deal with yet another meeting spiraling due to Danica's perceived notion that everyone owed her something.

"What is it you wish to speak to us about?" Morana said, leveling Danica with a flash of her own power, multiple colors pulsing around her.

Asteria rose from the chair, her feet hovering a few inches off the ground. Rod tracked her every move as she floated across the room to an opposite window from her mother. "I will not sit idly by while Gallus infects humans with an illness they don't deserve. I'll need to speak with you about a cure." Asteria looked at her mother as she continued. "When I spoke to Gallus, he told me to stay out of this, to remain neutral. By helping cure the humans, I'll no longer be removed from the situation. I'll be directly opposing him."

"So this means, as far as any Lyrans are concerned, you are siding with us on the matter of the prophecy," Morana guessed, and Asteria nodded solemnly.

"If you haven't spoken to Sybil, I'm pleased to inform you Eldamain is ready to take up any mantle you give them." Asteria pursed her lips as she squinted at Rod. "With that being said, they've asked for my assistance in meeting with the other thrones that will join this cause. They want to talk strategy with them without being found out by the Lyrans or opposing kingdoms, and a visit from me is expected with Riddling and The Northern Pizi. I will just have a... prince with me."

"Which prince?" Every muscle in Rod's body tightened, and Morana felt her patience dissolve.

Morana pointed to Rod and Danica as she said, "You two are insufferable. Could you please mind yourselves and attempt to stay on the course of the conversation without diverting?"

Asteria smirked from where she stood, mimicking Rod's stance against the bookcase. Danica and Rod simmered from their posts, glaring at Morana.

"As I was saying," Asteria drawled, dipping her head to Morana, "I plan to disperse the remedy for this illness before visiting Taranis and Dionne. I spoke with Dionne and Lumir at the gala, and I wasn't sure if you'd told them about what's happening with the Lyrans."

"In the vaguest sense, I warned them of the humans' vulnerability," Danica announced, shrugging. "It's best if you talk with them further anyway. They seemed rather perturbed when I showed up."

"Shocking," Asteria said with a straight face, reflecting Morana's thoughts. "Prince Quintin let me know you believe Phoebe can be swayed."

"She has a human husband," Rod clarified with a nod. "She cares for him and his family deeply. If what you say is true, she clearly had good intentions when researching this illness. I would venture that she respects the humans in her kingdom, too."

"If Gallus has spoken with her already, I don't know what good I can do," Asteria admitted, walking back to the chair she'd been sitting in. "He will offer her—"

"He will offer her humans safety," Rod finished, which only earned him a menacing glare. Morana reclined against the chair, closing her eyes as she tipped her head back. "We've come to that same conclusion. Based on your conversation with him, I expect he will offer that safety in exchange for her neutrality."

Silence descended over the room, and Morana peeked at Asteria. She was lost in thought, staring out the window overlooking the rest of Eonia.

Morana wished they could have talked more about her visitation with Gallus and what she was up to in Aveesh most recently. Especially as to why Asteria appeared disgruntled when she mentioned the Eldamain prince she would be working with.

Morana mainly wanted to know about *that*.

"What if this becomes a war?" Danica finally walked away from the window, turning her back on it. "What will you do then? How will Celestia stand?"

"Will you finally use the labrys I made you?" Rod smirked, but Asteria ignored him.

She didn't tear her gaze from whatever held her attention outside the house. "I can't believe for one moment Gallus will want this to escalate into a war. I know his words don't mean much to you all, but they mean something to me. He insisted war was not his agenda."

"It may not be his, but it's always Nen and Zephyr's." Rod took cautious, painstaking steps toward Asteria rather than floating over. Her body instinctively locked up at his approach, but she allowed him to stand just inches from her. "How long do you believe Gallus will be able to hold them off before they start wreaking havoc upon Aveesh?"

Asteria studied his face, a slight frown at the corners of her lips.

Morana wanted to take her into her arms from the grief in that pout, but Asteria was more than an adult now, even for a Lyran. She knew the internal war Asteria constantly battled between her father and mother, the desires of the Lyrans and her own, and the urge to fight her way through or just give in.

Too many times, she'd talked Asteria down from the ledge of her own despair—one that occasionally led to discussions of how one killed a Lyran. The girl only ever wanted to be accepted for who she was, not what they wanted her to be: an almighty Goddess, an idol, or a submissive partner. Few ever truly understood her and that desire.

Asteria sighed heavily, resting a hand against Rod's arm.

Despite Asteria's resentment of the male, there would always be something within her drawn to his familiarity, especially after spending nearly five hundred years as a pair. Whether she knew it or not, it could be grounding during turbulent, confusing times.

Morana dealt with similar sentiments toward Valeria, except they'd been together for as long as she could remember, far before they ever came to this Realm.

"Gallus can hold his own." Asteria's hand slipped off Rod as she straightened, her starfire brightening. "He's always been capable of holding himself against you lot and Nen and Zephyr."

Rod started to protest, but Asteria held up a hand. "*If* this leads to war, I believe Celestia would side with the protection of humans. They'll call on all Sirians across Aveesh to join. I've always taught them to respect all Beings, particularly those in need."

"You won't force them?" Danica clenched her fists at her sides, lips pressed into a thin line. "Asteria, you are Goddess of the Sirians. They will answer to you and you alone. You are *their* Goddess, and they should obey—"

"I am *nothing*!" Asteria shouted, the flames of her fire burning hotter as the edges closest to her body deepened to purple. "Just because I wield the powers of both Sirians, and just because I have an extra ability from the Universe, does *not* mean they owe me anything. I'm not their keeper. I'm not their parent."

"They will need someone to look to, Asteria," Danica scolded, marching across the room toward her, Energy swirling around her manically. "*When* this leads to war, you will lead your people."

"Then I'll be their General or Lieutenant or whatever the hell they call it!" Asteria threw her arms out, standing tall against Danica with her face drawn tight. "Not their dictator—" Rod opened his mouth, and Asteria jabbed a finger toward him. "And do not say another word about that fucking labrys, Rod."

Morana sighed as she abruptly stood from the chair, zooming across the room to slide between the two Lyrans. She faced Danica head-on. "Let it go, sister."

Danica pressed her lips together tighter, her Energy audibly buzzing. "You can't protect her from her position forever, Morana."

"Lyrans have always had the freedom to choose what we do with the power we are granted," Morana explained quietly, squinting at Danica. "If you insist she is a Lyran, then those liberties we were once granted extend to her. Let. It. Go."

With a jut of her jaw, Danica vanished with a pop, probably portaling to her or Dola's residence. Morana released tension from her shoulders she hadn't realized she was holding, dragging her gaze to Rod with a raised eyebrow.

His gaze flickered from Morana to Asteria behind her, but it lingered on Asteria every time with utter longing.

"This is not the time," Morana said quietly, offering him a softer expression than the one she doled Danica.

But as always, Asteria, ever the spit-fire, lived up to her nickname. "There will never be a time again."

Asteria vanished just as quickly as her mother, and Morana shook her head at Rod. "Don't mistake familiarity with affection."

"So, I'm to believe she offers me glimpses because…" He trailed off, pointing at the empty space where Asteria had been. "Why?"

"Why what?" Morana tilted her head. "She doesn't offer you glimpses, Rod. It's the familiarity of you she leans on. The very least you can do is support her as a friend rather than try to push the boundaries she's placed between you."

"I don't want her friendship," Rod whispered, sorrow coating his words. "I want *her*."

"You can't own her if that's what you seek to do." Morana scoffed, shaking her head. She rubbed her temple, squeezing her eyes shut. "Why can't you just move on, Rod? Even better, why did you cheat in the first place if you want her so badly?"

"How am I to explain it, Morana?" Rod sunk into one of the chairs, rubbing at his bare, gilded jaw. "I was just so tired of… Heavens, she fought me on everything. I just wanted one night without the pressure from her, from Danica—"

"From Danica?" Morana sobered at that, frowning. "What pressure?"

Rod ignored her question. "I know I fucked up, and I want her back no matter what anyone else wants from her or me. This side of her feels different. There's a passion I've never seen from her before—a light I always hoped would come to her one day."

"This has always been her, Rod." Morana shook her head slowly, disappointment weighing her down. "You just failed to see it, and Danica tried to suppress it."

Morana snapped her fingers, appearing in the safety of her own home. She was beginning to hate being every Lyrans' parent.

CHAPTER 23

ASTERIA

Asteria portaled directly to Danica's library within her residence. She'd always admired her mother's extensive collection and the way she displayed it. From floor to ceiling—well over three stories high—were bookcases filled to the brim with an assortment of books and tomes. The scent of old parchment was nearly overshadowed by another smell that was far too sweet, like burnt sugar.

There was only a single window to let in any light, and since they were in Eonia, that meant the illumination came only from the stars in the sky. Otherwise, a chandelier glowed dimly with the Energy.

Somehow, Danica managed to accomplish a foreboding ambiance within her library, which was only fitting for someone as unpredictable as her with a collection of history from two different Realms.

The snap of another portal echoed through the room with a flash to Asteria's right.

Danica stepped through with an incredulous glare, hands clasped behind her back and an eyebrow raised. "Trespassing is beneath you, daughter."

"Did you forget I require your assistance?" Asteria floated toward one of the far walls of books, her eyes skimming over titles both in Etherean and the language of the Lyran's home world. "I'm following up on that request since you walked away in the middle of a conversation."

"I walked away from an *accusation*." Danica stepped up beside her, brushing her fingers over the spines before them. She peered at Asteria through narrowed eyes. "There's a difference."

"Spare me," Asteria shot back, a tight-lipped grin plastered on her face. "I told you I needed your help, and you popped away like it was beneath you."

Danica didn't look at Asteria, keeping her attention on the stack of tomes. Asteria caught the flicker of those glowing gold orbs, though, the equivalent of an eye roll. "It *is* beneath me, Asteria. It's not my responsibility to research an illness plaguing humans, and it shouldn't be yours. That's what you have your Sirian Healers for. Task them with finding the cure."

Asteria's nostrils flared, power simmering beneath her skin. "You really can't help yourself, can you? Even when humans are dying, you still act like you're this supreme Goddess who can't spare a second of your immortal lifespan to assist the world you supposedly rule."

"They're humans. They're *always* dying from some sort of illness." Danica slowly twisted her head over her shoulder. "Why is this any different than the other illnesses you task your Healers with curing?"

"Because the Obsidian Decay is *divine in origin*," Asteria snapped between clenched teeth. Her flames waved erratically around her. "It's part of this prophecy you lot are so keen on trying to prevent. Something Gallus is responsible for. Or have you forgotten you're feigning compassion for the humans and threatened genocide of their entire race?"

"There's that temper." Danica finally flipped her gaze to Asteria, a sly grin spreading up her cheeks as she pulled the first book from the shelf. "Honestly, I don't know how you expect to save anyone when you're always moments from combustion."

"And you're being as helpful as ever." Asteria sighed heavily, resisting the urge to rub at her forehead being in her forsaken god-form. She needed Danica's help, not because she was incapable, but because she didn't know how to read the damn language in a majority of the books she'd likely find a cure. "Are you done posturing, or do I need to light something on fire to keep your attention?"

Danica pursed her lips, one book clutched in the crook of her elbow while her other hand poised against a second book halfway pulled from the shelf. "You're as exhausting as your father."

"And yet here I am, still asking."

There was a silent pause as something flickered behind the illumination of Danica's eyes. Recognition, or maybe even reluctant respect, but she slipped the second book from the shelf before jerking her head toward the dark mahogany table in the middle of the library.

Asteria wasn't sure where everything went wrong with their relationship.

There were fond memories with Danica, although they fluctuated between the more frequent, not-so-fond ones. When Asteria learned how to wield the Energy, Danica was elated at how effortlessly she caught on to conjuring and manipulating it. Despite her father being the one to wield the Aether and starfire, Danica was still ecstatic when Asteria mastered all three of her powers. It meant she was a powerful Lyran, arguably one of the most powerful amongst them, and that made Asteria *more than*.

If Danica wanted her child to be anything, it was to be the best—to be *more than*—so she could say this was her daughter.

"Tell me everything you've learned about the Obsidian Decay," Danica asked, her tone even. She flicked her hand over the tomes, pages fluttering as they revealed symbols and glyphs familiar to Asteria, if only because she used to watch Danica read through her old books when she was younger. "What does it look like? How does Gallus have it manifesting?"

The heavy weight of hostility slowly dissipated as Asteria sunk into the chair opposite where Danica stood. A desire to use the Energy to heal was a passion Asteria and Danica shared, putting them on an even ground where they could finally cooperate and relate.

Or at least pretend to.

"I've yet to see it in a live victim, but the dead one I saw in Ghita had hardened, black veins." Asteria rolled her head on her neck, shutting her eyes. "So were their organs. I believe that is where the plague has acquired its name. They truly look as though they've been replaced by obsidian."

One book ceased mid-flip, and Danica cocked her head at Asteria, squinting. "How long does it take to completely alter the body?"

"They're saying about a day or two—"

Something moved out of the corner of Asteria's eye, and she dragged her attention toward it just in time for a tome to carefully float directly into Danica's outstretched hand.

Danica gently laid it on the table and waved her hand over it. The cover peeled back and once again, pages began to turn of their own accord. Asteria watched her mother with scrutiny, trying to gauge her reaction.

"Why did you ask for my help?" Danica asked as she concentrated on the book, a slight frown furrowing the browless, light taupe skin of her god-form.

"I had my reasons." Asteria was fixated on the book, but it stopped flipping and she caught Danica glaring from her peripheral vision. She sighed, relenting. "Like I said, the illness is divine in origin, which means it needs divine unmaking. I don't doubt Gallus found how to do this in his—or your—plethora of tomes on the Aether. You can't tell me in the eons Lyrans have existed, not one who wields the Aether has never attempted to use it in such a way. You've had the Energy for who knows how long on top of your wealth of books on Energy-wielding. It's where we learned it could enhance healing in the first place."

Danica hummed as she resumed her scavenging, a low, amused

sound.

"Careful, Asteria. That almost sounded like admiration." One final page opened, and Danica's eyes glided over the ancient, foreign script. "You've always been so stubborn about distancing yourself from what you are. Yet here you are, asking the mother you loathe for help with *divine unmaking*." She raised an eyebrow, peering up from the text. "Funny, isn't it? How you always come back to me when the real work begins."

Admiration?

Asteria wasn't about to take the bait, but it caught in her ribs all the same. That smug lilt in Danica's voice always scraped something primal in her—something blistered and old.

Once again, Danica made this all about *her*. About power. About being right.

She always did.

Heavens forbid the deaths of innocents mattered more than her insistent need for attention and exaltation.

Which is why Asteria bit her tongue. She wasn't here to win an argument. She was here to end this illness, and if it meant enduring Danica's self-importance, then she would let the woman revel in her delusions.

Danica slid the tome across the table as if Asteria would be able to read the damned thing. Regardless, she pressed her fingers into the page and slid it closer while holding Danica's gaze, resisting the urge to let it burst into flames just to spite her.

If it didn't have the cure to the Decay, she would have.

"A sort of parasitic magic," Danica explained, waving her hand over the tome. "Just as ancient as our powers. Remember when we found enhanced blood of either Lyrans, Sirians, or Lemurians could amplify the effectiveness of any potions or elixirs the Healers and House of Echidna would develop?"

Asteria nodded slowly, staring at the markings on the page.

"The way to counter the Aether in the blood will primarily be the Energy," Danica explained, her fingertips barely braced on top of the table with her shoulders back. "Since we're dealing with mere humans, it can't be directly inserted into the bloodstream. It would likely do just as much damage to them as the Aether. It will need to be combined with an assortment of herbs to help gently coax it through their systems while protecting their bodies."

Asteria ignored the snide tone to Danica's words when she uttered *human*. She looked up at her mother, folding her hands in her lap. "What would the herbs need to do *precisely*, Mother?"

Danica bristled, her aura flaring.

It appeared both of their patience for each other's antics was thinning.

"They will need something to prevent inflammation," Danica began, drumming her fingers along the table. "They will also need herbs to support the nerves, immune function, metabolism, and liver and digestive health. If you can include something that provides mental clarity and antioxidants, it will help support their bodies against any complications."

Asteria schooled her face into a blank, slack expression, hopefully appearing deep in thought about what herbs would work.

That was all too easy. The thought came unbidden, curling through Asteria's mind like smoke.

Danica had gone straight to the shelf. No hesitation after Asteria told her what the victims suffered from.

No cure should come this quickly, especially one from something Gallus either found, made, or altered. It took them longer to learn any enhanced Being's blood could boost an elixir.

But what was she to say?

Why do you know this? Why aren't you all that surprised?

Danica would twist it, sneer, turn it into another deflection dressed as superiority.

Asteria tightened her grip around her fingers, but she bit her tongue, swallowing her lingering discomfort like ash.

She didn't want another war of words. Not now. Not when people were dying.

Maybe it was a coincidence or buried knowledge Danica hadn't realized she still carried.

Maybe...

She would deal with it later, after the mortals were safe and the world stopped unraveling.

"You always did have a talent for solving problems *after* they became catastrophes." Asteria offered a tight smile. "Still... Thank you."

"You know," Danica said, side-stepping the table, her hand trailing on top of it, "you would be a dangerous Goddess if you ever stopped pretending you weren't one."

Asteria met her gaze. "And you would've been a decent mother if you weren't so obsessed with being a Goddess."

CHAPTER 24

ASTERIA

Asteria waited with Sybil in the receiving room at Aggelos Palace, pacing anxiously as she held tight to the strap across her body. The vials clinked in the sack hanging at her hip, her gaze latching onto where Sybil gripped another. Two more satchels sat on one of the cushioned chairs nearby.

Combined, they had roughly two hundred vials prepared with the herbal ingredients needed for this elixir to cure the Obsidian Decay: chamomile, kava, skullcap, echinacea, ginseng, and turmeric. The last thing needed was to charge the ingredients with the Energy, which was why she needed Piers to come with them.

Sybil connected with her trusted Lemurians to find which cities would need the cure on the Main Continent. The next step would be treating the mortals without drawing too much attention from Gallus, Nen, Zephyr, Valeria, and whoever else they were working with.

"You can't prepare for the feeling of portaling, Wells." Gavril's voice carried down the hallway, and Asteria involuntarily locked up. "It's an absurd sensation—"

"He's being quite dramatic," Piers said as the three men entered the receiving room. "It's bearable compared to days' worth of travel."

"I'm sure I can manage," Wells assured, but he was no longer paying attention to Piers nor Gavril as he entered the room. A playful smirk already tugged at the corner of his lips as he made eye contact with Asteria.

As a greeting, he simply *winked* at her, and Asteria glowered.

"I've not left this castle in three days," Piers said, clasping his hands behind his back. His gaze bounced from Sybil to Asteria. The former pursed her lips as he continued, "I must say, I believe this level of seclusion may be a record for me since reaching adulthood over a decade ago."

Sybil snorted, and Asteria didn't miss the playful twinkle in Piers's eyes.

"I'm sorry to disturb your otherwise busy schedule, but people are dying who require our assistance," Asteria said, throwing her shoulders back. "I, for one, don't wish to search up and down this continent for wherever it is you might have ventured to."

"Even though it would only take you mere seconds?" Wells approached the chair where one of the satchels rested, picking it up and testing its weight.

"I would still waste time trying to find where in the Heavens you all went if you weren't here," Asteria explained, folding her arms over her chest as she cocked her hip. She raised an eyebrow at Wells, gesturing to the bag. "Are you sure you can manage?"

A roguish half-smile slowly climbed up Wells's cheek as his eyes glistened. His gaze dragged from the top of Asteria's head to her feet before returning to her eyes. He tucked the satchel over his head. "I think I can manage perfectly well."

Asteria's nostrils flared as heat flickered in her stomach at what should've been an innocent statement, but how Wells spoke was full of sin.

"What are we going to be doing?" Gavril interjected, his eyes studying the interaction. "The last time you spoke to us, you said you would require Piers's Energy?"

"Yes," Asteria confirmed, shaking her head clear of exactly what Wells could manage. She grabbed the second satchel and handed it to Piers. "Danica and I found a cure for the Obsidian Decay, and the vials in these satchels contain the required ingredients. The final touch that makes this elixir effective in battling the Aether within the bloodstream is the Energy. The other ingredients simply boost support of the body in various degrees."

"I'm not versed in healing techniques," Piers explained, shaking his head. "How do I add the Energy to this vial?"

"Simply charge the ingredients within the vial but not the vial itself," Asteria said, picking at the worn leather of the satchel. She felt Wells watching her from the opposite side of the chair. "Once it emits a white glow, have the individual ingest it immediately."

"That's all?" Gavril's gaze bounced from Piers to Asteria. "Where are we going?"

"To every village we believe is infected," Sybil said, her voice timid. "I was able to get in contact with different trustworthy Lemurians. Currently, besides a small village outside of Eryphus, we have Ghita in Allanis, Lolis in Sylvan, and Sado in Teslin."

Piers frowned in deep thought, lips pressed together as he stared toward one end of the room.

Wells eyed the four bags amongst them, frowning. "How many victims do you anticipate in each city? This can hardly be enough for three villages."

"I'm not sure." Sybil sighed, hanging her head.

"The ingredients needed are rather common for Healers to have on hand," Asteria explained, ushering them toward her. She opened a portal behind her to the Healer's quarters in Lord Caius's home. "I hope we can replenish what we use for each city from the Healer's supplies. Every lord has an appointed Healer in their home, and I'm positive they'll let me into their quarters to utilize what they have without a second thought."

"I'm concerned about Sylvan and Teslin," Gavril admitted just as Sybil went to step through the portal. "We're on opposing sides as far as we know. Will they not be angry that we're invading without cause?"

"We have cause, and we're not *invading*." Asteria nodded at Sybil to go through, offering her a tight-lipped grin. "We're healing the sick. That's all."

"Then why bring Gavril and me if you're simply healing the sick?" Wells asked, exchanging a glance with his friend. "Will that not raise suspicion? At least Piers has the Energy. Gavril and I, to any bystander, don't have a purpose."

"I'm not foolish enough to think the Lyrans won't send their people to harass us." Asteria scoffed, narrowing her eyes. "I would rather have the protection. Besides, you lot have a purpose." She smirked at Wells then, who had minimized the distance between them. "You're my lackeys."

Gavril let out a single harsh laugh, grabbing Piers's hand as the prince hauled him through the portal.

Asteria continued to glare at Wells, agitation simmering at how he studied her in silence.

"Your lackey..." Wells rocked back on his heels. "Lackey Orwell Carraphim has a ring to it."

"It's not a title." Asteria simmered, her eyes narrowing into thin slits.

"Whatever you say, Blue." He shrugged as he studied the portal's opening like a new sword. "So I just walk through?"

Asteria stepped up beside him, motioning toward it. "It's just an opening—" She cut off as she replayed what he said. She snapped her head to him, frowning. "What did you call me?"

"Blue." Wells gave her a full grin that lifted his features and brought a glow spearing through Asteria, knocking the wind from her. "I figured it was a fitting nickname after you nearly went Mighty Goddess on my brother last fall."

"I don't have nicknames," Asteria said between clenched teeth, even if that was a lie. Morana, Sybil, Dionne, and her father all had nicknames for her. In fact, Gallus had two.

"That appears to be a lie." She deadpanned, slightly impressed he caught it. "All my friends have nicknames."

"We're not friends."

"You may be reluctant, but I foresee us spending quite some time together moving forward, what with you joining our side and all." To her surprise, Wells slipped his hand into hers, the rough calluses rubbing against her palm as he interlaced their fingers. "But we can talk more about it another time. Our *friends* are waiting for us, Blue."

Wells tugged her behind him through her portal, the shock of his hand in hers—warm, stirring—and his sudden initiative causing her focus to waiver. The portal started closing just as half his body crossed the veil between Eldamain and Lord Caius's home.

"Wells!" Without a thought, she shoved them through, throwing the force of her body at him before it closed fully. They both gasped at her sudden attack, his hands latching onto her waist to steady them as they stumbled into their destination.

Asteria didn't know how she came to be in her position other than blindly throwing them through the portal, but she was enjoying it far more than she cared to admit.

Her arms wrapped around Wells's neck, elbows interlocked. They were both at a slight angle, his arms around her waist, holding her against him. Their faces were mere inches apart as their heavy, nervous breaths mixed between them.

"You—" She cleared her throat around the hoarseness, her heart fluttering as he rolled his lips together. "The portal was closing."

"Is that so?" he whispered, maintaining eye contact. She was lost in the deep blue ring around his beige irises—

"Did we miss something?" Gavril's voice interjected, his abruptness causing Asteria and Wells to jump apart, straightening their clothes. "You two took an awful long time to get through the portal."

Asteria whirled on them to find Piers, Sybil, and Susane stunned while

Gavril leaned against the table where the corpse was days ago with a damn grin spread across his cheeks.

"We were just having a discussion," Asteria hissed as she fought the heat rising to her cheeks. "Nothing amiss."

Gavril only hummed as he pushed himself off the table, keeping his eyes trained on Wells with an eyebrow raised in inquisition.

"Prince Piers was explaining how to use the elixir you created," Susane said, her gaze bouncing between Asteria and Wells. "I can be of use if you need me. Whether it be preparing as many of the ingredients as I can or helping administer them. I fear my fellow Sirian connections are still a day away."

"Your assistance in administering would be extremely helpful." Asteria nodded. "We will be able to cover far more ground that way. When we're finished here, whether those we can help are cured or we run out of vials, I anticipate you and Piers will likely be quite spent. I can make more elixirs to replenish our stack without depleting your herbal stock."

Susane nodded, interlacing her fingers in front of her. "Where do we begin?"

"Anyone complaining of symptoms within the last two days at maximum." Asteria gestured for Wells to hand Susane the satchel, unable to meet his eyes. "I'm afraid beyond that, it's too late."

"We have an old establishment we converted into an infirmary to house any who are ill and still able to get here." Susane grabbed the bag, but almost dropped it from its weight.

Wells pursed his lips and slowly took it back, quietly explaining, "I'll just stick by you as you administer if that's alright."

Susane smiled softly, nodding. "Thank you, Your Highness."

Wells curled his lip at the title, and Susane giggled with a slight blush, stirring something foreign and bitter in Asteria. She cleared her throat, drawing Susane's attention back to her. "What of those who can't journey from the outskirts of Ghita?"

"I suppose they're in their homes." Susane gnawed on her bottom lip, then held up a finger. "Lord Caius has records of the homes within Ghita's borders that venture far outside the main city. Perhaps you would be able to portal us there?"

Gavril grumbled something unintelligible under his breath, and Piers jabbed him in the ribs with his elbow at the same time Sybil knocked him upside the head. He shot a menacing glare at Sybil before softening his expression when he turned to Piers.

"I can portal you all," Asteria assured, her fingers tingling as Wells drew closer.

"I think I'll rather enjoy portaling," he said quietly, only for her to hear.

She gasped at the insinuation underneath the deep rumble of his voice, pinning her gaze on him. "*That* will not be a regular occurrence."

He simply offered the smile that took her breath away, adding a wink for good measure.

CHAPTER 25

ASTERIA

After hours of curing the sick within the provisory infirmary across the road from Lord Caius's manor, Asteria spent another few hours portaling their group to homes on the outskirts of town. Piers and Susane gave every bit of Energy they possibly could to the people of Ghita, and Asteria stepped in when they needed her.

And Heavens, did they need her.

While a Lyran, portaling as much as she was took its toll on her. Being able to portal from one location to the next was simple when done a few times within a day, but to do so consecutively over a few hours was draining and dangerous, not to mention using the Energy alongside the others. It could easily push her toward the brink of Fracturing, losing herself to her powers.

By the time they portaled back to Lord Caius's residence, Piers could barely stand. He rested all his weight against Gavril, his shoulders rising and falling with heavy breaths. Asteria nearly tumbled into Wells again, his hands shooting out to catch her. She had no choice but to let him steady her, their hands locked momentarily on one another's biceps before they broke apart.

"Princes," a male called as he descended nearby steps. He was rather round with a handlebar mustache curling at the corners of his lips. "I can't begin to thank you—" The man stopped short upon seeing Asteria, and he immediately bowed.

Asteria whimpered a plea. "You don't have to do that."

"Lord Caius," he said as he rose, holding out his hand instead. She accepted with a soft smile, his grip firm as he nodded. "I can't thank you *all* enough for coming to my village with the cure. I had the cook boil a batch of stew and warm up bread from the day for you. There are guest rooms upstairs that I encourage you to take advantage of before you go on your way."

Asteria sighed in relief. She wasn't sure if she could portal them all back to Eldamain tonight.

"Thank you, Lord Caius," Wells said in place of his silent older brother and Asteria. "That's very kind of you and most appreciated."

Piers mumbled something in Gavril's ear, and the latter said, "Would it be trouble to have the meal brought to our room? I fear the prince might keel over at any moment."

"Of course." Lord Caius ushered them toward the stairwell. "Come, let me show you to your rooms."

"I can bring it to you and let the cook know we plan to take ours from the Healer's quarters," Sybil said, resting her hand against Asteria's arm. She leveled Susane with a stern look. "You go to your room and rest. We'll take care of preparing replenishments and ensure we leave extra in case there are more victims."

Susane nodded without hesitation. "Take as much as you need. I have another batch of herbs in the garden that should be ready in the next day or two."

"Thank you again," Asteria said, gripping the Healer's hand. "Your service is greatly appreciated. I know you are aware of the possible consequences considering the state of the Gods and the kingdoms at this time."

Susane offered Asteria a grim, tired smile. "I'm a Healer. Be them a child, elderly, criminal, or saint, I won't turn someone away. That includes what type of Being they are in this world, but especially humans. They're forced exist with those who have power they can never attain. They don't deserve this, and I would rather die saving them than submit to a royal missive."

Susane squeezed Asteria's hand before gathering her skirts and climbing the stairs. Pride swelled in Asteria's chest, and she wondered if those morals were something Susane had always believed, or if it was because of what she tried to foster at the Academy.

"Shall we?" Wells interrupted, gently resting his hand on her lower back. He jerked his head toward the Healer's quarters.

Asteria frowned, curling her lip. "We?"

Wells deadpanned, a funny expression for someone who seemed perpetually playful. Asteria suppressed a grin, which he ignored. "I did nothing today compared to you, Piers, and Susane. The least I can do is follow a recipe to make more elixirs."

"I suppose." Asteria shrugged half-heartedly as she led the way into the Healer's quarters. She spotted a chair beside the counter and headed straight for it before her legs gave out. She moaned happily when she sank down, leaning her head back and staring at the ceiling.

The silence between Wells and Asteria was surprisingly not unpleasant. She caught him out of the corner of her eye in the chair next to her, tipping it back on two legs with his hands folded over his lower abdomen.

She could still feel the muscles of that abdomen clenching against her stomach as he held her against him, the thought sending warmth straight to her core.

Asteria shut her eyes to remove the highly inappropriate thought of what body lay beneath that shirt, admonishing herself internally. She wanted to rip her hair out in frustration from being unable to pinpoint why he was unraveling the self-control she typically exhibited when it came to males.

She'd kissed a handful over the last one hundred and twenty years, but that was as far as she ever let her curiosity with men venture. Allowing anyone the privilege of claiming any part of her only stirred disgust.

Except with Wells thus far. She found herself considering far too often what his hands and lips would feel like in places usually hidden beneath her clothing.

Wells cleared his throat as the two front legs of his chair plopped down on the ground. Asteria peeked out of the corner of one eye. "It's occurred to me that neither of my brothers has thanked you."

Asteria straightened in the chair, angling her body toward him as she frowned. "Thanked me? Heavens, why?"

"For siding with us," Wells said as though it were plain as day. "I can't imagine it's an easy choice, beyond your reasoning of Fate, to be stuck between Lady Danica and Lord Gallus—"

Asteria held up a finger, shaking her head. "No."

Wells raised an amused eyebrow, the corner of his lip kicking up. "No?"

"First and foremost, you must stop calling them Lady and Lord." Asteria chuckled, rubbing a hand across her forehead. "It's exhausting to hear. The next matter is that choosing a side has nothing to do with Danica and Gallus."

"Are they not your parents?" Wells leaned forward, resting his forearms on his thighs. Asteria nodded slowly. "Being split between your mother and father can't be easy to come to terms with."

Asteria sighed as she held his inquisitive gaze, maintaining a neutral expression.

There were very few people she talked to in this Realm. She could count those she truly trusted on one hand: Morana, Sybil, Odo, and her brothers. Although Erika was slowly making her way onto that list.

To Asteria, trust involved divulging one's inner thoughts and personal matters—for example, the complicated nature of her relationship with her parents.

She didn't care whether she and Wells were forced to work together for the foreseeable future or if they would never see each other again, but that last thought betrayed her. Something inside her twinged slightly at the thought of *never* seeing him again.

She wouldn't be sad but maybe disappointed.

He seemed to relent on his interest in the conversation as he leaned back in the chair, crossing his arms over his chest and rolling his neck.

Asteria remembered what Odo had said about Wells's wife, and she suddenly felt guilty for knowing something so intimate about him. She didn't know why she cared at all, but she said softly, "My relationship with my parents is quite complicated."

Wells startled as though he'd forgotten she was there. He sat straight, his attention entirely engrossed on Asteria. She swallowed against the strange nervousness of talking about Danica and Gallus and folded her hands in her lap.

"I'm not sure how much you know of Lyrans—or Gods and Goddesses to all of you—but it can be quite difficult for us to have offspring." She paused as she collected herself, old grief tickling the back of her mind. "At least with one another. It seems we have no trouble reproducing with humans, Sirians, or Lemurians.

"When Danica and Gallus found out they were going to have me, all the Lyrans were utterly stunned. Where they are from, there hadn't been a new Lyran born in quite some time. I was the first born in this Realm *and* the first to be born for as long as their memories served them."

"You were coveted," Wells said, and Asteria couldn't help the sharp exhale.

"I suppose you could call it that." She remembered the Lyrans' obsession with her and their expectations. Rod still pined after her despite her vehemence to remind him it wouldn't happen. "Danica was part of the Lyrans who demanded excellence from me. She wanted me to embrace being a Goddess and enact my will upon the Sirians—and still does. Her insistence has created a tense relationship between us because I didn't want that. I grew up alongside some of the Andromedans you are familiar with, so I felt more akin to them than the Lyrans.

"Gallus encouraged free thinking." Asteria blinked at the thought of her father. She had yet to mourn what she knew was the beginning of the end of their relationship. "He taught me how to use my Aether and starfire, and I became skilled at both. He encouraged me to choose how I wanted to go about my immortal existence rather than forcing something upon me I didn't want."

"So you prefer your father over your mother?" The way Wells watched Asteria had her leaning closer to him. His face was open and receptive, absorbing every word she uttered.

Seen. She felt seen.

"Like I said, complicated." She smiled at that, which had him mirroring the expression. She decided this was her favorite quality of his. Then she remembered she didn't need to favor anything about him. "Gallus has his faults like anyone, but those he does have are severe. He instigates, debates to cause an argument, and likes to experiment just to see what happens. He can be a dangerous man, but he was always a good father. The older I am, the harder it is to reconcile the two versions of him."

"That explains why you threaten to set fire to things when told what to do," Wells observed, and Asteria shot him a glare, but she couldn't suppress the smile on her face. "I have to admit, I was always curious as to why you refused the behavior the other Gods require of their subjects and why you spent more time on Aveesh than them."

"I'm glad we can come to the source of my stubbornness." Asteria tried to press her lips together. She waved a hand at him. "And you? What is the source of your impishness?"

Wells burst into laughter, pressing a hand against his stomach. Asteria stood corrected.

This was her favorite quality of his, especially because it coaxed a rare giggle from her lips. She slapped her hand over her mouth, stunned by the sound.

Wells looked at her with glistening eyes as his laughter faded. "I don't think I've ever heard laughter from you."

"It's a rarity." She stared at the door, even as his gaze penetrated the side of her face. "Must I ask again?"

Wells chuckled as he shook his head, and she dragged her gaze back to him as he let out a sigh. "I suppose it has to do with wanting more attention as a child. Being the third son sometimes means you are simply… the *spare*."

Wells glared at her, and Asteria rolled her eyes as he continued, "Quin was raised as heir to the throne, what with being the eldest son. Piers was taught combat and strategy and still attended some of the studies Quin was required to take. He was the next in line. Should anything happen to Quin, he needed to be capable of taking the throne.

"The crown prince and next heir are rarely ever simultaneously murdered or killed." Asteria's eyebrows twitched with a frown as he said those words, like it was an ordinary statement to speak of your siblings' deaths. "I was left to my own devices, I suppose. Sure, I was loved by my family, but I didn't feel as though I had a purpose. I didn't feel particularly wanted for quite some time."

"I'm certain your family wanted you," Asteria said, tightening her hands in her lap to keep herself from soothing him with a hand on his knee.

"I know. But as a child, the actions of your family can leave lasting impressions." Wells tipped his head side-to-side. "I suppose I was an untamed child because I wasn't given direction. I knew that about myself when I went to the Academy. That's why I decided to go the Warrior route—to learn a little discipline."

She smiled at that, lightly tapping her shoe against his ankle. "Disciplined, but still ever the mischievous boy."

Wells grinned, his eyes crinkling. "I find it rather condescending when the centuries-old Goddess calls me a boy."

It was Asteria's turn to burst into laughter, the sound echoing around them in the chamber. She buried her face in her hands to gather herself, her chest feeling lighter than it had in decades.

When she peeled her fingers away, Wells grinned broadly, his eyes flitting across her face. "A giggle and a laugh? I feel as if I should be rewarded for such an accomplishment."

"Don't push your luck, Prince." Asteria sank further back in the chair. "Did the Academy help you find your purpose in life?"

"I don't feel as though I have one grand purpose," Wells pondered. "But it was never the purpose I sought. I've always been a simple man. I desired to be wanted for who I was, for all my perks and flaws."

Asteria hummed because she could relate to him in that respect. She'd only ever wanted to be seen for who she was and what she wanted. "So, did you find that?"

She internally cursed herself when his smile broke at the corner, and she remembered Odo's words about Ruelle. While Wells tried to maintain a wistful grin, the joy behind it died. He stared down at his hands between his legs, absentmindedly nodding to himself.

"I did," he said softly, averting his gaze.

"Wells," Asteria said, reaching across the distance, nearly falling out of her chair to wrap her hands around his knee. "I'm sorry. Odo told me—"

"Don't apologize," he exclaimed, not unkindly, turning and grasping her hands in his as he leaned closer. "I suppose I didn't anticipate this conversation taking a turn in that particular direction."

He turned her hands up, his thumb skimming across the middle of her palm. It sent sparks up her arm and through her body. His face brightened again as he continued, "Ruelle didn't care who I was. The moment we met, she told me she'd heard a *lot* about me from Odo, and I almost brushed the meeting off until she tugged me into her and whispered she would rather learn for herself."

The fondness in his voice kept the smile on Asteria's face. "Clearly she enjoyed what she learned."

Wells chuckled again, his eyes crinkling as he shook his head. "I suppose she did. Her love for me not only accomplished the feeling I craved my entire life, but it made me truly realize how many people around me did love me for who I was.

"Just because I lost Ruelle doesn't mean I lost that feeling. My relationship with my brothers and even with Gavril has improved, and I have her to thank for that."

Asteria enclosed her hands around his again. "I'm glad you found that happiness then."

"And have you?" Wells paused, looking up at her through his lashes. "Found happiness yet?"

Asteria's mouth opened; she didn't know whether from shock or because she was instinctively going to answer, the comfortability with Wells locking her in the moment.

The door flew open, though, and they startled apart.

Sybil stood in the doorway with a tray of food, pursing her lips as her gaze bounced between them.

"I brought food," she said, moving straight for the empty space on the counter and avoiding the table in the middle of the room. After she handed a bowl to Wells, Sybil moved to give one to Asteria, an eyebrow raised.

She mouthed to Asteria, *What was that?*

Asteria silently accepted the outstretched bowl, ignoring Sybil's question, if only because she didn't have the answer herself.

CHAPTER 26

PHOEBE

Phoebe sat at the large mahogany desk, her gaze sweeping across the massive expanse of parchment surrounding her in a curved half-circle.

"Gods," she grumbled under her breath, resisting the urge to swipe every last item to the floor. "Can't find anything on this beast of a fucking—"

"Your Majesty?" someone called, and Phoebe held her tongue as she made eye contact with her newly appointed nursemaid. "You have some rather persistent individuals who requested lunch with you."

A warm smile spread across Phoebe's cheeks as she slowly rose from behind the desk. "I suppose I could be bothered for lunch. Send them in."

The Sirian nursemaid returned the smile. She tapped the office door in time for two small figures to barrel through. Phoebe made it around her desk just in time for both children to latch onto either side of her. They looked up at her with sea-green eyes, Marks stark against their foreheads, blinking innocently.

As if she didn't know they swindled their way into coming here for lunch.

"So we're having lunch?" Phoebe said to her children, squatting to their level. Jeremiah clamored into her lap, wrapping his small legs around her midsection and hands around her neck.

"We asked Maria if we could bring pastries for lunch, but she said we should eat something with more nutrition," Emmalina chided, throwing her head over her shoulder to glare at Maria. "Mother, tell her we can have pastries."

Phoebe failed to suppress the chuckle that fluttered from her lips. She attempted to muffle it by pressing a kiss to the top of Jeremiah's head. "Emmalina Abbott…" Phoebe held tightly to Jeremiah, reaching her other hand toward her daughter to tug on a black curl. "I'm not your father. I agree with Maria. Growing Sirians need ample nutrition. After you've worked your brain with your studies, pastries don't seem like a good way to do so."

Emmalina turned that penetrating gaze onto her and Phoebe raised her eyebrows in amusement.

This child…

Phoebe wished to savor every single year of their childhood, but she was fascinated to see what sort of queen her daughter would make.

"If you eat your lunch and behave like good children," Maria began, ushering in the attendant with the food cart, "maybe your mother will give me permission to grant one pastry each when we are finished."

"A pastry!" Jeremiah yanked his head back, hands flat on Phoebe's shoulders. "If I eat my lunch?"

Phoebe laughed again, peeling him from her as she urged both children toward the short table in the middle of the couch and chairs. "Yes, you can have *one* pastry if you eat your lunch." Phoebe lifted her gaze to Maria, shaking her head with a wistful grin.

After the unfortunate *incident* with Delilah, Phoebe had tasked Dustin with replacing the children's nursemaid. Being queen, Phoebe had the final decision on who that person would be. Lucky for her—and to the dismay of the Council—she and Dustin already had a replacement lined up just in case.

Maria was an old friend from the Asterian Academy. Phoebe had just been waiting for something to befall Delilah. It was a blessing from the Heavens that she was the one who doled out that Fate.

"How are things progressing?" Phoebe asked, observing her daughter over the rim of her wine glass while directing her question to Maria. "You know… unlearning some of the damage done by Delilah."

"Considering Delilah ignored Emmalina as she had done with you"—Maria gave Phoebe a knowing glance—"she's adjusting just fine. As for Jeremiah, I still think he cowers in anticipation. He doesn't seem to trust easily but is beginning to speak to me more instead of only Emmalina."

"It'll be bittersweet when he doesn't cling to me." Phoebe brushed a stray curl from Jeremiah's forehead. "When he stops, I'll know he's truly progressing past the scars Delilah left behind."

"We'll get there, Phoebe," Mariah said quietly, nibbling on a piece of bread. "Part of this journey will be letting him warm up on his own time, to let him know he's in control again."

"He's only five," Phoebe whispered, fighting back the burning frustration in her throat. "He shouldn't have to heal from so much—"

"I see the look in your eyes." Maria reached across the distance, laying her hand on Phoebe's. "Don't blame yourself. You're the queen of an entire country *and* a mother. It's not an easy balance, but you manage far better than others. Your children know you love them, which is most important of all."

Phoebe offered Maria a grim smile, even if her kind words did help quell some of the worry eating away at her heart. She desired to be unlike King Drogo, both as ruler and parent, but some days it felt like she must sacrifice one for the other.

Another knock on the door startled both Maria and Phoebe. She turned her head toward it without removing her eyes from Maria. "Who is it?"

"Miss Endora, Your Majesty," one of the guard's voices called, a hint of nervousness in the quiver. "She has another with her—"

The double doors burst open, and Phoebe and Maria leapt in front of the children. Phoebe's hands glowed white from her god-power while the Aether swirled between Maria's.

"You believe I mean harm, Your Majesty?" Endora feigned shock, a frail hand flying to the base of her throat. "After all we've worked for?"

"I would believe harm comes to my children when I'm interrupted so suddenly and with such impatience," Phoebe snarled, curling her lip as her power winked out. "Have you harmed my guards?"

"I'm unharmed, Your Majesty." The guard sighed from the doorway, his face gaunt.

"Your Majesty," Maria muttered beside Phoebe, her eyes bouncing between her and the children. "Do you need me to take them elsewhere?"

"I want to stay with Mommy," Jeremiah whined, his eyes frantic as he cowered beside Emmalina.

Phoebe kneeled before him, grabbing his shoulders in her hands to force his gaze upon her. "How about you and Emmalina go with Maria to the gardens with your lunch? I'll meet you there once I'm done with my meeting. Maybe I'll smuggle a sweet treat. What do you say?"

Jeremiah and Emmalina sprung into action with the promise of sweets, grappling onto Maria's outstretched hands. Endora and the Lemurian beside her stepped to the side of the room near a large tapestry depicting one of Phoebe's illegitimate ancestors to let them pass.

Maria glanced back with a sympathetic grin tugging at her cheeks before Phoebe waved the door shut.

Phoebe flung her arm out toward Endora, the Andromedan grunting at the force holding her in place. "Think critically before you tell me why you have so rudely interrupted one of the first days I've been free to spend with my children."

"If it weren't important, I would not dare a journey from the comforts of my abode," Endora bit out, and Phoebe released her. Endora nearly stumbled to the ground, but she caught herself on the back of one of the plush chairs. She shook out her flared sleeves before gently sitting on the edge. "You know Marin."

Phoebe picked up her skirts and maneuvered behind her desk as she eyed the Andromedan lurking near the door, squinting as she scrutinized him. Phoebe knew *of* Marin, who was a Lemurian and Andromedan, but she didn't recall meeting him before.

Like many Andromedans, Marin was over three hundred years old. With Phoebe being one of the youngest Andromedans in decades, they were all just as legendary to her as any other Being on Aveesh.

Marin reigned from the House of Argo—one of Nen's children—with the ability to shift into the sea creature known as the ketea, similar to a drakon except they lived in water and had a thicker tail instead of hind legs. In his mortal form, though, he was quite boyish, with smooth skin and an ageless face. Eerie, pale purple eyes blinked at her through gray lashes that matched his long gray hair.

Phoebe sighed as his bare torso glittered from the light of the sconces, pearly scales stretching over his arms and chest in patches like armor.

"You couldn't find him proper dress?" Phoebe glared at Endora, who sat at the edge of the chair like a glass doll. Phoebe slouched into her own, rolling her neck. "Endora. Why are you here?"

"First bit of matter," Endora began, her mouth twitching imperceptibly, "I've brought Marin because, as a ketea, he can speak the water language."

"I regret to admit I'm not certain what that means," Phoebe admitted, her gaze bouncing between the two Andromedans.

"Blood of Beings contains water," Marin spoke, his voice angelic like a harp. "The water language not only allows me to read the waters of the sea to communicate, but it also allows me to read the blood of any Being."

"Since you refuse to speak to Sybil about your immortality"—Endora paused, tilting her head—"or possible lack thereof, I have brought another who can tell you whether or not your blood sings agelessness. It's similar to prophecy in that it could give you what age you will die, except it can't account for external factors such as an assassination attempt."

Phoebe narrowed her eyes at Endora, pressing her lips into a thin line.

Endora held out her hands, the fabric of her sleeves swaying with the movement. "Do you prefer I bring someone from the House of Echidna to read your palm, scry, or shuffle cards?"

Phoebe groaned, but she ushered Marin closer to the desk. "What will it require?"

"Simply a few drops of your blood and saliva." Marin produced a small oyster shell from a pouch hanging at his waist, gently placing it on top of a stack of parchment. Phoebe eyed it and the Andromedan. "If you must know, I have to drink it. I will not use any of my findings against you by any means."

"I have to warn you, Phoebe," Endora interrupted as Phoebe reached for a letter opener. "He will also be privy to your familial heritage. I know our world whispers, but Marin will know."

"And you will keep your damned mouth shut," Phoebe snapped at Marin, taking pleasure in his flinch as her peripheral caught the white flash of her power. "Is that understood?"

"Of course, Your Majesty," Marin said calmly, no sign of the shock she saw on his face just moments ago.

"Very well." Phoebe quickly jabbed the end of her finger with the letter opener. She squeezed the tip over the shell, watching as three droplets smeared onto its white skin. She leaned over, collecting saliva in her mouth before allowing a generous drop to blend with her blood. She waved her hand between the shell and Marin. "Go on, then."

Marin moved as if he were still in water, his hand floating across the air as he gently reached down and cupped the shell. He met Phoebe's eyes as he lifted it to his lips, winking before downing the liquid.

Phoebe's lip curled involuntarily at the practice.

Marin's eyes snapped back to Phoebe, and she gasped in awe as his pale irises began to swirl, glittering with specks of white like stars winking in the night. They emitted a faint glow, casting a slight purple aura onto his high cheekbones.

"The secret Andromedan," Marin said, his voice still melodic and wistful, caressing the air around them. "Second daughter of the Evening Star."

Phoebe leveled a finger at him in warning, clenching her jaw.

He snickered, a trilling sound, before continuing and pocketing the shell back into its pouch. "Alas, while you may be Andromedan, it's only because you carry the blood of Gallus in your veins. You don't bear the signature blood mark of an Andromedan any longer."

"What does that mean?" Phoebe's heart hammered in her chest, her hand fluttering to it in hopes of calming the rhythm.

"The signature mark he speaks of is what grants us extended lifespans." Endora raised her gaze and hand to Marin, caressing the scales along his forearm. "Tell me, cousin, what does her lifespan say now?"

"You will not live beyond a century," Marin admitted, tilting his head at Phoebe. "If you are to die when your corporeal body gives out, you will live well into the standard lifespan of a simple Sirian."

Phoebe collapsed heavily into the chair behind her, a strange weight lifting from her shoulders she hadn't known had been there. She stared at where the shell once was on the parchment, soaking in the words of the Andromedan.

A simple Sirian.

She couldn't believe it. She'd maintained her Andromedan god-power but wouldn't outlive Dustin or the children.

"There is another thing," Marin interjected, her thoughts ceasing at the hesitation in his voice. "It seems there may be a side effect of the elixir, one I'm not sure Endora considered."

Endora snapped her gaze to Marin then, the cloudy mist of her own god-power glazing over her black eyes with agitation. "You question my potions?"

"There are plenty of potions that come with side effects, Endora, especially new ones." Marin scoffed, rolling his eyes. The movement startled Phoebe.

Until then, she was unsure if he was capable of anything other than an air of aloof mischievousness.

"What is the side effect, Marin?" The pounding in Phoebe's chest renewed its pace as she picked at her nails underneath the desk.

"The gift that allows Andromedans to outlive most is due to a consistent reproduction of the cells and lifeforce in our body," he explained, and Phoebe tried to remember what she'd learned of cells from the handful of Healer classes she took at the Academy. "It seems the potion has also targeted your natural reproductive abilities."

"You mean childbearing," Phoebe said, her hands ceasing to fidget. "I can no longer have children?"

"Phoebe—"

She held up a hand to cut Endora off, who rightfully appeared nervous.

"Unfortunately." Marin finally sat, easing Phoebe's anxiousness. "It has left you barren."

Phoebe pursed her lips, mulling that over.

In all fairness, she and Dustin had discussed the possibility of more children on occasion, but the conversation hadn't come up since she'd ascended the throne.

She wasn't too bothered that she couldn't have more children. There was already guilt for the children she rarely found time to spend with. She was unsure if she could handle more.

"Lucky for you, Endora, this isn't much of a disaster for me," Phoebe explained, folding her hands on her desk. "Should you offer this elixir to others, I would advise warning them of that information."

Endora simply bowed her head, relief lowering her shoulders from her ears.

"Was that all you interrupted my day for?" Phoebe asked, frowning. "Because I hardly see how I couldn't have come to visit you at your residence for a bit of blood reading."

"I have some information regarding the Obsidian Decay." Endora leveled Phoebe with a knowing look, something foreign flickering in her onyx gaze.

Phoebe stiffened at that, leaning forward as she flourished her hand over the desk. "Get on with it then."

"It appears the illness continues to stay with the humans, Your Majesty," Endora explained, blinking at Phoebe. "It has yet to spread to Sirians or Lemurians despite instances of close proximity."

"Why do we believe that is?" Phoebe shook her head, searching the strange look on Endora's face.

The hair on the back of her neck rose.

Endora sighed, shaking her head. The dramatics were similar to when she feigned shock. "It must have to do with their weakened bodies. They simply cannot withstand this illness at the rate a Sirian or Lemurian god-touched body can."

Phoebe frowned, the words which Endora spoke were suspiciously condemning.

Endora took her silence as an opportunity to continue.

"You see, Phoebe, my greatest concern is that if we don't handle this illness within the humans soon, it will eventually spread to Sirians and Lemurians." Endora slowly rose from her seat, towering before Phoebe as she pressed her back into her chair. "If the humans continue to harbor this illness, it will grow smarter and stronger. It'll learn how to use the humans as hosts, then infiltrate a Sirian's or Lemurian's stronger immunity."

"You're giving quite a lot of credit to a plague," Phoebe said, tilting her head as she studied Endora. Her hands were now clasped, concealed in her sleeves. She stood firm, her face open, which wasn't typical for her. "There's something you're not telling me—"

"Phoebe, if I may," Marin said, laying his hands palm up in a sort of supplication that Phoebe wasn't falling for. He rose, and Phoebe found it rather condescending that both Andromedans spoke to her—a queen—from *above*. "It all comes back to the humans. If Sirians and Lemurians are not catching it, then something about the humans has caused this plague to come to fruition. Whether it's their weaker bodies or poor habits, it raises concerns. I'm sure you are familiar with rats and how they, too, carry diseases into our crowded villages."

Phoebe set her jaw as her power hummed beneath her skin, buzzing like a bee.

"How is it we handle rats in the cities, Endora?" Marin asked innocently, but his words were sticky.

"I believe we set out poison to be rid of them, and also deter them from the streets—"

"Enough!" Phoebe splayed her hands, crossing them in front of her body.

The chairs they'd been sitting in flew across the room. They shattered against the walls, wooden chunks raining down around them.

Endora and Marin stood stoically, although Phoebe sensed an undercurrent of deception beneath the strange masks they wore. There was indeed something they weren't telling her, but to drag the humans into this and blame them for something so vile? Equate them to *rats*?

Phoebe wouldn't have this talk in her country, let alone her study.

She took a steadying breath, laying her palms flat on the desk as she peered at the two. "Let me make myself very clear, Endora. If I find you are poisoning or harming humans in an attempt to eradicate this plague, there will be no trials for your judgment.

"I won't need an elixir to rid you of your immortality." Phoebe leaned forward, lowering her voice as she sneered at Endora. "I will tear your heart from your chest and feed it to my hounds. Are we clear?"

Something dark and menacing flashed in the endless depths of Endora's eyes, the edges clouding over momentarily. "Of course, *Your Majesty*."

Phoebe straightened behind her desk, bowing her head. "Thank you for your time and gifts, Marin. I appreciate your candor, as well as your discretion. Should I find you have spread my name across the kingdoms, you will surely meet a similar fate as Endora."

Marin simply nodded with frantic eyes, peering at Endora, who was still simmering when Phoebe dismissed them both.

CHAPTER 27

SYBIL

L olis was a small, quaint community sitting on the perimeter of the Raven's Wood, just along the border of Sylvan and Etherea. Similar to Ghita, it was run by a human, Lord Broadus.

Also like Ghita, it was Sylvan's most heavily populated human village.

Sybil stood beside Asteria in the far corner of the receiving room, her gaze bouncing between the three men accompanying them. The Healer of Lolis, Davit, listened intently as Piers explained how to charge the concoction to treat the Obsidian Decay.

"Why must we wait again?" Asteria grumbled under her breath, leaning against the wall. Her head lolled back with a soft thunk, drawing Wells's attention to them. He shot Asteria a crooked smile, and she stiffened. "Time is consistently of the essence."

"What's going on here?" Sybil turned her back on Wells, studying Asteria's face. She only narrowed her eyes at Sybil, pressing her lips together. "Don't give me any of that. I see right through you, and there's nothing subtle about you and him."

"There's *nothing* about me and him," Asteria muttered, pushing off the wall to stand closer to Sybil. "Don't be meddlesome like—"

"You better not compare me to your mother." Sybil deadpanned, her right eye twitching. Asteria suppressed a grin, averting her gaze. "You know I have no judgement. You can't say there is nothing, Asteria. There is *something* happening between you two."

Asteria remained silent, her eyes dragging across the wall beside them, pretending to observe the tapestries hanging there.

"Maybe you don't even realize there's something." Sybil adjusted the satchel on her shoulder. "Or maybe you're under the impression if you pretend nothing is there, then it will simply vanish."

Asteria reeled her glittering eyes at Sybil, mischief playing at the corners of her lips. "You're the pot calling the kettle black—"

"Sorry to keep you lot waiting," a deeply accented voice called, multiple heavy footsteps shuffling into the room. "I had to fetch my guest who I believe is a great advantage in this situation."

Asteria and Sybil simultaneously wheeled their gazes toward the door, where two men and a woman stood. The man with a mop of bright red hair was Lord Eurion Broadus, that much Sybil knew. By the way the woman lingered close to him, she was most likely Lady Rhona, his wife—though Sybil hadn't known she was Sirian.

The third man Sybil knew for certain, although nearly a century had passed since she saw him last—

And he *looked* like every bit of it.

His skin was a rich brown, several shades lighter than Sybil's and far warmer. His hair was wavy and entirely gray, matching the stubble that shadowed his jaw. The rest of the short beard hugged his chin, while the hair above his lips had faded to black, like his thick eyebrows. His eyes—whiskey and bright—caught the light from the sconces.

The last time Sybil saw him, he had appeared in late adulthood rather than middle age.

"Garuda," Asteria said, tilting her head. "Why in the Heavens are you here?"

"Rod sent me a letter about what transpired with the Lyrans," Garuda explained, dipping his head to her and then Sybil with a wink. *Cheeky fuck.* "I tried to speak with the Mariandes, but they wouldn't see me."

"I thought they were devoted to you," Gavril said, eyes wide with disbelief. "They wouldn't see you at all?"

Garuda shook his head, hurt hidden beneath a grim smile. "I fear what Zephyr has fed them. Alas, I've lived in Sylvan for the last century since the House of Nemea held the throne. I have a connection to it, and I couldn't leave it entirely defenseless against the Decay."

"Well, you can help administer," Davit interjected, stepping toward Garuda. "We're partnering one Sirian with Energy and someone without. With Garuda here, Lady Rhona can assist with the Energy while he mixes the elixir and carries the supplies."

"However you need me, I'm more than happy to help." Garuda placed a hand over his chest, bowing slightly to Lady Rhona.

"We'll need more supplies and far more vials." Asteria sighed, her brow furrowed. She directed her question to Davit. "Do you have more here? We only brought so much."

"We'll scrounge up the last of any supplies we need." Davit rubbed the back of his neck and shrugged. "I fear we're quite overrun with the Decay. I don't know the state of it anymore because it's been difficult to track. Being such a close community in a confined perimeter, it has spread quickly."

"We'll do all that we can," Wells assured with a terse nod. "We can split up around the perimeter of the town in separate pairings and work our way to the center square through the houses." He looked to Asteria. "I believe that will help from expending your powers."

"It will hopefully help enough that I can portal us back to Eldamain after this." Asteria held her hand out to Sybil, who immediately knew what she was asking. "Davit and I will gather as much supplies as we can."

"Gavril and I will help to speed this along," Wells said, and Gavril whipped his head to Wells with a curled lip. "It's picking plants, Gav, not playing in muck."

"It's all the same to me." Gavril sighed, aimlessly waving a hand in the air. "Lead the way."

"Stay back and educate Garuda on the proportions," Asteria instructed Sybil before pointing at Piers. "And you explain how to use the Energy with the potion to Lady Rhona."

With that, the four left out the door, leaving Piers, Sybil, Garuda, Lady Rhona, and Lord Eurion.

Piers shot Sybil a wary glance before shaking Lord Eurion's hand and jumping into his demonstration.

"It's been some time, Sybil," Garuda said. Sybil jumped at his sudden proximity, swearing under her breath. "I believe a whole century, correct?"

"If my own memory serves me correctly..." She heavily sighed, rolling her shoulders back. She waved at the settee. "Let's sit. The measurements are quite simple. It doesn't take much to combine the ingredients."

Sybil adjusted her skirt as she sat back against the cushion. Garuda followed, leaving barely an inch between their legs. She would've snarled had she not felt Piers's heated gaze searing into her.

"There will be jars of chamomile, skullcap, and echinacea water as well as jars of ginseng and turmeric paste," she explained, holding her hands up between them. "You'll want to fill a vial halfway with water, then add the paste until the water reaches three quarters of the vial—enough to fit the stopper without overflowing. You'll add one teaspoon of kava root powder before corking it, then shake the vial to mix. Once done, hand it to Lady Rhona. Piers is instructing her on what to do from there."

"Asteria made it seem as though it were some radical experiment." Garuda snorted, reclining back against the cushion.

"It's the kava and ginseng that are dangerous due to their potency, so Asteria just wants to be safe—" Sybil stopped as he spread his legs enough for his left thigh to press against hers. He crossed his arms, one eyebrow raised. "What in the Heavens are you doing?"

"The moment I laid eyes on you, all the memories we have together flooded my mind." His dropped voice low, eyelids heavy. "I'm simply testing the waters."

"You are your father's son." Sybil snorted, shoving his knee away as she scooted over. "There's a reason our memories stop a century ago, Garuda."

"You can't still be angry that I sired more children." Garuda braced his forearms on his knees. "I wish to extend my bloodline as much as I possibly can until my body no longer allows me. It's only in my gryp nature to do so. It's also clear not just by our acts, but your acts the last six hundred and some years that you can't have children—"

"Is there a problem?"

Sybil snapped her head to Piers towering over her and Garuda. His tone was lethal, one she only heard him use on the knights beneath him when they left their posts or were caught in less than savory positions.

"What's it to you, Prince?" Garuda slowly rose from the couch, gaining a few inches on Piers as he looked down over the tip of his nose. "Are you that desperate to be a knight in shining armor?"

"For Heaven's sake," Sybil growled, lurching from the couch and squeezing herself between the men. She kept her back to Piers, planting both hands on Garuda's chest. "Go fluff your feathers somewhere else, you taloned mongrel."

Garuda glared at her through narrowed slits, his golden eyes flashing as if he was fighting the emotions of the gryp within him to protect his pride. She glared right back, shoving lightly against his firm chest to create more space between them.

He gave her a small, mischievous smirk at the display of strength, a sharp canine glinting in the light before he turned on his heel and strutted toward Lord and Lady Broadus watching the ordeal with utter fascination.

"You didn't need to—"

Sybil whirled on Piers, her fists clenched at her sides. "*You* didn't need to do that, Prince. I'm more than capable of holding my own against a fellow Andromedan, lest you forget."

"It wasn't for your sake I said something," Piers said, his voice dropping low as he stepped closer. She instinctively took one back, her frustration faltering as her scowl morphed into a frown. "I simply couldn't help myself."

Sybil scoffed in disbelief, shaking her head.

After the last few years of Piers nearly forcing her to watch him and Gavril fall in love, he had the audacity to act out of *jealousy*.

"That's absolutely preposterous," Sybil hissed, grabbing a fistful of his tunic and dragging him behind her as she hauled him to the corner of the room. He faced her head-on with darkened eyes, fighting his smirk. "First of all, you forget you're only twenty and nine while I am six hundred and nineteen. I have a lengthy history of partners that you can't possibly comprehend, including Andromedans who may or may not still be alive.

"Second of all, you can't be—don't have the *right* to be—jealous." Sybil jabbed a finger into his chest, squinting. "I don't belong to you, and you don't belong to me. Therefore, you can't interfere with the people I choose or choose *not* to bring to my bed. Do you understand?"

"Loud and clear, Syb," Piers said far too calmly for Sybil's liking. The door creaked open and before he walked away, he paused to whisper in her ear, "Just remember in that *lengthy* history, you only ever loved me."

She audibly gasped, twisting on her heel to stare at his back with her mouth open. He didn't look back as he approached Wells and Gavril, hands in his pockets.

"What was that you were saying about pretending nothing was there?" Asteria said quietly as she approached Sybil with a satchel outstretched between them. She had half the nerve to slap the coy smirk off Asteria's face. "Come, Bee. Let us continue *pretending*."

Sybil ground her teeth, breathing sharply through her nose.

One more village, she reminded herself. *Get through this and Teslin.*

Then she could go back to making herself scarce around Piers once more.

CHAPTER 28

ASTERIA

Asteria waited beside the portal as Piers and Sybil stumbled through into Aggelos Palace, exhaustion nearly taking Piers to the ground again before Gavril could catch him. Wells was the last through, and Asteria's arm shook as held it open, a tinge of blue tunneling her vision. The moment he was clear, the portal closed with a loud snap.

She released the power far too quickly, and it rushed to her head. It swelled, pressing against the inside of her skull, her vision momentarily going black as she lost feeling in her limbs.

In the next blink it returned, but she stumbled into Wells as the pressure released, leaving her lightheaded. He wrapped one hand around her bicep, the other braced against her waist.

Asteria could care less about the position they were in as long as her vision stopped pulsing blue.

She groaned, slamming her forehead into his shoulder, fisting his tunic at the sharp sting behind her eyes.

"You need to get her food and water now," Sybil snapped to someone—maybe Wells or Piers. There was a quiet grumble Asteria couldn't understand, but she knew it didn't come from Wells. "Asteria? I need you to look at me."

"Let me help you, Blue," Wells whispered, his breath tickling the top of her head.

Asteria inhaled deeply as his grip tightened, letting him do most of the work to steady her. She locked onto the freckles across his nose, blinking rapidly until the blue finally receded from her vision.

Sybil's hands clasped over Asteria's cheeks, and she twisted her head until their eyes met. Sybil searched for something, her eyes frantic. She pressed her lips together for a moment, but appeared pleased when she nodded once and released her.

"We'll stay at the castle tonight," Sybil announced, turning to Wells. "I'll find an attendant to prepare two guest rooms for us, then I'll make sure Piers and Gavril haven't snuck away from the kitchen."

"Stars above, I'm fine," Asteria drawled, rolling her eyes.

"I highly doubt that," Wells grumbled, gripping her shoulders as he guided her into a chair. He pushed against her until she carefully lowered. Once he knew she would stay, he lowered himself into the chair across from her. He braced his forearms on his thighs, studying her with a deep frown. "We should've stayed in Lolis."

Asteria slowly shook her head, sighing. "Not at the expense of Lord Eurion. They've suffered so much already and have exhausted their resources to keep Lolis from crumbling under the Decay. Besides, we don't have time."

Wells's eyes flickered across her face, the frown between his brows holding steady. "I would've rather we stayed one night for rest and replenishment over risking your own health to make it back. If we exhaust you, it'll take far longer to heal the humans."

Wells didn't know the half of it.

Asteria knew she was being irresponsible with this trip to Ghita and Lolis. Pushing herself to these extreme limits was testing her, especially over two consecutive days. If she Fractured, she feared the world would have a host of problems beyond the Decay and other Lyrans.

When a Lyran Fractured, the nature of their powers overtook their mind, erasing who they truly were at the core. While most Lyrans had one or two powers to fall victim to, Asteria had three: the Energy, Aether, and starfire—powers of the Universe.

She feared what would happen should the powers of the Universe have complete reign over her mortal body and god-form.

"If you feel yourself nearing exhaustion, say something," Wells demanded, leaving no room for argument. "Understood?"

Normally, Asteria would be furious at the tone and command he pinned on her. Instead, she was reminded of her childhood and the intense sincerity Gallus used to speak to her with.

"You know, you sound like my father—"

It was then she remembered Wells was *supposed* to be a father.

Like in Ghita, the joyfulness in Wells's eyes dimmed, this time far more drastically. Asteria opened and closed her mouth, unable to find the right words to erase what she'd said.

For the first time, Asteria contemplated setting herself on fire.

She found she didn't like this version of him—the depthless grief written across his face—and she hated even more that her irresponsible comment had caused it.

"Excuse me for a moment," he muttered, rubbing his hands on his thighs as he rose from his seat. Asteria's heart clenched, and once again, she let her mouth move before her mind.

"Wells, I'm so sorry." She flew from the chair to block his path, gripping both of his forearms. She blinked as her vision tilted, and Wells's eyes flared as he braced his hands on her waist to keep her upright. She whispered, "I didn't mean it maliciously."

"It's fine," Wells said, averting his gaze. "I suppose you've caught me off-guard... again. This topic is far more sore."

Before she knew what she was doing, Asteria lifted a hand between them, her fingers gently caressing his chin beneath his jaw. She gently drew his gaze to hers, and her heart nearly broke at the sorrow glistening in his eyes.

It seemed to fade the longer he looked upon her.

"Still, I'm sorry." Asteria sighed, her hand casually dropping to rest against his chest where his heart thundered. "I can't imagine your pain."

Wells blinked a few more times, clearing his throat. He nodded once before guiding her back to the chair she was sitting in. She kept a heavy gaze on him, ignoring the relief when he sat back down in his own chair.

"It's not that the loss of Ruelle isn't painful," Wells said quietly, hands twisting in his lap. He gave up with a heavy sigh and folded them together, bracing his elbows on the arms of the chair. "Time eases the wound, but it doesn't rid me of it. I'll forever miss and mourn her, but I cherish the time we had together. However brief it may have been in my life, I can look back and be grateful for her and her love.

"I never got that time with our child." Wells steadily inhaled, and Asteria wanted nothing more than to console him. This time, there was too much space for her to reach out. "I'll never get to hear his laugh, to show him how to wield a sword, to learn if he would prefer his mother over me… It's the things that couldn't be that are more painful."

Asteria fought back her own tears because his words hit too deep, and he deserved to have his moment of grief.

She'd wanted to be a mother when she and Rod were together. At times, she'd wanted it more than anything.

As Lyrans, though, conceiving was extremely difficult between them. She was a rarity, and the likelihood she and Rod would've had a child was even slimmer than Danica and Gallus having her.

Regardless, they tried. They were intimate, mostly for that purpose alone. There was rarely any excitement or passion in those moments because they were both so focused on getting it just right to strengthen their odds.

It's why his affair had hit her so hard.

A child was produced from it, and she was left broken.

She was left with the things that could never be.

"You knew it was a boy?" Asteria lifted her eyebrows to mask her own sadness.

The corner of his lip twitched imperceptibly. "I was able to put a name on his headstone beside hers."

Damnit. Asteria's eyes burned as she whispered, "What did you name him?"

"Ruelle wanted Cael." He pursed his lips, shrugging. "I didn't mind any of the names she'd picked out, so I went ahead with that as his name."

Asteria averted her gaze, and she didn't know why she asked her next question. "Do you think you would ever want children again?"

She felt his heavy gaze burning into the side of her head, the silence pressing a weight against her chest. She didn't dare look at him, if only because she knew she was toying with a reality that was far out of reach.

"With the right person." Wells's voice was tender as it echoed through the room. "I think I would."

CHAPTER 29

ASTERIA

"D on't you find it curious?" Piers asked Wells under his breath, eyes flicking over his brother's shoulders to meet Asteria's. "The towns..."

"The towns infected?" Wells hooked the bag of vials over his shoulder, shrugging. "I've not given it much thought."

"Three of the four towns are collected in the southwestern corner of our continent," Piers said, directing his attention back to Asteria. She opened the portal beside her to their next destination in Teslin, ushering Sybil and Gavril through as Piers stood beside her. "Then suddenly Ghita becomes infected? That seems awfully far north. You haven't heard of any other villages infected?"

"Not according to Sybil's connections," Asteria replied, squinting at Piers. How he furrowed his brow reminded her of Wells, who brushed her forearm as he paused before the shimmering portal, Teslin rippling in the background. "You think it means something?"

"You said if this was Gallus's doing, he would be calculated in how he allowed the illness to spread." Piers glared at Wells, who stepped closer to Asteria's side. Goosebumps rose on her arm where he nearly stood against

229

her, heart fluttering.

It was making it quite difficult for her to pay attention to the portal and what Piers was trying to discuss.

"Illness doesn't spread so sporadically," Wells interjected, and Asteria caught him nodding from the corner of her eye. "It would spread through trade routes and travel. Ghita isn't in a trade agreement with any of those villages. Not so directly that illness would spread. It would need to reach other cities before reaching them."

"I don't know what you're getting at," Asteria grumbled, rubbing her fingers across her forehead. "We should be getting to Sado, though. Maybe this is something we can continue to discuss once we help them. My mind is presently occupied."

Wells snorted, and she whirled her heated gaze on him, raising a finger in warning. He startled rather dramatically, throwing his hands up between them in surrender and slowly stepping backward through her portal. His smirk grew with each step he put between them.

After he vanished through the veil, Asteria took the opportunity to breathe, centering herself again. Despite the unhealthy heartbeat in her chest, her entire being simmered with excitement.

And for what?

"Wells was born with a single goal in mind." Piers stepped up beside her, staring at the portal. He smirked, too, shrugging. "To get under everyone's skin."

He went through the portal, but Asteria frowned at his declaration. She highly doubted Wells got under his brother's skin the way it felt like he was writhing under hers.

Or the way her mind only conjured images of his hands on her skin and her naked beneath him.

She growled, quickly moving into Sado and slamming the portal shut behind her—

Only to miss a stream of Energy skimming by her face.

"What the fuck?" Asteria quickly whirled to the scene before her, heart plummeting to the pit of her stomach.

Piers stood before Gavril, his veins, eyes, and Mark glowing the white-gold of the Energy. Wells's Aether snaked up his arms and pooled around him on the ground. Sybil stared at the figures blocking the street before them with her lip curled in a snarl, green eyes illuminated as she fought the shift to her drakon form.

"Curious," said a harsh, throaty voice. Unfortunately, Asteria knew precisely who the voice belonged to. "We didn't call for a Goddess, yet here she is with quite an unsavory entourage."

Asteria rolled her eyes, tipping her head to the sky. She sighed before drawing her gaze back down to meet rounded, bright purple eyes set back under thick black eyebrows.

"Caine." Asteria sneered, his name like acid on her tongue. "What a pleasure it is to be graced with your presence."

Caine was another Andromedan from the House of Echidna, a drakon like Sybil. The only difference between them was while Sybil was made, Caine was the offspring of a Lemurian woman and Zephyr. He was over three centuries old, and in Asteria's experience, the apple didn't fall far from his father's tree.

"I highly doubt that." Caine grinned, canines glinting in the sunlight piercing the haze Teslin frequently found itself under. "It appears I must ask, but what are you doing here in Teslin, Asteria? The last I heard, you were sequestered in Celestia. Although, there are rumors you have been fluttering in and out of Eldamain."

With that, Caine's eyes bounced to Piers and Wells. Asteria breathed through the territorial wave that rolled over her when Caine peered at Wells for far too long.

"It seems the rumors just might be true, Father," the male beside Caine said, his eyes narrowed on Piers. "Not one, but two spare princes? Not to mention their Lemurian pets."

Sybil growled at that, a low rumble that caused pebbles near her feet to tremble against the cobblestone streets. Asteria held a hand up between her and Sybil, hoping to ease the drakon until she felt the shift was absolutely warranted.

"I'm not sure if you or your employers are aware"—Asteria paused to glare at the three Sirians beside Caine and his son—"but there is an illness plaguing several villages across the continent. Luckily, I've found a cure with the help of Sybil and the Carraphims." She didn't dare mention Danica. "I saw fit to have them assist me in sharing this remedy."

"I don't believe the Seymours called for divine assistance regarding the Obsidian Decay," one of the Sirians said, tilting their head at Asteria. "I certainly didn't call for your help."

"You are the present Royal Healer, then?" Asteria asked, taking a cautious step forward between Piers and Wells. The Energy churned within all three Sirians before her. "I find it rather unfortunate that, as a Healer, you didn't consult me when you came across this illness. Especially given the nature of the disease and pace at which it spreads."

"We've found it's isolated to humans." The Sirian Healer shrugged, and starfire thrummed in Asteria's veins at the nonchalance from a previous student.

"One would argue all the more reason, would you not?" Wells asked, his voice steady. Asteria chanced a glance, intrigued by how he played with the Aether as he waited for danger to strike. "At least, if I remember correctly, that's what Healers are taught at the Academy, no? To heal all, no matter Being nor heritage nor prejudice?"

"The Seymours have instructed us not to intervene with what nature and Fate intend," one of the other Sirians said evenly. This time, Asteria couldn't hold back the starfire that licked at her fingertips.

"None of you can speak of what nature or Fate intend when you can't converse with either." Asteria curled her lip, appalled by their behavior. "You may wield the Energy, but don't mistake that for ownership of the Energy of nature and all things. You're but one of many who can wield it."

"As he said," Caine interjected, stepping closer, "we've been instructed not to intervene. Therefore, we must ask you to go back to whatever hole you lot crawled out of, or we will be required to act with force to remove you."

"Remove us?" Piers chuckled darkly, the Energy flaring brighter around him. "Are you threatening two princes of another country?"

"Two princes who have come onto our soil, seeking to undermine the rule of our king?" Caine genuinely pondered the question despite him being the one to ask it. This was why Asteria couldn't stand Zephyr and his children. They were tiresome, and it always ended with her wanting to remove *them*. "Yes, Your *Highness*. I am."

"I can't—in good conscience—leave your sick to die," Asteria snapped, fire swirling around her body, gently caressing every dip and curve. She felt Wells's eyes on her, the darkness in them sending heat where it most certainly didn't belong at this moment. "I seek to heal, and if you stand in my way, I have no qualms about cutting you down."

All three Sirians called to the Energy, balls of gold light sparking and twirling in their hands like moldable stars. Caine's son rolled his shoulders, black leather skin stretching under his collar.

Caine's purple eyes illuminated from within, his throaty voice rolling through the air. "How unfortunate."

Three tears echoed off the stone buildings encasing them. Caine and his son burst into black dragons the size of the two-story structures around them. Asteria felt the Energy soaring toward them before she saw it, throwing up a shield as she turned to meet Sybil's drakon form.

Dark green scales the same color as her eyes stretched across her massive form, larger than either Lemurian behind them. Beige horns ran the length of her spine and curled at the top and sides of her head, matching the hue of her belly and chest. She spread her taloned wings wide as she adjusted to her drakon form, slamming into adjoining buildings.

Asteria deadpanned, and Sybil huffed. "Get Caine and his offspring away from here. Take it to the skies. We're in a human section of town, and they don't need to rebuild with what they're already dealing with. So no fire. Understood?"

Sybil huffed another breath of hot air at Asteria, her long snout dipping. Asteria patted it with a mischievous grin before turning back to Wells, Piers, and Gavril.

With a hitch-pitched, grating call that rattled Asteria down to the bone, Sybil catapulted straight for Caine's son, taking out Asteria's shield in the process. In a blink, Sybil grabbed the smaller drakon in her maw and launched into the sky.

"I suppose that's one way to handle it," Asteria grumbled under her breath.

"You did tell her to take it to the sky."

She whirled on Wells at the same time Piers countered a burst of Energy, sending him backward into Gavril's chest.

"Don't mind me!" Piers shouted over the crackling of Energy bursting before them. "Not as if we're busy or anything!"

Wells actually laughed at his brother while the other Sirians fired at them. Asteria's lips curved at the sound and the absurdity of laughing in this situation.

Aether and Energy erupted around them.

Asteria focused on one of the Sirians before her, conjuring the Aether to swallow the torrent of Energy he sent toward her. The darkness swallowed the golden glow, but the Sirian was ready with another powerful stream of Energy.

Except Asteria knew this tactic. She'd taught every Warrior who graced the halls of the Asterian Academy for centuries—not to mention she could *feel* the Energy and Aether before it even neared her.

Asteria focused on misdirecting his moves and exploiting the Sirian's recklessness as he tried to fight aggressively, throwing powerful but precise impacts. She countered every ball of Energy he hurtled with Aether, a small shield, or her own ball of Energy.

Few knew the true extent of her Lyran powers. Danica could only manipulate, diminish, and manifest the Energy, and Gallus did the same with the Aether, aside from his ability to wield the starfire.

Sirians wielded one or the other, using their power to deliver an impact, generate and project, manipulate, and charge.

Asteria could do all that and more.

With the next explosive force of Energy from the Sirian she fought, Asteria let it come to her, arms outstretched in front of her. With a quick, sharp inhale, she siphoned the Energy into her, and it vanished with a wink.

"What in the Gods..." The Sirian stood dumbfounded.

"I know, I play pretend very well," she said calmly, admiring the tendrils of Energy and Aether twisting around both of her arms, "but you forget—I am your God."

Asteria shot a surge of Energy directly at the Sirian's chest, slamming him against a nearby wall. At the same time, she wrapped the Aether around the legs of the Sirian Wells was up against. She pulled their feet from beneath them so they landed flat on their back.

"How did—" Wells glared at her from the corner of his eye. "You absorbed the Energy."

"You saw that?" She flicked her hand, and the Sirian she sent to the ground tumbled forward when the Aether tugged his feet out again.

Wells grinned, shaking his head. "It may be unbecoming of me if I admit what watching you with your power does—Get down!"

Asteria squatted so her head was level with his waist, and she sent another burst of Energy around him at the Sirian approaching Wells from behind. The male skidded across the cobblestone down an alley.

"Fucking lycan," Wells growled, and Asteria glanced over her shoulder as she rose from her crouch.

Reigning from the House of Nemea, lycan were the equivalent of wolves but double or triple the size. Presently, two lycans prowled forward, their large paws crunching the loose gravel beneath them.

Asteria was impressed to find one whimpering behind the other two, a gash across its side. "Did you do that?"

"I'm wounded that you're so shocked." Wells chuckled under his breath but tipped his head toward where another lycan was emerging from the same alley she sent the Sirian, who now walked beside the giant dog with liquid malice glowing in his eyes. "You take one side, I take the other?"

"Works for me."

Asteria and Wells leapt into action. She wasn't worried about picking up any slack for Wells or conjuring her shield. Any time she was delayed in countering the Sirian or trying to distract a lycan, Wells intervened and vice versa.

She couldn't ignore how fascinating it was that her and Wells's abilities synchronized, especially when he would use the Aether and she the Energy.

"Shield on your right, Blue," Wells snapped from beside her.

She yanked on the vines of Aether wrapped around two lycans' before extending the shield in front of her, arching it around her right. She twisted to maneuver it so Wells was behind the shield, and a whirl of Energy ricocheted off its surface.

"Great timing." He panted, wincing as he threw his arms on the back of his head.

She stepped closer, her eyes scanning his face and torso, trying to find where he might be injured. His brow furrowed, but his lips twitched at her scrutiny.

"Oh, leave it," she grumbled, splaying her hand and swirling it over her head to encase them within the shield.

There were too many of them, and Asteria needed to portal them out of here without entirely expending herself. She searched the sky for Sybil, Caine, and his son, concerned when she only found one black and one green drakon.

"She better not have killed him," Asteria muttered.

"I'm not sure it would be such a bad thing!" Piers called over the growling and bursts of Energy between him and another Sirian. "We're outnumbered, Asteria."

"I'm well aware!" she yelled back, adjusting the shield to encase Piers and Gavril.

Piers sagged in relief against Gavril, his lids heavy. After using so much of his Energy the last two days to heal the sick, she wasn't shocked at how tired he was.

Wells didn't appear in any better shape, but since he couldn't help heal with the Aether, he still had the glimmer of fight in his bright eyes.

"You three," Asteria said as she threw open a portal beside them. "Go through the portal to Celestia, and I'll be right behind you. I need to wrangle Sybil. When you get through, let Odo know we're coming."

Piers hesitated, but Gavril didn't. With a nod, he yanked Piers's arm before dragging him through the veil.

Once again, Wells stood at the edge, waiting for her. She wanted to be angry that he was risking himself. For what, she wasn't sure, but the slightest inkling that maybe it was for her had her stomach twirling.

Until she remembered Sybil was a long-time friend of the Carraphims.

Asteria lifted her gaze to the sky as she held the shield and portal, squinting through the gray haze to catch any flash against bright scales. When she thought her heart would give out from anxiousness, a massive green figure shot through the sky with a black one not far behind.

"Shift back!" Asteria screamed over the rumbling growl of Caine, heart pounding as he inched closer to Sybil's hind legs. Her voice was ethereal as she tried to reach her drakon. "Sybil! Shift back, damnit!"

"Asteria," Wells warned as even more Sirians and lycan tumbled from the alleyways. "We have to get through the portal—"

"I'm not leaving her!" she shouted at him, the words melting into a cry of frustration. "By all means, follow Piers and Gavril. Then I can close it behind you and find a different place for Sybil and me."

Asteria twirled her wrists before her, and the shield transformed into a wall of starfire, encasing her and Wells from the onslaught while leaving enough room for Sybil to drop and shift into the portal.

"You have to be absolutely out of your fucking mind if you think I'm going to leave you alone amidst this chaos." Wells grabbed her forearm and yanked her closer to the portal, away from the wall of fire still burning around them. "I will throw you through that portal myself before I go without you."

"You mean without Sybil and me," Asteria said breathlessly, and it had nothing to do with expending herself to hold the portal and fire.

Wells smirked at that, gripping her chin between his thumb and forefinger. She held her breath as his thumb swiped along the edge of her bottom lip. "I mean you, Blue."

Asteria's chest heaved as her eyes flitted from his eyes to his mouth, unsure of what to do in this scenario. It felt rather inappropriate to want nothing more than to kiss him, but she chalked it up to the high of the fight.

Sybil's cry pierced the air, startling them. Their gazes shifted to the sky to find a jagged gash glistening deep red at the end of Sybil's tail. Asteria's vision pulsed black at the edges.

"The portal," Wells breathed against her neck, and she snapped her head to him. He lifted his arm over her shoulder and pointed at the sky where Sybil and Caine were swirling through the clouds. "Can you open a portal up there for her?"

Asteria blinked at him, contemplating the approach in her head.

"It's possible, but we risk Caine getting through it, too," Asteria said, biting her lip. "I would need to shut this portal and take down the shield to time it properly."

"I'll hold them off while you do that." Wells stepped around Asteria toward the shield of starfire until he winced at the heat.

"There are too many—"

"Just do it!" he shouted, rolling his arms. The Aether swelled around him, growing erratic and thicker.

She groaned, closing the portal behind her with a wave of her hand. Before she brought down the starfire, Asteria sent more Aether to intertwine with Wells's, tripling the size of the makeshift shield he was building. She thought she heard him chuckle as she snuffed out her flames.

Energy and Aether burst on the other side of their wall as she tracked Sybil in the sky, gauging the distance between the end of Sybil's tail and where Caine was still far too close for Asteria's liking.

She would be risking Sybil's tail and Caine's life. The last thing she needed from this uprising was an Andromedan dead by her hands. It was far too soon for casualties, and the first true casualties would paint the villain.

"Fuck it." Asteria threw open a portal mere feet in front of Sybil, who didn't falter at the veil before her in the clouds. Asteria's blood roared in her ears, but she kept her eyes on the beats of Sybil's wings as she tried to pick up her speed. "Come on, Bee."

"Asteria!" Wells shouted, but she couldn't pull her gaze away as Sybil was breached the veil. She had to time it perfectly. "Open a portal behind you the minute she's through."

"Get ready!" she shouted back, counting down as Sybil's tail wiggled at the edge of the veil, her heart pounding. "And... Now!"

She slammed the portal shut a breath from Sybil's tail, and Caine shot through the now-empty sky. Asteria released a sigh of relief as she waved a hand behind her to open the fourth portal of the day, only for the wind to be knocked out of her as Wells slammed into her, and they tumbled through the veil.

Before they hit the stone ground, Wells twisted so he landed on his back with Asteria on his chest. They both grunted at the impact, staring at one another in shock as they realized they'd made it out.

"This seems to be an occurrence for these two." Piers sighed, but Asteria swore she could hear a smile in his words. "They're late, tumbling through a portal."

Wells dared to *shrug* beneath her.

"I'm pleased to see them getting along, then," Odo voiced, and Asteria snapped her head up at him through narrowed eyes, her hands flat on Wells's firm chest.

"I'll have you know—"

Wells cleared his throat, cutting Asteria off before she could rip into the three men staring down at them. Her eyes widened when she realized how close they were and what position she'd arranged them into.

Asteria was *straddling* Wells on the ground, his hands squeezing her hips just above the fold of her legs.

"While this view is just as exquisite as I dreamed it would be," Wells said quietly, a blush heating her cheeks to a temperature that quite possibly matched the inferno between her legs, "I didn't anticipate an audience."

The reminder of the men standing over them urged her into motion. She slammed her hands on his chest with a snarl before rolling off him.

The door burst open, and Sybil marched through, her hair windblown, face manic. "What the *fuck* was that?"

CHAPTER 30

ASTERIA

They gathered in Odo's living room, each poised on various seats he and Erika pulled from their dining room to account for the extra bodies. The residences in Celestia varied from quaint apartments to small abodes complete with kitchens, dining spaces, and at least two bedrooms.

While the Hespers required one of the small abodes at the edge of campus, Asteria preferred a simple apartment with only enough space for a bed, a few chairs, and a small table. She didn't need much since it was just her, and she preferred to take meals with Odo and the other Elders.

A quiet giggle interrupted the tense silence, and Odo's daughter, Elle, waddled into the living room ahead of Erika. When she laid eyes on Wells, her giggles morphed into a squeal of delight.

Asteria's eyes widened in a strange, elated horror as the child attempted to scramble onto his lap, babbling in her high-pitched voice.

"Hello there, little one," Wells said as he gathered her into his arms, positioning her on one of his knees. "Will you be joining us for our chat with Momma and Papa?"

"Yes!" She bounced enthusiastically, grinning up at Wells as though he hung the sun.

At this point, Asteria couldn't help but look upon him that way either.

"I suppose since you lot stumbled directly into our home looking like you ran from shore"—Odo shot a glare at Asteria, and she flipped him her middle finger—"we have no choice but to entertain you."

Odo wasn't thrilled that Asteria portaled them directly into his home rather than somewhere on campus like her own rooms. She tried to explain it was more efficient to appear here since she planned on filling him in on what was transpiring across the Main Continent and with the Lyrans.

He set his jaw and gestured toward Elle in Wells's lap, nostrils flaring.

"What *were* you all doing?" Erika asked as she passed around teacups. "Asteria, Odo tells me you have recently been leaving Celestia to venture to Eldamain. I wasn't aware you knew the Carraphims so intimately."

"I didn't." Asteria dipped her head as she unintentionally side-eyed Wells, who watched her expectantly. Elle clapped his hands together against his will. "Some developments have forced me to work alongside Eldamain."

Odo hummed, his eyes twinkling. "Well, it's a good thing you had the chance to meet Wells beforehand."

Asteria snapped her head to him, narrowing her eyes. He leveled a finger at her as if he knew she was about to do something crude.

She'd planned on it, but Piers spoke up.

"Before we entirely derail this conversation into what might be a bonfire," Piers drawled from where he slumped in a chair, his eyes heavy-lidded. "I believe you might need to fill them in on what's occurring."

"I would also like to know what in the Heavens happened for them to know we were coming," Sybil questioned from where she sipped a healing tonic Erika whipped up for her. She winced at what Asteria knew was a bitter taste.

"We knew this was a possibility," Asteria explained, her head resting against the open window, breathing in the ocean air. "It's why I wanted to bring Wells and Gavril along on this expenditure to begin with."

"I thought I was your lackey." Wells's voice hinted at playfulness as his gaze bounced from Elle to her. "Can you say *lackey*, Elle?"

"Licky," the toddler attempted, and Asteria chuckled darkly.

"I would appreciate it if you didn't teach my daughter words she can't possibly understand," Odo grumbled, peering at Wells. He slowly slid his eyes to Asteria. "Or gestures."

"I'll teach her what it means." Wells shrugged, tilting his head. Elle mimicked him with wide, studious eyes and Asteria thought her heart would burst from her chest.

"I apologize for the intrusion, but what did you know was a possibility?" Erika asked, making the rounds as she poured hot water into everyone's teacups.

"It's not an intrusion," Asteria assured, sighing. "I believe it's time to alert you, as it seems things have escalated far beyond what I anticipated."

Asteria and Piers began to fill Odo and Erika in on the happenings of their world. Asteria summarized what was said about Sybil's prophecy, stealing glances with her to ensure she spoke correctly. Sybil jumped in to explain her vision of Nen and Zephyr, how she'd happened upon the Obsidian Decay and the interaction with Endora, as well as pinpointing the infected villages.

Asteria added in her conversation with Nen at the Patronage Gala, leaving out some of the more aggressive details.

As Piers explained the political side of things, Asteria recalled the thought he proposed before they portaled to Teslin. Piers was right that it was odd the illness suddenly appeared in Ghita after being contained to the southern end of the continent, especially without appearing anywhere else nearby.

While disappointed in Gallus, Asteria knew he spoke the truth. He was a calculated, strategic thinker. He would follow the natural pattern of plagues to pass this illness off as a normal disease aroused by humans. She didn't understand why he would jump from one end of the continent to another.

Until two things Rod and Sybil said rang through her mind.

Lord Caius insinuated the Rotherhams are detached from Ghita, quite possibly the situation.

How long do you believe Gallus will be able to hold them off before they start wreaking havoc upon Aveesh?

It appeared Gallus couldn't hold them off for long.

"Nen and Zephyr are diverting from the plan," Asteria muttered, aimlessly setting her teacup on a side table.

Wells stopped bouncing Elle on his knee, frowning at her. The toddler squeaked, scrambling off his lap. He pouted at her as she hobbled over to Asteria, his eyes tracking her movements.

"Is it my turn now?" Asteria rose from her chair, hands outstretched toward a grinning Elle. She hitched the toddler on her hip, catching Wells's eye.

They were blazing, and a blush unexpectedly rose to Asteria's cheeks as she turned away.

"What's that supposed to mean?" Sybil lowered her cup from her lips.

"I told you Gallus didn't want war," Asteria explained, lightly bouncing with Elle. "His goal was this convoluted sense of balance he believed he needed to correct. Nen and Zephyr were the first to goad the others about ridding the world of humans or enslaving them in some capacity. Nen was the one talking about war. Both men are reckless individuals who won't care about the consequences of said war."

Piers, ever the strategist, caught onto what Asteria discovered. "The pattern... Gallus was trying to make the Obsidian Decay appear like a natural phenomenon. Nen and Zephyr are growing impatient."

"Rod warned as much." Asteria cursed under her breath for having to admit Rod was correct. At the same time, she reminded herself that Rod, Danica, and Morana had millennia of experience with Nen and Zephyr. "I'm unsure if Gallus knows what they're doing. I think this is further confirmation they've spoken in great detail with the countries we hypothesized they would."

Sybil fiddled with the rim of her teacup, pondering. "The Sirians from Teslin essentially said the Seymours demanded they ignore the Decay."

"They did what?" Erika dropped her cup onto the saucer with a clatter. Elle's gaze locked onto her mother. "The Royal Healer in Teslin is aware of the Decay?"

"It appeared so," Gavril grumbled, folding his arms over the back of Piers's chair and hunching over. "That's why we got into some trouble. Caine, his son, and a few Sirians were waiting for us when we portaled to help Sado with the spread of the illness. They said if we tried to help, they would take action."

"I recall them saying they would remove us," Piers muttered, still miffed by Caine's word choice.

"Gallus may be the one who started this," Asteria said as Elle laid her head on her shoulder, "but Nen and Zephyr are running with it like a child might run with a knife."

"Please don't give her any ideas." Odo sighed, watching his daughter burrow her face into Asteria's neck. Her heart swelled, a soft grin tugging at her lips. "So Nen and Zephyr want the kingdoms pinned against one another? Are we to believe Sylvan has allied with Allanis and Teslin in this cause?"

"If we insinuate that, we certainly need to assume Thalassa is also allied with them," Gavril explained, his chin propped atop Piers's head. His eyes flickered to Asteria and Wells. "If Teslin and Allanis are already working together, we need to speak with your brothers *and* sister."

Asteria winced at the pinch of guilt, and Erika silently gestured for Asteria to hand her Elle. She passed the child along, her eyes staying shut despite the commotion.

She knew they needed Phoebe—now more than ever—and she could only pray her voice of reason was stronger than whatever Gallus had to offer.

"Taranis and Dionne won't argue against it," Odo said, a frown creasing his forehead. "But Phoebe, Asteria? You don't have the best—"

"I'm well aware of the task I have before me regarding my sister," Asteria snapped through her teeth with a tight smile. Fingers brushed along her forearm, and she startled slightly until she felt Wells's presence. Calmer, she added, "We're hanging on Phoebe's soft spot for humans."

The truth of the situation settled heavily over the room, Sybil shifting uncomfortably in her seat as she stared into her empty cup. Asteria wondered if she was reading the leaves, determining if the choices they were moving forward with were for the best or if they were making a grave mistake.

"Don't doubt yourself," Wells said quietly behind her, tugging harder against her hand. She dragged her gaze to him, studying his kind smile. "I can see you questioning your decisions. You're doing the right thing."

"I know." She nodded stiffly but softened when his thumb brushed over the top of her hand. "I would prefer not to be the one to make the first aggressive move. Speaking of which—did you kill Caine's son?" Asteria snapped her gaze to Sybil, yanking her hand out of Wells's grasp.

"No." Sybil scoffed, a tinge of regret in her voice. "I simply injured him enough that it would take a few hours for him to recover."

"One would argue Caine and the Royal Healer attacked *you*, meaning you didn't make the first move," Odo intervened, standing from his chair and sliding his hands into his pockets. "All kingdoms know when it comes to Healers, there should be no prejudice for what type of illness or Being it is. A Sirian who attended the Academy should most definitely know better. If they're refusing to treat their people, they can't retaliate against another for stepping in to help their sick."

"Until they cross the line, these scuffles must not have any casualties on our end," Asteria explained. "Nen and Zephyr will use any opportunity to get more Sirians and Lemurians on their side, no matter who started it."

"So why come here, Asteria?" Odo finally asked, his gaze bouncing across every individual in the room. "I know Celestia has been your home for the last fifteen years, but you didn't portal into your sleeping quarters. You portaled to my home."

Asteria gnawed on her lower lip, maintaining eye contact with Odo. He raised an eyebrow with expectation and a bit of apprehension. Erika shuffled into the room, breaking the increasing tension between them.

"Erika," Asteria said, not taking her gaze from Odo, "could you please show the princes, Sybil, and Gavril to a few empty rooms in the same building as mine? We need to rest before we reconvene."

"Of course," she replied quietly, resting her hand against Wells's bicep. He stared at Asteria for a moment longer before nodding and following Erika, the others close behind.

She waited until the front door of the Hesper's home clicked shut before slowly turning back to Odo, who now held an official Head Elder expression.

"What are you going to request?" he asked, clasping his hands behind his back. The guardedness of his expression sat heavily in Asteria's stomach.

"I anticipate Allanis and Sylvan will follow Teslin's lead in forbidding their Healers from helping the sick humans," Asteria began, reaching for the bag Wells left behind. "The cure for the illness is in these vials. Simple ingredients that need to be charged with the Energy."

Odo hesitantly took the bag from her, keeping his dark eyes on her face.

"You said as much, but the Healers of the Academy are taught to help the sick, no matter what." Asteria gestured to the bag, then waved a hand above her head. "We can't sit idly by while humans are dying. Putting aside the origins of the illness and the motive behind it, the bottom line is that humans are sick, and we have the cure. I want you to send any senior Healers to the villages we discovered or make contact with Sirians who wield the Energy who can get to those villages without raising suspicion."

"I agree with you that the Academy should help." Odo gently placed the satchel on the chair he vacated. He lifted his gaze, chin lowered.

"That's not all you've come here to say, though. I see it in your face and hear it in the words you're not speaking."

Asteria stood by her beliefs that she couldn't force Celestia to help in a war or choose a side, but she worried what would happen if Celestia decided to do absolutely nothing.

The options were few.

Either she forced the Academy to participate, allowed the Sirians to choose who they wanted to help, or forced them to stay out of it entirely as her father requested. She wanted to believe she wouldn't have to force Sirians to help, but the fact remained she'd already met three too many who were more than content to stand aside as humans died.

"I'm not entirely sure the allies we seek are enough," Asteria explained quietly, stepping closer to Odo. His expression was wary as he listened. "If this leads to a war between the Lyrans, my father's side will utilize their connections to support them. That leaves Eldamain, The Northern Pizi, and Riddling as allies against Allanis, Sylvan, Teslin, and Thalassa. We could have Etherea, but if Gallus has already bargained with Phoebe, we don't stand a chance without Celestia."

"Asteria..." Odo shook his head slowly, holding her gaze. "What you're about to ask... There are Sirians in those countries, too. They're not just Healers, but Diplomats and Warriors as well."

"I'm aware." Asteria sighed, shutting her eyes against the ache behind them. "But they're attacking humans, Odo. If we don't win, I fear for the future of this world. All that Celestia stands for could very well be in jeopardy."

"We've always remained neutral amongst the quarrels of the kingdoms," Odo explained, his back straightening. "It allows the Elders to run the Academy efficiently despite the countries we come from. It also allows the students to coexist peacefully, giving them the freedom and opportunity to put aside their differences. All that said, it's very difficult for us to choose a side while maintaining your created cohesion."

"This isn't a war amongst the kingdoms—"

"But it is." Odo chuckled, a hollow sound. "Whether intentional or not, Nen and Zephyr have made it about the kingdoms. The moment you spoke of allying with this country or that country, it became not just about the Lyrans but about the countries they find favor in."

Asteria's heart hammered in her chest as she shook her head vehemently. "You can't tell me you will damn the humans."

"No one is damning them, Asteria." Odo reached out to her, but she stepped back, leveling him with a glare. Her heart clenched at the hurt that flashed across his face. "We're agreeing to help heal them and offer them the cure for the illness. When it comes to war and fighting against each other on a battlefield, I'm not sure…"

He wasn't sure if Celestia could take a stance.

That's what he left hanging in the air, which had Asteria's stomach curdling with a thick emotion, irritation prickling beneath her skin.

If they didn't have Etherea *or* Celestia on their side, Asteria feared there would be no hope at all.

CHAPTER 31

ASTERIA

Asteria marched through the halls of the housing within the Academy, foregoing portaling to her apartment after expending herself yet again.

She didn't mind the time with her thoughts, though. Otherwise, she feared she would set something ablaze within her room, and she rather liked its appearance right now.

She was perturbed by Odo's words but more so startled. She hadn't anticipated his insinuation that it would be difficult for Celestia to get involved in a war with the Lyrans, especially considering the humans were the victims in this scenario. She'd always strived to instill the Academy with a drive to protect humans just as much—if not more—than their fellow Sirians.

Why would it matter if the kingdoms were pinned against one another, Sirians amongst the ranks or not? If this ended in war, Lyrans would face Lyrans, Andromedans against Andromedans. Brothers, sisters, and family members could very well find themselves on opposite side of the war.

So why did Odo believe it would be difficult to choose a side? There was only one right side, and it was beside her—their Goddess.

I won't stoop to that level. She hated the thought the moment it appeared in her head.

Asteria prided herself on coexisting with her people rather than being their omnipotent dictator. She wanted them to have free thought and their own minds rather than making decisions to appease her, hoping she would grant them some sort of benevolence.

Which meant she had to let Odo do his job.

She slammed through her bedroom door in frustration, her thoughts running circles over this.

She just wanted Celestia to choose good, whether or not she was on that side. That's all she ever wanted—for them to *do good.*

She snarled at no one in particular, momentarily wishing Rod would appear, if only to have an outlet for her anger. It would give her something to do—something to occupy her mind with.

Wells would be a worthy distraction… She stopped pacing in the middle of her room, gawking at the fireplace in horror. *Heavens above, where did that come from?*

He flooded her mind now that she opened the gate.

Dueling beside him in Teslin was exhilarating. They fed off one another, anticipating what move the other would make, supporting or amplifying it. He didn't try to overcompensate as she found most men do when training Warriors.

Wells remembered her shield and requested she use it rather than trying to be some hero. *He* was the one who thought of the portal in the sky for Sybil.

Asteria growled in frustration, throwing herself back against her bed, her shoulders bouncing slightly against the plush mattress. She laid on her back with her hands resting on her stomach, staring at the empty ceiling with more thoughts of Wells.

His jesting with her, his glee from portaling, his sarcasm, the feel of his hand in hers, his body under hers…

No man weaseled his way into her mind the way he had. It was the most infuriating yet intoxicating thing she'd experienced in a long time. She found herself admiring things about him, occasionally drooling over him, and even ticking off what she liked most.

One of those things—his crooked smile—popped into her head. The way it imperceptibly tugged at his cheeks, eyes darkened with heavy lids, and a slight incline of his head.

Heat gathered low, and her hand twitched on her stomach.

Absolutely not. She would not fantasize about him. The moment she did that, she would be admitting to herself the full depth of her interest in him, which would make avoiding her visceral reactions impossible.

Except she needed release to rid her body of this coiled tension that had built up from the moment she portaled him for the first time. How he effortlessly caught her against him when she threw herself at him, his strong arms wrapping around her—

Asteria groaned as she searched her memory for a pleasant face she had no connection to, landing on someone she knew was long gone. She bunched up her dress, shivering as the cool air hit where she was aching most. Her hand slowly slid down the front of her body, delving between the slickness already pooling.

She shut her eyes and almost snarled because she knew it was a result of Wells, which only brought those intriguing eyes back to her mind, the feel of his lips on the top of her hand conjuring thoughts about how those lips would feel against her.

Fuck it.

She stroked her damp fingers in a circle as she imagined his lips wrapping around her clit, sucking as he slid two fingers inside her. She dipped her fingers through her aching core, gasping softly at the tightness as she pulsed, wondering what he would say if his fingers were the ones caressing the spot that sent a flare of fire through her—

"Asteria?"

She felt the Aether on the opposite side of the door before it swung open, and she lurched upright, covering herself with her skirts.

Her skin flushed when she connected with the eyes she pictured in her head.

"Are you okay? I passed your door and saw a glow…" Wells trailed off as his eyes fell from hers.

She glanced down to see illuminated blue veins fading underneath her fair skin, silently cursing herself.

Too long, indeed.

"I'm alright," she assured Wells, her cheeks burning at the hoarseness of her tone. She cleared her throat, stumbling over her words as his gaze narrowed, and the smirk she envisioned earlier painstakingly climbed up his cheek. "I was just… I needed some time to… I was practicing some things—"

"Oh?" Wells stepped far enough into the room for the door to click shut behind him. He crossed his arms over his chest as he pitched against the frame. "Is that what ladies are calling *this* these days?" He flicked his hand between her and the bed.

Asteria pressed her lips into a tight line, avoiding his gaze. "I'm not sure what you mean. As I said, I was—"

"Practicing. Right." Wells pushed himself off the door, the muscles beneath his tunic flexing. He slipped his hands into his pockets and strolled across the room toward the chair in front of the fireplace. He shrugged, and their eyes connected. "Do you need help?"

Asteria blanched, her mouth dropping open. Heat immediately returned to where she'd just been touching herself. "What did you say?"

"Do you need help?" Wells repeated, slowly turning one of the chairs to face the bed. He waved his hand up and down, and her eyes fluttered at the way he said, "*Practicing?*"

Asteria hadn't been touched by a man in over a century, and she'd only ever let one man see so much of her in her entire existence. The thought of Wells helping her—whatever that meant—had her heart pounding in anxiousness and excitement, the traitor it was.

"I beg your pardon," she breathed, shaking her head as she realized what his offer truly meant. "I believe it's highly inappropriate for you to be offering—"

"We're friends." Wells slowly stepped one foot in front of the other, the click of his heels like a clock as he made his way around the chair. He lowered himself onto the cushion, his eyes never leaving hers. "We're mature adults."

"Debatable." She narrowed her gaze, but her heart still thundered, her body tingling.

His tongue flicked against his upper lip as he rolled it under his bottom teeth, then morphed into a smirk. "I've been told two is better than one. I know some women prefer the company of another woman, but something tells me you prefer men."

Shock, irritation, and desire all warred within Asteria as her chest rose and fell with short, rapid breaths. She scanned his face for teasing or condescension, but she only found amusement and something dark in his heavy-lidded gaze. He reclined, set his legs wide, and folded his hands in his lap.

Asteria wasn't blind nor deaf. She knew he was intrigued and attracted to her just as much as she was to him. The difference was she was a Goddess, everything about her meant to lure those around her in, especially the Sirians whose powers mimicked her own. They would feel the pull to her and the endless access she wielded.

She had no excuse as to why she was drawn to him.

Her stubbornness, as he so blatantly pointed out in Ghita, bubbled within her. She refused to back down and let him beat her in this game of wits. If he was challenging her, she would play.

Asteria lifted her chin, braced her hands behind her, and slowly lifted her knees. Her heart fluttered wildly in her chest as the skirt of her dress fell down her knees, bunching at her waist and exposing herself to him.

Wells's eyes darkened, but he kept those eyes on hers, tension amplifying the longer they stared at one another.

"I've not needed a man's help in over one hundred and twenty years," Asteria cooed, tilting her head. "What makes you think your cock inside me would be better than what I could do for myself?"

Those beige hues darkened further as Wells maintained his composure, a full smile breaking out across his face that was unadulterated mischief. "Who said anything about needing to be inside you to make you come?"

She let out a breath of disbelief as her stomach dipped, coiling tight. She swore the warmth between her legs dripped onto the mattress below, and it was only confirmed when Wells's attention finally dragged to where she was exposed to him, his smile slipping.

"Show me," he demanded gently, his eyes lifting back to hers. The heat in his gaze coaxed a soft whimper from her lips. He adjusted his slacks, and Asteria spotted him straining against the seam. "What is it you do to yourself that you haven't needed another?"

Asteria's mouth went dry. *How did I end up here?*

The youngest prince of Eldamain sat in a chair at the end of her bed, ogling her cunt as her arousal slid onto the bed.

"I enjoy learning," Wells whispered, his voice rough, skittering across her skin. "Teach me, Blue."

She swallowed, her senses coming alive as she brought a trembling hand to the apex of her thighs, once again sliding her fingers to find she was utterly drenched. Her eyes fluttered shut, her head lolling back at the soft pressure against her swollen lips.

Wells clicked his tongue from the chair, and Asteria's head snapped back down to him. Her movements paused as she glared. "As a student, I require my teacher's undivided attention."

Her eyebrows furrowed as she pursed her lips in confusion, but Wells's clarification was sinful.

"Eyes on me, Blue."

She locked with his gaze at the same time she slipped two fingers inside herself, moaning quietly at the pleasure rippling through her. It took all her willpower to keep her attention on him and not shy away.

It was a thrill she'd never experienced before, having someone watch her pleasure herself, and it took even more self-control not to give in and let him take her fingers' place.

Wells sank further against the back of the chair, propping one elbow on the armrest. He pinched his bottom lip between his fingers as he watched her, entranced.

Asteria lost herself in the dazed ecstasy brought on by Wells watching her pleasure herself, the intensity and attention with which he regarded her keeping her fully engaged. His breaths increased with her own, her vision tunneling as her body tightened everywhere in anticipation.

When the corner of his lips ticked up ever so slightly, the coil within Asteria snapped, her body teeming with pleasure as her walls shuddered around her fingers. She moaned drunkenly, her hips grinding on her fingers as she rode out the orgasm, all while watching Wells's bright eyes glaze over.

Asteria's body went lax as the climax subsided, her panting the only sound in the hushed room.

Wells rose from his seat and adjusted his slacks again. She stopped herself from looking at where she knew his erection would be. He walked to the edge of the bed where she was still propped up on one hand. She slowly removed the other from between her legs as she came down from the high.

Yet their eyes never left one another.

When she went to clean off her fingers on the nearest fabric, Wells's hand shot out and wrapped around her wrist.

She frowned at him, unsure whether to be thrilled or enraged.

He tugged on her stiff arm, and she relented warily, but it immediately morphed into wide-eyed elation as he lifted her hand toward him. He drew her fingers into his mouth, lips wrapping around them, as soft as she remembered. He slowly dragged them against his tongue, curving it around her fingers.

When he removed them from his mouth, he released her wrist at the same time she drew it to her chest. He winked at her with a sly grin and turned on his heel, hands clasped behind his back as he walked to the door.

"And you?" Asteria managed to say, lowering her legs.

He stopped before the handle, peering at her over his shoulder. He shrugged and answered simply, "This wasn't about me."

With that, he opened the door and snuck out like a thief in the night.

Asteria let her body fall back against the mattress, staring at the ceiling again. She lifted her fingers above her, rubbing her thumb along where his tongue had caressed her fingers.

What have I done?

CHAPTER 32

PHOEBE

After another day of fending off the Council, Phoebe managed to sneak away and trade with Maria to put the children to bed.

She ducked her head to place a gentle kiss on Jeremiah's forehead directly on his Mark, smoothing back his curls. Her heart warmed at the faint smile that graced his chubby cheeks. With a final pet, she moved on to the room next door where Emmalina lay in her bed, fighting her heavy lids as she offered a similar grin to Phoebe.

"Mommy?" Emmalina said softly, leaning into Phoebe's hand as she tucked her hair back. "Who was the merman and the ghost that came the other day?"

Phoebe chuckled under her breath.

Her daughter wasn't far off with Marin. She was still learning about the Lemurian Houses and the different creatures they shifted into. On the other hand, Endora could very well have been a ghost with her pale skin and sunken cheeks.

"She wasn't a ghost," Phoebe explained, keeping her voice lighthearted. The last thing she needed was Emmalina waking from a nightmare. "She's an Andromedan but also a Sirian like Mommy."

"Does she have a special power, too?" Emmalina asked, her eyes widening.

"She does, but maybe I will tell you about it in the morning." Phoebe leaned in and kissed her on the forehead just as she had Jeremiah. "Her power is not a bedtime story, I assure you."

Emmalina pouted, but Phoebe could see her fighting sleep. She rose from the bed and walked across the room, shaking her head at the dolls scattered on the floor. She slipped through the crack in the door and quietly closed it behind her before heading back toward her study.

Her shoes clicked against the floor as she reached into the pocket within her cloak, retrieving the letter she received from Eldamain earlier that morning. She was startled when she beheld their royal seal, even more so when she found Prince Quintin had signed it himself.

He was vague, which was ominous. She hadn't seen nor spoken to the male in years, let alone since she was crowned queen. He wrote in a tone that suggested they were usual correspondents, the phrasing relatively informal.

Though distance has grown between our thrones, my thoughts have not strayed far from our once-shared bond of trust and purpose.

It was odd to her because she and Prince Quintin had never once shared a bond. If anything, the former alliance would've been between King Drogo and Quintin's father. They weren't even friends before he entered her marriage games.

News of the human affliction has reached even my distant halls, and I fear this Darkness coils too near to your throne. One does not speak of storms to those who shelter the rain.

Endora mentioned the Obsidian Decay was now in Teslin and southern Sylvan, but Phoebe was curious about how Prince Quintin heard of it in Eldamain. What was even more curious was this Darkness he spoke of. She thought it meant the illness, since it manifested black like night, but he capitalized the word.

The last line was also troublesome. She didn't understand it, so she told Dustin she wanted him to meet her in her study to analyze it before they retired for the night. If anyone was good at deciphering poetic words, it was him.

Phoebe opened the study and stepped inside, quickly shutting the door behind her. A head peeked over the top of her desk chair facing the window. The room was rather dark, though, and her heart rate spiked into an unhealthy rhythm.

"Dustin, why is the room…" She trailed off as the chair twisted, and she realized just how *dark* the room was. She couldn't see the shelves or tapestries lining the walls, unnatural shadows crowding around her.

"Daughter," Gallus's voice sang. The form rose from her chair, and she connected with the frigid blue of his mortal form eyes. "It's been quite some time since we last spoke. I believe it was just before your coronation, when I hinted Drogo seemed rather mad."

"You didn't come to the coronation, though," Phoebe said, carefully slipping the letter into the sleeve of her cloak, distracting his attention as she adjusted a miscellaneous trinket on the side table. "I understand your hesitance to do so, but you didn't even visit after in private, which leaves me questioning why you're here now."

"Can a father not visit his daughter?" Gallus asked, a slight pout to his bow-shaped lips.

Phoebe clenched her teeth, envious of the unmistakable resemblance between her half-sister and father. Phoebe resembled her Sirian mother—nearly identical—furthering the space between her, Asteria, and Gallus, which felt as though it was never breachable.

"I'm not typically the daughter you visit on a whim in the middle of the night, cloaking my study with Aether," she said, holding her voice despite her chest fluttering erratically. "I won't ask again. Why are you here?"

Phoebe may have respected Gallus as a Lyran, God, and half her heritage, but she knew his affections never truly belonged to her. They belonged to Asteria—Gallus's true weakness—which left her forced to achieve greatness to win any favor from him.

Gallus sighed, the air thick with boredom as if he wanted her to play some silly game with him.

Phoebe wasn't moronic. Her sharp bite and intimidation might've been useful for Beings like Delilah, Endora, and Marin, but they would be futile against Gallus.

Her power alone would be no match for him, and one wrong move could be detrimental with him in her castle.

"I tried to be gentle with your sister," Gallus explained, and Phoebe tensed as the Aether around the perimeter of the room churned. "I insisted she stay neutral, remain an uninterested party, but she blatantly ignored my warnings, putting her and me on opposing sides."

Phoebe frowned, blinking at Gallus. "I don't know what you speak of. Opposing sides of what?"

Phoebe braced as Gallus raised his hands, but when he flicked his wrists, the Aether disappeared to reveal what lurked in the shadows.

Caine reclined against the wall on the left side of the room, inspecting claws that curled from the edges of his fingertips, peeking at her over them with a sly, venomous smirk.

She didn't care to acknowledge him, though, because Endora stood on the right side of the room with her hands clasped behind her back and a wide, sinister smile stretched across her sunken cheeks. Beside her, wrapped in swirling black tendrils of Aether, was Dustin with a rag tied around his mouth, bruises swelling the left side of his face, and scratches across his neck.

"What the fuck is going on?" Phoebe snapped, moving toward Dustin with a white glow emanating from her. Gallus held up his hand, a black wall of Aether pulsing before her in warning.

"Your sister didn't listen, child, but you *will*," Gallus snarled, his voice permeating the air in a cavernous echo as he flicked his pointer finger.

Phoebe fell back into a chair, suppressing the power thrumming in

261

her veins as Gallus wrapped the Aether around the legs of the chair and dragged her to the opposite end of the desk across from him.

Caine moved from the corner of her eye, and she tracked him as he walked across the room to stand beside Dustin.

Dustin muttered something around the cloth between his lips, eyes frantic, but Caine glared at him and punched his stomach. Dustin shut his eyes around a muffled grunt, attempting to hunch into the attack, but was forced upright by the Aether around his body.

"Don't!" Phoebe shouted, moving to get up again when Caine dragged a curved claw down Dustin's cheek. The Aether clenched tight around her wrists, burning in a way she'd never felt before. She shot her attention back to Gallus, her eyes wide. "I don't understand what's happening."

"If you listen, you will know," Gallus warned, sitting back down. Beneath his fair skin, the endless depth of his god-form swirled. "Sybil foresaw a prophecy that warned of the extinction of Sirians, Lemurians, Lyrans, and Andromedans. It says nothing of humans, though."

Phoebe's brows tried to press together in a frown, but her eyes were too wide and frantic as she simultaneously focused on Gallus and the other two Andromedans near Dustin. If she didn't glow like the moon in the sky when using her god-power, she'd be finding a way to use it to get Dustin free.

"Every Lyran has their theory as to what that could mean for the future of this Realm, but I know what it truly means." Gallus's eyes flashed, the black ring around his irises swirling with the icy blue before settling again. "With so many Beings, this world requires a precious balance. One that has tipped from the audacity of humans."

"Audacity?" Phoebe whispered, inclining her head.

"They think themselves greater—or at the very least the same level as the rest of us—but they would be *nothing* without us," Gallus explained, his lip curling. "Lyrans are the ones who saved them from the wild animals on this plane. Sirians were made to help protect them against such creatures. Giving the creatures the power to shift from mortal to animal and back again allowed everyone to coexist peacefully.

"But the humans now believe they are worthy enough to sit amongst the powerful who are the sole reason they have survived in this world." Gallus reclined, peering at Dustin as he shifted his shoulders to bury deeper into the chair.

"What are you going to—" Phoebe stopped herself, dragging her head to Endora. The necromancer just smirked, black eyes and Mark winking as she nodded her head once. "You're responsible for the Obsidian Decay?"

"It's the beginning of this balance, child." Gallus smiled, but it was laced with pity. "I don't seek to eliminate *all* humans. I just want them to remember they don't run this world. They need a reminder of how weak they are—that without all of us, they would be the ones to perish."

"If you don't want to massacre them, why are you infecting them?" Phoebe shook her head, swallowing against the burning lump in her throat.

"To remind everyone that humans are *rats*," Endora hissed, their conversation from the other day echoing in Phoebe's mind. Endora closed a fist, Aether squeezing tighter around Dustin. He shut his eyes but grunted against the pressure. Phoebe struggled against the tendrils when a slight crack echoed through the room, but it only served to dig the Aether deeper into her skin. "Helpless, useless rats."

"Endora," Gallus drawled, his face still turned to Phoebe. "How about we practice the control your mother seems to lack?"

Endora relented with a sneer as she stepped back from Dustin, releasing her fist, and he whimpered softly as he inhaled. Phoebe bit back a sob, but a tear tracked down her cheek.

"Use the mortals to spread an infection, make the world fear them." Phoebe breathed slowly as bile rose to the back of her throat. "Then what do you suppose will happen? The world will retaliate against the humans?"

"By keeping them in check." Gallus shrugged as if he didn't speak of indenturing an entire race of Beings. "Diminish their population, create prejudice against them, and ostracize them from positions of power. Sirians and Lemurians should be the only ones to rule." Gallus smirked as he met her husband's eyes, a devilish grin growing.

Phoebe couldn't fathom what he wanted from her if he insisted on harming Dustin. Why come to her when he knew those she loved dearest were human? Her husband was human, and his entire family in Chimbridge, another village in Etherea, was human. His mother and father had done more for her in the short time she'd known them than her own parents—all three of them.

"I won't turn my back on my family," Phoebe whispered, her lip quivering as she thought of turning a blind eye as they infected Dustin and his sisters. "You can't expect me to shut my eyes to the horrors you inflict on them, all the while knowing what was bound to happen."

"I don't expect you to either, my dear," Gallus said softly, his voice too sweet, like the poisonous nectar of oleander. "Which is why I wanted to come to you and offer kindness and compassion that will extend to the humans you care for."

Phoebe sat stoically, even if her heart rattled in the cage of her ribs, threatening to burst. She swallowed against the dryness in her throat, urging him to go on with a dip of her head.

Dustin garbled from the corner of the room.

"Remain neutral," Gallus demanded, standing. He slunk around the edge of the desk toward Phoebe, tucking a stray strand of hair behind her ear, his cold fingertips grazing her skin. "Don't intervene in the war the other Lyrans wish to incite, and your humans won't be harmed."

"War?" Phoebe snapped her head to where Gallus journeyed to the left side of her confined chair. "What war?"

"As I mentioned, Asteria finds herself on the opposite side." Something sharp and sorrowful flickered across his face. "There are some Lyrans who agree with me, but others do not believe in my campaign.

They seek to undo what I've begun with a cure and are rallying with other kingdoms to stop this. I fear they wish war upon us, although I'm doing everything in my power to keep that from happening.

"Should it come to that, though, I simply ask that you not get involved. Don't ally with your sister, and you also won't have to ally with the countries on our side. Simply stand aside and let me do my work."

Phoebe forced air into her lungs, willing her heart to calm. Her gaze bounced from Dustin to Endora to Gallus in that sequence repeatedly until she felt the room spinning as fast as her thoughts.

She had nothing against the humans outside of her family. Her human citizens were just as precious to her as the Sirian and Lemurian ones, and she wished for them to coexist peacefully. She never understood the prejudice other Andromedans harbored regarding them.

She wanted them to live, just as she wanted to protect her family at all costs.

Were her kingdom and family worth the lives of every other human on Aveesh? Could she live with the knowledge that she bargained with her father in exchange for neutrality?

"Think faster, Queen Phoebe." Caine clicked his tongue against his teeth. "I fear King Dustin may need a Healer."

Phoebe locked eyes with her husband. They were heavy and glassy, his black hair clinging to his face in inky strands.

She knew he needed a tonic for whatever internal injuries ailed him. He gently shook his head, barely perceptible. Her lower lip quivered as she shut her eyes, another tear slipping free.

The rest of the world wasn't her responsibility. If she didn't protect her kingdom, she subjected them to more of the Obsidian Decay and a possible war where victory wasn't guaranteed.

Her kingdom and family were her priority. The bargain would at least give her time to figure out how to help her people, those she loved with her whole self and those who gave her their unyielding loyalty.

"All my humans," Phoebe finally announced, and she heard Dustin try to shout around the gag. "Not just my family. I want the Obsidian Decay to stop spreading in Etherea. I want you to leave every human untouched within my borders, or you have no agreement."

"I don't think you have room to—"

Gallus held up a finger at Endora, tilting his head. "Anything else?"

"Swear to me," Phoebe whispered breathlessly, her shoulders rising and falling with every breath. She let her god-power finally spring forward, the room illuminating in a soft, white glow. Pieces of furniture levitated in the air, and Gallus's eyes bounced to each piece with something glittering in those icy hues. "Swear to me that you nor any of your partners will harm a single human in Etherea from this day forth. If you do, you will regret the day you ever stepped foot in my kingdom.

"You will also get me the cure for the Obsidian Decay."

Gallus's lips twitched at the corner as he slowly lowered his finger. Phoebe glimpsed an emotion she swore she'd never seen from Gallus before.

Pride.

"We're in agreement, daughter." Gallus nodded, swirling his hand above him.

Phoebe heard Dustin fall to the floor, and the burning retreated from her wrists.

"Dee!" She threw herself toward him, grasping his face as she pressed their foreheads together. He lifted a hand behind his head to untie the cloth gagging him before he grabbed her shoulders, his face scrunched in pain.

"Phoebe," he groaned, voice hoarse. "What have you done?"

She didn't answer him—couldn't answer him.

Instead, she extended her head as Endora and Caine stepped through the portal Gallus opened.

"Why are you doing this?" she asked him, clutching Dustin to her side as a wet cough wracked his body.

Gallus peered down at her as his mortal form slipped away, his god-form sending chills up her spine while simultaneously enchanting her. She lost herself in the never-ending night sky ofs his silhouette, her powers stirring beneath her skin.

"Power writes the laws of life, daughter." He tilted his head, observing her like a predator might stalk its prey. "You of all people should know that."

PART II

"BETTER TO REIGN IN
HELL THAN TO SERVE IN
HEAVEN."

JOHN MILTON, *PARADISE LOST*

CHAPTER 33

SYBIL

*T*he metallic atmosphere sat heavily on their tongues as the howls of horror echoed through the tarnished planes. A tear ripped open in the clouded sky, cracking at the jagged edges with blue and gold lightning. Deep within the chasm, a fathomless black pulsed endlessly, threatening to swallow them whole.

A flash of bright blue speared through the Realm, but none knew what they felt. A new God rose, taking up the post once placed before them. A sacrifice was made, conjuring a mother's despair and vengeful father's rage.

There was a knock in the dark.

It knocked and knocked, reverberating through a sphere swirling with colors—endless colors and faces and people and places and countries—

Sybil, it called. Sybil, come back—

Sybil gasped as she pitched forward, bracing her hands on the firm structure before her. She blinked to clear her vision, her head hanging limp as she greedily swallowed mouthfuls of clean air to wash the lingering metallic taste from her mouth.

"Syb," Piers said again, and her vision cleared enough to recognize the green grass beneath her feet, another pair of boots before hers. "Just take deep breaths."

Feeling crawled back into her limbs, needles prickling her skin.

She reminded herself that she was in Celestia, that Piers was with her, and somewhere, Asteria was also on the island fetching breakfast or conversing with one of her Elders.

Her fingers twitched against the structure she clung to, which she realized was Piers's biceps. His hands cupped her elbows, the only thing keeping her off the ground as feeling returned to her legs.

"I'm back," she assured him softly, her voice hoarse. She cleared her throat as she tightened her grip, fighting the bile rising in her chest. "Help me..."

Sybil didn't need to finish her thought. This wasn't the first time Piers was there to help her through a less-than-pleasant vision.

His arms stiffened as he positioned them for her to use as a brace, and she hoisted herself upright. She uncurled from her hunch with Piers's assistance, carefully lifting her head to meet his thoughtful gaze. Those green and brown eyes flickered over her face, grounding her until her vision stopped wavering.

"Was this one new?" he asked quietly, his thumbs brushing along her triceps. "Or have you seen this one before?"

Sybil cleared her throat, blinking away the overwhelming grief lingering from the vision. It startled her—not just because of the amount of grief she felt but that her own grief echoed from this Path.

"This was new," she whispered, loosening her grip but not letting go entirely. "Every decision made on either side creates a new Path for me to see."

"Are they all different Paths, or are they steps on the same Path leading to the outcome you foresaw already?" Piers lifted an eyebrow.

A muscle ticked at the corner of Sybil's lips.

She had spent so much of her immortal life living in Eldamain. The Carraphim line had been on that throne for over six hundred years, and she knew every ancestral line rather intimately. She befriended the families who ruled the throne, watching generations take up the mantle set before them by their ancestors.

She refused to interact with the new generations when they were still young. The idea of watching them grow from younglings until the day they died made her ill. She preferred to befriend them once they reached a reasonable adulthood, transitioning from one line to another.

These Carraphim princes were no different than any others...

Except Piers.

From the moment Sybil met Piers, something about him was different. She'd never quite placed what it was, but she was infatuated with him. Too fast they fell for each other, growing too close.

She cut it off years ago, but it never changed their deep friendship and understanding of each other—nor the tension that flared whenever they were near one another. Piers knew the right way to ask questions about her visions so she could speak around them enough for him to potentially decipher.

Piers was always piecing puzzles together, even when others didn't see the patterns.

"*Same Path, same outcome,*" Sybil muttered, her voice monotone.

Piers nodded slowly. They let go, fingertips brushing before falling to their sides. "Do you know what you saw yet?"

Sybil pressed her lips together, squinting. She shook her head, and that was the truth. Sometimes the visions came in vague images like the one he pulled her from, while others were clear as day.

Like when she saw Endora's death.

Piers sighed heavily, but it wasn't from agitation. It was relatively serene, and she tilted her head at him. He pursed his lips and shrugged. "Well, it appears there's nothing we can do about it at this moment. Do you agree?"

Sybil deadpanned, even if her chest lightened at hearing the reminder aloud. "I suppose you're correct."

He hummed, and the way the sound rumbled through her chest reminded her of how close they stood in this courtyard where anyone could walk by. She took a small step back as she brushed off her skirt in an effort to alleviate any inelegance from the gesture.

"How's the scratch on your tail?" Piers asked in an attempt to mask his slight flinch as he slipped his hands into his pockets. "Did the elixir from Erika help?"

"The drakon doesn't seem as disgruntled anymore, so I think it healed," Sybil explained, folding her arms across her midsection. "Although I won't know for certain until I shift later."

"Are you coming with us on our journeys to The Northern Pizi and Riddling?" While he averted his gaze, squinting at something over her shoulder, he couldn't hide the lilt of excitement in his voice.

"It's not my place to journey with you lot." Sybil offered Piers a small smile when he frowned at her comment. She reached across the short distance between them, laying her hand against him. "You must journey on your own. Both because I have no true purpose on the journey like I did with helping administer a cure, but I also feel Fate would prefer it that way."

Piers's eyes dropped to where her hand barely grazed his chest, directly above his heart. He stepped closer, forcing her hand to flatten against the hard muscle beneath. Sybil held her breath as one of his hands lightly gripped her fingers, the other skimming her waist.

"And if I prefer you came?" Piers asked, eyes searching, stripping her bare. Her breasts brushed against him as she inhaled sharply. "Would you defy Fate to please me?"

She bit her tongue as the urge to remind him she knew many different ways to please him tried to force its way from her lips. A smirk that resembled one Wells always wore climbed up his cheek, eyes twinkling.

He knew exactly what she wished to say.

"What would Gavril prefer?" Sybil asked softly, the words merely a breath of air between them.

He narrowed his eyes, but the smirk didn't falter. He raised the hand at her waist, toying with the end of a white braid draped over her shoulder.

"I hardly see how Gav would have anything to say about it. I believe if the roles were reversed, you would have far more to say about his company than he ever has to say about yours."

"I don't pretend to miss your insinuations, Piers." It was Sybil's turn to glare at him, using her palm on his chest to push him back to arm's length. Her braid slipped from his fingers. "You know precisely what I mean when I ask what Gavril would prefer."

Piers rocked back and forth from his heels to his toes. He opened his mouth to speak but Odo's voice carried to them from a nearby pillar. "Sybil!"

She snapped her head over her shoulder, glaring at the Head Elder.

Odo gave her a stiff wave before ushering her to where he stood. "Erika requests your presence. Something about a final dose of the healing elixir."

Sybil held up a finger at Odo before directing her attention back to Piers.

He was already backing away from her, hands back in his pockets.

"I suppose I'll see you when we reconvene after meeting with King Taranis and Dionne," Piers called as the distance grew between them, dipping his head. "Until then, Syb."

With that, the prince turned on his heel and strutted off toward Heavens-knew where, which only had Sybil's irritation bubbling deep in her drakon form.

He'd managed to get the last word on her.

Again.

Sybil gathered her skirt before marching up beside Odo. He waved a hand before leading her to wherever Erika was. They journeyed a mere few feet before Sybil could no longer stand Odo's eyes lingering on her face.

"What is it you'd like to say, Odo?" Sybil grumbled, curling her lip and flashing him a sharp canine.

She knew Odo well enough from his time as Royal Healer of

Eldamain and his relationship with the Carraphim princes. Their acquaintance level was equivalent to her and Gavril's, although arguably less combative.

Which had absolutely nothing to do with Gavril being Piers's lover.

"I find your behavior rather curious is all," Odo explained with a curt shrug, pushing his glasses up the bridge of his nose. "From my understanding, you insisted on ending any relations with a particular prince, yet I find the two of you quite close. Alone in the courtyard, I might add."

"I'm not some princess whose virtue is at stake." Sybil lifted her chin, side-eyeing him. "When you are over six hundred years old, no one bats an eye to find an old Andromedan alone with any male. Or female, for that matter."

"I don't question your virtue or lack thereof." Odo winked at her, and a low growl rumbled deep in her chest. "Oh, hush now. There's no need to get primal about it. I was stating my observation."

"I didn't end *all* relations with Piers," Sybil said quietly, gripping her skirts tightly. "He's still my friend. We've only recently been shoved into proximity because of our roles within all this nonsense."

"I didn't see any forces shoving either of you in the courtyard." Odo chuckled under his breath, clearly pleased with himself.

"You're a busybody," Sybil snapped, which only coaxed a louder laugh from Odo. "For a Head Elder, you think you'd have better things to occupy your time with."

"I'm a bored married man." Odo's laugh trailed off, even as his grin remained. "I miss the drama of Eldamain amongst you lot. It was always an entertaining treat to witness an immortal involve herself in the debauchery of mortal men."

Sybil scoffed, shaking her head. "You must leave this island once in a while if this is your state of mind within your first year of being Head Elder. You have a decade more to go."

"As long as you and Asteria keep bringing me exciting news…" Odo gave Sybil a sidelong look, cracking her hard exterior. "I'm sure I won't need to leave as frequently as you believe."

CHAPTER 34

ASTERIA

Asteria stood alone with her statue towering over her in the garden of the Asterian Academy. The fresh spring breeze brought the salted air of the ocean amongst the lavender and sage brushes swaying down a nearby aisle. Small conversation was echoing around her from various halls of the Academy as she stared at the smirk carved into her marble face.

How quickly her sentiments of the world had changed.

"It bears a striking resemblance," Wells said from behind her, but she didn't startle. She'd felt him behind her before he said a word—and not because of the Aether within him. "They mastered that smirk. Not too jovial, just a hint of amusement and slyness."

"Hm."

When Wells echoed the sound in a mocking tone, she noticed she'd instinctively leaned back against his chest. She peeked from the corner of her eye to find his face directly beside hers. Her stomach fluttered, and she couldn't identify whether it was excitement or bashfulness.

"I told Odo it was provocative," Asteria grumbled, fighting the heat in her cheeks. "I would never dare wear a sheet as a gown."

Wells chuckled low, the sound wrapping around her. She shut her eyes against the tickle of his breath caressing her neck as he spoke. "You know, Blue... I think you're lying. Maybe in your youth you wore such a gown—"

"In my youth?!" She whipped around with a scowl, fully facing him with a raised finger. "I will have you know—"

The coy grin on his face stopped her short.

He'd purposely riled her so she would look him in the face because, now that she was, all playfulness fell away when she realized which finger was between them.

The same finger he'd had in his mouth the night before.

"You were saying?" he asked, eyebrow arched, grin remaining. He took a step closer, her finger jamming into his chest. "What must I know? I already learned quite a bit last night."

Her breath shuddered as she recalled her senses. "You may have learned *something* last night, but you don't know much about me."

Wells shrugged as he took her hand in his. "I suppose you may be right. I can't possibly comprehend all six hundred years of your existence."

He lifted their hands, and Asteria frowned. He tugged her hand around her head. She followed the path of his arm with a wary glare until he drew her back against him, crossing his arm over her chest. His warmth wrapped around her, and her eyes fell shut at the odd sensation settling over her.

"That doesn't mean I don't know you," he whispered, his lips brushing her temple. "What do you think I've been doing anytime we're together?"

Asteria couldn't answer. She was caught in his arms and didn't want him to let go.

There was a quiet, imperceptible hum of something familiar, warm, and steady. Everything dimmed around the edges, only leaving behind his soft heartbeat against her back.

She couldn't name this, but she just knew it was easier here, like maybe she could rest for a moment.

Maybe longer.

"I've been watching and listening to you." His fingers lightly traced her collarbone from one shoulder to the other, brushing her hair back. "I quite like what I've found."

She slowly twisted in his arms, fighting the swirling in the pit of her stomach as she met his burning gaze. "Is that so?"

He dipped his head without breaking her gaze. "If my presence last night didn't give you any indication, I'll just have to be more convincing."

"And what if I've not found what *I* like?" She dragged her gaze up and down his body, stepping away and crossing her arms over her chest.

"Oh, love…" Wells laughed, his eyes crinkling at the corners as he shook his head. "We both know that's not true. If you hadn't found what you like, you wouldn't have been dripping—"

"Please stop agitating her," Piers called as he and Gavril strolled down one of the aisles carved from the hedges. "I can't continue to make excuses for you. I would rather not have to explain to our dear brother how you became charred remains."

Asteria normally would've appreciated Pier's acknowledgment of her common threat if her mouth hadn't dropped open at what Wells had been about to utter aloud for anyone to hear.

A smug smile stretched across his cheeks.

Piers didn't seem to initially discern the tension simmering between them wasn't malice, but Asteria caught how Gavril watched her and Wells. There was a slight squint to his eyes, lips pursed as he scrutinized them both with nothing short of fascination.

Wells held his ground when he found his friend studying them. Asteria fidgeted, linking and unlinking her fingers.

"What's our plan?" Piers asked, crossing his arms. "Home and then off to the countries?"

Asteria nearly thanked him for the change of topic. "I know the original plan was for Wells and myself to be the ones to talk with my brothers and sister, but we're far closer to a possible war than we originally anticipated. As two Lieutenant Generals for Eldamain, I think having you and Gavril with us would be beneficial."

"I'm inclined to agree," Wells said, and Asteria was transfixed as he spoke. "I honestly question whether I'm useful at all in these endeavors."

"You are," Asteria said far too quickly. Wells turned his attention to her, his face alight despite no smile. She fought to explain herself. "I mean, your brothers have both... expressed your need. Your presence would be beneficial with—"

"I love him, but Piers has the personality of a doorknob until you get to know him," Gavril interrupted, but Asteria knew better. The way both Gavril and Piers watched her with intrigue revealed her quick response wasn't missed. "Wells is the charming brother who has a way with words."

Asteria scoffed, and all three of them stared at her. She cleared her throat, shaking her head. "As I was saying, Piers and Gavril should come.

"We head to The Northern Pizi first. Taranis will be simple since he's still King. Dionne will also be easy, but one of his various levels of grandsons is King of Riddling now. He can't summon their army at will, no matter how much they listen to what he says. We'll need a meeting with the current king, and Dionne can help."

"What are we telling them?" Gavril asked, resting a hand on the sword strapped to his waist.

"Everything." Asteria nodded once, meeting the eyes of each male. She questioned again how she'd got herself in this position. "The Obsidian Decay, the Lyrans to avoid, what to prepare for, and possibly strategizing how best to get them to the Main Continent should war break out amongst us."

"Quin and I prepared the treaties before I left," Wells explained, patting his coat.

"We can't waste another moment." Piers sighed, shaking his head. "Lead the way, Asteria."

She ignored the bristle of irritation at his command, only letting him off because he handed her the charge. She waved a portal open. "You lot know the routine but stay close."

Asteria stared at the veil shimmering before them, her brother's study blurring on the opposite side. She took a steadying breath, shifting into the mentality required to deal with him.

"I thought you got along with your brothers," Wells said, directly behind her again.

"I do," she drawled, glancing at him. Their noses brushed at the proximity, and her breath hitched. "Taranis requires a specific level of patience. Speaking of my patience, you seem to find yourself behind me quite frequently. Is this intentional?"

"Trust me, Blue." She suppressed a gasp, biting her lower lip as he dragged his finger up her spine with a featherlight touch. "Finding myself behind you is *quite* intentional."

"Heavens above," she grumbled as she shut her eyes and walked through the portal.

CHAPTER 35

ASTERIA

Taranis's study was less of a chamber for quiet reflection and more a stage set for performance.

Rich walnut paneling lined the walls, dark and polished to a gleam. Above the hearth was an oil portrait of her brother—top buttons of his shirt open, smirking, one hand resting on his hip, the other cradling a chalice.

The sprawling desk was littered with letters, a golden inkpot shaped like a skull, and a chessboard with the white king knocked over.

She rolled her eyes because she knew it was a pointed message he hoped any visitors would get.

"So we just wait here until he appears?" Gavril asked, flopping into one of the chairs beside Piers. The prince scowled as he nestled in. "Do you know how often your brother comes to his study?"

"Part of my abilities allow me to sense the Energy or Aether within a Sirian," Asteria explained, shutting her eyes. "I can sense my parents and siblings more specifically once I'm near them."

"So you needed to be in The Northern Pizi to sense him?" Wells asked, a bit of awe in the question.

"I needed to be in Castle Ashe," Asteria corrected, peeking an eye open at him. Sure enough, he watched her with a twinkle that tightened her chest. "Now, let me work, Prince."

Asteria shut her eyes again and opened herself up to the Energy, searching the castle for Taranis's signature. His god-power gave his Energy a sharp edge, like static tickling her fingertips.

It tasted like rain before a storm.

"It appears he may have found us," Asteria announced just as the door to the study swung open. "Little brother."

King Taranis Beaumont was Asteria's youngest brother, but that didn't mean much for an Andromedan. He was eighty-two years old, but the male barely looked over forty. He had light brown hair streaked with silver pieces, one side shaved while the rest flipped casually to the other. His groomed beard matched his hair, silver eyes glittering with a roguishness that was the source of her kinship with him.

"What has our mother done now?" Taranis asked in his deep Pizian accent as he closed the door behind him. "And what have I done to deserve an audience with two Carraphim princes?"

"What has she not done?" Asteria grumbled, sighing heavily as Taranis approached her, arms wide.

He engulfed her in a suffocating hug, pinning her arms to her sides. He shook her back and forth, and Asteria caught Wells's gaze over his shoulder.

She glared in warning at the half-smile that tickled her chest.

"Are you two really related?" Gavril asked as Taranis released her. She snapped her head to him with narrowed eyes, her jaw dropping as he blatantly scanned her brother from head to toe. "There's no way this beautiful, broad man is your brother."

Gavril leveled Asteria with a sly grin, wiggling his eyebrows. Her entire body stiffened and she raised a finger, marching toward him, "I swear to the Heavens, Gavril—"

"You can have a shot at him later," Wells muttered, snatching her wrist in his firm grasp as he tugged her to his side. Her face warmed at the contact, and Taranis tilted his head from the corner of her eye. "We have important things to discuss at the moment that don't require a bickering match."

"Really?" Piers whispered harshly at Gavril, smacking him on the chest with an incredulous look.

"Which part are you flabbergasted by?" Gavril asked, a playful frown scrunching his face.

"Ladies," Wells drawled, and an unexpected smile spread across Asteria's cheeks. His attention was wholly on her, and she cursed herself as the twinkle in his beautiful eyes brought warmth back to her cheeks.

"Fascinating," Taranis murmured, pulling Asteria back into the moment. She blinked at her brother, dread seeping into her at the sight of his raised eyebrow.

Taranis was unpredictable—and bound to bring this up later.

"I'm not sure if you're familiar with all of these men," Asteria began, reeling back the conversation. "Taranis, this is Prince Orwell and Prince Piers Carraphim, the two spare heirs of Eldamain's throne. The other *strapping* fellow is Lieutenant General Gavril…"

"Faris," Gavril inserted as he bowed to Taranis. "Sir Gavril Faris, Your Majesty."

"I don't like that." Asteria curled her lip at Gavril, but he winked at her.

"Like it or not, sister, just because you don't follow proper etiquette doesn't mean the rest of us will follow your stead." Taranis walked around his long wooden desk, hands clasped behind his back. "I've had the pleasure of meeting Crown Prince Quintin Carraphim in the past, enough to hold a conversation, but I've merely met the brothers in passing. It's nice to formally make both your acquaintances, as I'm sure the reason you lot have come will require it.

"This has to do with the other Lyrans, does it not?" Taranis lowered into the large black velvet chair behind his desk.

Asteria nodded as Piers and Gavril sat back down in the chairs they previously occupied. She stood beside the remaining one, but Wells gently rested his hand against her lower back, the contact burning through her clothes. He cocked his head at the chair with an encouraging nod.

She frowned but still found herself slowly sitting on the soft cushion as he held her gaze the entire way down.

"If you're here"—Taranis leveled Asteria with inquisition, and she clenched her teeth—"I take it we're going down the Path of war."

Asteria sighed heavily, slouching. "I'm afraid it feels quite inevitable at this rate."

"And you're sure it's not our mother's doing?" Taranis smirked, but it was short-lived. He leaned forward, resting his forearms on the corner of his desk. "I suppose your presence also means that Gallus is partaking in this?"

"He's the one responsible for all of it." Asteria's voice came out flat, but a hollowness echoed in her chest with her next breath.

There was a featherlight touch across the top of her shoulder, but she didn't dare draw more attention to the *something* happening between her and Wells until she had a moment to understand it better herself.

"How do you feel about his involvement, Asteria?" Taranis's gaze flickered rapidly across her face, and her brow twitched imperceptibly.

"It's neither here nor there." This time, her voice was quieter than she wanted it to be.

"Alright then." Taranis reclined against the chair as Asteria's chest tightened with her aching heart. "What's to be done?"

What *was* to be done?

Asteria tried to push away the thought of what this all meant for her and her father, just as she'd been doing since learning the Obsidian Decay was because of him. Still, she couldn't stop the thoughts from flooding her mind.

Deep down, she knew her resentment toward her father about his *technical* infidelity was petty and had no true basis. In time, the resentment would've continued to fade.

After all, it was over thirty years ago, a blink in her six hundred years of existence. Despite that tiny seed in her heart, it was simply that.

A measly seed.

Now she feared what this deliberate separation meant.

She loved her father dearly. A part of her still didn't believe he'd gone to this extent to achieve his strange experiment. At the same time, she couldn't say for sure whether that was what all of this was about. He'd tried to explain it to her, and while she understood what he was saying, she didn't *truly* understand.

Asteria struggled to reconcile this version of Gallus with her father—the same man who'd taught her to fight with her Aether and starfire with patience. The same man who'd held her when she'd learned Rod impregnated a human. The same man who'd encouraged her resilience...

He couldn't be the same man trying to incite harm against humans.

"Asteria?"

She snapped her gaze to Taranis's piercing silver eyes as he inclined his head.

Her mouth propped open, but words failed her.

"Start training your men," Piers interjected from beside her.

"Oh?" There was intrigue hidden in Taranis's bright eyes as he dragged them to where Piers sat.

Asteria dropped her gaze to her lap, picking at her nails until a gentle caress passed over her shoulder again, and they relaxed away from her ears.

She didn't even realize she was tense.

"I'm sure they're trained well for defense and minor skirmishes." Piers rested both hands on the arms of his chair, his voice level, body relaxed. "You have a land advantage with your entire continent being your country. Unfortunately, the majority of the fighting will likely occur on the Main Continent."

"Minor skirmishes?" Taranis scoffed. "They're trained for war."

"But a war with Gods?" Piers offered a somber grin.

Taranis drummed his fingers on the desk as he pursed his lips, scrutinizing each of the men individually before peering at Asteria. He blinked once before inhaling sharply. "Why are all of you here? My sister could've delivered this news without the assistance of Eldamain's... finest."

Piers stiffened beside her, and Taranis's taunting sobered her instantly.

"Danica, Morana, and Rod sent Sybil to Eldamain shortly after the meeting with the other Gods went poorly," Wells explained, the rumble of his voice a strange but welcome comfort. "I'll assume Danica warned you about what occurred, but Eldamain was tasked with corralling the countries most likely to protect humans."

"Who are those countries?" Taranis rubbed at his beard as he observed the map of Aveesh on his wall.

"We intend to ally with yourselves, Riddling, Etherea, and Celestia." Wells swiped a finger down Asteria's arm as he adjusted his grip on her chair. She was unsure if he meant to keep her calm at the mention of Celestia, but that was precisely what the gesture did. "We had a brief conversation with Celestia before coming here, and we plan to journey to Riddling and Etherea next, in that order."

"Is Celestia not yours to command, sister?" Taranis didn't move his head from where it was angled toward the map, only his eyes peering at her. "Is your presence not evidence of your allegiance?"

"You know better than that," Asteria said, glaring at him. "I'm not our mother, nor am I the other Lyrans. I give them a choice and hope they do the right thing."

Taranis hummed, tapping a finger against his nose before placing his palms on the desk and slowly rising from his chair. "None of these countries have ever been allies, at least not as far back as my knowledge serves me. What say you, sister?"

Asteria searched her memory, glimpses of the past flashing rapidly through her mind. She searched her entire existence as best she could but realized Taranis was correct.

Celestia had always been a neutral country, but the other four had never allied before—not in a way to guarantee support in war.

There was never such a war. Not one that involved the entire world.

"We march to war hand in hand…" Taranis trailed off, raising his eyes to Piers and Wells. "Tell me, Prince Orwell. What happens after we succeed?"

Heavens above. Asteria rolled her eyes, but she wasn't entirely shocked.

She wanted to believe a war that threatened an entire race of Beings would be enough for kings to set aside bargains and treaties. They required recompense for their help because they couldn't fathom drawing up arms together for the simple matter of doing what was right.

"You know, brother, it's due to entitlement and ambition that the world is even in this predicament," Asteria voiced, tilting her head as her hand rested against her collar. "I'm disappointed."

Taranis let out a harsh laugh as he shot Asteria a look that meant he knew disappointment was not what she felt, nor did he care. "You may have spent most of your existence on Aveesh amongst the Beings rather than with the Lyrans in Eonia, but you've never been a diplomat.

"You've never needed to be one." Taranis leaned forward on his desk with a crooked grin. "You may deny it with your every breath, but you *are* a Lyran and, therefore, a Goddess. The world kept you out of diplomatic matters until it involved Lyrans. Besides, your baby brothers have taken up the diplomatic mantle for you."

Asteria flicked her hand at Taranis, a stream of black Aether soaring toward him. She heard a gasp beside her, but Taranis smirked and pointed his hand at the Aether. A spark of lightning danced across its surface, obliterating it.

She flipped him her middle finger, and Wells snickered behind her.

"Tell me why we continue to acquaint ourselves with the children of Gods," Gavril grumbled low to Piers.

"Prince Quintin has proposed a treaty between Eldamain, Etherea, The Northern Pizi, and Riddling." Wells reached into the pocket of his cloak, retrieving a rolled parchment. He moved to the desk and passed it to Taranis. He unrolled the parchment as Wells explained, "There are five articles outlined within the treaty. You're more than welcome to keep this copy for yourself. It's a draft and can be amended if need be.

"The first article outlines maritime cooperation amongst our countries. The second expands the military and defense pact beyond this war and ensures peace between us." Wells stepped back, his hand resting on the arm of Asteria's chair.

She couldn't tear her gaze from him. Despite being the youngest brother, the way Wells spoke commanded the room. How he presented the articles—the authority in his voice, the air of virility around him—made even her want to partake in the agreement.

"Article three proposes an exchange of culture and knowledge," Wells continued, his damned finger skimming her arm again. All her attention honed in on that single point of contact. "It even proposes establishing a grand library in one of our countries. The fourth article simplifies the trade of goods dependent on the resources each country has to offer over coin, and the final article proposes a council molded after the recent amendment to the Academy's Council of Elders. Two representatives from each nation meet each year to maintain the bond."

Asteria startled, her mouth parting. Wells must have felt her eyes on him because he peeked down at her with the ghost of a smile.

"I thought you'd like that." He winked, but she was distracted by the flutter in her chest—low, soft, and deep. Her throat ached, startling her, and not because she was hurt.

Why does this mean something to me?

"This is quite the treaty." Taranis perused the parchment outstretched before him. Even if he hid his excitement from the others, the Energy swirled in him as he read it. She knew her brother well enough. He was intrigued, possibly impressed, and those wheels in his head were turning. "How long would this stand before it's renewed or dissolved?"

"One hundred years," Wells answered, tilting his head. "While none of us from Eldamain will be alive to continue this treaty, we anticipate you and Phoebe will be. There's a strong possibility Dionne would also be alive. If anything, that puts your countries at an advantage."

"Are the terms negotiable?" Taranis rolled up the parchment, carefully placing it on his desk as he stared intently at Wells.

"Once the countries agree to join, we'll have a meeting where you can discuss any negotiations or preferences you have for some of the terms outlined in any of the articles, Your Majesty." Wells dipped his head as he stepped back behind Asteria's chair.

"I'll provide timber and steel." Taranis paused, narrowing his eyes. "But only if Riddling provides shipwrights and Etherea volunteers their scientists who created their irrigation system."

"You don't require anything specific from us?" Piers's tone was not subtle, laced with suspicion.

Taranis shrugged with a devious smirk, sitting back in his chair. "It seems my beloved sister favors your country." His gaze briefly bounced to Wells. "I won't inconvenience you by requiring something extra. I'll leave the trade choice to your king and crown prince."

Piers's frown deepened, but Asteria felt it directed at her.

She wished with her entire being—if only briefly—that she could set Taranis on fire.

"But wait"—Gavril paused, a long moment of silence as he contemplated what he was about to say—"Dionne is just as much your brother as Asteria is your sister."

"Dionne no longer sits on Riddling's throne. I also find the old man is far too bored with his grandson ruling." Taranis grinned, and Asteria knew what that grin meant.

Taranis was the youngest of Danica's children. There were well over one hundred years between Dionne and Taranis, yet they acted like common brothers by how they picked at and teased each other.

The men loved nothing more than antagonizing one another for sport.

"Are there any major plans set in place?" Taranis looked at Piers and Gavril. "If my memory serves me correctly, you're also a Lieutenant General, Prince Piers."

Piers nodded once. "It's a hypothetical plan at the moment, but we anticipate any battles to occur within Sylvan since Teslin and Allanis have the ocean on a majority of their coastline. Sylvan has a neutral climate compared to our winters up north or the intense heat in the south.

"In a perfect alliance, we would have your army support Eldamain's, and Riddling would support Etherea. We would attack in waves to tire them, and it would also ensure you don't send your entire military and leave your borders defenseless. Thankfully, Etherea has an extensive and talented army, so we would rely on Riddling to attack Thalassa. With their expertise in shipwright, we feel they are the best offense for that island."

The first thought Asteria had was how extensive this plan was to be thought up on a whim. Eldamain must have conducted a plan the minute Sybil spoke to them, which means either Sybil or the Carraphims had faith in Asteria joining.

She wasn't entirely sure how she felt about that.

The other thought was how formidable the plan was. While she wasn't a diplomat, she was a warrior, and one well-versed in strategy. There were a few holes, but she would wait until the agreement was settled between the four countries before vocalizing.

Hopefully, by then, they would have Celestia's agreement as well. She could use Odo's knowledge on a plan of attack.

"I commend you." Taranis pressed a hand to his chest, bowing to Piers in his chair. "You've given this quite some thought in a short amount of time, which proves to me you are the country to be leading the charge amongst us."

Taranis turned to Wells, and Asteria held her breath. She didn't like the playful gleam behind her brother's glowing eyes.

"I also tip my hat to you, Prince. I believe the treaty is something of your work. I know your brother, the crown prince. He has the face and appearance of a diplomat, but I'm not sure how his knowledge as one fairs."

Asteria felt Wells stiffen behind her at the comment, and she filed it away to inquire about later.

Taranis turned to her next, and her stomach dipped, contrary to how it did when Wells smiled at her. "I see what attracts you to him, sister."

Piers and Gavril sputtered simultaneously. Asteria breathed calmly as she reminded herself that Taranis was her beloved brother and she couldn't kill him.

Harming him seemed within reason, though.

CHAPTER 36

ASTERIA

After taking a moment to collect herself, she accepted Taranis's invitation for them all to rest before journeying on. He then forced them into another study meant for hosting.

Asteria was not sure what her brother typically hosted in this room, but it appeared Piers, Gavril, and Wells did when they reacted with various degrees of shock and surprise.

Circular mahogany tables were scattered around the right side of the room, each surrounded by four chairs with a lantern placed in the center. On the opposite side of the room were various velveted chairs, chaises, and settees—more so of the latter two.

Taranis beelined for the wall of cabinetry and proceeded to collect various glasses of wine and liquor. Asteria accepted the wine before setting off to one for the chaises by a grand window facing the Northern Mountains.

The men took to a few nearby chairs, talking amongst themselves. Asteria occasionally listened in on their conversations about travels and politics as she observed her second favorite view on Aveesh.

From this room's location in Castle Ashe, the twin peaks of the

Northern Mountains reached high into the endless night sky like two shadowy beacons. Stars dusted the sky, her blue starfire humming contentedly at the speckles of blue amongst the red and white.

"So, the two of you?" Taranis's voice climbed a pitch higher, something like fascination in his tone. Asteria whipped her head toward the lounging men, following his gaze to Piers and Gavril. "Well, I thought you were simply co-Lieutenant Generals—possibly very good friends."

"Did you not catch Gavril flirting with you in your study earlier? When he also used the phrasing to insult Asteria?" Piers's ankle balanced on his knee, and he swerved it to his left to kick Gavril in the leg.

The corner of Gavril's lips ticked up, and he gently rested a hand on Piers's thigh. Piers rolled his eyes but lost to his own smile.

"I mean no offense," Taranis explained, a glass of whiskey dangling from his fingertips. "It's not common in our culture for males to…"

"Fuck each other?" Gavril interrupted, and Wells choked harshly on his sip of whiskey.

Asteria burst into laughter at the horrified expression on Piers's face and the lack of emotion on Taranis's. Wells continued to sputter as he turned his head to her, flashing her a look of amusement.

"For lack of a better term, I suppose." Taranis righted himself, adjusting his collar. "I have also heard the women will… *fuck* each other."

Asteria snickered under her breath, tipping back her wine at this turn in conversation.

The Northern Pizi and Riddling did vary in cultures, not just from each other but from the Main Continent. The Northern Pizi was far more closed-minded when it came to anything sexual—or at least who could be involved in a sexual endeavor. Perhaps they were not as *creative* as the majority of the world.

Not that she had any room to talk.

Things were changing more with each generation, but both countries were still behind the Main Continent, so to speak. Riddling shared a similar mindset as The Northern Pizi but had a slight difference in how they took sexual partners. Riddling stuck to the traditional version of partnership with one husband and wife, while The Northern Pizi praised males who took multiple wives at once.

"Some, like our prince here, will take either male or female," Gavril said between sips, earning a rather pointed glare from Piers. "What?"

"It's not your place to air out my sexual life with a foreign king." Piers's eyes narrowed into thin slits, even as he briefly addressed said king. "No offense, Your Majesty."

"None taken at all," Taranis assured with a shrug, twirling his glass before directing it at Wells. "And you, Prince Orwell? Something tells me you definitely hold interest in women. Do you also accept men?"

"Are *you* flirting with *me*?" Wells grinned coyly over his glass, eyes twinkling in the light of the fireplace as Taranis's low chuckle reverberated through the room. Asteria was far too fixated on Wells. She found it unfair how easily he stunned her and sent her heart into an absolute fit. "I solely prefer women, unfortunately. Gavril tried to kiss me once when we were younger. I like to think when he learned I was only interested in our friendship, he went to the next best thing."

"You're not always charming, you know." Piers shot Wells an even deadlier glare than he'd pinned on Gavril. The latter only chuckled before throwing back the rest of his liquor.

Asteria was far more interested in what Wells said. "Gavril tried to kiss you? When was that?"

Gavril and Wells locked gazes, and Gavril started laughing like a jester as he journeyed to Taranis's expansive liquor cabinet to pour himself another glass.

"Gods…" Wells sighed, tapping the glass against his stubbled jaw. "It was right before I went to the Academy, so it must have been over ten years ago."

"How long have you two been together?" Taranis turned his attention to Piers just as Gavril sat down beside him.

"It's been four years." The way Piers looked at Gavril with such a soft expression made Asteria wonder why in the hell he was fraternizing intimately with Sybil.

"So you wield the Aether, like your eldest brother," Taranis mulled out loud, pointing at Wells. He gestured to Piers and Gavril next. "You inherited the Energy, and you are Lemurian from the House of Argo."

The men nodded or grumbled their agreement, and Gavril muttered, "Nereid."

"Do you know how long you'll live with your extended lifespan?" Taranis suddenly blurted, and Piers locked up.

While Andromedans could live hundreds and hundreds of years, most humans and Sirians lived anywhere from eighty to one hundred years if no ailments or disasters befell them. When Rod created the first Sirians, he modeled them after the humans already found on Aveesh, making their lifespans similar. Their forms simply withstood the power to hold the Aether or Energy, unlike the humans.

Lemurians' bodies were *more*, though. They mainly inhabited mortal-esque bodies, but their true nature mimicked the animals and creatures they shifted into, who had different lifespans and aged slower than mortals. Each House's qualities even peeked through their mortal forms, like scales on their skin, sharp canines, vertical pupils, and gills.

Lemurians lived anywhere from two to three hundred years, depending on the houses they reigned from.

Except the House of Argo.

Their averages hovered around four hundred years.

"Piers," Gavril said, but the prince lurched from the couch and slammed his glass on a nearby table as he stormed out of the room. Gavril offered a hollow glare at Taranis before exchanging a pained grin with Wells. "I have him."

Asteria focused on Gavril until the door slammed behind him, her heart aching for the two.

She knew far too well the trouble of extended lifespans. While she rarely connected intimately enough with mortals to be crushed by the grief of loss, she'd befriended enough to feel sadness when they passed.

She expected more from Taranis, what with him being an Andromedan. He was only eighty, and his first wife was still alive. While his other two wives were in their late twenties or early thirties, she was a woman in her seventies. All the while, Taranis had barely grayed or wrinkled, passing more in the age range of his young wives.

"You know better than that," Asteria scolded, sweeping her legs off the chaise to sit straight. "That was rude."

"I was merely curious." Taranis tipped back his glass to drain it. She deadpanned as he rose. "I can empathize with the Lemurian. I understand what it's like to come to terms with the fact you will outlive those you love. I thought perhaps the prince would have also prepared himself, especially considering he comes from the Carraphim family."

"What's that supposed to mean?" Wells asked, not unkindly.

"Your family has befriended Sybil rather intimately for many generations." Taranis set his glass beside the one Piers left behind. "Your family must be prepared to have those you love watch you wither while they don't age."

Wells only blinked, but Asteria simmered.

Then she understood precisely what Taranis was getting at when he turned his gaze on her before sauntering out, an eyebrow raised.

He was making a jab at *her* and whatever he thought he saw between her and Wells.

That stupid cunt.

"Stay out of it!" Asteria shouted as she jumped from her seat, pointing a condemning finger at the closing door. She pressed her lips in a tight line, nostrils flaring as she inhaled a forced breath.

"This day went far differently than I imagined it would," Wells muttered as he rose from the couch with his empty glass. He walked over to Asteria and held out his hand before her. "Another, or are you finished?"

She frowned at him until he eased the glass from her hand, and she realized it was empty. She cleared her throat and brushed off her skirts. "I think I'll need another."

He chuckled under his breath, nodding in agreement.

Asteria slowly lowered back onto the chaise, her eyes stuck on Wells's back, transfixed by the muscles that stretched beneath his tunic. He reached for the cabinet and grabbed the whiskey and wine, sleeves tightening around the tops of his shoulders and arms. Something wicked but wonderful curled low in Asteria's stomach and she remembered what transpired last night.

Was that only last night?

"You have a heavy gaze," Wells suddenly said as he turned around with their now-fulled glasses. "It's how I always know when you're watching me."

Asteria's mouth dropped open. He extended her wine glass, which she silently accepted. He smirked as he pressed his glass to his lips and sat beside her on the edge of the chaise.

"I don't watch you," Asteria finally said, albeit weakly. She poured a generous mouthful of the tart liquid down her throat.

"You don't seem too convinced by that statement." Wells rested his forearms on his legs, hunching forward. He still angled his head toward her. "If it's any reprieve, I enjoy you watching me."

"Of course you do." She scooted closer to the back of the chaise, leaning her elbow on it as she narrowed her eyes on him. "You were the one who admitted earlier that *you* watch *me*."

"I also said I listen." That reminder did nothing good for the control she attempted to reel in on this conversation. Wells tipped the rim of his glass to her, adding before sipping again, "I also don't try to hide it."

"That's plenty obvious." Asteria turned her gaze away, attempting to spot the dark peaks outside as a distraction.

It didn't work because Wells was far too good with his words. "I don't hide my affections and attraction, if last night was any indicator."

Asteria stiffened, and heat immediately gathered between her legs. She shut her eyes as she swallowed before painstakingly swiveling her head back to Wells.

If she were a weaker woman, she might've folded at the sight of the damned smirk he constantly flashed her, but she knew how to outwit many—especially men.

Except she was far too aware Wells was winning the battle of wits between them.

Asteria set her wine glass on the stone ground beneath the chaise before adjusting herself. She sat crossed legged beneath her skirts, facing him fully.

"Since you're the one to bring it up once again, I suppose we should discuss last night." She breathed through the swirling in her chest at the memory.

Teach me, Blue.

"Only if you want to discuss it." Wells set his glass down before twisting his body to her, bracing his hand behind him. "What is it you would like to discuss?"

"Why did you come to my room in the first place?" She believed she knew the answer, but she wanted to make sure.

"There was blue light coming from beneath your door," he explained with a shrug. "Naturally, after battling Sirians in Teslin, I wanted to make sure there was no danger."

"Erika had already showed you to your quarters, though." The sly grin ticked at the corner of her lips. "Had you not retired for the night?"

Something flashed in his eyes, and while brief, she knew immediately what it was when the Aether churned recklessly in his chest.

Disbelief.

"Were you coming to my chambers, Wells?" She sat straighter, hands tucked in the gap between her legs. "What were you coming to my chambers in the night for?"

"To speak with you," he answered immediately, startling her.

She anticipated a deflection, or even a temporary explanation to divert from her leading question. After her interactions with Wells over the last six or so months, she should've known better.

"And what did you wish to speak to me about?" She tilted her head, squinting.

"I enjoy your company," Wells admitted, his eyes searching her face and drawing down her neck. Chills broke out across her skin as she straightened her back further. "We spent most of yesterday fighting beside one another, and I wanted a moment just to talk with you."

She blinked rapidly, unable to counter.

Asteria hadn't expected that at all.

"That startles you." He frowned, and she jumped at the contact on her knee. She glanced down to see his hand slide closer to her, his thumb caressing.

In fact, his entire body inched closer.

"I'm not accustomed to men searching me out at night just for"—she latched onto the freckles spattered across his nose—"conversation."

"I thought you said you hadn't needed a man in one hundred and fifty years." Heavy lids peered down at her.

"One hundred and twenty." She was breathless, her eyes unable to focus on a single thing about him. The freckles, the ring around his irises, his lips, his broad shoulders…

When she recalled him watching her last night, she was certain she would combust from the heat spreading through her body.

Wells only hummed, either at the correction in time or silent tension between them, nodding his head slowly. "Was there something else you wanted to talk about regarding last night?"

Asteria blinked herself out of her transfixion, leaning back from him, but only a little because she felt the heat radiating from him. "You said you learned a lot last night."

"Quite a bit." His smile widened as his eyes darkened.

"I should test you." She gently brushed her fingers against his on the chaise, batting her eyelashes. "To see how well you were paying attention."

"You had my *undivided* attention, Blue." His hand moved from under hers, but it wrapped firmly around her knee. It traveled up her thigh as he angled closer. "There were a few things I would've added to the curriculum. Despite that, there was still a lesson to be learned."

Asteria fought the fire growing inside her and her raging heart. She wasn't sure which direction she wanted to take this conversation. He laid out two paths for her: the curriculum or the lesson.

"What's going through that beautiful head of yours?" He was inches from her now, breath mingling between them.

"What would you have added to the curriculum?" Her heart hammered in her chest as she waited in frenzied anticipation to see if this was the right question to ask.

A tiny piece of her considered Wells was cunning enough to spin the same answer for either way the conversation went.

"The one thing that can only be learned through a hands-on demonstration." His gaze fell to her lips, and they began to tingle. "I learned how you like to be touched, but have yet to learn how you like to be kissed."

Oh.

She didn't expect a kiss. By no means was she disappointed—or at least that's what her body told her. No, according to her body, she *yearned* for a kiss.

Then she realized it was her move now. This was him asking to kiss her.

She enjoyed this playfulness too much.

"I suppose…" She couldn't breathe. Her lungs filled too quickly and not enough. She couldn't remember the last time she'd kissed someone and was suddenly quite conscious about it. "I suppose I have availability for a brief demonstration."

The corner of his lips twitched.

Wells's hands slowly slipped to the side of her neck, and her eyes shut involuntarily, body humming. He tucked his thumbs beneath her temples and brushed his nose against hers. She tipped her head when his lips neared, his breath caressing her upper lip. The blood in her veins heated to an unbearable degree, her core clenching. Her want took over, shattering her patience.

She pressed her lips firmly against his.

Wells stiffened, and neither of them moved for a moment, testing this brief press of lips.

The same feeling from the garden at the Academy creeped back in, but this time, it was accompanied by a single word.

Safe.

She was safe here with him.

Too soon, he pulled away. Asteria wondered if it wasn't what he expected until his arms flexed beside her, still holding her head, his rapid breaths matching her own.

He was holding himself back.

Something swelled within her; the only thing that could stop it was his lips on hers once more.

"Again," she whispered, barely audible. She swore a low rumble rattled between them before he kissed her with more purpose.

Sparks shot through her veins when their lips connected this time, a jolt that released a heavy breath. Her shoulders relaxed as she clung to his wrists, his tongue tentatively stroking the seam of her lips, asking for permission.

She granted it, and she came *alive.*

Everything fell away; she forgot where they were and didn't care. His lips parted with hers, and she followed an instinct within her, allowing him to guide her. Every time his lips moved, desire instinctively drove her, the heat gathering low in her stomach rising higher and higher.

When Wells's hand slipped into the hair at the back of her neck, she wanted to feel his. She needed to find out if his curls would wrap around her fingers, if they were soft or coarse.

She was the one to disconnect them, but it wasn't for long. Her breath trembled in the silence between them, and her hands drifted up his forearms, tracing the subtle lines of muscle. When her palms skimmed the curve of his biceps, something fluttered low in her belly.

She lifted to her knees, and Wells's pupils pulsed once as he watched, ever so still as if she were some wild thing he feared would vanish if startled. She smirked as she swung a leg over his, settling in his lap. All that drove her was the need to be *closer*, to feel *safer*.

"Blue," he whispered.

No—*prayed*.

She pressed her forehead to his, sliding her hands across his shoulders and up the nape of his neck, finally tangling with his curls.

They did, in fact, wrap around her fingers, arguably the softest hair she'd ever felt.

His eyes shut with a quiet, tender moan, like her touch had undone something in him. The sound went straight to her core, unraveling her restraint.

The third time their lips met, they kissed as though they were starved—like they'd come across something so inimitable they wished to be consumed by it.

Tongues tangling and lips parting wider, they devoured one another. She tugged his hair harder, tipping his head just right to deepen their angle. He answered with his hands at her back, sliding down and pressing her against the hard planes of his chest.

When she rolled her hips against him, his teeth grazed her bottom lip, and she nearly gasped at the wave that shot through her. The need bloomed, sharp and sudden.

More.

Her body cried out for more in every nerve with every breath.

Everywhere. Anywhere. Now.

But that last word stopped her, plunging her back into reality.

This was want, and it was too much, too fast because wanting him felt like more than just a kiss.

Wells must have sensed her hesitation because they pulled back simultaneously. Asteria was pleasantly surprised to find the same bewilderment reflected on his face. They searched each other for the answer to how they'd gotten here, her hands still stuck in his hair and his firmly gripping her waist.

"Did you—" She panted, absolutely breathless. "Was that—"

"If you're going to ask if I enjoyed that"—he paused to catch his breath, his grip flexing—"it's taking every drop of restraint right now to be respectful."

If any other man had said something like that to Asteria, they would've found themselves flung across the room.

From Wells's lips, though, that tension coiled deep within her pulsed.

"It's late, though," he whispered, his hands journeying back up her body and neck to frame her cheeks. "We have another eventful day tomorrow."

Asteria only nodded. He smiled lazily before bringing her back for a quick kiss.

Fleeting, but it still felt like *more*.

Wells held her hands as she clamored ungracefully from his lap, averting her gaze when she caught the slight strain against his slacks. He guided her to the door, his hand stuck to her lower back until they entered the hall. From there, he stuffed his hands in his pockets but remained beside her, their shoulders brushing.

They walked to her room in silence, and she stayed in front of her door as he journeyed to the one beside hers. He bobbed his head as he opened it.

"Until tomorrow, Blue." He disappeared into the dimly lit room, and she took that as her cue to enter her own.

Asteria fell against the door, her head lolling back once it shut.

She knew, without a doubt, that she'd started down a path from which she feared there was no returning.

CHAPTER 37

MORANA

Morana journeyed up the many steps to the second floor of her abode, the emerald green stone glistening with streaks of gold cast from the chandeliers.

She could've easily portaled or glided through the air to travel around her home, but something about the mortal act of walking allowed her to think better, running through the ways everything they were doing could go absolutely wrong.

She didn't understand at what point in their ruling over this Realm that it'd all gotten out of hand, so much so they were now on the brink of war.

When Morana first agreed with Danica and Gallus to go on their quest across the Universe, she never believed this would be the outcome. There were so many tales of Lyrans who established themselves in various Realms to share the gifts they were granted.

So where had they gone wrong? How had they become so divided?

Morana refused to believe the catalyst was when she'd placed Sybil's soul into the drakon. As far as she knew, she was the only Lyran granted the power of Life and Death who never used the ability to reincarnate souls.

It was inconceivable that the first and only time she'd truly used her gift, the act hurtled their world into chaos. It didn't make sense when others across the Universe could use such a gift without complications.

Then again, they rarely ever learned what became of those who traveled beyond their home. Most never came back, and those who did spoke vaguely of the worlds they'd left behind.

As she rounded the corner toward the room she once thought would hold souls waiting to be reincarnated, Morana stopped in her tracks just within the doorway, blinking at the figure within.

"Valeria?" Morana clenched her fists as she inched closer to where the Lyran stood rather ominously in her mortal form. "You can't be here."

"This was once my home, too, Morana," Valeria said, shrugging one shoulder, her long, cherry red hair shifting with the movement. "I do miss it some days. Don't you miss when we lived together?"

It was a trick question, one she found herself asking occasionally. She never knew how to answer. "I cherish the memories of our life before you betrayed me, if you must know. But I don't miss you presently."

"That is very unkind to say to someone you love." Valeria pouted those full, pink lips, tilting her head to the side and blinking deep red eyes that reminded Morana of blood. "Why do you treat me so?"

"Valeria." Morana deadpanned, unfazed by her attempt at seduction. "I've known you for as long as we've been alive. Most of my existence was spent with you, save for the last five or six hundred years." She gently caressed Valeria's jaw, her fingers tracing the pointed bone to her chin. "I don't easily fall for your feigned innocence."

Morana walked away from Valeria toward the empty pillars lining the farthest wall.

"Don't be so drab, Morana." Valeria scoffed, quiet footsteps echoing behind her. Morana stilled when Valeria's presence vibrated behind her, warm breath tickling her neck. "Gallus tells me you have never taken another."

At the mention of Gallus, Moran's eyes widened. She whirled around, finding Valeria mere inches from her face.

That son of a bitch.

She peered down at her, eyebrow raised. "First of all, telling me you're spending time with Gallus doesn't gain you favor. Second of all, it's not his business to tell you because it's not *your* business."

"But it's true?" Valeria's eyes pulsed once as though she contained fire within her. "You've been celibate since?"

"I have no interest in others." Morana didn't fully understand why she felt the need to elaborate. Maybe she wanted to incite guilt within her former partner, no matter how unlikely that emotion was for Valeria. The other part wanted to rub it in Valeria's face that she was better than her. "You were the only one I ever loved, ever shared a bed with. Unlike you, I never fathomed loving another. I still don't."

"Yet you say you don't miss me despite holding to your virtue because you have no draw to another," Valeria whispered, her hand reaching up to cup Morana's cheek. She lurched away, snaking around Valeria's form to create distance again. "You see my confusion."

"Your confusion has nothing to do with my actions and everything to do with your inability to acknowledge who and what you are." Morana pivoted to face Valeria, pointing a damning finger at her. "As far as I'm concerned, the woman I once loved no longer exists. The minute you betrayed me and had a child with another was the moment I realized you'd truly lost yourself to your power. You're still that stranger who wears the skin of the love of my life."

Valeria's face remained neutral, but the flicker of red glowing behind her mortal eyes revealed Morana struck where she intended.

It didn't give her as much satisfaction as she would've liked.

"I never meant to hurt you, Morana," Valeria insisted, her voice drawing with a plea. "You have to understand that."

"I will never understand because that's exactly what you did." Morana shook her head, her two braids whipping her shoulders. "I don't know what you thought would happen when you cheated on me with a Sirian male."

"It was a mistake!" Valeria rushed upon Morana far too quickly, her cold hands gripping her face. "It was one mistake in our entire existence with one another. You can't condemn me for eternity because of that."

Morana's heart palpitated wildly in her throat. She couldn't remember the last time she was this close to Valeria, let alone the last time she touched her. She regretted it immediately because Valeria's peppermint scent wrapped around her, soaking into her senses and amplifying them.

"I can, and I will." Morana's eyes flicked across Valeria's face, her mortal form's soft, pale skin flawless. She always enjoyed this form, but contrary to what Valeria believed, she didn't shy from her altered god-form.

"Remember what it was like raising Sybil in this home together?" Valeria asked, leaning in as she used her grip to lure Morana closer. "She was so small when we saved her."

Morana's eyes shut briefly as she recalled the memories of their daughter. It was centuries ago, but Morana would never forget a single year of Sybil's life.

Valeria always loved helping the small children of Aveesh, whether human or Sirian. It was one of her more endearing qualities Morana favored—and missed.

Valeria adored children, and there was always a tiny twinge of guilt within Morana that they were two females in partnership. If it wasn't already difficult for Lyrans to have children, they ensured the probability was zero when they fell in love.

The children of Aveesh made Valeria happy, though, and Morana never once questioned how much time she spent with them. The only concern Morana ever had was how often she found Valeria healing the children she favored from deathly diseases or fatal wounds.

It was dangerous for Lyrans to use their powers so frequently and grandly in such a short amount of time.

When Sybil was attacked by a young drakon, Valeria was already weakened and couldn't repair the damage to the child's poor body. She begged Morana to save Sybil and find another form to put her in. Morana explained the repercussions, that she couldn't take the soul out of another living child to put Sybil's in its place.

It was then Valeria showed Morana she had infected the drakon with a disease that had stalled its heart. Morana was unsure if putting a soul into a damaged creature would ensure resurrection.

Valeria said she could heal the empty vessel so Sybil could live.

That was exactly what she did, and it cost them both.

"Her giggles when we would chase her through the halls," Valeria reminisced, her thumb stroking Morana's cheekbone. "Her persistence to master flying in her drakon form. She was adorable as a little drakon and has made a magnificent grown one. The largest of this world."

"She is beautiful," Morana whispered, blinking at her former lover. "She turned out to be an incredible Being."

"The first of her kind, her prophecies near the magnitude of Dola's." Valeria pressed their foreheads together, chills spreading from the point of contact through Morana's body. Her heart continued to hammer in her chest. "Maybe we could live that life again. We could raise another child together."

Morana frowned, pulling back enough to survey Valeria's face. "What do you mean?"

"I know what I did was unfathomable," Valeria explained gently, inhaling sharply. "I just wanted another child to care for, and we couldn't repeat what had happened with Sybil. I sought someone to give us a child we could care for together."

Morana's face slackened, because this was the first time Valeria had ever accepted what she did as a fault, even if there was still no apology.

"I should've spoken to you about it, but I wanted to surprise you." Valeria tapped her nose against Morana's, breath skating across her lips.

"I know how foolish that was of me."

"You want to bear another child?" Morana warred with the emotions in her chest. She had her daughters, Sybil and—for all intents and purposes—Asteria. Neither were of her blood, but she loved them as her own. "I couldn't live through—"

"I wouldn't bear the child." Valeria smiled, but it was tight. "You could this time, so you have a child of your own blood."

Morana's mouth dropped open as she realized the deception this was turning into.

To think she nearly fell for the bullshit spewing from Valeria's mouth.

"I *never* wanted children, Valeria," Morana exclaimed, shoving her with all her strength. Unexpectedly, Valeria tumbled to the floor on her ass. "That was *you* who wanted children. When you saved Sybil, I saw how badly you lost yourself to your powers, healing and curing children for so many years. Infecting and healing the drakon pushed you over the edge, Fracturing you. You couldn't be the mother Sybil needed. I had to step in for both of us."

"So you don't even love Sybil?" Valeria curled her lip, and her mortal eyes morphed into deep red, glowing orbs.

"That's not what I'm saying!" Morana shouted, throwing her arms out. "I love Sybil. I would never and will never turn her away. She's my daughter, and I happily give her my motherly love. I give her the love she deserves from me and the love she should've received from *you*."

Morana's heart thundered for a new reason as her veins illuminated in a kaleidoscope of colors. She lowered her arms, taking steady breaths as she watched Valeria rise from her position.

Her mortal skin slowly shed from her body, revealing the god-form beneath. Her skin paled to a stark white, like bone, her cheeks hollowing and features shadowing. The skin drew tight over her face, black veins stretching up and down her forehead and cheeks from the dark eye sockets glowing red from within. The red mist swirled around her, leaking from her hair until the strands were colorless.

"So there's no hope for us?" Valeria's words were cavernous, thrumming through the air.

"No, Valeria." Morana shook her head as a heavy weight settled her chest. "It can never be what it once was, and you have to accept that."

Valeria screamed in frustration like dozens of ravens screeching in the night. The mist pulsed violently as it thickened, a sinister grin pulling at her thin black lips.

"So be it." Valeria narrowed her eyes at Morana, and something foreboding wrapped around her, cutting off her air supply. "You took my daughter away from me. Now, I will take her away from you."

CHAPTER 38

SYBIL

S ybil unclipped the clothes from the line stretching overhead in front of her home, haphazardly tossing them into the wooden basket at her feet. A cool spring breeze whipped through the clustered abodes around her, voices carrying from every which way on the outskirts of Heridy alongside the faintest hint of lilies from a nearby bush.

As she gathered the final blanket, a quick image flashed through her mind just before it occurred.

"Hello, dear sister," the grating voice announced from behind her.

"You're quite far from home once again." Sybil gathered the basket in her arms, conjuring her patience to appropriately manage whatever it was Endora had come for. She twisted on her heel with a pained grin. "To what do I owe the pleasure, Endora?"

"Can one sister not visit another?" Endora stepped onto the lawn, her hands clasped within the ridiculous sleeves of her cloak. "You and Asteria aren't even sisters, yet you spend nearly every waking moment together."

The weather was far too warm for Endora to be wearing such a dark, heavy piece of clothing. Sybil supposed the Andromedan was perpetually cold as someone who surrounded herself with corpses.

"We don't," Sybil corrected, hitching the basket on her hip. "If my memory serves me correctly, you called me useless the last time we saw one another."

"Oh, come now." Endora giggled through tight lips, and Sybil scowled. "You know I mean no foul. I meant your gift seems useless when you can't tell people what you see."

Sybil blinked, using every ounce of will to keep her face schooled in neutrality. "Right."

Endora sighed heavily, taking another step forward. "I don't wish to quarrel with you. I simply wish to hold a conversation. I understand Asteria and her Sirians at the Academy have concocted a remedy for the Obsidian Decay."

"If you're telling me you traveled all the way from Etherea to retrieve the ingredients from me, you've wasted your time." Sybil turned her back, walking toward the propped front door of her home. She called over her shoulder, "The Healer of Etherea should've received the potion by now."

"They did," Endora drawled, her feet shuffling behind Sybil. She stopped in her doorway, Endora only a few feet away. "That's not why I've come. I wish to speak to you about what I've discovered regarding the Obsidian Decay, especially regarding Queen Phoebe's involvement."

Sybil narrowed her eyes at Endora, something prickling in the recesses of her mind. The hairs on the back of her neck rose, but she wasn't sure what the drakon within was alerting her to.

Knowing Phoebe's involvement could answer whether or not she would side with Asteria and Eldamain. If Phoebe knew the entire time about the source of the Decay and was directly involved, it also meant it may not be safe for Asteria and the Carraphims to portal into Etherea at all.

All she saw was Piers's smile, and she relented with a heavy breath.

"You can come in," Sybil said, jerking her head toward her home. "Don't make me regret this, Endora."

"Thank you." She followed behind Sybil, stilling just within the door as Sybil dropped the basket before the settee in her living space.

Sybil eyed Endora with suspicion weighing on her shoulders. She chose to stand in the kitchen, leaning back against her counter , arms crossed over her chest.

Maybe she should've stayed outside in case she needed to shift into the drakon.

"Out with it, Endora," Sybil snapped as Endora's gaze perused her home. "Might as well make use of the time you took to travel here since whatever it is you need to say couldn't have been a letter."

"Why didn't you listen to what I told you to do in Allanis?" Endora asked, tilting her head. Sybil scowled, but Endora continued, "I told you to leave it alone and let me take care of the Obsidian Decay."

"I trust my instinct." Sybil shrugged, pursing her lips. "It told me to contact Asteria. Fate must've known Asteria could come up with the cure."

"It appears so." Endora squinted, her black eyes crawling across Sybil's shoulders. "Well, I suppose Aveesh will know the cure for the Decay now. Queen Phoebe will be pleased."

If Phoebe would be pleased about the cure, it meant she wasn't nefariously involved with the Decay, which only had Sybil anxiously pondering what in the Heavens Endora wanted, if not to discuss Phoebe.

"Are *you* pleased?" Sybil asked, flicking a white crimped curl behind her shoulder to mask the tremble of her hand from trying to restrain the thrashing drakon in her chest. "You don't seem like you're pleased. From how you spoke in Ghita, I thought Phoebe tasked you with searching for a cure."

"She did." Endora nodded, rolling her lips together. "The Decay appeared in Etherea first. Queen Phoebe has a positive relationship with her humans, considering her husband is one. They came to her immediately with the news, and she sought to rectify the illness. She knew I was the most skilled at identifying diseases, with our mother being the

Goddess of Healing and Disease."

"Indeed." Sybil simmered, a muscle ticking in her jaw.

She couldn't determine where Endora stood within this looming war. She'd mentioned Valeria, and yet she claimed to be assisting Phoebe. Regardless, Phoebe wanted to protect—not harm—the humans.

Either Endora had asked Valeria for assistance and she denied her, or Endora hadn't actually researched the disease as her queen asked of her.

The latter was more likely.

"Despite Valeria being the Goddess of Healing and Disease, it wasn't you who discovered the treatment, now was it?" Sybil straightened from the counter, stepping closer to Endora.

"Don't you mean despite *our mother* being the Goddess of Healing and Disease?" Endora mimicked Sybil's step, but it wasn't nearly as predatorial.

"Oh, no." Sybil chuckled low, sneering. "I mean Valeria. She's no mother of mine."

"How disrespectful you have grown with age," Endora chastised with a bite to her tone, those beady eyes penetrating as the Aether flickered in her Mark. "You consistently choose Morana over Mother and never refer to her by her matronly title. It wounds her."

"Oh, quit the act, Endora." Sybil waved a hand between them, shaking her head fiercely. "Valeria can only be wounded when she doesn't get what she wants. She isn't hurt by my denial of her love, but by my refusal to acknowledge her as my other adopted mother by name."

"You wouldn't be alive if it weren't for Valeria's pleading." Endora righted her even tone, as though what she said was fact and not opinion. "You know better than I that Morana refused to keep your soul on this plane until Valeria nearly lost herself to preserve the drakon body for you."

"She *did* lose herself!" Sybil laughed then, the sound broken. "That's why she's not my mother. She was too Fractured to be bothered with me. I don't care who was responsible for bringing me back from the dead, or who did or didn't want me to begin with. What matters is who cared for me when the time came, and Valeria wasn't there."

"Did you ever think Valeria wasn't there because Morana didn't give her the chance?" Endora minimized the space between them even more, and Sybil lifted her finger in warning. "It was Morana who believed Valeria had become Fractured, but she was too blind and selfish to see Valeria just wanted to be your mother. That was why she left and had me—because she never got to be yours."

"Valeria should know there were plenty of opportunities to make amends with me and establish some sort of relationship." Sybil rolled her eyes, rubbing her forehead. "Yet she sends *you* to… what? Attempt to rectify her wrongs when she and *my* mother stand on opposite sides of a prophecy? Mind you, *my* prophecy."

"No." Endora sighed, pouting. "Unfortunately, Valeria is well aware the sides are solidified."

"For fuck's sake," Sybil grumbled, throwing out her hands. "Why are you here, Endora—"

Endora tapped into that enhanced speed, moving faster than Sybil could catch, and Fate gave her no warning.

Suddenly, the Aether lashed around Sybil's wrists, yanking her arms wide and burning against her skin. She barely had time to blink before Endora's face surged into view, eyes alight with satisfaction and something crueler. Sybil grunted, her mouth falling open in silent disbelief as her eyes dropped.

Endora held the hilt of a blade, buried in Sybil's abdomen. Blood slowly leaked onto the fabric of her dress, crimson blooming in a slow, spreading halo.

"To send a message," Endora whispered, leaning toward Sybil's ear. The blade sunk deeper, that sting pulsing and screaming as Endora twisted it. "What better way to weaken a Lyran than to kill their child?"

Sybil should've known this was a trap. The first divide amongst the Lyrans was because of her, so it was only fair they would use her as the first true act of betrayal.

Endora yanked the blade out, and Sybil screamed at the unnatural friction as her muscles and tendons resisted. She was able to glimpse the gray-toned sheen before Endora plunged it into the other side of her abdomen.

This time, it wasn't just pain.

Lightning shot through her and her skin tore before it faded to numbness. Something inside her cracked. Not physically, but fundamentally.

Her limbs trembled from th sudden absence of strength, her power going dormant beneath her skin. The front of her gown dampened far more rapidly than it should have with her accelerated healing abilities.

"I'm not sure if you saw what type of blade this is," Endora said, smirking with malice as she stepped back, leaving the blade within Sybil's abdomen.

"Hematite," she whimpered as the Aether tightened around her arms, keeping her from pulling the tainted stone from her body.

Even if she hadn't seen it, she could feel it. The tainted element of the blade threaded into her veins, corrupting any enhanced capabilities. Her connection to Fate frayed and the drakon recoiled, both of them retreating deep within where she couldn't reach.

"The weakness of the Lyrans and Andromedans." Endora picked up a nearby cloth, wiping the blood off her hands and inspecting them in the light. "Do you feel it? The quiet inside you?"

Sybil groaned around the ache in her stomach, the urge to vomit rising in her throat. Her knees buckled, but the Aether bindings held her upright.

Hematite was a stone found within the Black Avalanches, an unknown element to the Lyrans until they journeyed to Aveesh. It reminded them of obsidian, except where that rock had an endlessness to its depths, hematite had a gray sheen when twisted in the light.

The stone was once mined and gifted as a ring to the First King of Aveesh, Enki, a son of Rod. He found that when he wore the ring, he didn't heal as quickly, and his enhanced strength and stamina were diminished.

A few more tests were conducted amongst the Lyrans and Andromedans, and they found the hematite muted or canceled out their powers and abilities when worn. Henceforth, the mining of hematite became outlawed in every country.

That didn't stop people from doing it, though.

"It will only be a matter of time before you pass out from your pain since you're not used to feeling it so acutely," Endora explained, and her body wavered as Sybil's consciousness fought for consciousness. "By then, you will have lost enough blood that I'm sure it will be near impossible to heal yourself. You will die from your wounds while Eldamain burns around you. Without Eldamain or Etherea, your side can't possibly win."

Sybil squinted, trying to keep her eyes open. She wanted to snarl, to fight Endora, but her jaw only locked, fingers twitching uselessly against the restraints.

Terror bloomed where fury once lived.

Her mother was an agent of Death, and yet she'd never felt closer to the force.

The deafening roar of a drakon shook the foundation of her home. Dust and debris rained down from the ceiling, and the ground beneath her feet trembled, followed shortly by a chorus of terrified screams.

"Just in time." Endora grinned, clapping her hands together as she stalked closer to Sybil. She inhaled short, quick breaths since any deeper ones stretched her stomach, sending spears of agony through her. "Tell me, sister, did you see your own death? Did you know it would be by my hands, or were you not privy to that information?"

"No." Sybil grunted as she forced her head up, the edges of her vision blurring as the wound stuffed with the blade burned like her blood was boiling. "But I saw yours."

Endora flinched, recoiling from Sybil.

So this was why Sybil couldn't tell Endora she'd seen her death when they ran into each other in Ghita.

Another roar penetrated the air, jars shuddering in the cabinets behind Sybil, and Endora's gaze shot to the ceiling. It sounded like logs rolling down a hillside somewhere within town.

Then again, everything felt far away.

"Let's hope Morana can find your body amidst the cinders."

As Sybil's vision faltered, Endora released the Aether from around her arms. She hit the ground with a sharp sting that rocked her entire body before succumbing to nothingness.

At least with the hematite stuck within her, she wasn't plagued by visions of what was to come from this decision.

CHAPTER 39

PHOEBE

Phoebe slammed her elbows onto her desk, the candle flickering wildly from the sudden motion. She rubbed her hands up and down her face and forced deep breaths through her fingertips, but it was useless to quell the nervousness and edge that had plagued her since Gallus graced her with his presence.

She'd barely eaten since, secluding herself within her study or spending time beside Dustin in the infirmary. The guilt of leaving her children with Maria weighed heavily on her shoulders, but the deal she'd struck with Gallus and the Andromedans curdled her stomach.

Phoebe couldn't muster the courage to look upon her children without tears welling in her eyes.

She'd convinced herself the protection of her family and country superseded the safety of humans in other countries. They weren't her responsibility; that belonged to those countries' royal families.

Bile burned the back of her throat, and she washed it down with the remainder of the harsh burning liquor.

A knock on the study door startled her far more than it needed to, and she swore under her breath as the glass shattered in her hand. She reached for a cloth on the bar cart, staunching the bleeding from the shards that cut her.

It would be my own fault for the first wound since losing my immortality.

"Fuck it all," Phoebe grumbled under her breath, throwing her body against the back of her chair. The same one Gallus had sat in. "Come in."

She was surprised to see Dustin limp into her office, sporting a cane in one hand, clutching his side with the other.

"What in the Gods' names are you doing here?" Phoebe jumped up from her chair, holding her hand out in front of her.

Dustin stilled, proceeding to roll his eyes as she lifted him an inch off the ground. She gestured toward herself, and he floated across the room until he stood before her desk.

"Was that entirely necessary?" he groaned, leaning his weight on the cane. "I'll need to rehabilitate my body back to working order eventually."

"You aren't supposed to be out of the infirmary yet." She leveled him with a glare that he averted, pretending the bookcase was far more fascinating. Her heart ached at the dim light behind those sea-green eyes, hoping it would brighten again with time. "What are you doing here?"

"Thorne informed me you've been in here since the incident." He lowered his voice, eyeing her. "You haven't been with Jeremiah or Emmalina."

The same guilt clenched her heart, and she had half a mind to fire Thorne for tattling to Dustin.

"Don't you think they're frightened?" he asked, studying her face. "They can't see me like this, or it will scare them more. Not having you there to assure them we're both okay will worry them into fits."

"Don't *you* think I know that?" The Aether coiled beneath her skin. "What would you have me do, Dustin? How am I supposed to look at my children after having to make the decision I did? How am I supposed to look at Emmalina as the heir to this forsaken throne and tell her that Mommy bargained with the bad people so they didn't massacre the humans she will one day rule? Or her family or her father—"

Her voice choked off into a sob as the weight of the last few days crumbled in her chest. Phoebe's hand clutched the column of her throat, and Dustin left his cane aside to slide across the corner of the desk. He pulled her into him, wrapping his arms around her shoulders and grasping the back of her head, trapping her arms between their bodies.

The tears flowed then, burning a path down her face and soaking his tunic. She trembled as her body forced her to accept this reality, fearful of the decision she'd made out of desperation and love.

"We'll figure it out, my moon." Dustin placed a rough kiss to the side of her head, resting his cheek against her hair. He held her closer, arms tightening around her like the safety net she needed. "We can't solve the world's problems—let alone our own—in a few days' time. There are people we can speak with and try to get messages to or from. There are things we can do to outsmart them. You are far more intelligent than Caine or Endora."

"I'm not smarter than my father," she muttered quietly into his shoulder, laying her palms flat on his chest.

He pulled back enough to tuck his finger under her chin, lifting it to force her gaze to his He peered at her over the tip of his nose. "Gallus may be some ancient Being not of this world, but you are *clever*. His arrogance will be his downfall. You don't need to know more than him to be smarter."

"We are siloed, Dee," she whispered, tears leaking from the corners of her eyes. "We can't speak with the countries publicly defending Gallus and his Lyrans. It will appear as though we are siding with them, and then we'll be forced into this war. I can't reply to Prince Quintin's letter, or it will appear we are going against Gallus's wishes, and they will attack us."

Dustin sighed, cupping her face as he brought his lips to her forehead. "We'll figure it out, Phoebe. We might not figure it out immediately, but we can do our best to start."

Her hands trailed down his abdomen, and she blanched when his eyes flashed in pain. She tore his hands from her face, hauling him toward her chair. "Gods, Dustin. You need to be resting. You can't help me if you're trapped in the infirmary for the foreseeable future or die…"

Dustin held her wrist tightly, gazing up at her from where he sat. He frowned at her still-bleeding hand between them. "We're both as mortal as any, Phoebe. You're just as susceptible to the injuries I've incurred."

She ripped her arm from his grasp, sighing as she hopped onto the edge of her desk. Dustin grumbled with a heavy breath, rolling his head. He dragged the chair closer, guiding her feet onto the cushion between his legs. Her heart nearly burst when he wrapped his arms around her legs beneath her knees, resting his chin on top.

"I didn't come here to only talk about what we will do and lecture you about our children." Dustin pouted, batting his sea-green eyes at her. "I'm sorry, love. I know you're under pressure more now than ever. I'm just as fearful for the kids as you are."

Her lips proved traitorous as they ticked up at his pleading expression. She stroked the side of his face, running her hands through his long black hair.

"What other news have you brought me?" She tucked a strand behind his ear before bracing her arm behind her around the massive pile of parchment.

"Asteria and Sybil were spotted fighting Lemurians and Sirians in Teslin," he blurted, startling her. She warred with confusion and anxiousness, possibly a twinge of jealousy. "They had the two younger Carraphim princes with them and one of their Lieutenant Generals."

Phoebe's face fell then, heart hammering in her chest as Gallus's words rang in her head.

…she blatantly ignored my warnings, putting her and me on opposing sides…

The sting of jealousy pulsed within her again, and it only got worse as Dustin continued. "We also have a reliable source that believes she was in The Northern Pizi with the two princes shortly after."

She was speaking to her brothers first.

Phoebe shoved the hurt down. The jealousy was warranted, but the hurt wasn't. She knew very well that if Asteria was helping Eldamain collect allies, she would go to King Taranis and Dionne first because she was closer to them and trusted them more.

But I'm the one with the human husband.

"Phoebe," Dustin said softly, his hands running up and down her calves. His chin lifted an inch from her knees. "You know she'll come here despite the strain in your relationship. She knows you respect humans just as much as the others, if not more."

"She'll save me for last." Phoebe cleared the hoarseness from her voice, averting her gaze. "She'll talk to Dionne and King Savaric Basu in Riddling next before coming to Etherea."

Dustin studied her intently. She knew he would find the emotions she was desperately trying to hide.

Phoebe hadn't seen Asteria since she'd graduated from the Academy, which was well over a decade ago. Her own sister didn't even attend her coronation last year, which only poured salt in the wound Gallus created by not attending either.

The people who were supposed to care for her—her actual blood—appeared to want nothing to do with her. When they did show her attention, they were harsh.

King Drogo was just a cruel, absent man who saw any form of fatherhood as a nuisance. Even in a reality where Phoebe actually was his daughter, she didn't foresee that changing the way he acted with her. Whenever he remembered that she was his sole heir—however illegitimate—he scrutinized her for her empathy and compassion.

Her mother, Petra, was a drunk who died a few years ago from her addiction. There was never a relationship there to begin with since she was either days deep into a bottle or sleeping off the liquor before heading into another stint.

When Phoebe finally went to the Academy, she thought finally getting to meet her half-sister would be her savior, pulling her away from the edge of the world she lived in—one that was keen on reminding her she was never truly wanted. She'd heard so many stories of Asteria's kindness to Sirians and her relationship with her other half-siblings, she'd thrived on hope.

How quickly her hope had burned underneath that blue starfire.

During Phoebe's first two years at the Academy, Asteria taught Warrior classes. As a newly married princess at the time, Phoebe was required to take the Diplomat class, but she'd took on other electives to fill her time.

Except she had no choice in the matter. Asteria had *demanded* she take Warrior classes because of her god-power, and she'd always sat in on them.

Her sister had never fully instructed Phoebe, though. Instead, she'd criticized her any time she practiced using her gravitational manipulation. Asteria would coach her for ten minutes before she went back to the shadows.

Once Odo Hesper appeared at the Academy, Phoebe had stopped existing. She didn't know how, but he'd cracked Asteria, and her sister spent all her time with Odo until he graduated.

"How do you feel about her coming here last?" Dustin squeezed her calves to get her attention. "Don't try to lie to me because you know I'll call you out on it."

She narrowed her eyes, her lips thinning.

"Phoebe—"

"It doesn't matter how I feel about it." Phoebe sighed, toying with the quill on the desk. "This is how things are. Asteria will come here on her own time as she normally does. Unfortunately, our father got here first. Even more unfortunate is that she didn't think he would come for me before she did."

"Be clever when she comes." Dustin lifted her feet, gently letting them fall to the ground. She held out her hands, and he firmly gripped them to boost himself from the chair. "You know she's powerful, and if she has King Taranis and Dionne on her side—not to mention Celestia—we would not need to fear your father's wrath."

Phoebe gnawed on the inside of her lip, chest tightening with all the possibilities of how Asteria's presence within Etherea could go terribly wrong for her kingdom. Before Asteria even arrived, she needed to find a way to let Gallus know. To maintain this neutral facade, she would have to hear her sister out at the least.

From there, though, she wasn't sure what she would do. The Carraphims no doubt would bring a treaty of sorts, but what good would a treaty do if the world as they knew it was about to change inevitably?

"Come with me to see the children," Dustin pleaded, minimizing the space between them so she was stuck between him and the desk. "You know they'll distract you from all this. They bring you so much joy, and I want to see that joy in you again."

Phoebe softened, leaning her head against his shoulder without putting too much weight on him. He wrapped his arms around her again, and she let him hold her, absorbing his level-headedness and patience.

She feared she would need a lot of it in the coming days.

CHAPTER 40

MORANA

M orana portaled into Eldamain immediately after donning her mortal form, and her heart plummeted at the sight of Heridy.

She spun to assess what was happening around her, the city a blur. A large drakon soared overhead, silver fire heating the air. The acrid stench of charred earth filled her nostrils, mingling with the sharper, sickening odor of overcooked meat.

She covered her mouth, eyes burning as ash drifted like snowflakes through the air. Around her, it was a nightmare of shattered homes and foliage consumed by flames, people fleeing from the wreckage. Screams echoed through the chaos, people running in every direction.

Eldamain was under attack.

A burst of Energy lit up beside Morana at the same time she spotted Sybil's open door. She tore her gaze away to peer at the Sirian beside her who was attempting to aim at the drakons flying above.

Morana's hand shot out, grabbing the Sirian by the shirt and yanking him to her. "Who do you serve?"

The Sirian male stared wide-eyed, and his heart thundered against

Morana's knuckles along with the throbbing panic of his soul. "Lady Morana—"

"Not the time!" she shouted over a nearby explosion. "Don't make me ask again."

"Eldamain," the male blurted, holding his hands up in surrender. "I serve Eldamain."

"Use the Energy and summon Asteria," she demanded. "Reach in and yell *Sybil*."

He nodded, and Morana threw the Sirian away from her, sprinting into Sybil's home.

Her heart stopped at the sight of her daughter sprawled motionless on the floor in a small pool of her own blood, vibrant crimson staining the tips of her white hair.

"That stupid bitch," Morana hissed through clenched teeth.

Rage ignited in her chest, mingling with the sharp-edged terror that threatened to tear her apart. Her mortal form shattered under the weight, the ground trembling beneath her feet as her god-form surged to the surface, a multitude of colors projecting across the walls in a burst of light.

She skidded to her knees beside her daughter, heedless of the blood soaking her gown as she gathered Sybil's head into her lap. Tears gathered at the corners of her eyes, and she couldn't recall the last time she'd cried.

But cradling the broken form of her child, Morana didn't care.

"Sybil," Morana cooed, petting the hair off Sybil's clammy forehead. She hovered a hand over her daughter's chest, but her familiar soul flickered restlessly as it fought the hand of death. "Please, no."

Inspecting the wound, Morana's heart hammered against her chest as blood continued to seep out. She tore off a strip from the sleeve of her gown, balling it up to staunch the bleeding. She considered leaving the dagger in to help with the second wound, but she did a double take at exactly what type of dagger this was.

"*No*," Morana gasped, ripping off another strip to prepare to pack the second wound as her entire being hallowed out.

If her instincts were correct, this blade *had* to come out.

Her hand wrapped around the hilt, and she immediately felt its wrongness. Slowly, she drew it out of Sybil, and launched it across the room. She quickly stuffed the cotton into the wound, muttering encouragement under her breath in hopes Sybil could hear her. Her chest tightened at the shallowness of Sybil's each breath.

A snap echoed through her home.

Morana jerked her gaze up to the now-cramped living area, eyes flitting over three males—a Lemurian and two of the Carraphim princes—before connecting with a frenzied Asteria. Her eyes widened as she beheld Morana, one eyebrow arched.

But she dropped her gaze to Morana's lap, and wrath flashed across her face with the endless night of her god-form briefly beneath her mortal skin.

"What the fuck happened?" Asteria growled, throwing herself to her knees beside Morana. Tears lined Asteria's eyes as she scanned Sybil's body. They stopped on the wound before registering the blood on the floor with another blue flash. "Why isn't she healing? Is she—"

"Hanging on." Morana's voice cracked as something damp and scalding tracked down her face. "The dagger. Hematite."

"Son of bitch," the Lemurian with purple eyes gasped, and the Carraphim princes' jaws dropped at the sight of Sybil.

The taller one with greener hazel eyes locked up, his skin ashen. He fell to his knees and crawled to Sybil opposite of Morana and Asteria without taking his eyes off her daughter.

"Morana!" Asteria snapped, forcing her attention to Asteria's wild, swirling blue eyes. "What. Happened."

"I don't know." Morana held in a sob as Sybil's soul vibrated. "I mean... I don't know the specifics. Valeria came to me and said she would take my daughter from me. I knew I had to come here immediately. I found her like this. I don't know who did it, but I have no doubt it's

Valeria's doing."

"Valeria?" the Lemurian muttered, frowning. He looked to the other Carraphim prince, speaking quietly. "I thought that was also Syb's mother."

"Not now, Gav. It's complicated," the prince grumbled to his friend.

The second joined them in the kitchen, squatting beside Asteria and placing a hand on her shoulder. She jolted and drew her attention to the male. Something passed between them, and she turned back to Morana. "You need to take her to Celestia—"

"Her soul," Morana whispered, veins pulsing brightly along with the sob lodged in her ribcage. "The body is failing it."

"Get her to Celestia *now*," Asteria repeated, her breath quivering as she tried to quell the panic in her voice. "Ask for Odo and Erika Hesper. Tell them I sent you. Tell them about the dagger—"

Sybil tensed in Morana's arms as she gasped for air, but the breath transformed into a heartbreaking cry that tore through her as she no doubt agitated her wounds. Morana's heart launched into her throat as her grip tightened, holding Sybil's shoulders down.

Her usually bright green eyes were too dull for Morana's liking. Her lips quivered at the sight of Sybil's heavy-lidded gaze bouncing slowly between her, Asteria, and the Carraphim prince kneeling at her other side.

"Momma—" A sob broke through Sybil's lips, and she trembled. "Endora…"

Morana hushed her, leaning down and pressing her lips to her forehead. "We're here, my drakon. We're going to help you."

"I'll kill her," the Carraphim snapped at his brother, his eyes and Mark pulsing with the white-gold light of the Energy. "I swear to the Gods—"

"Don't swear too hard since there's at least one in this room," the other responded, earning a glare from Asteria. "I didn't say two, but I left the option open in case you want to be one right now."

"I can't stand you," she grumbled before drawing Morana's attention back to her. "Morana, you need to go now—"

Screams pierced the air as the ground quaked in rhythmic thuds, a deep, guttural bellow clogging the air.

"What in the *fuck* is going on out there?" Asteria shouted, lurching to her feet.

"I'll go with them," the Carraphim opposite Morana said, and Sybil's slack, heavy-lidded gaze stayed on him. Her hand twitched, and he caught it, slipping his bloodied hand into hers. "I won't leave you."

"We have to go help with whatever's going on outside," the second Carraphim interrupted, his gaze bouncing between the Lemurian and Asteria. "I have a terrible hunch about who those heavy steps belong to, and we'll need a Lyran's help to protect Eldamain right now if our favorite drakon is down."

Asteria's nostrils flared, her head swiveling between Morana and the male. "Okay… Piers, go with Morana, and if *anything* unfavorable happens, you call for me. Do you understand?"

"Of course," he agreed quietly, nodding once. "And Riddling?"

"We'll take care of it," the brother said, nodding. "Stay with them."

Asteria held her attention on Sybil for a heartbeat longer before she stormed out of the home, the other two males following closely behind. The Lemurian paused at the doorway, his eyebrow raised at who she now knew was Prince Piers.

"Don't die out there," Piers said to him, his voice cracking. "That's an order."

The Lemurian smirked, his lavender eyes glittering. "As you wish, Your Highness."

"Grab her," Morana commanded, rising to pull a portal open in the middle of the kitchen. It swirled manically, blurring the stone structures on the other side. Piers gathered Sybil against him, apologizing softly as she whimpered. "You love her?"

His eyes flashed at Morana, jaw clenching. "It's complicated."

Morana scoffed as she stepped through the portal. "It always is."

CHAPTER 41

ASTERIA

Asteria emerged from Sybil's home, the sky ablaze with smoke and silvery flames from the drakon. A gold one soared above, wings outstretched like sails against the blackened sky.

With a thunderous roar, it lunged forward and sank its massive jaw around the throat of a pale blue drakon mid-flight. It thrashed, letting out a keening, wounded cry that echoed off the jagged cliffs of the Black Avalanches. Blood poured from its torn throat, raining down on the snow-dusted peaks.

The gold drakon released its grip, and the blue one fell from the sky, limbs limp and wings folding in. It struck the mountain slopes, the impact rippling through the earth.

"Gods," Wells breathed beside her, staring at the scene in horror. Gavril walked up beside him, sword drawn. "What am I looking at, Gav?"

"War, Your Highness," Gavril muttered, peering at Wells and Asteria with a tightly drawn expression. Wells deadpanned, and Gavril shrugged. "I believe this is officially war."

"Which drakon was yours?" Asteria's gaze bounced from Wells to Gavril, the Aether and Energy tingling restlessly around her from various battling Sirians.

"The blue one," Gavril bit out, his jaw clicking. "His name was Benjamin."

Asteria may not have known the drakon, but Gavril's anger echoed within her.

Beyond Celestia, Eldamain had always held a special place within her heart. The country was important to Sybil—not to mention they'd had Sirians on the throne for *centuries*, even before she was born when they were uncivilized settlements.

Seeing them under such a devastating attack for the first time in hundreds of years incited a heat beneath her skin that rolled like the flames from the drakon's mouth.

Not to mention seeing another fall reminded her of the attack on *her* drakon.

"Fuck me," Wells drawled, and Asteria snapped her gaze to him.

She followed his line of sight toward the southwestern ridge of the Black Avalanches to find the source of the rhythmic thumping they'd heard in Sybil's home.

Drakons weren't the only scaled creatures who reigned from the House of Echidna. Another reptile, the thirío, was larger than any drakon—including Sybil. While it didn't have wings or breathe fire, its sheer mass alone was enough to cause catastrophic damage, not to mention the two curving horns protruding from its head.

It walked on hind legs like a mortal, a thick muscular tail behind it for balance, about half the length of a drakon's. Its body was encased in firm, leathered skin, a dark, mottled gray that shimmered faintly beneath light. Across the back of its head and down its shoulders were jagged, overlapping scales layered together like armor. Unnaturally long and curved claws curled from its hands, thick enough to break the hide of a drakon and carve out craters in the Black Avalanches if it so chose.

It was arguably the deadliest creature of any House—and also one of the rarest.

It appeared to be coming from Allanis, which didn't bode well for Eldamain.

"When was the last time you saw one of those?" Wells asked Asteria, his eyes wide as the blood drained from his face.

"Well over two hundred years," Asteria answered, sighing heavily as she shook her head. "Heavens, I can't even recall who it was that could shift into a thirío. What I do staunchly remember is they were from Allanis."

"Clearly." Gavril tossed his sword from one hand to the other, rolling his shoulders. "Without Benjamin, and with Sybil down, the rest of the drakons we have can't take this thing out on top of whoever that gold cunt and white bitch flying around are—"

A petrifying roar split the sky, trembling through the air. Gavril let out a sharp curse and clapped a hand over one ear. Wells grimaced, eyes hesitantly scanning the sky.

A colossal blur soared overhead, its shadow nearly blotting out all the light over Heridy, a rush of wind following its wake.

Asteria's pulse pounded in her ears, jaw clenching so damned tight at the sight of the abnormally large drakon she *swore* winked at her from above.

"Please tell me that's not who I think it is," Wells interjected, his gaze flickering from the drakon to Asteria. "Asteria—"

"If you're asking me to tell you that *isn't* Zephyr gliding through the clouds…" Asteria groaned, angrily running her hands through her hair as the sound morphed into an irate shout.

Wells and Gavril startled, gawking at her like she'd lost her mind.

There was only one way to stop the thirío without proper time to summon *any* reinforcements.

She only hoped Zephyr wasn't here to cause even more problems.

"Fuck the Heavens," Asteria snapped, throwing her hands out at her sides. She inhaled deeply before pointing at Wells and Gavril without taking her eyes off the thirío, who appeared to be debating whether to scale the Black Avalanches' peaks. "When I finish, I'll meet you in Sybil's home. I'll need a new dress."

"What do you mean…" Wells trailed off as Asteria shut her eyes, calling to the cold heat buzzing beneath her skin.

Shedding her mortal form was never easy. It was like trying to peel away a thin layer of wax that had hardened over her flesh. She preferred it far too much over her god-form, which only meant her soul had begun to identify more with the imitation than with the truth of what she was.

The starfire erupted around her in a bright flare, her clothes incinerating within a blink from the unnatural heat. Her black hair simmered to an ethereal blue as it morphed into living flames around her, her silhouette an endless night tinged with twinkling blue, purple, and gold.

A sharp stab of grief pierced her.

Her form resembled Gallus's, but the grief was short-lived as the Aether lured her in.

It called to her louder than the Energy, which was buried beneath it and the starfire. The Aether sang to her the songs of all: the calls of her ancestors, the burn of a star born, the flash of one dying. Asteria wanted to light the world up in flames of—

"Blue." His voice pulled her from the endless depths of her power, and she twisted her head to where Wells stood beneath her. At some point, she'd begun to levitate. "Is this your…"

"Stay here," she demanded, then flew toward the Black Avalanches where the thirío lifted a claw against a rising stone wall.

Asteria twisted her hands in front of her as she slowed and threw a ball of Energy at the belly of the thirío. It screamed with a high-pitched wail, staggering back from the mountain range into the empty land bordering Eldamain and Allanis. She neared it as she floated above the mountains, redirecting its attention to her.

"It would do you well to stand down," she warned, her voice echoing through the caverns below. "I take it you know who I am now."

The beast snarled as it curled its claws into fists, spittle dripping from its sharp teeth—ones that released a deadly poison if desired.

She shot a stream of Aether at the thirío's, wrapped it around its thick neck, and tightened until its shout tapered into a choke. Asteria yanked her arm down, and the beast's head slammed into the dirt at its feet.

"Don't be a fool," she muttered as the beast shook its head, trying to regain its senses. "Retreat."

The beast suddenly launched into the sky, its claw barely swiping the air Asteria tamed as she shot to the side. With its hind legs elevated from the ground, she released another burst of Energy that hit it from the side. The creature slammed into the ground *hard*, the terrain concaving beneath its weight.

Asteria curled her lip as she stared down at the beast and the crater it now lay in.

Now she'd have to ask Rod to fix the ground she'd shattered.

She counted the shifter's breaths as its chest heaved. Asteria needed the thirío to stay down or retreat. Otherwise, she would have to get more aggressive with her assault.

Historically, thiríos could only be defeated by Lyrans long before they could shift to mortal forms. Once they could shift, Zephyr still needed to train them. They lost themselves to their primal call more often than other Lemurians.

"Damnit," Asteria fumed as the reptile rose to its four legs before unsteadily uncurling from its hunch. "You're untamed."

Either Zephyr didn't help train this Lemurian on purpose, or it simply went without for far too long. It could explain why Zephyr was here, seemingly hovering over Heridy in predatory circles rather than decimating the thriving village with his minions.

Asteria straightened in the air as she leveled out. She pinned her glowing eyes on the narrowed sneer of the thirío, hot, heavy breaths huffing from its snout. It dipped its head, pointing one of its horns directly at her.

Really?

It charged, but Asteria was faster. She shot into the sky just as the horn nearly nicked her—if only to challenge herself—and conjured a shield beneath her to act as a barrier between the beast and the mountain range. The creature bounced off the shield at full force.

Asteria felt *that*.

With its heavy frame, the collision knocked the wind from her, the shield dissipating. The thirío fell to its back, and the ground rumbled once again from the impact.

Her heart thundered in her chest, but not from exhaustion. It was the thrill of utilizing her powers, wielding them to an extent she rarely got the chance to do—not unless a fellow Lyran felt like challenging her. The only other Being who could match her outside of a Lyran appeared to be the thirío.

It roared, louder than the beating wings of the drakons drawing closer.

"I'm so sorry," Asteria said loud enough for the creature to hear.

It loosed a deafening screech as Asteria's arm lit up blue and white-gold, the colors swirling and crackling. She raised her hand above her head, breathing in.

Once again, she conjured one of the powers only she had—one she hated using.

With her release, she jerked her arm, palm aimed directly at the thirío. Blue and gold light streaked from her outstretched hand directly into the center of the beast's body. The creature's eyes flared once upon connection, its body stiffening. The light vanished as it flopped to the ground like a burlap sack of grains, the bones in its body entirely liquified.

She closed her eyes in a brief moment of silence for the fallen creature, then whipped her head toward the oncoming drakons, her brow set rigid. The three—gold, white, and a black one that reminded her of Caine's son—stopped mid-flight, flapping above the peaks.

Zephyr hung back, observing with a tilt to his pointed head.

"This is your warning," Asteria called to them, clenching her hands into fists. "Retreat now, or I'll do the same to you. No matter who your father is." She shot a glare at the black dragon.

It narrowed its vertical pupils, snarling as it revealed menacing, sharp teeth. The black dragon roared at her, only further convincing her it was Caine's son, before Zephyr huffed a breath of air at it. It snapped its head to him, bearing its teeth, but nothing happened as they stared each other down.

She knew Zephyr was more than likely using his gift to speak through minds to communicate.

Another beat passed before the three drakons launched higher into the sky, one after the other, their flight taking them toward western Allanis.

Leaving her and Zephyr in a stare down.

I forget how beautifully you fight when you actually wish to be a Goddess, Zephyr projected into her mind, a glimmer in those royal blue eyes, pupils vertical in his drakon form. *I know Danica always wanted to combine your gifts with Rod's, but imagine if you had my child. Starfire, Energy, Aether, and shifting into any wild animal—*

"If you don't want the same Fate to befall you as your little pet down there, I suggest you stop now." Asteria narrowed her glowing eyes, starfire twining with the Aether beneath her form. "Lest you forget I can easily lay you out."

I'd like to see you try, Little Lyran. She swore she could hear that maniacal laugh in her head. *Unfortunately, as enticing as a tussle with you sounds, your father would absolutely obliterate me with my choice of starfire should I touch a single hair on your head.*

Enjoy the fallout of that, though. Zephyr jerked his snout toward the leather lump that was the thirío. *Nen will love to hear you played right into our hands.*

He shot past Asteria with one flap of his wings, following the same route as the other drakons.

She didn't know what Zephyr meant by playing into their hands, but concern burrowed into her chest at the thought of exactly who that thirío was.

Asteria portaled back to Sybil's home, choosing the bedroom over the living room. She hissed as her mortal skin rolled back into place, the Aether and starfire seeping deep into her bones. The first gown she spotted was a deep navy piece, its flowing, layered sleeves trimmed with a gold cord that tied beneath her breasts and circled her waist.

She exited the living room just as she finished tying the cord. Not a second later, Wells and Gavril clamored into Sybil's home.

"You act like one of us so frequently I forget you're a fucking Goddess!" Gavril shouted, laughter bubbling from his lips. "I've never seen a Lyran battle, but if that's any indication of what your father or mother can do, we're in for a—"

"Silence," Asteria snapped, narrowing her eyes.

"I'm giving you a compliment, you nutter," Gavril retorted, his lavender eyes glittering.

It was then Asteria took in the state of the two men. Gavril was covered in blood, dirt, and soot, and she couldn't decipher whether it was his blood or not. His shirt was torn in various places, and the hem appeared singed.

Wells was in a similar state, except there was an angry cut across his forehead, blood rolling down his temple. Asteria advanced on him instantly, her hand reaching for the wound.

"You're hurt," she whispered, eyes wide.

He chuckled, a lazy grin tugging at his lips. Wrapping a firm hand around her wrist, he stopped her fingers just before they touched the cut. "Hardly, Blue. I must say, I'm rather jealous you're entirely unscathed."

She curled her fingers into her palm, a sinister smirk lifting her lips. "It was a small challenge, but I had quite an advantage."

"I would say so." Wells snorted, his grin faltering as he winced. "I will also say…"

His body swayed, and he nearly stumbled into her. Her hands shot out immediately, bracing against his hard abdomen.

"I believe you're concussed," Asteria managed as she steadied him. Gavril stepped in, slipping Wells's arm over his shoulder.

"I found another one of our lieutenants a few streets down," Gavril explained as Wells unhooked his arm and shoved his friend away with a scowl. Asteria glared at Wells, but he winked at her only to groan from the gesture. "Do you realize who that monstrous thing was?"

"I found it difficult to inquire while it was in beast form," Asteria grumbled, opening a portal in front of the blood she refused to acknowledge was Sybil's. Unease sat heavy in her stomach from Zephyr's comment. "Are you telling me you learned who it was?"

"You might not like it, darling." Gavril cringed, angling his body away from her. "They're saying it was the spare heir to the Allanis throne, Prince Clause Rotherham."

"Fan-fucking-tastic." Asteria nostrils flared as she rolled her shoulders.

"Can't imagine how they kept that secret," Wells grumbled with his eyes closed.

Zephyr's comment made a lot more sense now.

He and Nen purposely sent Prince Clause in his thirío form because they knew he was untamed, and Asteria would put him down to stop him from harming Eldamain. While their side might have committed the first blow to a Lyran's child, she was the one who committed the first important death.

An heir to one of their thrones, no less.

A warm, callused hand slipped into hers, squeezing once. She met Wells's gaze as he offered her a soft smile that loosened the tightness in her chest.

"We have to keep going," Wells said, pulling her closer to his side. "Gavril knows the military plans to share with Dionne, and I'm the diplomatic representative. We can collect Piers when we're finished with

Dionne and King Savaric, but we must gain these alliances if they're making these bold moves on us already."

"He's right." Gavril stepped up to the edge of the portal. "I told the men to relay to Quin that we helped but are on our way to Riddling now."

Wells nodded at Gavril just before the Lemurian vanished through the portal. He raised an expectant eyebrow at Asteria.

She sighed, eyes lingering on his cut as her shoulders deflated. Luckily, the bleeding was slowing. "You're okay?"

Wells's gaze softened, and he pulled her into his arms, gently kissing her temple. She shut her eyes to his warmth, her hands pressed to his sides, unfazed by the dirt and grime covering him simply because he was holding her.

"If I knew any better, I'd believe you're concerned for my well-being—"

"I regret this immediately," Asteria said as she shoved him away and through the portal into Dionne's private residence in Riddling.

CHAPTER 42

ASTERIA

Gavril was standing in the middle of the hallway in Dionne's home in Kabal when Asteria and Wells stepped through the portal. She waved it shut behind her, ignoring Wells's penetrating gaze as she released his hand and walked toward the thin double doors before them.

She already felt ridiculous for the immediate concern that stunned her body when she saw him injured. She told herself it was only because he was a prince, therefore a very important person who couldn't be injured while in her entourage.

It had nothing to do with how he was quickly becoming an important person to her.

And she refused to acknowledge how much she enjoyed him just holding her.

The double doors flew open, and the courtyard in the middle of his small home was bathed in the golden light of sunset, dramatic shadows cast across the walls from the thick palm trees and vibrant floral bushes blooming beautifully in the height of spring.

Dionne sat at a small, wrought iron table—one built more for decoration than actual comfort—sipping tea from a dainty ceramic cup that looked like it might belong to one of his great-grandchildren.

He stopped the cup just below his lips, the handle pinched between his thumb and pointer finger. His golden-hazel eyes lifted to Asteria, and that was it.

Laughter burst from her lips.

She stopped a few feet from her brother, doubling over, gripping her stomach as the wheezing cackle took over. She'd be embarrassed about it later, but how could she not laugh?

Her two-hundred-year-old brother was perched precariously on a small iron chair that could very well snap if he shifted his weight, one leg crossed over the other at a dramatic angle since the table was too short to keep his legs stacked beneath.

"Why do you appear…" Asteria giggled as she tried to collect herself. "You do know that isn't a *real* table to sit at, correct?"

His glittering eyes narrowed briefly, flashing red and orange like the churning, liquid fire of his god-power. The corner of his mouth betrayed him as a smirk creased his deep, olive-toned skin.

"I swear to the Gods, Asteria," Dionne grumbled in his thick Riddling accent. "You can't appear without warning."

Asteria wiped her eyes as he rose from the chair, dabbing at his grayed beard with a cloth. "Don't give me any of that. I know Mother Dearest told you I would be coming with a Carraphim or two in tow at some point."

"That she did, but she didn't say when." He strolled over to stand before her, and she realized he and Wells were the same height. "You've interrupted evening tea."

"A grown man sitting alone at a decorative table isn't the image that comes to mind when you tell me I interrupted *evening tea*." Asteria giggled again as she mimicked his deep voice, trying to suppress her smile as her lips quivered.

"You can be such a bitch sometimes." He roughly clasped his hands around her shoulders. The Mark on his forehead and his eyes flashed orange and red again, and she hissed at the intense heat. "This is no way to say hello, especially because I haven't seen you since the Patronage Gala months ago."

"Hello," she half-whimpered, half-yelled, whacking his hands off her only for him to swallow her in a hug that echoed the one she'd received from Taranis. "What is with males and smothering me with your hugging? You and Taranis—"

"Oh, so you saw your least favorite brother first?" After letting her go, Dionne ran a hand through the hair that matched his graying beard.

"I only have two brothers," she grumbled as Dionne peeked around her with an inquisitive eyebrow. "And neither of you are my favorite."

"Who are they?" Dionne jerked his head toward Wells and Gavril.

The two stood in silent fascination, just as they had when they saw her interact with Taranis. The only difference this time was a twinkle in Wells's bright eyes that had Asteria's stomach dipping.

"Prince Orwell Carraphim," Wells said as he strode forward with his hand extended. "It's a pleasure to formally meet you, and I won't bother you with the tales I've heard of your firepower." He swung his arm toward Gavril. "This is one of Eldamain's Lieutenant Generals, Sir Gavril Faris."

"Yes, Prince Orwell," Dionne drawled, bowing at the waist. "I believe you're rather familiar with whichever level of grandson sits on the throne."

Asteria wheeled her gaze to Wells, frowning. "You're *familiar* with King Savaric?"

"Familiar in the loosest of terms." Wells shrugged, slipping his hands into his pockets. He flashed her a princely smile before redirecting it to Dionne. "Do you, by chance, have any sort of healing tonic to obliterate this wicked headache I'm presently suffering from?"

"Let me grab an attendant." Dionne patted Wells's shoulder as he went to the door they'd come through. He glanced down both ends of the hallway before turning right with his hand up.

"If you already knew King Savaric, why would we need Dionne?" Asteria asked as she stepped into Wells, searching his face. "Why would you need me?"

Gavril sighed dramatically as he leaned against a nearby wall, scratching at the dark curls gathered on his head.

"Again, know in the most minuscule sense of the word." Wells pinched two fingers together in front of her face to emphasize his point. She curled her lip as she slapped his hand down. "We met twice over two other diplomatic ventures, and I might have gotten him drunk on the second one and lost him—"

"You *lost* the King of Riddling?" Asteria scolded under her breath, but an open-mouth smile spread across her face.

"That's beside the point." Wells battled his own grin, blinking rapidly as he held his hand palm-up between them. "The point is I don't know him well enough to get an audience in the urgency we need to speak. I'm aware the royal family will drop all they're doing for Dionne. Therefore, the fact you're Dionne's sister gives us an in. Not to mention your portaling minimizes the amount of time it would've normally taken to acquire an audience with him."

He stepped closer to her, his fingertips brushing hers in a whisper she questioned whether it'd actually occurred.

"Besides"—he lowered his voice, glancing over his shoulder to where Gavril had his eyes shut—"I have a *list* of reasons why I need you."

"Oh, do you?" Gavril called loudly, opening one eye.

Asteria blanched as Wells rolled his eyes.

Dionne walked back into the room with a corked vial, but he stopped before Asteria and Wells, studying their proximity—or lack thereof.

"Your elixir," Dionne said, thrusting the vial at Wells, but keeping his gaze on Asteria. She didn't appreciate her brother's heavy judgment in the lift of his eyebrow. "I have to ask... Why are you all so filthy? Well, except Asteria."

She lifted her chin, but it was Gavril who answered, "We were leaving The Northern Pizi when a Sirian called for Asteria through her communication vortex." Asteria glared at him, and he waved her away. "Someone stabbed Sybil with a hematite dagger at the same time a host of drakons set fire to the southern borders of Heridy. They also had a thirío, which happened to be Prince Clause Rotherham of Allanis. Oh, and Zephyr showed up, but he merely hovered."

"Well, when you put it like *that*"—Asteria batted her eyes at Gavril with a clenched jaw— "I guess Zephyr politely left and war hasn't just begun."

"So you believe Allanis and Zephyr purposely attacked Eldamain?" Dionne's gaze bounced between them as he methodically paced the room. Her face fell, and she nodded once. "They're moving rather quickly then. And you said Prince Clause Rotherham is a thirío?"

"It appears so," Asteria said at the same time Gavril blurted, "Asteria killed him."

"Damnit, Gav!" Asteria shouted, wheeling on him. "Do you ever think before speaking?"

"No," he and Wells answered together. Gavril smiled gleefully at Wells, whispering, "She called me *Gav*."

"You killed the spare heir of Allanis?" Dionne pinched the bridge of his nose. "For Heaven's sake, Asteria—"

"Don't chastise me!" Asteria squealed, throwing her hand toward where she believed the Main Continent was. "He was feral, and he wouldn't stand down. I tried to lay him out, but the fucking imbecile wouldn't *stop*."

"Filthy mouth," Wells muttered, and Asteria ignored him for her own sanity.

"She became a full, almighty Goddess," Gavril explained. Asteria would've throttled him for his interjection if the wonderment in his voice didn't catch her attention. She swung her head toward him. "What? I've never seen you do that, nor have I even heard tales of what your god-form looks like."

"I have to agree with him." Wells finished off the vial, shivering at the taste before pocketing it. "I didn't know that's what you looked like."

"I've only seen you use it once," Dionne added, frowning. "That was in private on Celestia, though, and because I poked at you until you transformed."

"I have not donned it publicly for Aveesh in a *very* long time," she whispered, twisting her fingers. "I was barely in my first century the last time I used it here, and that was because I got into an argument with Zephyr—"

"Naturally," Dionne grumbled, and she glared before continuing.

"It terrified the settlement we fought over, and they called me the Hollow One for three generations before they stopped associating the tale with me." She shut her eyes tight, shaking the memory from her mind. "If I frightened anyone…"

"I can't speak for those in Heridy who saw it." Wells shrugged, but something familiar darkened his eyes. "From where I stood, *frightened* is not the correct word."

"From where I stood, something else might've stood—" Gavril broke off with a grunt as one of his legs gave out beneath him.

Asteria sensed the Aether diminishing in Wells just as quickly as it flared.

"We'll get an audience with Savaric first thing in the morning." Dionne walked back toward the double doors, ushering them to follow. "Until then, you lot look like you could use some rest. I have a guest room in the east wing, although it's more like a shared quarter."

"What do you mean by shared?" Asteria caught up with Dionne, walking side-by-side.

"There's a very small common room, and two other rooms are attached," he explained, one hand tucked behind his back, the other splayed between him and Asteria. "I'm sure the men will offer you one of the rooms and they will share the other, or the Lemurian will take the couch. Unless you plan to share with the…"

He trailed off as Asteria's eyes flashed in warning. He chuckled under his breath, and Asteria peered over her shoulder to check on Wells and Gavril. They appeared to be conversing, but Wells's brow was furrowed.

"What's that about, Azzy?" Dionne asked quietly, leaning into her. "I haven't seen you like *that* with a male since Rod. I would venture even then—"

"Stop," she hissed, her shoulders tensing. "I don't know what you're referring to."

"Oh, spare me." He rolled those golden eyes, the left side of his mouth curling to reveal a dimple. "The glances of yearning, the brushing of limbs and appendages, unintentionally finding your bodies leaning toward one another—"

"You've made your point." Asteria jabbed him with her elbow, and he yelped.

"Do we need to separate you two?" Wells chided, and the playfulness of his tone sent Asteria's heart into an unhealthy pattern.

"Nothing out of the ordinary." Asteria waved without turning just as Dionne curled his arm around her neck, tucking her under his armpit against his chest. "Stars above, Dionne. I still have starfire left if you want to feud."

"You would think they're teenage siblings squabbling rather than centuries-old Beings," Gavril muttered, which coaxed a snort from Wells.

"We can hear you!" Asteria and Dionne said at the same time. He squeezed his arm tighter around her neck.

"Would you—" She struggled embarrassingly as she slipped out of his grasp.

"You're treading deep waters, Azzy," Dionne taunted with a knowing look. He lowered his voice again as he stepped closer. "What are your plans with him?"

"Heavens, he isn't a dame in need of courting." Asteria ran a hand through her knotted black hair, tugging it over her shoulder. "I don't have plans, Noni. I'm over six hundred years old. I'm... letting it play its course."

"Right." Dionne stopped before a set of doors, producing a key from his pocket. "Says the Lyran who's only had one relationship before she swore off men for two-thirds of the time I've been alive."

She hummed under her breath—although it resembled more of a snarl—just as Wells and Gavril joined them before the door.

"Do you have a large bath or possibly a lake nearby?" Gavril asked, his voice wary. "I expended quite a bit of energy in my mortal form and need to shift into my nereid one for a few hours, or I'll become quite ill against the desires of Prince Orwell."

"I have a large bathing chamber beneath my home," Dionne explained, dropping the key into Wells's outstretched hand. "Perhaps I'll join you, and maybe you can fill me in on some of the more strategic ideas of this war."

"As long as you don't mind keeping the water on the cooler side..." Gavril's voice faded as he followed Dionne down the hallway.

"Are you hungry?" Asteria asked, her body tense as Wells unlocked the door.

"I could possibly eat." He shoved the door open with a raised eyebrow. "Will you be coming in, or do you plan on planting yourself outside this door?"

"You should wash up," she insisted, nodding her head. "I'll go to the kitchen. If Dionne was already having tea, it's past supper here. I can throw something together."

"That's not a bad idea." Wells stepped into the room, pausing to throw his head over his shoulder. "Knock before you come back in."

She blinked, her cheeks heating. He closed the door just as an utterly indecent thought flew into her head. Before it clicked shut, Wells gripped the wood, yanking it back enough to rest one hand on the frame.

"Or don't." He winked and shrugged, then shut the door in her face.

Asteria wanted nothing more than to dunk her body beneath the frigid waters of Orion's Lake.

CHAPTER 43

ASTERIA

Asteria sat before the warm glow of the fireplace, plopping another berry into her mouth. Spring in Riddling may be warmer than countries like Eldamain and The Northern Pizi, but being a desert continent, the cold at night seeped into her bones chilling her blood.

The glow of the fireplace also amplified the alluring and almost sensual mood of the room, the ceiling shadowing the dramatic hues and provocative tapestries littering the walls. Her eyes trailed Wells throughout the small common room as he perused various pieces.

She wasn't entirely sure what this wing functioned as. She doubted Dionne placed his family in a room where the figures in the painting above the fireplace were participating in an act Asteria was positive children shouldn't bear witness to.

"I'm beginning to see a commonality between the children of Danica," Wells said without looking at her, his head tilting at a tapestry where a feminine figure had her head lowered into a masculine figure's lap.

"I'm not sure I know what you're getting at," Asteria shot back, gently bouncing her feet where they were draped over the arm of the chair.

He peered over his shoulder, scanning her position. The action was far more sultry than it needed to be. "You and your brothers have quite the tongues."

"Ah." Asteria tipped her head up to the ceiling. "When your mother does nothing but claw at your skin, you must sharpen your teeth and tongue to protect against her delusions."

Wells chuckled, his footsteps growing closer until his face appeared upside down over her. "Is it because of your mother, or because they learned from their older sister?"

Asteria scoffed, ducking from beneath him and shooting up from her seat. Both of his eyebrows rose as she pointed her finger toward the door. "Didn't you see how Dionne teased me to no end?"

"I also saw how Taranis teased you," Wells observed, slowly stepping toward her again. "You may be shocked to hear this, but just because you're a Lyran and your brothers are Andromedans, you're not excused from brotherly and sisterly banter. Even with the hundreds of years between you three."

"Taranis is the most vexing." She folded her arms across her chest as he continued toward her. "He pesters Dionne just as much as me. He likes to get a rise out of us so we fight him. Someone always walks away with a split lip."

"Even you?" He stopped directly in front of her, trapping them between the chair and short table.

"Who do you think taught them to use their god-powers?" Asteria smirked, flipping her hair over her shoulder.

"Dionne acts differently with you than Taranis, though." Wells tilted his head. "Gentler, I suppose, despite the headlock. You have nicknames for one another."

"Because Dionne is older and has lost his jovial spirit." Asteria sighed fondly, remembering when Dionne was Wells's age. "The older he gets, the stronger our kinship grows. He knows what it's like to live far longer than most."

Wells nodded as he rocked from his heels to his toes, hands clasped behind his back.

"What about you? What's the dynamic between you and your siblings? Don't think I forgot about Taranis's comment regarding the treaty."

"It's exactly as it sounds." Wells shrugged one shoulder, head dipping to it. "A figurehead can't be good at *everything*. Quin has always looked the part and controls himself better than Piers or me. On the other hand, he doesn't strategize well. Luckily for him, Piers thinks everything is a puzzle. I'm far better with words than both of my brothers."

"I can't deny that," she grumbled under her breath, but his eyebrows shot up as a grin stretched across his face. "Although, I have to disagree. You seem to control yourself well in political situations."

Asteria waited for him to say more, but he continued to stare at her in silence, eyes flickering across her face. She straightened her back, frowning as her stomach coiled. "What is it?"

Wells took a step closer, his hand trailing from the curve of her jaw to the point of her chin where he tucked his finger underneath. "Does it make you nervous when I stare?"

She jerked back, ignoring the fire kindling between her thighs. "You don't make me nervous."

He cocked his head, taking another step into her. She retreated a single step but the back of her thighs hit the chair. "Don't you fidget when you're nervous?"

She frowned but glanced down at where her hands ceased intertwining. She snapped her head back up, her attention latching onto the smirk lifting his lip.

A mistake, because she immediately remembered the feeling of them against hers.

"You see, Blue." Wells paused to close the distance between them, his abdomen brushing her hands. Her body betrayed her—her heart hammering to reach him as her finger stroked imperceptibly against his shirt. "I'm an observant male. For example, how your eyes fall to my lips leads me to believe you're thinking about when we kissed."

A breath of disbelief morphed into one of shock when he gently unlocked her hands, using them to tug their bodies together.

They were as close as they'd been during the kiss.

His firm chest pressed against her breasts, the heat of his body seeping through the thin fabric between them. Their hips hovered close, separated by a pinch of space, tension crackling in the air. Wells slowly tilted his head, but at the last second, he shifted. His lips ghosted just behind her ear, his warm breath brushing her skin.

"You've been fascinated by my lips long before we kissed, though." He pulled back only to snake around her head, caressing the other ear with his whisper. "How many times did you fantasize about my lips on yours?"

He brought his head back, finally brushing said lips against hers. Her body responded instinctively, arching into him. A low, guttural groan of satisfaction rumbled deep within his chest, his hands sliding to rest firmly on her waist. She clung to him, her fingers gently digging into the hard muscle beneath his tunic.

"How many naughty fantasies have you had about me?" His lips moved against hers as he spoke.

"Far too many."

It was she who closed the distance once more.

Asteria sighed softly when their lips met, that familiar wave of safety returning. His arms wrapped around her waist, and a sharp throb stirred low in her core from the simple weight of him pressed against her.

Seizing the moment, she deepened the kiss, her hands tracing the strength of his arms and broad planes of his shoulders, memorizing the contours beneath his skin. She dove her fingers into the wild, damp tangle of his curls, tugging gently to anchor herself.

She couldn't understand her fixation with his hair.

Asteria gasped when he spun them and sank into the chair, tumbling ungracefully into his lap. She giggled quietly as he helped right her so she was straddling him. She gripped his stubbled jaw in her hands, lowering her lips back to his.

How was a male so addicting? Asteria drank him in with every swipe of their tongues, her body rolling against him in subtle grinds.

She moaned softly against his mouth as his hands lit a tingling path from her waist, over her hips, and curving around the back of her legs. He dug his fingers into the soft skin where her ass and the back of her thighs met, pulling her down onto his lap and rolling his hips. She keened at the pure desire she felt from his stiff length beneath her.

As Wells brought his lips down her jaw and neck, teeth and tongue skimming across skin she didn't know was sensitive, she realized how entirely at his mercy she was. Even if she was the one straddling him, something about letting him guide every step of this intoxicating dance only ignited a foreign thrill deep within her.

The same thought from their first kiss sprung on her abruptly.

She wanted *more*, but her nerves still lingered in the back of her mind. *Another small step wouldn't hurt…*

Besides, she was safe with him—that much she was certain.

Asteria swallowed around her dry mouth, and Wells pulled his head back to look up at her, eyebrow raised.

"You once said you wouldn't need to be inside me to make me come," she whispered, rolling her hips to test that boundary. "I've wondered how that could be when it seems all men do is think with their cocks."

"I see." Wells clicked his tongue against his teeth. He pursed his lips as his gaze searched the room. "Ah!"

Wells adjusted his grip so his hands tucked behind the back of her knees and stood with fluidity. She clung to him as she yelped, her thighs tightening around his hips.

"Wells!" she yelled, and he moved across the room toward the bedroom they'd decided she would sleep in. "Wells, what are you—"

He stepped under the threshold, crouching to avoid hitting her head on the paneling around the door and went straight for the bed, gently laying Asteria on her back. "Do you trust me?"

The question caught her off-guard.

Is that what this was?

Asteria searched Wells's face, her breath quickening the longer she looked. For what, she didn't know, but she repeated his question over and over in her head, the answer immediate each time.

Maybe it had happened when he defended her with his Aether in Teslin or how he didn't force whatever happened between them in Celestia and The Northern Pizi to go further—between watching her pleasure herself and the kiss.

It could've been all the ways he pushed at the walls she'd fortified around herself, but with a gentleness, never to the point of disrespect. There was also the fact he found so many parts of her astonishing that others found cumbersome.

For all those reasons and the unspoken moments between them, Asteria found she trusted Wells, and that recognition spoke volumes to her heart.

"Yes," she whispered, and he crashed his lips to hers.

This kiss was different from the others.

It was deeper, laced with heat that stole the air from her lungs and left her thoughts in disarray. It wasn't soft or tentative; it was charged, exhilarating, every draw of his lips igniting sparks along her skin. Her mind was heavy with need, dizzy beneath the weight of it.

He devoured her, mouth slanting over hers with fierce intent, his tongue sweeping along her bottom lip in a slow, claiming stroke that coaxed a soft, breathy moan from her. She wove her hips underneath him, her core throbbing as his hard cock ground against her through their clothes.

Her breath caught as she rocked against him, and the way he responded—a low growl vibrating in his chest—only deepened the rush coursing through her.

To her surprise, Wells removed his lips from hers and pressed their foreheads together. The most beautiful smile broke through his husky chuckle. "I ask this a final time. Do you trust me?"

"Yes," she said without hesitation, tugging on his tunic.

"That trust is safe with me." Wells's hand slid up the middle of her body. "You have my word."

Asteria nodded, swallowing the lump in her throat as her thumb swept across his jaw.

"Now"—he tugged the cord at the front of her dress, his movements languid—"before we begin, what you must know about me is that I'm a patient man, Blue."

Fuck.

Asteria was unsure why that statement melted her into the bed. She clenched her thighs together for a bit of friction, because she wasn't patient.

"There are many places on your body I can touch or kiss or lick that will have you begging to come," Wells explained, his tone and words bringing a fiery blush to her cheeks. He tugged the collar of her dress, sliding it over her shoulder and down, exposing her breast. The cool air pebbled her nipple. "There are some of the known ones, like the lips, neck, and ears, all of which I've already shown attention to." He trailed the tips of his fingers down her chest to the peak, circling. "There are even more known ones, which include these."

He pinched her nipple between his fingers, pain mixing with pleasure, the ache between her legs burrowing deeper. Her hands squeezed the sides of his arms, pleading for more. His hand clutched her arm, slowly pulling her wrist toward his lips.

"There is the wrist." He tenderly dragged his teeth along the faintly glowing vein. "The palm." He placed a gentle kiss in the middle of her hand. "The fingertips." He flicked his tongue along the pad of her pointer finger.

Asteria whimpered because whatever he was doing had every

nerve—every cell—coming alive in her body. It was like he'd awakened something buried deep within her, and now every part of her was singing in response.

"So many places"—he painstakingly bunched up her dress until the fabric gathered at her hip, the cool air ripping a gasp from her lips—"that will continue to wring *that* sound from you."

Somehow, the coil within her wound tighter as he glanced down, watching his hand drag from the inside of her knee up her inner thigh. Asteria panted with anticipation, hands trembling as they returned to his brown locks, twisting within the curls to ground herself.

She didn't care if he entered her so long as he granted her release from the maddening need inside her.

His fingers drew a burning circle below her navel, taunting. "The most sensitive part is that pretty cunt you so graciously bared to me."

Wells slipped a hand into her undergarments, sliding his fingers against her. He groaned as he felt the wetness gathered there and dropped his forehead to hers, the sound rumbling against her chest. He applied pressure as he moved his fingers back to her clit, circling in slow, methodical motions. She tugged on his hair as blinding ecstasy washed over her, fingertips tingling as the starfire responded to her increasing arousal.

She couldn't bear it any longer.

Asteria yanked his lips to hers, desperately urging him to continue. She'd never felt so much from so little, and she felt greedy for wanting even *more*.

His tongue swept into her mouth as his fingers continued circling her clit, occasionally gliding through her slickness but still not sinking into her, which only drove her yearning into a frustration that tore a whimper from her. Her raving desire took her thoughts to places she hadn't journeyed in a long time.

She wanted to feel him thrust into her, stretching her with his fingers, his cock—anything.

She wanted to touch *him*, to see how he would respond to her hand wrapped around him, her mouth, even if she'd never done that act before.

She found she just *wanted*, and yet that word wasn't strong enough. His words from earlier sounded in her head.

I have a list of reasons why I need you.

Was that what she was experiencing? Was he a need? Something she wasn't sure she could live another moment without?

Wells moved his lips across her cheeks and down her jawline before drawing her ear between his teeth. "Remember what I said, Blue?"

She threw her head back, silently pleading with him to sink inside her, for those expert fingers to dip into her blazing heat. He only dragged his teeth across the pulse at her neck as he pinched her clit.

Release speared through her, her body shuddering as waves of pleasure sent her mind reeling, breathy moans fluttering from her lips. Wells groaned into her ear as she tightened her grip on his hair, continuing to draw out her pleasure.

When the last throws faded and her moans returned to normal breaths, she opened her eyes with heavy lids. Wells gazed down, the dark blue ring around his eyes brighter than usual. He bent to kiss her as he slowly removed his hands from her clothes.

When he rolled away and rose from the bed, she thought he would remove an article of clothing that granted her the view she'd only conjured in the fantasies they spoke of earlier, but he only adjusted his slacks.

She shot upright, pulling the fabric of her dress back over her shoulder as she frowned at him.

Wells winked, thumbs tucked into his pockets, drawing her gaze to his cock straining against his pants. "Goodnight, Blue."

With that, Wells shut her door behind him, leaving her alone and completely satisfied.

"Son of a *bitch*," she growled.

He'd done precisely what he'd said.

She had come without him having to be inside her—not even a finger.

More importantly, she realized Dionne's words rang true as she acknowledged her care, concern, and trust in Wells.

There would be nothing simple about what was happening between them.

CHAPTER 44

SYBIL

Sybil's eyes fluttered open as she returned to her body.

Directly above her was a beige stone ceiling, light peeking through the white curtains concealing the window. The air was dry and carried the layered scent of something earthy with a sweet, slightly peppery undercurrent. Then, cutting through like a blade came a quick, sharp note— eucalyptus, or something close.

Her senses sharpened. She blinked slowly, assessing her body. Pain still lingered, though dull and manageable, but there was no more detachment or disorientation. Fate's weight tickled the back of her mind, and the drakon rested within her chest.

Her own knowledge of healing allowed her to conclude she was more than likely being treated in a Healer's infirmary or private room of sorts.

Her gaze fell down the wall to continue inspecting, but she held her breath when something brushed her arm. She dragged her attention toward it to find a familiar male resting his head on the mattress.

Piers was here beside her—wherever *here* was.

"Piers—" She swallowed, wincing at the dryness scratching her throat. "Piers."

He startled awake, pinning those hazel eyes on her, the whites bloodshot.

"Syb," he said softly, inhaling as he wiped a hand over his face. "How are you feeling?"

"Water?" she asked, her eyes flickering to the small table nearby.

He nodded, carefully pouring a glass. He angled it toward her, and she groaned at the stiffness in her stomach when she tried to sit up. He frowned but tilted the rim to her lips so she only had to lift her head. Sybil wrapped her hand around his and the glass, blinking with inquisition.

"We're in Celestia," Piers explained as he set the glass back on the table. "Morana went to get some air. She's been here the whole time, hovering as Erika worked. I urged her to go see if she could find out anything about what happened after we left Eldamain."

The whole time…

Sybil didn't care about her mother at this moment nor what happened after she'd blacked out. She only cared about the man sitting beside her.

Dark circles hugged Piers's eyes, the deep purple beneath his skin strangely accenting the green hues of his irises. His mouth was downturned, drastically different from the firm line he usually kept. His stubble looked like it had a day or two of growth.

"You've also been here the whole time," she whispered, raising a hand. She brushed the backs of her fingers across his cheekbones, and his eyes fluttered shut. "You could've left. I'm okay."

Before she could lower her hand to the bed, he clutched it, dragging it to the front of his face. He kissed her knuckles firmly, then tucked them under his chin.

"But you weren't okay," he said, agony echoing in the lines of his frown. "You're supposed to be the invincible one."

"I'm not *entirely* invincible." She lifted a finger, dragging the tip along his bottom lip. "Age may not plague me, but I can still be wounded enough to incite death."

"I'm not supposed to fear the loss of you, remember?" He leaned forward, caressing her cheek with his other hand. The warmth of his palm shot through her. "You fear the loss of me."

Tears pricked her eyes, and one slipped down the side of her face to the pillow. Piers tracked its movement, blinking as he released an unsteady breath.

"You still shouldn't fear for me." Sybil shook her head to avert her gaze, but Piers kept a firm grip on her cheek. "I'm not your responsibility."

"Syb…" Piers frowned, appearing cross. "Caring and fearing for you have nothing to do with responsibility. Above all, despite our past, you were and still are my dearest friend. I don't have many of those, a sentiment I know you share."

She cleared the emotion from the back of her throat before speaking again. "You should be with Asteria, Wells, and Gavril not just because it's your *responsibility* to help with these alliances, but also because your place is with Gavril. You love him now."

Piers pressed his forehead to hers, their noses touching. "Just because I love him doesn't mean I stopped loving you."

Her breath caught in her chest, burning. She scrunched her face, resisting the overwhelming urge to kiss him just once.

Maybe Piers was right.

Maybe she was torturing him with subtle brushes of affection and seductive tones, if only because she felt tormented by the desire to be near him while knowing they would cause each other pain.

She was already in pain trying to keep herself away, so what did it really matter? Sybil only needed to tilt her head up…

Piers closed the distance, their lips sealing together with a relieved, desperate groan from them both.

The kiss was an unraveling.

It felt as though they kissed for the last time only yesterday, and yet the ache between them made it feel like centuries had passed since they'd last touched.

He deepened the kiss, hunching over the bed as if trying to fold himself around her. His hand found the side of her neck, warm and steady, thumb brushing beneath her temple in a gesture both reverent and possessive. Then his mouth parted hers, tongue sweeping between her lips with strokes that spoke of longing, regret, love, and a thread of desperation.

Sybil met his urgency, even as he loosened his grip on her hand. She traced it down his chest, fisting his tunic while her other hand latched onto his wrist. She ground herself in this moment, in the solid feel of him, as if anchoring to a truth she knew could be taken away at any moment.

Her moan sounded more like a purr when he curled his tongue against hers, remembering what that tongue felt like plunging between her—

Someone cleared their throat.

Piers jerked back, falling into the chair he'd previously been in. Sybil swiveled her head toward the intruder, her face heating when she met Morana's pale blue mortal eyes.

"I'm glad to see you're feeling better," Morana said, stepping into the room, hands clasped behind her back. She tilted her head at Piers. "Unless she required resuscitation. In that case, I should thank you—"

"*Morana*," Sybil snapped between clenched teeth, her eyes widening. Piers pinched his lips to hide his smirk, and she swatted his arm. "Don't encourage her."

"How about I leave you two?" Piers offered, slowly rising from the chair. Sybil's heart clenched, and she reached for his hand without a second thought. He glanced down at it, his tense expression softening before lifting it to his lips. "I'll come back when you're done speaking."

He shimmied around Morana, who stood like a statue in the entryway. Her eyes tracked him until he disappeared through the doorway. She slowly dragged her gaze back to Sybil, those eyes narrowing in scrutiny.

"You'll have mercy on your daughter who was just *stabbed* in her own

365

home by her sister," Sybil said, wincing when clenching her abdomen brought a throbbing ache of pain to two individual points. "Gods*damnit*."

"I would lecture you on cursing your own mother, but alas"—Morana paused as she helped prop Sybil at a slight angle with extra pillows—"I'll show you mercy, as you so thoughtfully put it."

Sybil sighed heavily as she settled, taking the undistracted silence to lower the blanket gathered around her. Just as she thought, a thin strip of cloth was wrapped around her breasts and down her abdomen, pinned by her hip. The fabric was stained faintly pink in two small circles.

"You mentioned your sister." Morana gently laid a hand on Sybil's forearm. "I don't want to make you relive it."

"It doesn't matter." Sybil's voice was softer than she intended as she drew her gaze to Morana's face. "This is but one day in my centuries of existence."

Morana sighed, rubbing her thumb along Sybil's skin. Her pale skin was such a contrast to Sybil's darker ebony hue, yet she'd never once doubted Morana was her mother.

They looked the same age now, both perpetually in the first three decades of life. It was a strange experience, but Sybil caught a glimpse of the age in Morana's mortal eyes every once in a while. It was the lazy twitch or curl of an expression, as though Morana used them so frequently they'd lost their depth.

"It was Endora," Sybil confirmed, averting her gaze to the open door. "She tricked me and used the Aether to hold my arms..."

"Details like that don't matter to me." Morana stroked the side of Sybil's face and into her hair, fanned around her head like a white veil. "I think Valeria sent her."

"I don't doubt she did." Sybil's voice cracked, emotion clogging her throat.

Sybil was young when she'd nearly died, somewhere in her very early childhood. She vaguely remembered how motherly Valeria was before the drakon had attacked her. If her memory was correct, Valeria had favored her over other children since she'd been an orphan.

All her favorites were, their parents victims of various diseases and illnesses.

What Endora said wasn't incorrect. In the end, Valeria was the one to beg Morana to save Sybil.

The difference was, when it came to raising Sybil, Valeria was absent. Morana took on all the responsibilities and love.

It didn't quell Sybil's desire to have her other mother's love.

"I'm so sorry, my drakon." Morana slipped her hand into Sybil's, and she fought the tears that burned her eyes. "Valeria came to me in Eonia and tried to... I really don't know what she was trying to do. Seduce me into something? Spewing nonsense about me carrying a child and raising another one together." Sybil recoiled. "You think I wanted that?"

Her distaste was short-lived anyway. She mewled at the deep ache the movement caused. She would have to rely on her face and hands to express distaste—or any emotion, for that matter.

"When I didn't give her what she wanted, she said she was going to take you from me like I took you away from her." Morana shook her head, gaze locked on the open door.

Sybil squeezed her hand to get her attention. Morana slowly drew her gaze back, those mortal blue eyes glittering with anguish. "She wasn't successful. You got to me in time, and I'm assuming you called Asteria."

Morana nodded, stroking her thumb over Sybil's hand. "I grabbed a random Sirian off the street and made them call Asteria through the Energy. Or the Aether... I can't recall now."

"It doesn't matter." Sybil stared at where their hands were interlocked.

She vaguely remembered the drakon's roar before she passed out, which had her wondering...

She poked around her memory for something Fate would let her speak to her mother about the prophecy.

[The True Path blooms.]

"I'm very worried, Morana."

Morana snapped her head to Sybil again, searching her face as she waited for Sybil to elaborate.

"If things continue this way…" Sybil swallowed against the bile and aftertaste trickling in from the vision she saw when she was in Celestia just days ago. "We're going to lose so much."

"Is it because of what Asteria is doing?" Morana waited, but Sybil deadpanned. It was far too vague a statement. Her mother rolled her eyes. "Okay. What do you believe the vision is telling you about the Path we are headed toward? Can you tell me that much?"

Sybil waited to see if Fate would deny her, but it was quiet. She wondered if Fate was just as afraid of what she saw, and it wanted to throw them a bone.

She jerked her head toward the open door, her eyes flickering between it and Morana. Understanding registered, and Morana waved her wrist, the door shutting quietly.

"When we were here a few days ago, Asteria filled Odo and Erika Hesper in on what was happening on the Main Continent," Sybil explained, still lowering her voice to a pitch she knew only Morana could hear. "Asteria told me Odo was extremely hesitant about choosing to help. He expressed it would go against everything Asteria has built the Academy on."

"Danica is going to have a fit," Morana muttered, rubbing her forehead.

"Morana…" Her mother waited but didn't appear to want to hear what Sybil was thinking. "I don't think Celestia will choose a side."

"Is that what you've seen?" Morana straightened in her chair. "Is it final?"

"I don't think it's final yet, but the Path burns brighter than the one where they choose to support Asteria." Sybil gnawed on her lip, tuning into her hearing to ensure no one was eavesdropping. "I fear if Celestia decides to remain neutral—regardless if we win or lose—something horrific will still happen."

CHAPTER 45

ASTERIA

Asteria took a deep, steadying breath to calm the unwelcome, unfamiliar nerves fluttering wildly in her chest. She reached for the handle, honing in on Wells and Gavril's voices rumbling outside the door. She hoped Gavril being in the room would lessen the intensity she knew would come from seeing Wells.

This was different from him watching her. He'd *touched* her where no man had touched in arguably far too long, and she felt a certain way about it. What was happening between them was more intimate than the fun she knew other Lyrans had with other Beings.

Get a hold of yourself.

She swung the door open and stepped out.

Their gazes locked instantly.

The corner of his lips twitched.

"Oh," Gavril drawled dramatically, pausing with a pastry halfway to his mouth. He narrowed his eyes as they bounced between Wells and Asteria. "You know, I'm not naive. Now that Piers isn't here to distract my every waking moment with that marvelous ass of his, there *is* something happening here. Right?"

"That's my brother," Wells grumbled under his breath, frowning at Gavril before raising an eyebrow at Asteria expectantly.

"I have such a burning desire to dissect this right now." Gavril stared at them, wide eyes alight. "And if one of you doesn't start talking, I'll continue to fill the silence."

Wells only stared at Asteria with the ghost of a grin, and she realized with irritation—and a small drop of amusement—that he was waiting for her to answer Gavril. Either he wanted to hear her answer first, or he was letting her decide how to explain this.

Unfortunately for him, Asteria was too stubborn to do either, so she crossed her arms over her chest and blinked repeatedly.

"I clearly know Wells's entire sexual history," Gavril began, waving the half-eaten pastry at his friend and pinning his eyes on Asteria. "From the day he lost his virginity to his most recent—"

"I think she gets what *entire* means." Wells's eyes briefly bouncing to Gavril, and Asteria's lips twitched into a smirk at the glare he gave him.

"Just wanted to be sure." Gavril held his hands up, then slowly lowered them as he studied Asteria. Her starfire burned at the back of her throat. "To be fair, I'm not sure there are any tales about the Goddess of Sirians and her sexual endeavors like there are of your fellow Gods. That leads me to conclude you're a virgin—"

"No." She pointed a finger at him, the word coated in poison. She pressed her lips into a thin line, breathing through her nose. "Not that what I do behind closed doors is any of your business, but I'm by no means a virgin. I'm just more private than my fellow Lyrans. And selective."

Wells's brows twitched into an imperceptible frown, his mouth downturned. Her stomach twisted into a knot because she knew he would ask her about it the next moment they were alone.

The only reason the world knew about the Lyrans' various sexual relationships with different Beings was due to the children born from those relations. The people of Aveesh knew Morana and Valeria were once together because of their connection to Sybil, just as the only way they knew about Gallus and Danica was because Asteria existed.

Very, *very* few on Aveesh knew of Asteria and Rod outside of the Lyrans.

So few that Asteria could count them on one hand.

It wasn't even Asteria who'd wanted privacy in her relationship with Rod. He'd wanted it, and while she'd thought it endearing at the time, now she questioned if it was so he could play around with Beings without them fearing her wrath.

All to say, Gavril and Wells were amongst the majority who *didn't* know.

"So, not a virgin Goddess." Gavril smirked, his pale eyes glistening in the sconces. He slowly lowered to the arm of the settee Wells sat on. "But the two of you haven't—"

"Gavril," Wells snapped, his eyes narrowing. "Silence."

Asteria's eyebrows rose at the fierceness in his tone and flare in his eyes. She should've been wary of the unfamiliar vehemence from him. Instead, she found herself extremely curious about the reaction—and possibly aroused.

A knock on the door startled them, but the visitor didn't wait to be invited in. Dionne's head popped inside, his golden-hazel eyes glistening. "It's now or never, General."

"You don't need—"

Dionne cut Gavril off. "I was talking to Asteria."

"Don't start this bit again," she grumbled, pinning him with a heated, glowing blue gaze.

"I want to be in on the bit." Gavril snickered, but she whirled her threat on him next. He only smiled with mischief.

"I believe you wish for death this morning, friend," Wells said as they all met in the open space of the living area, cupping his hand over Gavril's shoulder.

"He wishes for death every day," Asteria muttered, although she couldn't suppress her wistful grin. It was short-lived when her skin began to itch under Dionne's watchful eye.

She opened a portal beside them without another word. Her brother gave her a knowing look before stepping through first, then Gavril followed, leaving her and Wells.

Per usual.

"I don't know if I ever have the energy to—"

Fingers digging into her waist, Wells hauled her to his lips. She squeaked but melted into his embrace, hands resting on his forearms. He ended the kiss before she could think any further about it.

"We shouldn't keep them waiting," he whispered before stepping through.

She followed him with a roll of her eyes as she called out, "You realize you're the one causing us to always be delayed."

Asteria walked into the receiving room in Krishna Castle, nearly ramming into Wells's back.

The white walls were adorned with intricate, swirling patterns of maroon, gold, and black. Luxurious velvet and plush furniture was perfectly placed around the room, large floor-to-ceiling windows letting in natural light reflecting off the golden sand outside and casting a subtle glow against the artwork hanging on the wall.

Asteria enjoyed the natural scent of Riddling just as much as she enjoyed the view of the mountains in The Northern Pizi. It was a dry, earthy scent, mineral-rich with a hint of straw and greenery mingling together. The memories it evoked had her shoulders relaxing as the days of Dionne's early reign flitted through her mind.

She turned around the room inspecting the new pieces on display since the last time she'd been here, spotting the guard standing by the doors. He held a spear propped upright beside him, though he appeared relaxed.

"The other knight and Dionne went to fetch King Savaric," Gavril explained, already lounging in an armchair. "He wanted to make sure he could receive us. It was a rather quick exchange. I think they knew he was coming."

"All Dionne's descendants know of his relationship with me." Asteria clasped her hands behind her back, slowly strutting toward one of the sofas backed against the clear windows. She peered out, catching a glimpse of Sitara's central city a few miles out. "If Dionne is portaling into the castle, it typically means there's business to be had."

"Does he have you portal him often?" Wells raised an eyebrow, shoving his hands into his pockets.

"Hardly." She snorted, shaking her head. "Which is why it alerts them that something is amiss. There's also a chance that once Dionne heard from Danica, he warned Savaric and his Council there may be a visit in the future."

The knight by the doors grunted.

She took that as a confirmation, yet scrutinized him and thought she caught a tug of a smirk at his lips.

"Cheeky," Gavril muttered, his eyes glittering. Wells smacked him upside the head, and Gavril hissed, glaring. "What was that for?"

"Ogling," Wells said, but it was full of mirth. "Keep your hands to yourself."

"You know, friend, I could say the same to you."

"If you know what's good for you, Gav, you'll be silent." Asteria shot him a warning look over her shoulder, letting her eyes flash once.

"There it is again!" Gavril flung a finger toward her, his attention on Wells. "She's calling me by my nickname. I'd like to believe this is a lovely sign, but the rational part of me equates it to a lion playing with a mouse."

Wells chuckled mischievously under his breath as he walked up beside Asteria to stare out the window. He ever so slightly leaned into her, muttering under his breath, "You know it's unkind to taunt him."

"I don't taunt him," Asteria said slowly, dipping her head. "He pokes, and I simply offer ample warning there will be consequences for doing so."

"That's taunting him." Wells deadpanned, his eyes twinkling.

"I suppose." She fought her smile, twisting on her heel to face him. "Besides, no one said I was kind."

Wells opened his mouth to either concur or protest, but the doors opened, revealing Dionne and the knight Asteria assumed had escorted him to Savaric.

"This knight will escort both of you to King Savaric's private study," Dionne said, sweeping his hand toward the hallway. "Asteria and I will stay here and wait until you've spoken to him."

Asteria frowned, something restless twirling in her chest at the thought of Wells and Gavril alone with the king of a foreign country, one of her many great nephews or not.

Although, most of the concern lay with Wells being out of her sight.

She didn't know if he sensed her apprehension, but Wells pinched her chin between his thumb and forefinger, forcing her gaze back to him.

"You fretting about me is kindness," he whispered, his smirk tugging at an invisible string in her sternum. "While I appreciate the sentiment, I did attend your Academy with a Warrior specialty. I think our time in Teslin also proves I'm more than capable of holding my own."

"I wasn't…" She huffed a frustrated breath. There was no use denying it. She pursed her lips, contemplating whether what she said next would blatantly confirm her genuine care for him. "If anything seems off or suspicious, use the Aether. Summon me."

His face softened with a slight pinch of his brows. He nodded sternly before tapping underneath her chin and following the knights and an intrigued Gavril.

The moment the door shut, sealing her and Dionne in the room alone, he ushered her toward the two chairs in the middle. "I have much to ask you, Azzy. It's been some time since we were able to speak alone, open and honest with one another."

"I don't want to have one of our open and honest discussions," she whined as she fell into a chair with a whoosh of her breath. She leaned her head back, shutting her eyes. "I wish to revel in a moment of silence

I rarely seem to find these days."

"Ah, yes." She didn't have to look to know Dionne was nodding. "Is it because you have companions to portal, or because you share your down time with the spare heir?"

She jerked her head up and over, glowering at her brother.

"We'll come back to that." Dionne chortled, resting an elbow on the arm of the chair and plopping his chin into his palm. "So, you stand on opposite sides of a war from Gallus?"

"I didn't seek to do so if that's what you're implying." She let her gaze roam, unable to withstand the intensity of his.

"That wasn't what I was implying." His voice was softer than usual. "Are you okay with it?"

She let her reserves slip, her answer open and honest, like they'd always agreed. "No."

Other than Sybil, Asteria was closest to her brothers—especially Dionne. Odo was a friend, but he didn't know everything about her. Her siblings did, though, and they were among the only few who truly understood her.

Wells was making his way onto that list, but she refused to acknowledge that.

She and Dionne were four hundred years apart, but there was a connection between them, a mutual understanding. They didn't need to speak every single day or even every month to maintain their relationship. Whenever they came together, they fell back into a rhythm, teasing and playfully insulting, but always there if the other needed to speak candidly.

"Do you wish to talk about it?" Dionne picked at the pilling on the chair.

She shrugged, drawing her gaze to the Sirian Mark on his forehead. "This is reality, and I doubt anything will change it. I'm hurt, I will admit, but no amount of speaking deeply on the matter will help me."

"I disagree, but I won't push you." Dionne seemed to mull over something before speaking again. "What will you do about Phoebe?"

She blew out a harsh breath of air. "I have absolutely no idea. I'll be lucky if Gallus has yet to speak to her, but the longer I go without talking to her the more I fear he has made a move. They may not have a close relationship, but the one between me and her could very well be weaker than what lies between them."

"You're concerned about the resentment she might harbor for your mistreatment of her?" Dionne tilted his head, bouncing a foot on his knee.

"I didn't mistreat her…" She trailed off as Dionne leveled her with a glare, memories of Asteria teaching Phoebe at the Academy flashing through her mind.

It wasn't that Asteria hated Phoebe. She did love her sister, just in a very different, far more complicated way than she did Dionne, Taranis, or even Sybil. She loved Phoebe for the sheer fact they shared blood, but she didn't know much about her.

That was no one's fault but her own.

"Phoebe wants to be accepted by both of you, possibly more so you than Gallus. You can't underestimate her. She's married to a human, and her husband's family is human. She has a soft spot for them."

"That's what I'm afraid of." She shook her head at him. "If Gallus has spoken to her already, I know he'll use her love for them to his advantage. He may offer protection or manipulate her into thinking they are protected from whatever madness the Lyrans are trying to incite."

"Open and honest, Azzy." Dionne tapped his chest above his heart. "That's the only way to make any improvement with her."

"How often do you still speak with her?" Asteria asked, squinting.

Dionne occasionally helped teach at the Academy, especially when any of he or Taranis's descendants attended. He happened to be teaching Savaric privately on navigating his inherited god-power when Phoebe attended, and the two formed a rather interesting bond when Dionne picked up her teachings after Asteria had stopped.

"You anticipate I'll be forthcoming about my personal relationships when you brush me off?" Dionne snorted, and Asteria launched a small ball of Energy at him. He countered it with his own, a small pop fizzing through the otherwise quiet room. "Trust me on this. I firmly believe the repair of your relationship will ultimately be what can turn her to our side and get her to sway from Gallus if he's spoken to her already."

Asteria groaned with a rumbling undercurrent that had a smile springing across Dionne's face.

He always knew what to say, and despite her being hundreds of years older, his moments of wisdom frequently had her questioning herself. She admired him for it.

Until he opened his mouth again. "So tell me what's going on between you and the boy."

"The *boy*?" Asteria gawked at him, her eyes wide. "He's not a boy—"

"If my memory serves me, he is twenty and eight, no?" Dionne's eyes glittered with his devious grin. "You're six hundred and—"

"Don't." She held up a finger at him, simmering. "You have no place to speak, Noni. How many women have you taken since your first wife aged and passed? Being immortal—or damn near immortal—changes things when it comes to age. Besides, he's not immature by any means. He's already been married before."

Dionne fought another grin.

Damnit.

Asteria had fallen right into his trap, immediately hopping to the defense and alluding to something deeper. She ground her teeth and steadied her racing heart.

How was she to answer the question when she was avoiding it herself? Dionne had already pried at the topic yesterday, and the events of last night between her and Wells complicated things even further.

A small part of her whispered things became complicated the moment he took her hand in his.

"I didn't ask for this." She rose from the chair, picking at her nails. She made her way to the opposite side of the room. "I was doing fine on my own, living in Celestia, visiting Sirian events I was invited to. There were so many opportunities I know we could've met in passing, and yet it had to be now?"

Dionne's heavy gaze weighed on her. "Is it because of the proximity you share as of late?"

"I would be lying if I said no, but that's not all. That seems to be secondary." She brushed her hand over a woven tapestry hanging on the wall beside an oil painting. "We met nearly right before Eldamain asked for my help. He's friends with Odo, and he just... appeared."

"Let me guess..." Dionne dragged out the sentence as he rose, clasping his hands behind his back. "He took your breath away? You couldn't stop thinking about him? He's charming and witty?"

Yes, yes, and yes. But still...

It was the way he looked at her, the way he *saw* her and listened that officially locked in her interest. Of course, he was stunning, but there was far more to it than that.

"No one has spoken to me the way he has," Asteria whispered, squinting at the painting. "He's extremely challenging at times, but I find myself softening under his gaze and from his words."

"I know Dola converses with Fate," Dionne said as he stepped up beside her, trying to draw her gaze. "There is no Lyran who convenes with Destiny. There is a difference between those two forces."

She frowned at him.

"Don't look at me like that. You and I think of Fate in similar ways. It's a predetermined outcome driven by our choices, even after one knows Fate. It's all a cycle, and we usher it in by trying to change it.

"I believe Destiny works far differently." He bumped her shoulder, and she curled her lip. "Destiny is a choice we're given. An outcome that *can* be but doesn't *have* to be. We can shape it into what we want."

"You believe he is some sort of Destiny for me?" Asteria raised an eyebrow.

He shrugged, studying her. "I think Destiny has given him to you and wants to know what you will do with him. It doesn't mean you must accept him or that he's your future. He could be temporary, or he could be everything."

"I'm beginning to believe you converse with Destiny." Asteria huffed a breath of disbelief. She crossed her arms and faced Dionne fully. "What are you getting at?"

"Don't fight it." Dionne mimicked her, but instead of crossing his arms, he held hers to keep her in place. "I've loved many times, each partner as genuine as the last. I've always told you the relationship between you and Rod wasn't normal. I still firmly believe it was arranged between Danica and Rod. You might not want to believe me, but I've always had my suspicions.

"You deserve a greater love than that, and the way this man looks at you…" Dionne squeezed her arms. "Something tells me he could offer it if you let him."

"If I let him." She paused, uncurling her arms and letting them fall to her sides. "He's a *mortal* Sirian."

Dionne frowned as if that hadn't occurred to him. She couldn't blame him because she frequently associated herself with Andromedans or Lyrans, so this was likely the first time Dionne had experienced her around actual mortal Beings.

"How do you do it?" She stepped out of his grasp, holding her hands to her sternum. "If I continue to let him in, I fear where this goes, so I need you to tell me how you watch the ones you love die one after the other."

"Mannah was the hardest." He sighed as he dropped his gaze, referring to his first wife. "I remarried in hopes of replacing the hole she'd left behind, and it worked for a moment. When Leia died, it was another hole dug into my heart. After that, I knew I couldn't continue to marry. But I could have partners, and there was nothing wrong with that. I suppose I have enough love to go around."

Asteria rolled her eyes at the sly grin he flashed her, turning her back as she walked to the window. His soft footsteps followed, his radiating presence heating her back.

"We're different, Asteria." He wrapped his arms around her shoulders, kissing the back of her head. "You don't willingly share your love. You keep it hidden, and very few truly glimpse it in its entirety. Sometimes I wonder if I even have."

She tried to wiggle out of his embrace, but he held her tighter, warming his arms to a comforting degree.

"I also knew this would be my life at an early age. Sybil and Enki prepared me for the ever-fleeting love that came with being Andromedan. I stand by what I said—that they tried to groom you for Rod. With both of you being Lyran, they thought you'd be together for eternity. There was no need to prepare you to watch your loved one age."

"What is your advice then, Noni?" Asteria sighed heavily, lolling her head against his so it bumped aggressively into his cheek. She smirked when he grunted.

"I amend my suggestion from before. Be careful how close you get, Azzy."

She finally tore herself from him, whirling with a frown. "Do you have a reason not to trust him?"

"It's not him I don't trust." Dionne patted her head like a mut, and she shoved him with the Energy. He stumbled back, chuckling darkly. "It's *you* I don't trust not to get yourself hurt. Those you do love, you love deeply. As you said, he is *mortal*. I love you, but I don't believe you're ready to face the true extent of what that means."

Asteria knew this was where her frustrations came from when it came to Wells. She wanted to win against the care she'd developed for him, to be able to withstand his charm and pull.

Speaking of her care for him...

"What's taking them so damn long?" Asteria whipped out of Dionne's grasp, heading for the guard at the doors. Dionne followed close behind, his feet shuffling as she flicked her hand at the guard. "Move."

"Let him do his work, Asteria," Dionne said as he saddled up beside her, grabbing her arm.

She yanked it out of his hand and, without looking at the guard, wrapped the Aether around the male's torso, and tugged him clear of the doors.

"Fucking Gods," Dionne swore under his breath as she shoved open the double doors and entered the hallway. "Asteria, wait—"

She ignored Dionne's calls, marching toward the study he used to occupy when he was king. Asteria wasn't about to let the Basu family bully the Carraphims into something they didn't need to do, especially after the way Taranis had greedily insisted on the treaty before Wells even presented the option to him.

Again, she also didn't know Savaric like she knew Dionne or even his oldest sons. Her trust was far and few these days, especially considering the state of the world, and she wasn't about to leave Wells in a room for longer than she deemed necessary.

While Asteria knew the signature of Dionne's Energy and god-power, which passed down to any of his descendants, she was curious if she could decipher Wells's from any other Sirians wielding the Aether in Krishna Castle. She dug into the vortex—as Gavril so conveniently named it—reaching for anything familiar.

She nearly stumbled at how immediate it was.

Sure enough, beside the Aether she knew Wells wielded, there was a smoky signature similar to Dionne's, just a little fainter and mingled deeper within the Energy. That was Savaric.

As she neared the study, the signal grew stronger. It was the deep, thrumming of the Aether, but there was something warm and inviting about its connection to Wells. Like a familiar, sweet blanket draping around her, seeping into her bones and filling her chest.

Asteria stopped just outside the door, about to burst in when Wells's voice carried through the deep wood separating them.

"We don't mind that you want to house the library here at Krishna Castle," Wells explained, that even and calm tone of his stern but alluring.

"But those from Eldamain, The Northern Pizi, and hopefully Etherea should have access to the records without question. We're all part of the treaty, contributing the knowledge we share to stock the library. It won't only be your scholars."

"If we share the library, then I propose each country that signs the treaty also help fund the construction." Savaric sounded far too much like Dionne, his voice the same caliber and tone. Again, Asteria felt slightly nostalgic for the times when Dionne was still king.

Everything was far simpler.

There was a subtle thrumming, and if she closed her eyes, she could see Wells drumming his fingers on the arm of the chair where he sat.

"Lady Asteria, are you—"

Asteria wrapped a strand of Aether around Dionne's throat and gave a gentle but firm squeeze to silence him. He grunted as he stumbled into her back from shock.

"Spying," he finished in a hushed, slightly strangled tone.

"I don't spy," she hissed quietly, shrugging. "I'm observing."

Dionne snorted, and she squeezed tighter without entirely choking him.

"I can agree to that," Wells finally said with a pause before he added, "Again, though, there will be no arguments should someone—and I mean *anyone*—from one of the allied countries come asking to use the library as a resource. Whether that be diplomats or common folk, you can't turn them away."

There was a heavy, rather dramatic sigh, but then King Savaric spoke. "Fine. I can agree to that."

Pride swelled in Asteria's chest, warming every extremity and pulling a wide grin across her face. Listening to Wells in his element was absolutely fascinating, and watching him succeed in each negotiation—not with a single argument, but with calm, calculated conversation—had her ready to fall at his feet in surrender.

Which was a problem because she didn't want to surrender to this pull. She wanted to win against it.

Her conversation with Dionne made her realize it wasn't because she was stubborn and simply needed to win for the sake of it.

She needed to win the fight because if the interest and attraction won, she couldn't fathom falling in love with someone who would grow old without her.

CHAPTER 46

PHOEBE

"It was surely a warning." Phoebe paced the empty Council room, shaking her head as she nibbled at the edge of her nail. "Sybil and Asteria went against their parents, so the first attack was on the things they love. Sybil loves Eldamain, Asteria loves Sybil."

"Phoebe," Dustin drawled, trying to grab her, but she twisted out of his reach. "I highly doubt that was the entire motivation behind the attack on Eldamain. This *is* war, and Gallus has made the first move."

"They know damn well Asteria and the Carraphims are traveling between The Northern Pizi and Riddling." Phoebe shook her head, wagging a finger at Dustin. "They could have attacked either of those countries first. If it's a war strategy, you want to threaten a potential ally. You hit them in a way that causes them to pause. It's exactly what they did with us! That's why I think Eldamain's attack was purely emotional."

"Eldamain is also leading this charge against the other Lyrans," Dustin explained, leaning onto the cane to lift himself from the chair. "Their strategy could've been to chop them off at the head and keep the other countries complicit."

"If Eldamain fell, Dionne and Taranis would still very well enter this because of Danica and Asteria." Phoebe stopped pacing, her vision swaying from the constant back and forth. She rubbed at her forehead and down her face, growling as a pulse of her god-power shot through her veins. "It's a demonstration of what happens when you go against your parent, who's an all-powerful Lyran."

Dustin sighed, and Phoebe felt his presence before she saw his feet enter her view on the ground. She slowly raised her head, peeking through her fingers, body trembling. He rested the cane against the nearest chair before gripping her shoulders.

"If Asteria has spoken to Taranis and Dionne already, the chances you're next are quite high," he said gently, his thumb brushing her sleeve. "I think it's *still* worth hearing what she has to say."

"What happens when Gallus, Caine, or Endora find out I've accepted Asteria and the Carraphims into the castle?" Her voice cracked, and she ground her teeth. "Dustin, I feel like I'm falling apart. Pieces of me are being chipped away with every move made on either side."

"Gallus asked you not to get involved, to stay neutral," Dustin explained, his hands dropping to hold hers. He lifted her knuckles to his lips, muttering into them. "A proper neutral party will hear both sides. You've accepted Gallus into your home for his side, and now you must offer Asteria the same courtesy."

"I can't tell the Council what I've done." Phoebe shook her head, shutting her eyes. "What am I to say?"

"Lead them as you normally would through any other meeting and guide them to the conclusion to stay neutral." Dustin cradled her head in his hands. "You're extremely brilliant, resilient, and strong. You don't need my help, but know you have it if you need me."

"You have yet to speak entirely on what you think of my decision." Phoebe gauged his reaction, searching those beautiful eyes. She raised her hands, brushing a stray black strand of hair behind his ear. "What are your thoughts?"

"It doesn't matter what my thoughts are." He shook his head, face revealing nothing false. "You're queen. The decision is ultimately yours, and you made the best choice for that moment."

"You think I should change my mind at some point?" She squinted at him, waiting for *anything* from him. She loved Dustin for his level-headedness and ability to think beyond clogged emotions. Except for moments when she wanted to know exactly what he was thinking. "So you do believe I've made the wrong decision."

"It's not what I think you should or shouldn't do, Phoebe." Dustin brought his lips to her forehead directly over her Mark. "Sometimes there isn't a right or wrong answer. It's just what is, and you must make a decision and wait to see the outcome. You already have the answers in your head. I see what you're distracted from right now."

"Then help me see clearly." Her plea was fragile and broken, tears threatening to spill. "Don't let me drown here."

Dustin frowned, a quick blink as if she'd slapped him. She didn't mean it as an attack, but it was how she felt, and he had to know.

She may be queen, but he was also king.

"I think…" His eyes darted over her face. He sighed, shaking his head. "I think you know staying neutral is not the way. You don't have respect for humans only within our borders, but across the world. If you didn't, you wouldn't have ignored the Council's requests to renew treaties with countries historically known for bullying humans.

"I also saw your request from our scout in Eldamain." His mouth turned into a sad smile. "You asked them to report the *human* casualties from the attack—not any others."

Phoebe bit the inside of her cheek, averting her gaze. She had nothing to say because he was right.

"You can't protect mortals by only protecting one country." Dustin reached for his cane as he released his grip on Phoebe, clearing his throat and straightening his back. "I want you to also consider whether you trust Gallus's promise. He may very well be manipulating you."

It was Phoebe's turn to lurch back from his words. He leveled her with a knowing glare.

"Come now, Phoebe." Dustin sighed, his shoulders deflating. "I love you, and I know you yearn for his acceptance and acknowledgment, but this isn't the way to get it. Gallus is thirty-five years too late, and a God doesn't suddenly change overnight. Especially on the brink of a war he's responsible for.

"I will leave you with the Council. Remember, it's one step at a time. You first need to speak with Asteria and the Carraphims and see what they will offer to help protect the humans here. We will assess the best move from there."

Phoebe accepted Dustin's quick kiss just as the double doors to the Council room gently swung open. He offered a reassuring wink before walking out.

The moment his figure disappeared around the corner, the Council members filed in one after the other and bowed as they passed her to their chairs. The last thing she wanted to do right now was talk to the Council members about what had transpired.

The Council barely took her seriously now, and she had to portray this failure as intentional.

Phoebe felt weak because of her decision; she should've done something more. Being bested by Endora and Caine, seeing Dustin dangling between them, was a heavier blow than Gallus telling her to stand down.

"Your Majesty," Gareth began, each man following his lead as they slowly lowered to their seats one by one.

Phoebe stood beside her chair at the head of the table, refusing to sit. She needed to maintain the upper hand and advantage in this meeting, and that meant appearing grander than them. "Hello, gentlemen. I'll forego introductions as I fear time is of the essence. I presume you lot have heard the rumors of Heridy?"

"Are they rumors?" Lucius sneered, wrinkling his beak of a nose. "Or is it the truth?"

"The attack on Heridy by Allanis and Lord Zephyr is in fact true," Phoebe confirmed, and the men grumbled their discontent.

"Why in the Gods would they do that?" Edric scowled, and while he kept his back straight, his eyes darkened with what Phoebe knew was fear. "It seems rather unprovoked. Do we have any idea what led to this? Did the two countries have a falling out of sorts?"

"We just spoke a few months back on how Allanis, Sylvan, and Eldamain were nearly sister countries," Noel interjected, pinching the bridge of his nose. "Were we led so astray as to believe such a thing?"

"I don't believe you were," Phoebe said, resting her fingertips on top of the stone table. The crack in the middle of the stone was still there from the meeting Noel referred to. "Something else entirely has occurred."

"Have we received word from any royals?" Lucius narrowed his eyes at her, ever suspicious. "What has occurred that the world doesn't seem entirely privy to that *you* are aware of?"

Once again, she would have to quell entirely true rumors by misleading and manipulating them.

How was she any better than Gallus?

"This is far bigger than a simple squabble between two countries," Phoebe carefully explained, navigating her words. "From what I've learned, there is an argument amongst the Gods that has broken them into two separate factions. The Gods have saw fit to involve the kingdoms in such an argument, so they're pinning us against one another."

"What are they arguing about that requires an attack on another country?" Gareth's mouth hung open rather comically, but Phoebe was too focused on how she needed to present the information.

"Humans," Phoebe admitted, her eyes flicking over each member of the Council. She was surprised when Ronan snapped his head to her, the drunken haze briefly clearing from his vision. "There are some Gods who wish to eliminate humans or enslave them at the very least. Thus far, it appears Allanis, Sylvan, Teslin, and Thalassa are in agreement with the

Gods who want to commit such an atrocity."

"How do you know this?" Ronan asked, squinting. His voice was clear and strong.

Phoebe tilted her head. She'd never known a drunk to suddenly become sober in less than a second.

"Lord Gallus came and spoke with me privately after I heard of a scuffle between some folks of Teslin and Lady Asteria." Phoebe suppressed her neck roll at having to use her sister's formal title. At the mention of Lord Gallus, though, Lucius rolled his eyes, slumping in his chair. "He came to me in an effort to ask for Etherea's neutrality so that we stay out of this situation between the other countries."

Silence weighed heavy on her shoulders as the men exchanged curious glances. They raised their eyebrows, tilted their heads, and muttered to one another. For a moment, Phoebe wondered if they would take that request as is and be happy with neutrality.

But Ronan stared at her with an intensity she'd never experienced from him before.

"You have something you would like to say." Phoebe didn't expect Ronan to be the one to lead the campaign she hoped they'd take. She needed the Council to ask to hear both Gallus *and* Asteria's side of things so she could use it as an excuse should Gallus or the others come poking around.

"You simply agreed to neutrality with no benefit to our country?" Ronan bit out through clenched teeth. This was an entirely different male than the one she'd come to know over the last year. Granted, he was younger than the other Councilmen, but she thought he was just as flippant and pompous as the others. "A God doesn't simply ask without a bargain."

"He did offer something in return." Phoebe nodded slowly, clasping her hands behind her back and digging her nails into her palms. "He offered protection for our humans. He said so long as we stayed out of it, our humans would remain unscathed."

"We should accept that offer," Lucius blurted with a half-crazed chuckle. "Save us the fight and unnecessary death—"

"Did you accept?" Ronan's bright eyes were alight with worry and a slight glimmer of panic. Phoebe pursed her lips at the emotion. "Tell me you didn't accept that."

"It appears you have far more to contribute to this discussion than usual, Lord Ronan," Phoebe said, carefully dragging out her chair and lowering into it, maintaining eye contact with him. "I would like to hear what you have to say."

Ronan inhaled slowly, his shoulders stiff. "I have plenty of thoughts on the matter, but first, I hope you plan to hear what the other Gods may offer, Your Majesty."

Phoebe nearly chuckled in relief, but she swallowed down any emotion that would give away her reaction. "You believe the others have something to offer?"

"If the countries you speak of are on one side, we must consider the countries on the opposing side." Ronan angled toward her, every muscle drawn tight. She even caught the Energy glowing faintly beneath his skin. "That leaves The Northern Pizi, Eldamain, Riddling, and Celestia."

"Perfect!" Noel shouted, throwing his arms up. "Four countries against the other four, and we can stay neutral to ensure safety for our people."

"We should still hear them out," Ronan snarled, curling his lip. "If Lady Asteria was seen fighting Teslin, it means she is on the other side of whatever war might ensue. You forget she is *our* Goddess."

Phoebe was fascinated and quite curious about Ronan's reaction. He was normally the quietest, the drunk who held his seat and nothing more. Something about this topic—this situation—ignited a flame within him that she didn't think a single Council member was capable of wielding.

"I'm happy to hear Asteria's side should she come," Phoebe explained, resting her forearms on the table. "Until then, I agree we should remain neutral. Once we've heard both sides, we can act to protect our people to the fullest capacity. If we can avoid war, we can protect our people far longer and devise a better strategy if the antagonizers come out successful."

The men seemed content with that answer and rather pleased Phoebe had shouldered the responsibility of this hard decision rather than leaning on them for further input.

Except Ronan.

As the men filed out of the room at the conclusion of the meeting, Ronan was the last to rise, shaking his head and slowly following the others. Phoebe watched him carefully as what she now realized was a drunken facade stayed off his face.

"Ronan," Phoebe said gently, grabbing his wrist to stop him from going any further. He startled, glaring at her hand before pinning it on her face. "I wish to speak to you for a moment."

His body relaxed as he nodded once, lips pressing into a thin line. "Sure."

Sure?

Ronan continued to transform before her eyes. She thought maybe he was beyond his middle ages, but the longer she looked at him and the more the mask he wore slipped away, he appeared to be in his early fifties—if that.

He had a few streaks of gray in his dark brown hair, a patch of it on the chin of his beard and scattered through his mustache. Dark brown eyes were surrounded by wrinkles, but they weren't made from decades in the bottle.

She realized they gathered at the corners of his eyes.

"What can I do for you, Your Majesty?" Ronan hauled those dark eyes to hers, wary and tired.

The corner of Phoebe's mouth twitched. "How long have you been on this Council?"

He frowned, blinking. "A decade or so—since my father passed."

"You inherited the position?" She raised an eyebrow. She'd never paid much attention to her father's Council until she finished her time at the Academy, which would've been around the time Ronan took his father's place.

He nodded slowly, keeping his mouth in a tight line as he waited for her to elaborate.

"I think you deceived my father, and you continue to deceive the Council." He startled at the accusation, opening his mouth, but she stopped him with a raised hand. "Ronan, I don't blame you. But I think you have far more to contribute to this position if you showed your true self. What you've been showing me is certainly not that."

He didn't answer, just continued to study her face, possibly searching for any deception.

She couldn't fault him for his choice in maintaining distance. He didn't know her, not in the year she'd been queen, and that was because she'd purposely kept her distance from them.

That was when she believed every one of the Councilmen was a piece of shit.

"You care for humans," Phoebe concluded, folding her hands in her lap and leaning back against the chair. "Genuinely?"

Ronan sighed with the ghost of a grin, nodding. "You and I are quite similar."

Phoebe smiled then, her chest lightening.

"My husband is human, if you started to piece that together," Ronan said gently, folding his hands on top of the table. "My parents were rather absent most of my life, and our human staff contributed far more to my upbringing than they did. As you can imagine, humans are just as important to me as they are to you."

"Were you the one who told the others about the Decay all those months ago?"

He shrugged, pursing his lips. "I figured it would've been worth it. I didn't know you'd been working with Endora on a cure. Although, if you'd asked me, I would've suggested someone else to work with. In the end, it seems the Sirians I trust are the ones who came up with the cure."

The blood drained from Phoebe's face, and she was stunned into silence.

Ronan didn't just care more than he let on. He was smarter, too.

"I don't mean this in a threatening way, Your Majesty, but I know who your real father is." Ronan slowly stood from the chair, his head hung low. "I know there's more than you're letting on about this argument and the way in which Lord Gallus came to you. I don't presume to know the inner workings of your relationship with the other demi-gods or the Gods, but I'm sure it's strained."

The other *demi-gods.*

This was the first time a Councilman had verbally acknowledged Phoebe being a demi-god. In fact, it was the first time anyone had. Those who dared to speak about her heritage called the demi-gods Andromedans.

She'd never thought of herself as god-like before.

"I can't forget you pretend to be someone you're not," Phoebe admitted softly. "Why do you hide?"

"Why do you?"

Those simple three words yanked the air from her lungs, her mouth dropping open.

"I hope you do hear Lady Asteria's side, Queen Phoebe," Ronan said as he moved toward the door, his eyes no longer on her but straight ahead. "I fear nothing good will come from remaining neutral, despite Lord Gallus offering something in return that *sounds* appealing."

Before Ronan made it to the door, Phoebe found her voice again and blurted out the first thing that came to mind. "What did you specialize in at the Asterian Academy?"

She shot her head over her shoulder to find him frozen in place, hand poised on the doorknob and head hung low. She vaguely caught the slight smirk at the corners of his lips.

If he was born into a lordship, he should've taken the Diplomat route, but Phoebe had a hunch that wasn't what he'd done.

"Warrior, Your Majesty." Ronan met her eyes. "I bargained with Lady Asteria to take the Warrior route."

CHAPTER 47

SYBIL

S ybil peered into Quin's study, chuckling when she spotted the male behind his desk. His arms were propped on top, his head shoved into his palms. She snuck in and shut the door, the click echoing through the silent space.

Quin's head shot up, and the desire to tease vanished from her. His eyes were bloodshot and heavy-lidded with dark circles like Piers's. She frowned as she approached, tilting her head.

"I apologize for the unusual greeting," Quin said, sighing heavily before rising. "One could say I've been a tad overwhelmed as of late."

"It's unfortunate timing for your ascension to the throne," Sybil agreed, nodding. "A war, treaties, an attack on your country—"

"Attending a private meeting with *Gods*." Quin laughed, the sound hollow. "What sort of times are we living in, Syb? Any advice?"

She chuckled as he rounded the desk. "I can't say I've experienced any events quite like this in my existence thus far. I've even faced death more personally than I'd care to."

"Are you well?" Piers's voice permeated the air, and Sybil spun on her heel to face him.

He stopped a few feet away, his gaze studying every inch of her. Her skin warmed wherever his eyes fell, and her suddenly dry throat made it difficult to smile.

"Heavens," Quin groaned, rubbing a hand across his stubble. "I'm sorry, Syb. I didn't forget your injury, although it seems to have evaded me momentarily. How are you?"

"Two small scars I believe are permanent but entirely healed otherwise." Her stomach lurched with a phantom pain. She winced, covering it with a shrug, but Piers's hazel eyes lit with repressed anger. "My enhanced healing kicked in once the dagger and effects of the hematite were countered."

"I'm more than happy to hear that." Quin rubbed a hand against her shoulder with a grin that didn't quite reach his eyes. "I fear I'm not ready for the losses that will undoubtedly come from this war. I already lost villagers, and while I may not have known them personally, it feels like such."

"I wish I could offer words to prepare you." She shook her head, white braids brushing her waist. "Unfortunately, there are none that lessen the blow of loss, even for the immortal."

There was a crackle of static like embers popping in a fireplace. The three turned to the shimmering portal waving in the middle of the room.

"Is that a portal?" Quin eyed the veil warily.

"Morana said she would open one for us to walk through," Sybil explained, and Piers's fingers gently brushed hers as she led them to its edges.

"You just walk through," Piers said to his brother. "It may be slightly unpleasant."

Sybil stepped in to avoid being alone with Piers. The strange tugging sensation slammed into her sternum and pulled, the veil kissing her skin like dipping herself under a current of water charged by lightning. It was mere seconds before it vanished as their scenery changed to what Sybil knew as the Hall in Eonia.

"Holy shit," Quin whispered, and Sybil couldn't conceal her giggle. "This is Eonia."

Sybil forgot that few mortals ever stepped foot in Eonia. She'd spent half her childhood and adolescence in Morana's home, sometimes in Gallus and Danica's with Asteria. As far as she knew, she'd been the only Andromedan raised within Eonia. The rest were raised by their non-Lyran parents in whichever country they were conceived in.

Despite that, she knew plenty of Andromedans visited Eonia with their parents at some point in their lives. Since she'd reached adulthood, Sybil rarely visited. The last time she was here before her most recent meeting with Dola had been over a century ago.

She was sure it was when Asteria had ended things with Rod.

"Which Carraphims are these?" Rod called from across the room, leaning back against one of the tables surrounding the gold statue in the center.

"Crown Prince Quintin Carraphim, Lord Rod," he introduced himself as Sybil guided them to where the Lyrans gathered. When they were only a few feet away, Quin and Piers bowed at the waist. Sybil rolled her eyes, and Taranis observed them with interest from two tables down. "This is my younger brother, Prince Piers."

Rod released a quick breath, his mortal eyes bouncing between Sybil, Piers, and Quin. He landed on Sybil, raising an eyebrow. "How come you don't greet me as such?"

"Do you truly wish to know the answer to that question?" Sybil countered with her own eyebrow, the drakon growling in her chest as her vision pulsed green at the edges.

Rod sighed heavily, throwing his head over his shoulder to where Morana and Danica sat at a table together. "You let her speak to me this way?"

"Come down from your pedestal, Rod," Morana chided, her face flat. "I wouldn't put it past her to shift into her drakon to prove a point."

Rod shot Sybil a glare, but she caught the playfulness beneath.

She'd honestly never minded the Lyran, especially because his teasing only ever matched her own, similar to how siblings might interact. The only thing that kept her from admitting her preference for him over any other Lyran—besides Morana and Asteria—was the hell he put Asteria through.

"King Taranis," Quin greeted from where he stood, dipping his head before his eyes latched onto the other two Lyrans. "Lady Morana and Lady Danica, I don't believe I've had the pleasure of meeting either of you Goddesses."

"I understand you're not far from rising to king in your father's place, correct?" Morana asked, but her eyes shot to Piers with a wicked grin. "It's nice to see you again, Piers."

Sybil huffed a breath of disbelief, glaring at Morana as Piers sputtered beside her. She glared at him from the corner of her eye, and he gave her a sheepish, heart-clenching wince of a grin.

"Why must we have *both* princes present?" Danica asked, studying the men from her seat. Rod floated away from his table toward her. "I suppose I understand the soon-to-be king, but a spare heir?"

"He's not just a spare heir," Quin explained, not unkindly. "He's my highest Lieutenant General beside his partner, Sir Gavril Faris."

Morana's mouth dropped, the mix of shock and disappointment dropping a lead weight down Sybil's chest and into her stomach. Her mother's lips thinned, and she knew immediately what was going through her head.

Sybil watched the people around her fall victim to cheating, and here she was, letting Piers kiss her while still with his partner. She could feign ignorance that she didn't know how their relationship worked, but she knew it didn't make it right regardless.

"I understand Asteria is arriving with this Gavril and your youngest brother?" Danica narrowed her eyes. "What sort of position does he hold?"

"They brought him with to The Northern Pizi to discuss the more technical aspects of their treaty," Taranis said, his thick arms crossed over his chest. "It's my assumption he was the one to come up with the treaty in the first place, so I will guess that's his use."

Piers shrugged, sliding between two empty chairs at the table beside them. "We use him when we need to form alliances or negotiate agreement terms with other countries. He's a bit of a smooth talker, if you will. A charmer. He tends to get us what we want."

"An honest spare heir." Rod snorted at that, and even Taranis smirked. Sybil's heart picked up its pace. "How boring."

Quin paused halfway down to his seat, attempting to school his face. Tension rolled from him and Piers at the slightly disrespectful comment from Rod.

Sybil shook her head and reluctantly took one of the empty seats beside Piers. If Rod was already in a tizzy and had yet to see Asteria and Wells interact...

As though on the same mental plane, Taranis and Sybil snapped their heads to each other just as the clap of a portal resounded through the room, their faces saying the same thing.

This meeting could turn hostile quickly.

Taranis must have seen the interactions between Wells and Asteria when they visited him, which was not a promising sign. If he'd picked up on it from just a day or two with them, there was no way Rod wouldn't see the undoubtedly romantic tension.

"You need to get Wells to keep his mouth shut," Sybil hissed as she grabbed Piers's wrist and tugged him close. Gavril's laugh traveled to them, followed by what Sybil knew was Dionne's deeper timber.

"Why?" Piers asked, his eyes flickering over her face.

"I can't say." Sybil met Asteria's gaze, her stomach knotting at the proximity between Asteria and Wells. She imperceptibly jerked her eyes over to Rod. Asteria followed, stiffening and halting in her stride. "Just know if you don't want a problem with Rod, you need to separate Wells and Asteria."

"I don't—"

Gavril fell heavily into the seat on the other side of Piers, and Sybil released his hand. He planted a kiss beneath the prince's jaw.

Sybil swallowed against the burning jealousy at the heat in Piers's darkened eyes when Gavril whispered something in his ear.

"I would like to make this quick and painless," Asteria said as Dionne looked at her with a burning gaze, no doubt thinking the same thing as Sybil and Taranis. He waited for her to catch up with him and casually swapped places with Wells, slipping Asteria's hand into the crook of his arm. "I have things I need to be doing. Not that you lot would know, given you're hiding in Eonia while Aveesh is being assaulted."

"Watch your tone," Danica warned, her gaze trailing Dionne and Asteria as they sat at the same table. Sybil relaxed some when Wells shook Taranis's hand and sat beside the Andromedan without a second glance at Asteria. "You don't want to start this meeting off with disdain."

"I beg to differ." Asteria shot her mother a mischievous smirk, and Sybil heard Wells snicker under his breath.

Sybil immediately tensed up again. Piers eyed her with a frown before she recognized his studious expression fall over his face.

"This is a meeting to assess where we are and what still needs to be done," Rod said, rubbing his forehead. Morana shot him a look of disbelief. "I, for one, don't have the patience for a fit between Danica and Asteria or myself and Asteria, so let's just begin."

Asteria narrowed her eyes at Rod, but Sybil's heart rate didn't slow. She kicked Piers under the table when he tilted his head, gaze bouncing between Asteria and Rod.

Piers glared at her for striking him, but his lips twitched.

There was no doubt in Sybil's mind that Piers would figure out the history between Rod and Asteria by the end of this meeting. The male was brilliant, always connecting the world together like a puzzle.

"Thank you," Morana said, dragging out the words. "Where do we sit with your alliances and a military plan?" Morana looked to Taranis,

Dionne, and Quin for an answer.

"I believe my brother already agreed to the treaty's terms," Dionne said, gesturing toward Taranis. He dipped his head at Quin next. "I'm delighted to report King Savaric also agreed to join this alliance—with his own modifications to the treaty, of course."

"I heard the additions King Taranis requested regarding Etherea, should they join," Quin confirmed with a nod, folding his hands on the table. "What has Riddling requested?"

"The library of shared knowledge outlined in the treaty," Wells interjected, earning a slight glare from Dionne. "Riddling wishes to house such a library within their capital's borders, and in order for any other country to access it, they hope the allied countries will help fund its construction."

"I have no problem with that." Quin shrugged nonchalantly. "It's harder for war to come to their shores, anyway. I would have proposed Riddling or The Northern Pizi, and it makes perfect sense we would all help fund it just as we will help stock it."

"I don't care about a library." Taranis copied Quin's shrug, and Wells chuckled with amusement.

"Then that means Eldamain, The Northern Pizi, and Riddling pledge to support the cause we stand for," Rod said, reluctantly dragging his gaze to Asteria with apprehension.

Asteria raised her eyebrows, blinking innocently. Sybil feigned rubbing her nose to cover the grin she was losing against.

"What am I looking at, Syb?" Piers whispered from the corner of his mouth, not tearing his attention from the current staredown between Asteria and Rod. "Do they have some sort of feud?"

"You could say that." She met his eyes, the wind knocked out of her when they dropped from her eyes to her lips. His knee gently rested against hers under the table, and she knew she should draw it away, but the warmth went straight through her.

"What of Celestia?" Morana interrupted, lessening the blow of the question compared to it coming from Rod or Danica. "I know I was just there not too long ago, but I didn't get the chance to talk of war with them. Have you?"

"They are aware of all the events that have occurred." Asteria nodded slowly, but Sybil caught the tension in her neck. "I'll be talking to them next."

"Why not Etherea?" Danica questioned at the same time Morana asked Sybil, "What have you found on Phoebe?"

Everyone snapped their gazes to Sybil. She startled slightly at the attention, but Piers bumped his elbow against her arm.

"As most of you know, Endora stabbed me before the attack on Eldamain," Sybil explained, her stomach clenching. She shivered, and Piers rested his arm on the back of her chair. She shot him a look of warning, but even Gavril offered a tight-lipped grin. "She said something that stuck with me. I don't think it was said lightly, whether she believed I would die or not."

Sybil turned to Asteria, her eyes pleading. She tensed, jerking her head back.

"Not only did my connections in Etherea tell me that King Dustin was in the infirmary for quite a few days with rather extensive injuries"—Sybil paused, swallowing—"but they also said shortly after he was there, Phoebe pulled any Etherean military from the borders of Sylvan."

Piers bristled, his arm flexing behind her. She shut her eyes, preparing herself for Asteria to lose it.

"Between that and what Endora said to me, I have reason to believe Gallus and the others have already convinced Phoebe not to get involved."

The room went silent, and not just from everyone stilling around them.

No, the Universe churning outside of Eonia waited to see what the Goddess of Sirians and blue starfire would do as her power thrummed throughout the room.

"Blue," Wells whispered, but not quietly enough. Sybil and Piers both heard, but a quick glance at Rod told Sybil he hadn't registered the nickname.

Then something incredible happened that Sybil hadn't yet seen between Asteria and Wells.

Asteria's starfire immediately retreated from her veins, her mortal form holding steady, body visibly relaxing.

"Did you see that?" Sybil asked Piers, leaning around him to address Gavril. "What just happened?"

"Long story," Gavril replied without looking at Sybil, his eyes narrowed on Wells. "All I can say is something is happening between those two beyond flirting." Gavril glanced at Piers over his shoulder, something akin to awe on his face. "Wells has been acting in a way I haven't seen in over two years."

Two years...

That was when Ruelle had died.

"Do you think..." Piers trailed off, gauging Gavril's reaction. The latter shrugged, but it was a confirmation. "Out of all the women, he picked the Goddess?"

"What did Endora say to you?" Dionne suddenly asked Sybil.

She pressed her lips together, watching Asteria again. "She said we couldn't win without Eldamain *or* Etherea, right before the attack began in Heridy."

"They thought they would level us," Quin explained, straightening his back. "Not only did they send drakons—one I believe to have been Caine's son—but they had a thirío and Lord Zephyr."

"When was the last time Aveesh saw a thirío?" Rod asked, glancing between Danica and Morana. Both Lyrans were dumbfounded. "How did you manage to ward off a thirío attack?"

"I killed it." Asteria's voice was emotionless as she stared at Rod. The corner of Danica's lips twitched, and Sybil was instantly unnerved by the strange almost-smile. "Low and behold, it was the spare heir of Allanis, so that more than solidified my own stance if the fight in Teslin hadn't."

Rod chuckled at that, shaking his head, his eyes darkening. "Murderous."

Asteria's flashed blue at him.

"Oh," Piers drawled quietly, his wild eyes staring at Sybil. "*Oh,* they—"

Sybil shot out a claw, jabbing him in the leg hard enough for the tip to pierce his flesh.

"Fuck," Piers grumbled, but his eyes danced with excitement at his newest revelation.

"If you don't secure Celestia, we don't have a chance," Danica exclaimed, her aura pulsing gold. "It's time to stop playing with your Beings, Asteria. If they resist you, then you must command them to come to your aid."

Asteria's shoulders rose and fell rapidly as she stared at Danica, but her eyes flicked to where Wells sat a few feet away at the opposite table with Taranis. He nodded imperceptibly, and Sybil held her breath once again as she waited for Rod to catch on.

At this rate, Rod *would* catch on because it seemed Asteria and Wells couldn't keep themselves discreet.

"I don't want to force them to do good," Asteria explained, rubbing her forehead. "I want them to help because it's the right thing to do. If I force them into submission, it won't bode well for future conflict."

"If you rule them with a firm hand now, you won't have to worry about a firm hand later." Danica slammed her hand on the table, and every Sirian in the room jumped aside from Dionne and Taranis. Gavril simply jerked his head and frowned.

"Danica," Morana said quietly, firmly grasping her wrist. "Settle. Not in front of the mortals. Save this."

"Danica is right, though," Rod interjected rather calmly, wincing at Asteria. "This won't work without them now that we've lost Etherea."

"How have we lost Etherea?" Piers asked suddenly, the room quieting. Asteria narrowed her eyes at him, but Sybil's heart skipped. "People can change their minds. If I were in Phoebe's position, I would accept whatever Lord Gallus was offering because to me, there is no other option. Asteria has made it clear she has no real relationship with her sister, so why would Phoebe think she's coming to offer something?"

"That's all grand, but the problem remains that this is Asteria we're talking about." Rod mimicked the glare she attempted to level him with. "Don't give me that look. Given your history with Phoebe, and as this Carraphim prince has pointed out, you said so yourself you're not sure what sway you have with her. I don't see you going to Etherea and winning her over—"

"I firmly believe Asteria is more than capable of switching Phoebe to our side."

The silence following Wells's declaration was far different than the one that had followed Piers. Where that silence had indicated those in the room were mulling over his question, this silence thundered against Sybil's ears.

The calm before a storm.

CHAPTER 48

ASTERIA

Asteria's heart swelled uncomfortably in her chest as Wells pinned those piercing eyes on her with the ghost of a grin. It instilled a confidence in her, one she didn't know she needed when approaching Phoebe.

"What are the grounds of your *beliefs*?" Danica sneered, her eyes flashing behind the mortal hazel. "Asteria herself has mentioned plenty of times she doesn't believe she could sway Phoebe, and that was before we knew of Gallus. Somehow, you believe otherwise?"

Wells snapped his gaze to Danica, tilting his head as he observed her. Asteria clenched her fists in her lap, chest tightening for a whole different reason. "If I've learned anything about Asteria, it's the compassion she bestows upon those she cares for most. It's a rarity in this world worth more than gold."

Asteria wanted nothing more than to throw her arms around him, kiss him, and be as close to him as possible, but Rod ruined the moment as he spewed liquor across his table.

Asteria snarled at him, slamming her hands on the table and creating a crack beneath her palms.

"You're utterly ignorant," she snapped, curling her lip at Rod as he wiped droplets from his chin. Dionne sighed heavily beside her. "You know that, correct?"

"You've made that point once or twice," Rod grumbled, narrowing his eyes not on her but on Wells, and Asteria reeled in the anger humming beneath her skin.

"As long as you know."

"I apologize for my outburst, but it's rare to hear males call Asteria *kind*." Rod scoffed with disbelief, although it was a borderline crazed chuckle. His mortal eyes faded to their molten, pure gold the longer he looked at Wells, fist flexing around the glass.

Fuck.

"I guess I'm fortunate enough to have witnessed such compassion." Wells shrugged, and Asteria san further into her chair. "The way she treats Sirians, her relationship with Sybil and her brothers, the soft spot she's developed for *my* brothers—and even Gavril. I've also been lucky enough to receive her favor."

Asteria glanced at Sybil, who looked ready to implode from anxious anticipation.

"*Favor?*" Rod sneered, and Asteria rolled her eyes when the glass shattered in his hand. "What—"

"I would like to echo my brother," Quin interrupted, and Asteria wanted to kiss *him* on the mouth for the interruption. *What has Wells done to me?* "Asteria refused to join a cause based upon rumors. Despite those rumors being true, I found it admirable she didn't act from fear. She sought proof and validation before making a decision. That level of patience and compassion may sway Phoebe away from whatever Gallus has offered."

Asteria swallowed the emotion clogging her throat. She'd never had many people defend her against those like Danica and Rod, and she wasn't sure what to do with that sort of support.

"Patience." Danica deadpanned. "I've never heard that term used when describing my daughter. I have also never witnessed such a quality."

Morana propped an elbow on the table and rubbed at her forehead, scrunching her face.

Asteria ground her teeth harder when Rod spoke again. "I most certainly have never witnessed patience."

"Have you ever asked yourself if you taxed Asteria's patience?" Wells interjected, and while Asteria appreciated the defense, the last thing she needed right now was for Danica and Rod to see she'd acquired a mortal weakness. "Everyone—man or God—has a limit that never quite restores once it's been breached."

"Who do you think you are?" Rod lurched from his seat, leaning over the table. The youngest Prince of Eldamain simply crossed his arms over his chest and reclined on the back legs of his chair, earning an appreciative glance from Taranis. "You dare speak on a Goddess's behalf, presuming to know things about her that even her own mother disagrees with—who, mind you, is also a Goddess."

"Enlighten me then, *Lord* Rod." Wells plopped his chair down to fold his hands over the table. "What qualities of Asteria do you believe I've not been privy to that you must have been at some point in her six hundred years of life?"

"Wait…" Gavril muttered, looking between Piers and Sybil. "Something's happening. How are Asteria and Rod related again?"

"Would you shut it?" Sybil growled between clenched teeth, reaching around Piers to claw at Gavril.

Gavril frowned, caressing his arm as Piers failed to suppress a low chuckle. Even Asteria had to bite her tongue and take a deep breath.

"Petulance," Danica declared with an air of confidence that set Asteria's aforementioned patience on edge. "Asteria continuously displays unruly, childish behavior when told by anyone what she should or should not do, particularly when it's against her personal desires."

"If I had people regularly telling me how to live my life, I too might throw a tantrum," Wells mumbled, bumping his elbow against Taranis, who only snickered into his chest.

"I'm quite surprised you haven't threatened to set people aflame from the path this conversation has taken," Dionne said under his breath, leaning against Asteria.

"It is an effort," she answered between clenched teeth, taming that fire beneath her mortal skin. He joined the rest of the men in attempting to suppress their chuckles as Rod took it upon himself to finally answer Wells's question.

"What Danica is trying to so eloquently say is that when there are negotiations of any kind to be had, it's like going to war with Asteria." Rod's gaze bounced between Wells and Asteria, and she willed her face into a neutral mask to protect Wells. "If you truly knew Asteria, you would know she threatens to set someone on fire when she doesn't get her way."

"I have to admit she has threatened to set Quintin, Gavril, and even myself on fire. I would like to believe we are past that point." Wells's gaze snagged on Asteria, the corner of his lips twitching in that smirk she loved, and her heart skipped a few beats.

"And what *point* might that be?" Rod curled his lip, eyes no longer their mortal shade.

Asteria glanced at Quin and Gavril, their faces a mix of fascination and confusion.

Not Piers, though, because of course he'd already caught on to Rod's behavior and the words he wasn't saying.

No—Piers looked directly at Asteria with an eyebrow raised in question.

"I know her for who she is," Wells said as though it were the simplest matter in the entire Realm. Asteria melted when he peered into her soul and added, "I see her."

"You *see* her?" Rod laughed, throwing his head back as it echoed around the heavy silence, shattering the moment. "Please. You've known her for less than a year."

"And how long have you known her?" Wells cocked his head, drumming his fingers on the table. "Hundreds of years? And yet you only see the woman you wish she were."

A tense silence filled the space, clothes rustling as someone shifted in their seat.

If Asteria had to guess, it was probably Sybil.

"I understand, now," Rod muttered, slowly nodding his head, the movement sending Asteria's heart rate into the Heavens as he carefully turned his gaze to her. "So you finally found someone to fuck after one hundred and twenty years?"

Asteria launched from her chair, but Dionne wrapped his arms around her midsection, yanking her back against him as Gavril burst into a fit of coughs.

"You son of a bitch!" Asteria snarled, trying to wiggle free of Dionne's hold. He only tightened his grip, heating his hands to an uncomfortable degree. She pointed a finger at Rod. "It's none of your business who I decide to share my bed with! I could fuck every man here, and it still wouldn't be your concern."

"I would prefer it if you didn't," Gavril mumbled hoarsely as Morana whispered, "Heavens above."

"It's my concern when you've done nothing but put me through absolute hell over what I did!" Rod shouted, knocking his chair to the ground as he shed his mortal skin. His gold form flew toward Asteria from across the room to stand toe-to-toe with her.

She shrugged off Dionne as she snarled, "You cheated on me, you stupid fuck."

"Oh my fucking Gods," Gavril muttered from somewhere.

Rod shot him an irritated glare, his gilded skin pulsing. Asteria's power flared when he drew his gaze to Wells, and her mortal skin nearly slipped from her body as she shot a glowing blue shield around the table Taranis and Wells occupied.

"We're no longer together." She wrapped the Aether around Rod's ankles and jerked it back, nearly taking him to the ground. "We haven't been for over a century, which not only means that you can go fuck whoever you please, but so can I!"

"I'm not talking about when I cheated on you!" Rod shook his head as he righted himself to his full height. "You placed an impossible task upon my shoulders that if I were to stop taking women to my bed, you would consider discussing our future together. Yet here you are, taking a *mortal* Sirian to your bed after reiterating your missive just months ago?"

"For Heaven's sake, Rod." Asteria rubbed her forehead, veins glowing blue. "I hurled you through my office door after that."

"I have not bedded a single Being since then!" Rod threw his arms out, his face falling. "For you. I don't want any others, Asteria, and I'm sorry it's taken me so long to realize that—"

"Congratulations! It's a miracle your cock hasn't fallen off from lack of sex." Asteria narrowed her eyes as she shoved her god-form down. "It's not my fault you believed simply not bedding anyone for a few months meant I would take you back after what you did to me."

"That is a load of bullshit," Rod said, turning his back on her.

"Is it? Because it seems like you apologize for not realizing how much you love me, but you can't be arsed to apologize for *fucking cheating on me!*" This time, when Asteria wrapped the Aether around Rod's legs, she tugged hard enough to send him to his hands and knees.

She had half the mind to demand he grovel, just to see how far this supposed love for her truly went.

"This is typically how family dinners unfold," Taranis muttered, and Asteria gawked at her brother with wide eyes. Her temper dimmed when her eyes connected with Wells, her breath hitching.

Wells only studied her with interest and something he was attempting to hide as his gaze bounced between her and Rod.

A slight panic wiggled into her chest at the thought of Wells misconceiving this situation as her purposely keeping this from him. There was also guilt in this misconception, because what if he thought she'd withheld this information even after he'd been so vulnerable with her about Ruelle and his son?

Asteria was startled by how much it mattered to her.

"As per usual," Morana said, slipping between Asteria and Rod, "it seems we need to take a recess to breathe and collect ourselves."

"I don't need to meet again." Asteria shook off her stupor, clenching her teeth as she waved a hand to remove the shield. "I have my next moves. Wells, Gav, and Piers will come to Celestia with me to convince Odo and Erika. We will go to Etherea from there."

"As long as someone portals us home," Dionne said from behind Asteria, "the rest of us can prepare our armies for the first fleet."

"Each of us will portal one of you back," Morana assured with a nod. "Give Danica, Rod, and myself a few moments alone first."

"Could we…" Piers caught Asteria's eye, bouncing between her and Sybil. "Could we see Eonia?"

"I can take them," Sybil said softly.

Asteria's breaths came too quickly, her chest rising and falling heavily. She only held Sybil's gaze for a moment longer before shooting Rod a glare, the desire to harm him nearly greater than her willpower.

She clenched her fists at her sides to quell her emotions and twisted on her heel. A burst of starfire shot from her hand at the Hall doors before she strode out.

CHAPTER 49

ASTERIA

Asteria's god-form pressed behind her mortal skin as she battled the mess of emotions running through her veins. She hadn't experienced so many at once since Rod had cheated on her.

She growled to herself at the thought, only encouraging the anger burning in her chest. It was strong, but something else was stronger that scared her.

It was the regret and shame for not telling Wells about Rod sooner.

As far as those who existed on Aveesh, only Sybil and her brothers knew. Even Odo didn't know of her past with Rod, although he may have assumed there was some history there.

So why did she feel the need to explain herself to Wells?

Even more, why in the Heavens did she feel guilt? The realization only fueled her anger because guilt meant she cared how her choices and actions made him feel. It was her subconscious acknowledging how much she genuinely cared for him.

Asteria couldn't deny it to herself any longer. She liked Wells *a lot*, and the thought of losing him to something as trivial as her history with Rod didn't just feel like an inconvenience—it felt devastating, like a loss that had yet to occur.

That was better than where she knew these affections could develop, and maybe it was time to create some distance. She could very well use this revelation as an opportunity to add a barrier between them, especially if he was angry with her for not reciprocating the vulnerability he'd graciously handed her.

"Asteria!" Soft, quick footsteps echoed in the thick silence of Eonia. She was all too familiar with the voice. "Asteria, wait."

"I thought you lot wanted a tour of Eonia?" She sneered over her shoulder, but made no effort to stop. Heavens, her heart wanted to, but she knew it was best if she kept walking.

"I thought by now you wouldn't mistake me for my brother." Wells caught up with her. She expected him to walk alongside her, but he picked up his pace and suddenly blocked her path. "Stop for a second."

"You're in the way," she snapped, moving to sidestep him, but he followed. "You know I can very well portal away from you."

"Maybe I will tumble after you." His voice had a playful lilt, but his eyes were heavy with concern.

She tried to step around his other side, but he grabbed her shoulders. She stiffened, narrowing her eyes. "Remember how you said we may be past the threat of fire?"

"I *pray* you prove me wrong," Wells said, emphasizing that prayer by tilting his head to the stars.

"Let me go," she said gently, though it was laced with a hint of venom.

"You don't want me to," he countered, quirking an eyebrow. "If you wanted me to let you go, you're more than capable of making me."

She frowned at that, blinking. Her eyes burned uncharacteristically, and she was perturbed by it. The idea of making him go away burned her to her soul. "Wells…"

"You're angry, rightfully so," he said quietly, minimizing the space between them with a step closer. "You're hurt with what seems like old wounds. I don't know why, but you also seem embarrassed."

She shut her eyes as she resisted the warmth radiating from him, threatening to swallow her. How could he see through her and the act she was failing at? "You shouldn't know all that after a few months."

"So you'll push me away?" She wanted him to snap at her, to yell, but the tenderness in his voice only made her want to cave faster. "Why? What about all that happened in there suddenly changed this?"

"I don't need you to defend me or my honor, nor fight my battles for me."

"I know you don't *need* me to," he said, his thumbs brushing her shoulders, "but I want to. I saw your face in there, Asteria. You can't deny it felt good to have someone fight beside you instead of with you for a change."

That swelling emotion she experienced with him returned, her eyes burning again. Asteria sighed, glancing over her shoulder at the Hall. If they were to talk, this was the last place they needed to be.

"Come with me," she said softly, opening a portal behind her as she fisted his shirt and backed through it.

The scenery morphed from the middle of Eonia to a much darker, more familiar room. One she hadn't been to in over one hundred years.

Wells's eyes dragged over every inch of the walls and ceiling as she released him. He slowly stepped further in, awe and wonder lighting up his features. Asteria smiled as her chest lightened. She folded her hands in front of her, following him.

The walls were a deep brown wood, nearly black. One wall was entirely stocked with books up to the second level. From there, a small balcony jutted into the room. Even the wall of the balcony was stocked with books. Flourishing greenery adorned the others and bent around the stained-glass windows. They depicted nothing special, just a flower found in Eldamain.

A lily.

Above them was a chandelier lit with Energy. Below that, directly in front of them, was a curved, deep red sofa with a blanket draped over one of the cushions.

"Is this..." Wells trailed off, his hand stroking the blanket. He twisted to face her, his expression soft. "This is your home."

"Was my home," she amended, heart clenching. She glanced up at the ceiling with a woeful smile. "This was my childhood home, and then it belonged to me and Rod."

Wells stilled, and a wave of unease seized her.

"Sit," she whispered, sweeping a hand toward the couch.

He lowered beside the blanket, his eyes never leaving hers. She took the spot beside him, folding her hands in her lap as she drew a steadying breath.

Wells cupped her knee, studying her face. "You're not obligated to share anything with me. Your business was aired publicly for us back there, and I understand if you're not ready—"

"I am, though." She met his beautiful, bright, caring eyes, drawn in by the freckles beneath. "I found that once it was out in the open, I wished I'd told you sooner."

He nodded with a slight grin, his thumb brushing once before drawing his hand back.

"I haven't shared this with anyone in decades. Taranis asked once after Dionne made a side comment when they were younger." Asteria stared at the wall across from them where an oil painting hung above an empty marble fireplace. "It's a story, to say the least."

Wells waited patiently, letting her gather her thoughts. She found herself aching to lean against him, wanting his arms around her, his radiance seeping into her to calm the wounds he'd mentioned before.

"Legs," Wells whispered, wiggling his fingers at her.

She frowned but obliged, lifting one of her legs. He chuckled low but faced her on the couch and urged her closer, scooting her between his thighs. He draped her legs over his folded one, then threw his arm over the back of the couch. In this position, she could nestle into him and still easily tilt her head toward him as she talked.

His fingertips brushed her shoulder, and she relaxed into it.

Toying with the skirt wrinkled around her knees, she began. "When they left their world, Danica and Gallus had one another, and Morana and Valeria had each other."

Asteria never knew what Morana and Valeria were like in their prime, and she barely remembered a time when Danica and Gallus were happy together. "Dola and Irena were never interested in sexual partnerships, and I think the prospect of intermingling with other Beings intrigued Rod, Nen, and Zephyr the most.

"I mentioned in Ghita it's very rare for Lyrans to have children."

"Were you promised to Rod?" Wells frowned, his finger twisting a lock of her hair. The question sat in her stomach, remembering Dionne's hypothesis. "Like kingdoms do when they promise marriage between their children?"

"Not quite," she grumbled, then cleared her throat. "Gallus, Danica, and Morana primarily raised me, while Dola and Irena were something like aunts. Nen, Zephyr, and Valeria were... I'm not even sure. I don't favor any of them. Rod kept his distance for quite some time as I grew older.

"I'm not sure if that was his plan." Asteria shrugged, shaking her head. "I don't think I'll ever know. Regardless, because he kept his distance, I was fascinated by him. I believe it was around my seventieth year that he finally started to show me interest. When he looked my way, I felt quite special. I was infatuated, and I suppose we fell in love."

"You suppose?" Wells fought a smile, but it was one of incredulity. "One doesn't *suppose* they are in love, Blue."

"How does one know then?" She stopped toying with her skirt, narrowing her gaze. "He was everything I ever knew. He helped me create the Academy, even raising the island for me to build on. He made me smile, he let me speak my mind with the other Lyrans and either backed me up or showed me my fault.

"Lyrans don't marry as mortals do." Asteria sighed, tearing her gaze from Wells as she stared at the stained glass. "I spent over four hundred and fifty years with him, believing he was my partner for eternity."

Wells choked, and she whipped her head to him with wide eyes. He waved a hand between them. "I apologize. That wasn't polite. I don't think I was ready for the amount of time you spent together."

She pursed her lips and rolled her eyes. "Time is a strange thing for immortals. I don't know what that would equate to in your time, but it's been one hundred and twenty years since we separated. It feels just as long as when we were together."

"You said *believing* he was your partner?" Wells lowered his arm, wrapping it around her bent knees. "And you both said he cheated on you?"

Asteria ground her teeth, inhaling slowly. She expected the typical flash of anger she usually experienced when discussing this part of the relationship. Just as it rose, it was extinguished by the gentle touch on her calf. She blinked at where his hand was moving idly, and she wondered if he knew he was doing it.

"You know I don't wish to be looked at as a Goddess, at least not in the way the Lyrans expect a Goddess to behave." Asteria leaned further into the couch, resting her cheek on the back. "I don't wish to be tyrannical, and I don't wish for Sirians to be these hollow Beings. Love, obedience, virtue—they have no meaning unless they're chosen freely. Yes, I instill certain rules for them, but ultimately, they have a choice in the matter.

"I don't desire to control them, and from how they know Gods and Goddesses work thus far on Aveesh, I never want them to look at me and think I want to simply rule over them."

Something breathtaking lit up Wells's eyes, the ghost of a soft grin lifting the corners of his lips ever so slightly. It brought a warm blush to her cheeks, and she averted her gaze to avoid the intensity.

"So I've denied being a Goddess because I never want the Lyrans or the world to get the wrong idea about the type of person I am."

She snorted, earning a low chuckle from Wells. "Heavens, my mother is relentless, though. I don't think she'll give up my Goddesshood even after she's a memory in the stars. Rod always pushed me to accept it, too. He encouraged me to implement a strict hand with the Sirians, to discipline and instill fear rather than build a relationship with them on mutual trust. Over the decades, this topic strained us.

"I started to spend more time on Aveesh than Eonia. I would ask Rod to stay with me on Celestia, but he always refused and got me to come home to him somehow." Asteria's throat tried to seal shut, but she pushed on. "I will never know what led him to cheat. You said something in the meeting… It may be the source of all the questions I've asked myself since."

He mimicked how she laid her head on the couch, blinking innocently. "And what is that?"

A lock of his hair fell in his face, and she couldn't resist. She slowly lifted her hand, brushing it back, the touch just a whisper against his forehead. A deep, endless emotion flashed in his eyes, a permanent admiration.

"He had an expectation of who he wanted me to be, and I couldn't meet that…" The admission choked her, and she swallowed the lump in her throat. "I think centuries of trying to force me into that mold and me fighting it finally caught up to us. Instead of ending things, he cheated with a human, and Bodhi was born from the affair."

Wells's mouth dropped, but he quickly closed it. Asteria chuckled at him, though, his gaze empty now. "Gods. And the world has no idea."

"None." Asteria nodded, then wagged her head back and forth. "It's for the best. I would rather the world make their assumptions of me rather than gossip about something I try to move on from."

Wells held her gaze, his neck tense.

"So, Lyrans have a difficult time having children with each other"—Wells raised an eyebrow—"but not with any of the other Beings?"

"Apparently not." Asteria shrugged into his chest. "From what I understand, it was like that in their home world as well."

She lifted her hand again, tracing the still-flexed muscle below his jaw. His eyes fluttered, but he remained serious. "Can I ask you something without creating offense?"

"I make no promises." She smirked as he jovially rolled his eyes.

"I fear I have no better way to go about this." He sighed, lifting his head. She dropped her gaze, busying herself with the cuff of his tunic. "You said you hadn't needed a male in one hundred and twenty years, and I couldn't help but notice… you haven't had a partner since him."

Her heart hammered in her chest. "That doesn't sound like a question."

"I suppose not." He dropped his head back, staring at the ceiling. "I should've given that more thought as I pursued you."

"Why?" She frowned, her heart stilling. "Does that… Is that a problem?"

"Gods, no!" Wells shot up, and in a breath, he gathered her entirely into his lap, her legs now draped over both of his. "What I mean is maybe I shouldn't have been as… aggressive."

She laughed, throwing her head back as she wrapped her arms around his neck, scooting deeper into his lap. "You forget I've spent that time warding off men. If I wasn't interested in you, Wells, I would've forced you to back off."

His face softened, lids lowering. The hand resting on her hip branded her. "How far does your interest go, Blue?"

The question caught her in its grasp and squeezed the breath from her.

She'd been asking herself that very thing quite a bit recently.

Asteria could try to deny it all she wanted, but her interest in Wells had grown beyond physical. She wasn't sure how to say it at that moment, but she wanted to try.

"I haven't been interested in men like I am you," she admitted, squeezing his arm wrapped around her. "Every day I learn more I like about you and find myself continuously... drawn to you."

Wells angled her closer, dipping his head to her neck and peppering it with featherlight kisses between words. "I told you I'm patient. I'll only do what you ask of me."

He constantly melted her with his lips and words. She wondered how a man could be so interested in her that he was foregoing sex in favor of conversation and whatever they were presently doing...

Cuddling. They were cuddling.

"I want you to know I take your interest in me earnestly, and I meant what I said, Asteria." His use of her full name jarred her, and she pulled back to look at him. "I see you for who you are. I had no expectations meeting you, and I still have none. Every piece of you that you're comfortable enough to show me lures me in more. I find it astonishing that a God is so ignorant and blinded by his own image of you that he's missing out on just how incredible you truly are.

"To be honest, I'm slightly miffed he would dare try to change you." Wells tucked a finger beneath her chin, tilting her face toward his. "He is a *stupid fuck*, as you so gently put it. If I wasn't secure in myself enough to admit he would beat me in a fight, I would throttle him myself for how he's made you feel." He kissed her nose, adding, "Although I know you're more than capable of doing that. I would only ask you to allow me to watch the next time you want to teach him a lesson."

Asteria giggled blissfully as she shook her head, clasping his between her hands. "Where did you come from?"

He squinted, pondering the question. "Eldamain."

She laughed, bringing her lips to his and kissing him through the grins they both wore. He drew his arms tighter around her as the kiss turned passionate.

Asteria had never planned on letting anyone in again, but her heart opened to Wells now that they'd vocalized their interest. The way he spoke of handling her with care only had the shield she kept around it cracking enough for him to slip through.

The way his hands tightened around her had her wondering if he knew. They slid around the flare of her ribs, thumb skimming the side of her breast.

She arched into his touch, marveling at the deep moan it coaxed from him. It called to a primal part of her, urging her to wiggle in his lap and press her breasts against his firm chest. His fingers dug into her flesh, a heavy breath ticking up the corners of his lips.

"We always only go as far as you want." He kissed up her jawline. "Just know I'm more than content to stay right here and continue kissing you."

"Well, I think I'll enjoy having this memory here now," she whispered breathlessly, pressing her forehead to his and trailing her fingers down his chest. The desire to see beneath his tunic burned. "I'll think of kissing you on this couch when I visit instead of arguments I once had with *him*."

"Hm." Wells's eyes bounced between both of hers before sweeping up the wall. "How many rooms are there?"

"Heavens, I have no idea." She curled her lip, tipping back to get a better glimpse of his face. "Why do you ask?"

"How long do you think we have before Piers and Gav come looking for us to go to Celestia?"

"I don't know—" She yelped as he stood with her in his arms, slowly lowering her to the ground.

"I have an idea." He slipped his hand in hers and threw his shoulders back. "I would like a tour of this place."

"Okay," Asteria drawled, tapering off with a sigh as she led the way, only slightly disappointed the kiss wouldn't continue.

The disappointment was short-lived, though.

In every room they journeyed to, if she frowned or went quiet, Wells found a new way to kiss her. Pinned between him and the wall, her body dipped low as his lips met hers, holding her back against his chest as he kissed her from behind. They varied from slow and steady to deep and frenzied. They were only kisses, nothing more.

Except they were *so much more* to her.

Wells managed to erase every bad or mournful memory tied to her old home by kissing or chasing her around, reminding her of a childlike glee she'd thought gone.

No, what he did for her...

It was everything.

CHAPTER 50

ASTERIA

Asteria stood outside the temple on Celestia near Morana's statue. The Academy stretched down this side of the mountain and extended toward the island's northern tip where the ocean water glittered a bright, nearly teal blue. The plants across the island were in full bloom, beautiful flowers complimenting the green grass and ocean hue.

Depending on their designations, Sirian students bustled about, weaving through hallways, the fields, or the gardens. Her shoulders rose with a heavy inhale as she closed her eyes to the salty air, the wind gently whipping her hair around her.

"I have to say," Piers said, his voice steady, "for someone who refuses to accept her title, you're the image of a Goddess right now."

Asteria peered over her shoulder, softly scowling as he shuffled beside her with his hands in his pockets. She averted his inquisitive gaze, staring out toward the ocean before them. "Anyone can look the part. It's whether you can be what they expect of you or what they need from you."

Piers hummed, the sound so similar to one Wells consistently made. She glanced around one of the pillars behind her, smiling to herself as

Wells's laugh echoed through the temple.

"Do you think you can't be what the Sirians need?" Piers tilted his head. "Is that why you refuse your title?"

"I told your brother this already." She sighed, shaking her head. "I deny my title because of the ideology the Lyrans have attached to the term Goddess. I never wanted worship—only love freely given. If I must rule you to earn it, then it isn't love at all."

"Have you ever thought what the Lyrans believe makes a God or Goddess is different from what we think here in this world?" Piers asked as she met his greener hazel eyes. She frowned, raising an eyebrow. "The Lemurians have an idea of how their God acts, like the House of Argo and Thalassa. The world knows how the others act, how detached they are, when they decide to actually involve themselves, and what they get involved in—"

"What are you getting at?" She whipped her head forward, rolling her shoulders back. His gaze locked onto the side of her head.

"Despite what you say, the Sirians will always see you as their Goddess," Piers explained, his voice steady and calm. "You wield the Energy and the Aether and float, Asteria. You spend your time with *your* people at the Academy. They come to learn and master their gifts at a school run *by you*. Not to mention, they know you're the most powerful of them.

"We know how our Goddess leads." Piers shrugged, pursing his lips. "We think she is the best of the Lyrans."

Asteria swallowed against the lump in her throat, thanking the wind for drying the dampness gathering in her eyes. "I refuse to rule you."

"You don't need to rule to be a Goddess." Piers stepped closer, forcing her to meet his gaze again. "Leave the ruling to the kings and queens of the countries. You run the school and attend monumental events. You help, guide, and teach us. The way you interact is more than enough. *You* are enough."

The emotions shot to her head, tickling her throat as a tear threatened to slip. She held up a finger at Piers, shaking her head rapidly to clear it. "Why are you telling me this?"

"Plenty of reasons." His attention drifted to the temple. "For one, I, too, was at the meeting this morning. I saw how Danica and Rod spoke to you, and you have no need to be ashamed or embarrassed. Wells sees you, and I believe I *understand* you."

To be seen and understood was all Asteria had ever wanted.

Pity it took six hundred years to find it.

"To be fair, I wasn't sure if you even trusted me," she grumbled, facing him. "What changed?"

"I was curious about you at first. What had me watching you was Wells showing a particular interest." Her cheeks heated, gaze dragging to said male greeting Odo and Erika along with the other Elders filing into the temple. "My little brother is the world to me, despite what our bickering may imply. He's always been mine to protect, whether or not he ever noticed. When he started giving you far more attention than he has given anyone since…"

"Ruelle," Asteria said gently.

Piers nodded slowly as they walked into the temple to meet everyone. "There's a light in him I haven't seen in two years. If you are what has brought that part of him back—a part we thought lost—then I owe you a great deal."

"You owe me nothing, Piers." She cracked a soft smile, resting her hand on his shoulder. "Wells has brought me an equal—if not greater—amount of joy. He brings out a side of me I didn't know existed, which is more than enough."

"Oh, do I?"

Asteria startled as Piers chuckled under his breath and continued toward the gathering of people seating themselves at the benches within the temple. The blood drained from her face as she met Wells's glittering eyes, a broad grin spreading across his face.

"I was… We were just—" Asteria's shoulders drooped as he bubbled with glee, rocking back and forth from his toes to his heels. "You clearly heard what I said, so I don't need to repeat myself."

She made to move around him to the nearest bench, but he snagged her forearm and drew her to his side, arm snaking around her waist.

"Joy doesn't even begin to describe what you've brought back into my life," he whispered, his lips brushing against her temple.

She shivered against him and nearly brought her lips to his until someone cleared their throat behind them.

Asteria shot her head over her shoulder, meeting Odo's eyes with a glare.

He winked before saying, "As entertaining as I find this, I think there are rather pressing matters we must discuss, unfortunately."

Wells quickly kissed her cheek before releasing her, walking up behind the bench Piers and Gavril sat at. Asteria approached the space before them, her gaze sweeping across the attendants.

"I thought it best to address you all as the Council of Elders and collectively fill you in on what's been happening as of late," Asteria began, her voice steady as she met Erika's gaze. She smiled, but it didn't quite reach her eyes. "Sybil received a prophecy that split the Lyrans down the middle. One side believes the humans are to blame for the outcome of this prophecy, while the others don't think it has anything to do with them. The antagonistic side is attempting to eliminate humans from Aveesh, and those Lyrans have recruited countries to implement laws restricting them.

"To prevent them from doing so, Eldamain is leading a campaign to collect other kingdoms to the protagonists' side in hopes of countering them." Asteria met Piers's gaze, and he nodded encouragingly. "As it stands, Allanis, Sylvan, Teslin, and Thalassa are on one side. Eldamain, The Northern Pizi, and Riddling are on the other. For now, Etherea claims neutrality."

"Can Etherea not be swayed?" Philomena, the Diplomatic Elder *from* Etherea, asked. "Phoebe is married to a human."

"We have reason to believe Lord Gallus persuaded her to remain neutral with the promise of protection for the humans within Etherea," Wells interjected, his attention on Philomena. "We plan to speak with Etherea next to assess the situation and see if we can sway her."

"Even if Etherea were to join our side, we fear it will be a long, deadly war." Piers rose from the bench, hands clasped behind his back. "It splits the world in half, but the dilemma we face is the amount of powerful Andromedans and Lemurians found in Allanis and Sylvan. There's a chance we could still lose with Etherea, jeopardizing the safety of humans on this plane."

"What are you asking, Asteria?" Isadore squinted, his shoulders tense.

Odo mentioned the problem she could face asking them to choose a side. There were so many Sirians from every country who attended this school. Not only that, but she changed the rules to require a representative from each country to be on the Council.

Isadore was a Diplomatic Elder from Allanis, and Malcolm, the other Healer Elder like Erika, was from Teslin.

"I know I've instilled a stance of neutrality within Celestia no matter what the other countries are doing," Asteria said calmly, breathing through her nervousness. She didn't know where this conversation would go, and she was worried they wouldn't do as she hoped. "I've briefly spoken with Odo, and he's expressed the desire to stay unaligned. I proposed bringing this to all of you because I don't believe it is the best choice. I want to hear everyone's opinions."

"What will happen should the outcome sway in favor of the opposed Lyrans?" Conrad's gaze bounced between them. "Eldamain may have The Northern Pizi and my homeland on their side, but should they lose, then what happens?"

"We're not sure," Asteria admitted with a terse shake of her head. "They could force laws or conquer, instill new leadership on those thrones. The truly terrifying fact of the matter still stands that, despite collecting Riddling and The Northern Pizi, the grim prophecy Sybil foresaw remains the Path we are headed down."

"You're trying to change Fate." Philomena frowned, curling her lip. "You've never meddled in such an endeavor, Asteria. Why now?"

"What is the prophecy?" It was Isadore who asked, but his usual playful manner was missing. There was a mask guarding his expression.

"It foretold the extinction of Lemurians, Andromedans, Sirians, and Lyrans." Asteria swallowed, gauging the room. The Energy and Aether swirled within every Sirian aside from Piers and Wells. She rubbed her sternum at the sudden, unexpected assault.

"So they believe the humans are responsible because their extinction hasn't been foretold." Serena, the Warrior Elder alongside Conrad, rubbed at her temple as she stared off toward one of the statues.

"If you want us to put it to a vote, you have my support," Conrad said, crossing his arms over his chest. "This isn't some petty argument between countries. This is a war of our entire world to protect a species. I think we're obligated to be involved as powerful Beings on this plane. All the designations at this school prepare our Sirians for this event."

"Not on a mass scale involving every country." Isadore scoffed, shaking his head. "They're meant to exist within their home countries or the country they accept roles in. If we vote on a stance and stand against half of the countries these students come from, what sort of atmosphere are we creating for future generations should the side protecting humans emerge victorious?"

"This was Odo's perspective," Erika said gently as she rubbed her stomach, gaze shifting between Wells and Asteria. "I fear this is mine as well. Regardless of the outcome, we must consider the repercussions of taking a side. It would alter the future of what the Academy stands for. We have to be a safe place for all."

"What of the humans, then?" Philomena chastised, clenching her fists. "We just leave those innocents to the wolves and hope the right side arises victorious? As you speak, you're even acknowledging one side is preferable over the other."

"Of course we believe that," Odo said, standing with Wells, Asteria, and Piers. "There's no question about it, but we were built on neutrality above all else. It keeps our balance here at the Academy. Isadore is right. If we force those from Allanis, Sylvan, and Teslin to stand against their homes—possibly their own families—the Academy will forever be altered."

"So we sit and do nothing?" Conrad shouted, waving his hands around. "We're a Council. We should be voting on this matter. That's what we do at the Academy. We *vote* together."

"There must be a discussion before we vote." Odo sighed, adjusting his glasses as he shook his head. Erika reached for his hand, the other still on her stomach.

"Isn't that what we're doing?" Asteria glared at him, attempting to reel in her powers as they rose with her emotions. "This is the time for a discussion."

"You need an answer now?" Odo chuckled darkly, facing off with her. "This decision can't be made in a day, Asteria. This is something we must think about and evaluate. We must consider the Sirians as a collective and not based on the countries they reside in or come from. That's why you have us—that's why you have me."

"We're running out of time, Odo." Wells's brows furrowed, and he looked wounded by Odo's words. "Allanis already attacked Heridy. We lost two of our drakons and nearly lost Sybil, as you recall. Before that, we were bombarded in Teslin from administering a cure. The other side is moving, and we don't have enough forces to counter."

"We need to be proactive, not reactive," Piers interjected, frustration and disappointment shadowing his face. "The longer we take to rally, the more we must stop to react to whatever offensive maneuvers countries like Sylvan and Allanis attack with."

"I understand, but this is how it's done here." Odo's eyes pleaded with his friends before he looked at Asteria. "This is what you put me in place for—to ensure we uphold the rules and principles you've implemented despite what you may do or say."

"I didn't teach you to leave innocents to fend for themselves," Asteria hissed, strutting across the space as her god-form pressed against her mortal skin. She stood before Odo, her frustration growing. "Sirians have always been advocates for humans against the old mythical creatures the Lemurians shift into. They're volatile, just like Nen and Zephyr, and the Sirians were meant to balance the scales. Moves are being made against the humans, and you should defend them."

"Not before I defend the Sirians." He shook his head, jaw clenched. "The Sirians are my priority before the humans, and we must make a decision that's beneficial to *them*. As of now, telling them to stand up or down is not beneficial to them or this school. I'm not saying we'll force the Sirians *not* to help their countries, but we'll also not force them to stand against them."

Asteria's power thrummed beneath her veins, flashing under her skin. "Then take the time to think about *your* decision, Odo. Just know that while you flounder, people are dying."

"Asteria," Odo implored, but she was already opening a portal that led to the housing and guest suites, jerking her head at Piers, Wells, and Gavril. "Think logically for one second—"

"Don't speak to me like I'm a child, Odo Hesper!" she shouted, her eyes burning from the intensity of their shift as her voice echoed through the temple. She breathed slowly through her nose, growling. "I chose you for a reason. Taught you better than this. Don't disappoint me."

Without another glance back, Asteria followed the men, leaving the Elders in the temple surrounded by the idols of the very Lyrans who'd brought this upon them.

CHAPTER 51

ASTERIA

"**B**lue!" Wells's voice carried as she marched through the stone building toward her quarters.

She clenched her fists to quell her anger and the urge to take this out on him. The Aether within him swirled, alerting her just how close he was. Her door came into view as his hand wrapped around her arm, twisting her.

"Talk to me," he begged, his hand dragging down to intertwine their fingers. He gently skimmed her other arm, repeating the movement. "Talk it out with me."

"It shouldn't be you who needs to *talk it out* with me." She shook her head, a strand of hair falling in front of her face. "It's not your burden."

"It's not a burden." He frowned, gently tugging her closer until their chests nearly pressed together. He lowered his voice, the timber matching the vibration of her power and naturally urging it to settle. "I can't stand to see this franticness you hurtle toward. I know you're frustrated and that it comes from a place of care. You shouldn't have to stay in this state. Not if I can help."

Her breaths were heavy as she looked into his eyes, but her heart rate already had calmed at his presence, the call of the starfire growing quieter. Her guilt for using him this way still simmered beneath the surface, the tightness in her chest nearly unbearable.

"Okay," she agreed with a nod, "but don't feel the need to."

She kept one of his hands in hers, guiding him toward her room. A flick of her hand opened the door before them, and she immediately slammed it shut once they both were inside.

"It's not that I feel a need to, Blue." She tried to tug her hand from him, but he only used his grip to bring her to the chairs in front of her fireplace. He lowered into one as he spoke, "I want to. I desire to."

"You desire?" She raised an eyebrow, finding the way his thumb brushed over the top of her hand quite comforting. "Do you desire fixing people?"

"I don't seek to fix you if that's what you're getting at." He chuckled lightly, looking at their hands. His face was calm, and Asteria was transfixed by how beautiful he truly was. "I prefer you just as you are. Your panic is not who you are. It's just one of the qualities that sneaks up on you during unfavorable situations."

"You wish to rid me of my panic." She searched his face to gather his motivation.

He scoffed playfully, resting his elbow on the arm of the chair and lifting her hand beneath his chin. "What's troubling you about that?"

"It's not that I'm troubled." She wanted her hand back, but tucked under his chin, she felt oddly secure. "I just don't understand what sort of benefit you gain from relieving me of my panic or frustrations."

"Hm." That sound calmed her frayed nerves. He tipped his head back and peered down at her, rolling his lips together. It was such a simple movement that managed to scatter Asteria's senses.

"Come here, love," he whispered, urging her closer.

She frowned as she stood between his legs. Wells leaned forward, his hands gripping her hips as he stared up at her.

Something about this position felt intimate, especially when she lowered her hands to his shoulders, gently resting them. Wells looked at Asteria like she was divinity. While she technically was, it wasn't to covet, but to worship and adore.

"Is it surprising to know I've come to care for you?" he asked, thumbs tracing her hip bones. Her stomach dipped and knotted and heated. "When you're upset or hurt, I want to help you feel better simply because I care for you and don't like to see you that way. I enjoy seeing you smile because it's rare. I like knowing I make you smile—that I bring you joy. It satisfies my cumbersome male ego."

Asteria's face softened as she stared down at Wells's freckles stark against his skin in the dim light. Her hands lifted to both sides of his neck, thumbs brushing his stubbled jaw.

Wells's eyes fluttered shut, his hands flexing against her hips.

She couldn't remember the last time she'd confessed feelings to a male. She was positive she'd never told Odo she cared for him. She did, of course, but this was different. When Rod had courted her, there was never any declaration like this. Indeed, she and Rod had said they loved each other, but she no longer remembered when she'd heard it the first time or how she'd felt when he said it.

Wells handed her something precious, and his words brought a fulfilling elation unlike anything else.

"You don't have to say—"

"I'm not sure how something like this works," she whispered, shaking her head. His brow twitched, and she had the urge to climb into his lap.

He must've seen the desire in her eyes because he fisted her skirts, tugging her down as he slowly leaned back. She followed his lead, letting him guide her. She tucked both legs between his hips and the sides of the chair as she straddled him, then carefully lowered herself.

"What are you not sure about?" He searched her face, his voice tender and curious, which only warmed her.

"What's growing between us." She gnawed on her lower lip, and his gaze snagged onto it, his bright eyes darkening. "I find I care more for you than I thought I would, differently than I have for a male before."

"Well…" He sighed, sliding his hands up to squeeze her waist. Despite the rather sexual position, the way he held her was endearing. "In all my wisdom, I've found there are no rules to follow regarding how this is supposed to go. Besides, neither of us are fair maidens whose virtues must be guarded. We're quite grown."

She narrowed her eyes and lost to the smirk tugging at her lips. "While you may not speak it, I know what you think."

"Oh, do you?" Wells straightened in the chair, his hands flattening against her back. "And what is it you think I mean to say?"

She smiled broadly now as she dipped her head to him, her nose brushing his. "Something about my age."

Wells laughed, his head tipping away from her. The power his laughter had over her coaxed out a giggle and spread warmth through her limbs, lifting her spirits.

"Let me kiss you," he whispered, pinching her chin between his fingers and drawing her lips to his.

Asteria would never tire of kissing Wells.

His kisses were deliberate and sensual by nature. His lips traced hers as their tongues danced between them. With each caress, the kiss deepened, their bodies moving closer, hands searching for purchase.

Wells tipped his head and one of his hands cupped the back of her neck, holding her to him as he thoroughly devoured her. No matter where he put his hands, they never failed to send that aching heat straight to her core. She moaned into his mouth when his teeth dragged along her bottom lip, his tongue easing the slight sting of pain.

Her need took hold of her.

Asteria dove into his curls, twisting her fingers through them as she rolled her hips and angled his head back. She rubbed along his hardening length through her clothes, ripping a strangled groan from Wells. Smirking against his mouth, she tightened her grip.

"Do you like finding how hard I am for you?" Wells asked, barely breaking the kiss.

Asteria's cheeks heated at his filthy words, but that wasn't all that heated. Especially when he twitched his hips up to rub against her, eliciting a ragged gasp from her.

"The way you feel in my arms reminds me of how it felt when I made you come, and Gods, does that have me thinking about what it would feel like to have you come around me."

Asteria couldn't breathe as his lips trailed down her jaw and neck, nipping at sensitive places along the way. He tightened his grip on her, and suddenly, they were moving. Without breaking their kiss, he carried her across the room to her bed. He gently laid her down just as he had in Riddling, journeying back to her lips.

Heavens, she wanted him so badly, and he'd barely touched her.

"Wells," she mumbled around his lips, her fingers toying with the collar of his shirt. He pulled back to look down at her, waiting. "I think… Do you… I want—"

"Don't be nervous," he assured, tucking her hair away from her face. "Trust me when I say I don't believe there's anything I would deny you."

"I want you to touch me," she blurted quietly, meeting his darkened gaze. She swallowed as she caressed the side of his neck. "Inside…"

He smirked, his fingers trailing from her jaw to her chin, tilting it closer. He placed a kiss on her lips, still smiling. "Your wish is my command."

Everything intensified, and Asteria knew she'd never been kissed like this. Not with this kind of reverence.

Wells parted her lips with his, tongue stroking against hers in slow, coaxing motions that made her toes curl. His lips moved in long, purposeful strokes, drawing the tension from her until a deep, persistent ache throbbed through her. Her body responded before her mind could catch up, a low heat blooming in her core and spreading like wildfire.

His hand trailed down the side of her body, following every dip and curve. Every place he touched came alive, tingling and sparking like the

Energy. Asteria arched into him, her body silently begging for more, for him.

I'm a patient man.

She tightened her grip on his collar and her breath hitched as he toyed with the top of her skirt, his fingers barely dipping beneath the waistband.

"Are you trying to test my patience?" she mumbled, nearly cursing herself at how much that question resembled a whimper.

"I'm trying to behave, and your begging doesn't stifle my need for you," he growled, his hand slipping beneath her waistband and undergarments. He dove straight for her clit, and she gasped at the touch, already sensitive. "That sound doesn't help, either."

"If you expect me to apologize"—she keened as his hand traveled lower, his finger barely dipping into her—"you'll be waiting for eternity."

"I think I can manage." Wells peppered kisses down the side of her face, jaw, and neck, coating his fingers with her arousal. "So Godsdamned wet."

Wells gazed down at her, his beige hues nearly brown from desire. Then, ever so slowly, as if savoring the moment just as much as she was, he slid one finger into her.

Breathtaking pleasure surged through her, the blood in her veins replaced by fire. She unabashedly cried out as he dragged his finger back out in a deliberate curl that sent sparks radiating from her core to every limb.

Touching herself was one thing, but to have someone else touch her—to have *Wells* touch her—was a euphoric sensation she could no longer live without.

He set a steady rhythm, *patient* and practiced, his single finger stroking her with just enough pressure to stoke the fire within. It danced along the edge of release, teasing her, denying her just enough to leave her mind hazy and nearly writhing in anticipation.

Heavens above, he knows exactly *what he's doing.*

She forced her heavy gaze downward, locking eyes with him. That damned smirk curved the edge of his mouth, which only enhanced the throbbing ache between her thighs. Her breath grew shallow, lips parted in a quiet gasp as her lashes fluttered.

Still watching him, she slowly drew one knee up, her thigh sliding along his side as she opened herself further to him. His eyebrows lifted, but the only answer he gave was a low chuckle against her skin as he dipped his head to her ear. He nipped at the curve just beneath, and her body jolted, lightning striking straight through her with a pulse of pleasure.

"Greedy, Blue," he murmured against her throat, but he didn't deny her.

Wells withdrew his finger almost entirely, but when he plunged back in, he added a second. The slight stretch and added pressure ripped a breathy cry from her as she bucked into his hand in response. He ground his palm against her clit, leaving her clawing for more.

"Wells," she cried, no longer breathy but throaty. She tangled her fingers in his hair, encouraging a rumbling chuckle from him that brushed her skin and settled in her core where his fingers rubbed against that spot. "Heavens above..."

Asteria clenched tighter around him as he drove her higher, a carnal instinct rolling her hips in time with his movements, riding his fingers. He groaned softly, pressing his forehead to hers as his hips rotated, his firm length grinding against her.

That same instinct drove her next decision.

She snaked her arm down between them and ground her palm against him through his pants.

"That's—You're..." His rhythm faltered, his length twitching beneath the fabric as she dragged her palm farther down. She bit her lip to suppress her grin as he inhaled sharply. "*Asteria*."

He shuddered when her fingers traced the head of his cock. He angled his finger deeper, and she whispered, "I want you to come with me."

He groaned as he slammed his lips to hers. He pressed his fingers within her, and it stole the air from her lungs as release hit her deep and sharp. Her muffled cry morphed into heated pants, Wells's mingling with hers between them as she rubbed him through his slacks.

His fingers stilled, and Wells buried his face into her shoulder as he breathed through his release, whispering her name like she was his salvation.

Once they both stilled, he lifted his head and glared down at her with dark, narrowed eyes and a faint grin. He removed his fingers, clearing his throat before speaking. "I don't think I anticipated you…"

Heat rose to her cheeks, but she managed a nonchalant shrug. "It felt applicable."

"It felt *applicable*?" Wells laughed, his eyes crinkling. The sound forced a small giggle from her. He pinched her side, a proper laugh bursting through that lit up his face. "Well, your *applicable* decision means I now must embarrass myself journeying to my room."

Her heart pinched, a frown dropping her smile. Wells tilted his head, taking the opportunity above her to study the shift. She didn't quite understand it herself, but the longer they stared at one another in silence, the more she realized…

She wanted him to stay.

"I could open a portal for you," she said quietly, fingers tracing the muscles tugging beneath his tunic, averting her gaze. "Don't feel like you have to leave…"

His eyebrows flew up in surprise, and her cheeks warmed once again. She sputtered over her words as she attempted to correct herself.

"I mean, I know it's late… I'm sure you're tired from the day and would like some peace and quiet. I know I would—but not like that! I could have peace and quiet with you here just as much…" Her mouth stopped working and went dry.

Wells firmly pressed his lips to hers, slipping his grip behind her neck and curling his tongue around hers. A brief but passionate kiss that left her breathless when he pulled away.

"Here's what I propose," he said, his smile returning. "You open a portal to my room, keep it there, and I'll change into a new pair of slacks. Then, if you desire, I'll stay with you."

"Do *you* desire?" She braced for disappointment, shrinking into the mattress. "To stay?"

"Yes, Blue." His thumb stroked the curve of her ear. "I want to stay."

Her heart swelled in her chest, body relaxing as a warm smile lightened the anxiousness threatening to fuse her into the bed. Her answer was a snap echoing in the room, a portal glowing by the foot of the bed.

Wells glanced over his shoulder at it, and she nearly melted in his arms at the serene expression on his face.

"I'll be back shortly," he whispered, quickly kissing her temple as he jumped off the bed and through the portal.

Asteria made quick work of changing into a nightgown—a light, too-sheer chemise. Just as she untucked the blankets from the side of the bed, the portal hummed.

Wells stepped back through with a new pair of slacks. She waved her hand, and it clicked shut, but her attention was latched onto Wells as he brazenly examined her nightgown.

"You wish to test my self-control," he muttered under his breath, running a hand through his untamed curls. He took her in, eyes lingering on her breasts.

She smirked as she slowly crawled onto the bed, slipping her legs beneath the covers. "I wish to see how much of a gentleman you truly are."

He chuckled, rolling his eyes as he worked on the top strings of his tunic. "You know, Blue, it's not kind to treat your guests..."

Asteria stopped listening the moment he pulled his tunic over his head and tossed it aside, revealing the body beneath she'd only fantasized about in her mind.

"My eyes are up here, love," Wells muttered, his face suddenly appearing before her. He rested his palms on the mattress as he bent to her level. "You know, I'm more than just something pretty to look at."

She flattened her palm on the middle of his chest, gently urging him back. She inched closer to the side he stood on and rose to her knees. She continued to observe him, eyes following where her hand trailed.

His sun-kissed skin was taut against the swell of muscle across his shoulders and biceps, dotted with freckles that matched the ones on his face. Dark hair spattered across his defined chest, tapering into a line down his lean abdomen. Another trail of hair began lower, disappearing into his slacks.

What really grabbed Asteria's attention was the faint scars across his chest and littered across his abdomen. There was one that wrapped around him in a jagged line following his bottom rib.

"What happened?" she whispered, tracing that risen lighter patch of skin.

His abdomen flexed at her touch, the muscles beneath quivering with heavy, uneven breaths.

"Sparring lessons, jousting competitions, skirmishes with my brothers…" She held his gaze, retracing the scar she was most concerned about. He sighed, grabbing her wrist and kissing her palm. "Last year, I was traveling with Piers and Gav through Sylvan. Thieves ambushed us, and I made a foolish move that nearly cost me. Gav had to sew me up until we made it to a Healer in a nearby town for proper medications."

Her brows pressed together tighter as her throat burned. She wanted nothing more than to hurt whoever had marred him.

"Blue," Wells said quietly, grabbing her face and lifting it to his. "I'm okay now. Piers took care of them immediately. Believe it or not, he tends to be quite protective of me."

"Immediate execution was too swift a punishment," she muttered, startled at the words. Even Wells stared at her in shock, blinking. She had always been a little murderous, as Rod liked to say, but she'd never said something so sinister. "I believe you'll be happy to know I'm just as startled by that admission as you are."

He huffed a breath of relief. To her surprise, he yanked her lips to his in a slow, thorough kiss before whispering, "You're remarkable. I hope you know that."

She smiled at his words, but it vanished when she yelped as he lunged for her in the bed. They fell into a tangled mess of limbs as he repeatedly kissed her cheek, and she attempted to wiggle free.

"You're like a dog," she grumbled, trying to shove him off. "You have an unholy amount of energy and an infectious level of glee that I seem unable to ward off."

"Then don't fight it." He kissed her one final time before rolling onto his side next to her. He curled his arm over her midsection and tugged her flush against him. Her back curved into his chest, and he nuzzled his nose into her hair, inhaling deeply. "I know I don't."

"I'm well aware," she whispered, but exhaustion lay heavily on her. He tucked his leg between hers, and she slipped her fingers over his, entwining them. When he accepted, locking their grip, something sharp stung her eyes.

As she succumbed to sleep, Taranis's teasing words and her conversation with Dionne replayed in her mind repeatedly. Her stomach twisted at the thought of Wells's mortality, something wet slipping from her eye and dropping onto her pillow.

CHAPTER 52

PHOEBE

Phoebe stood rigid beside Dustin, hands stacked firmly against her sternum and stomach as she attempted to keep her face neutral. The guard waited patiently for her signal, his hand poised on the door.

"It's a simple discussion," Dustin reminded her in a low tone. "Nothing more, nothing less. Just hear her out and think about what's best for your kingdom first."

Phoebe peered at him from the corner of her eyes, nodding once. She flicked her gaze to the guard and repeated the gesture, loosely locking her fingers together and letting her hands hang limp before her.

The door swung open wide, and she didn't waste another moment. She schooled her face into an expression of indifference and passed beneath the threshold.

All in the receiving room rose from their seats except the figure already standing, gazing out the window. She turned her head over her shoulder, vibrant blue eyes glittering, accompanied by a slight grin.

Asteria looked no different than when Phoebe had attended the Academy over ten years ago. The only deviation between that version of her sister and the one now was the serene spirit within her gaze as opposed to the lines of her face drawn tight.

"My Queen and King," the guard said, gesturing toward each individual as he spoke, "I would like to introduce to you the following—Prince Orwell Carraphim and Prince Piers Carraphim of Eldamain, Lieutenant General Gavril Faris, and Lady—"

"If you would like to keep your dignity, I suggest you stop there," Gavril interjected, his hand raised toward the guard. "Besides, I heard she also goes by General—"

"If *you* would like to keep your dignity…" Asteria leveled Gavril with a menacing glare, pointing a finger at him. There was something odd about the exchange.

Phoebe's mouth dropped open in shock and dismay.

Asteria was being *playful* with this male, a characteristic she didn't think belonged to her sister.

The jealousy burning the back of her throat tested her decorum, god-power thrumming once under her skin. Asteria snapped her head to Phoebe, tilting her head.

"Thank you for the introduction," Phoebe said tightly to the knight, nodding. "I believe I know most of the individuals in this room, including Asteria. You're free to leave. These people mean no harm, and Dustin will stay with me."

Phoebe rested a hand on her husband's shoulder for emphasis. The guard bowed before leaving, and Phoebe waited until the door clicked shut behind him.

"You believe you know most of us in this room?" Gavril asked, folding his thick arms across his chest. "I don't know you."

"You're the only one I don't know," Phoebe explained with a glare. "I met Prince Orwell at his wedding and my own, where I also happened to meet Prince Piers."

"You didn't tell me you've met before." Asteria frowned at Orwell as she spoke, and Phoebe perked up at the questioning.

He leaned into her as she stepped beside him, his voice quieter. "Would you like a list of all the people I've met throughout my life, Blue?"

Blue.

The youngest Prince of Eldamain had a nickname for Asteria.

They also looked at one another like Phoebe believed her and Dustin looked at each other, which had three things flying into her mind.

The first was how she would need to fight tooth and nail to hold her temper at the envy trying to eat her alive. From her understanding, Asteria had never been personal with the Carraphims. Yet she'd managed to form close relationships with them in just a short amount of time while she'd never had one with Phoebe.

The second was Phoebe didn't think Asteria had shown romantic interest to anyone in the past, let alone a Sirian *mortal*. The third was the last time she saw Orwell was at his wedding, and she remembered hearing about his wife's passing.

"I know I'm a couple years late, Prince Orwell," Phoebe said, dipping her head and resting a hand against her chest, "but I wish to extend my condolences on the loss of your wife. I can't imagine what that was like."

Phoebe expected Asteria to bristle with irritation at the mention of his wife. Instead, she offered Orwell a soft smile as he bowed slightly at the waist and murmured, "Thank you, Queen Phoebe. I appreciate the sincerity."

"Must we continue to refer to one another in our formal tones?" Dustin asked, hands spread wide in front of him as he met each person's gaze. "I believe we're mature enough to deal with familiarity. Besides, I don't believe it's fair Asteria gets to forgo her formal title while the rest of us must continue to use them."

Asteria pursed her pale pink lips and narrowed those ethereally bright eyes at Dustin. There was a predatorial glint hidden beneath her sister's pale skin, which had the Aether swirling around Phoebe's arm.

Asteria raised an amused eyebrow at her, blinking rapidly.

"I agree!" Orwell clapped his hands together, jerking Asteria out of whatever she was considering. "For the sake of those in this room and the privacy here, I would also like to believe we can refer to Phoebe as Asteria's sister and Gallus as their father."

Gavril slowly slid his gaze to Orwell. "What the fuck did you just say?"

"Why do you think everyone is obsessed with my relationship with Phoebe?" Asteria threw an exasperated glare at Gavril.

"You mean lack thereof," Gavril muttered, rolling his eyes. Phoebe clenched her jaw, eyes widening. "So Taranis and Dionne are Danica's children—therefore, they're your half-brothers. Phoebe is then Gallus's daughter, making her your half-sister?"

Asteria curled her lip at Gavril, fists clenching at her side. Orwell pinched the bridge of his nose, sighing heavily. He rested a hand on Asteria's lower back, and she visibly softened, her face relaxing once more.

This was possibly the most fascinating thing Phoebe had seen in quite some time. There was no longer a single doubt in her mind that what Asteria had between her and Orwell was romantic.

"Phoebe," Asteria said, jolting her, "I wish to speak to you alone about why we've come."

"I know very well why you've come." Phoebe scoffed, shaking her head. Asteria stiffened, but she held her gaze. "Alas, it'll be better to speak privately as it's clear some of those in attendance may derail the conversation."

"You're supposed to be the one who's good at talking, Wells." Piers chuckled under his breath, shooting his younger brother a wary glance. "When did Asteria become the one to speak to the diplomats?"

"When they're her siblings." Orwell lowered into his chair, sinking into the back and throwing an ankle over his knee. "We'll just wait here and do what men do best."

Asteria glared at Orwell, but there was a tilt to the edges of her mouth. "I hope I won't be long."

447

Phoebe snorted with an eyeroll, and Asteria deadpanned. She barely caught the whisper of touch between her and Orwell before she approached Phoebe. She gestured for her sister to follow her to an adjoining room.

The small study sported a fireplace against the far wall and armchairs in the center, a short bar cart settled in the corner. There was a frail desk on the opposite side of the room, but that was all. The only source of light was a single, dim chandelier and oblong window.

Asteria followed her in, and Phoebe waved a hand to quietly shut the door behind them. She turned before one of the chairs in time to see Asteria looking over her shoulder at the door.

"Did you forget I have a god-power?" Phoebe raised an eyebrow as she lowered into the chair, her skin prickling.

Asteria threw her an incredulous look, sighing as she approached the chair across from Phoebe. "I didn't forget. I just wasn't ready for the door to abruptly shut behind me as soon as I stepped past the doorframe."

Phoebe hummed, reclining in her chair and resting her arms on the side as she squinted. Asteria lowered into her own, mimicking Phoebe's position.

Asteria may not have forgotten her god-power, but Phoebe had forgotten just how much Asteria looked like Gallus. They had the same fair, blemish-free skin and tall, lean figures. They even had the same black hair with a blue-purple sheen in the light. Phoebe would argue it was presently the same length. High cheekbones and pointed angles typically gave the two a very intimidating appearance, but Phoebe never knew if it was because of their supposedly mortal features or the powerful aura reverberating from them.

Asteria shifted, and Phoebe met her gaze. "You say you know why we're here."

"You want my kingdom to fight alongside Eldamain," Phoebe explained, smirking. She balanced her elbow on the arm of the chair, hand posed in the air. She rolled her wrist, toying with the Aether. "I'm sure it's appropriate to also include Riddling, The Northern Pizi, and Celestia, as well."

"If you're trying to intimidate me with my own power, you're wasting your energy," Asteria said. She cleared her throat as she forced out the next words. "Not Celestia, though."

Another bit of information Phoebe had a passion to know. Alas, they had other matters to discuss, and she was sure Asteria's island would be brought up eventually. "Regardless, you come to ask me to join your cause."

"Something tells me your answer will be no," Asteria guessed, her lips drawn tight.

"If you were to ask me the question this very moment without any further discussion, my answer would be no." Phoebe folded her hands in her lap and leaned forward. "I'm not entirely incompetent. I know the Carraphims will offer some treaty involving the countries they ally with in exchange for our assistance. Which is fine and well until you consider what this war is about."

"Let's not jump around and act like we're two diplomats attempting to come to an agreement." Asteria slowly rose from the chair, pacing toward the fireplace with her gaze on the portrait of Drogo. "We both know the entire truth of not only our relationship but your relationship with Gallus. I'm not naive—I know he came and spoke to you already.

"He probably offered protection for something you love dearly as long as you don't get involved in the war." Asteria twisted, leaning against the wall and crossing her arms. "He wouldn't dare ask you to pick a side but rather remain neutral."

"Of course he has." Phoebe threw her hand up to mask the agitation itching at her skin. She hated the way these immortals spoke. "He vowed to leave the humans within my country unscathed when it comes to whatever they have planned for the humans of Aveesh."

"You can't tell me Gallus came to you and had a simple, civil conversation, Phoebe." Asteria shook her head, eyes downturned, which did nothing but anger her more. Asteria had no right to pity her. "I know he came here and threatened Dustin—"

"You don't know anything," Phoebe snarled, lurching from her chair, but Asteria spoke over her.

"—on top of offering protection for your humans." Asteria pinned Phoebe with a knowing look. She was suddenly hurtled back fifteen years to being belittled by her sister during god-power lessons. "Open and honest, Phoebe. We owe one another that."

"Oh, do we?" Phoebe advanced on Asteria with a finger pointed at her.

Asteria easily absorbed the streak of Aether Phoebe flung at her, bright eyes briefly engulfed by the black from the flex of her power. Asteria's arms only fell to her side though as Phoebe came toe-to-toe with her.

"Why do I owe *you* anything?" Phoebe shoved Asteria's shoulder, and her sister's nostrils flared. "You've resented my existence from the moment I was born." She shoved her again. "You've treated me with nothing but contempt any time I'm in your presence." Phoebe shoved her one final time, Asteria's back bumping against the wall. "You chastised me and bullied me when I attended the Academy until someone *better* came along who you could mentor because your resentment went so deep you refused to take *your own sister* under your wing!"

Asteria startled, her eyes widening. "Phoebe... I don't—"

"Open and honest, Asteria." Phoebe chuckled, resting one hand on her hip and rubbing her temple with the other.

"We're not talking about our past right now, Phoebe." Asteria's shoulders slumped as she shook her head. "What we need your help with has nothing to do with us and everything to do with the future of Aveesh."

"He forced my hand, Asteria." Phoebe whipped around, pacing before the fireplace as her hands gestured wildly with her words. "You might have this exemplary relationship with our father, but I've never had a relationship with him. I suppose like father, like daughter in that regard." She leveled a glare at Asteria, who only returned it with more malice. "Gallus showed up in *my* home with *my* husband, bound by the Aether, beaten and bloodied to a point he now has permanent damage in the bones of his leg that will never heal."

Where most would've paled, Asteria's skin thinned, a dark blue glow flashing briefly beneath.

"He threatened my family and said it would be in my best interest if I listened to him, unlike you who didn't heed his warning." Phoebe threw a hand at her sister, heart pounding against her chest. "So unfortunately, Asteria, this has everything to do with us because it is our father behind it. Unlike you, with an army of Andromedans and Sirians and Lyrans at your back, I have no one to protect me and my family other than myself and the few I trust here who can actually do something.

"If you paid me any mind when I was at the Academy, maybe things would've gone differently. Maybe I would have the confidence to stand against him." Phoebe shook her head, huffing a breath of disbelief. "At least I would know you have my back."

"I do have your back, Phoebe," Asteria pleaded, closing the distance between them. She reached for Phoebe's hands, but she held them up in warning. The corners of Asteria's mouth and eyes wrinkled. "I still have your back if you decide to go against him. You have me and all those who come with me."

"How do I know that?" Phoebe snarled, their noses nearly touching. "How can I trust you when there's no foundation to build upon?"

Asteria sighed heavily, throwing her head toward the ceiling and clenching her fists at her sides. Phoebe's shoulders heaved with each breath, her vision tunneling from the frustration and years of jealousy and suppressed hurt.

Phoebe no longer cared why Asteria or the Carraphims had come. While she had her sister within her kingdom and castle walls, she would force Asteria to look her in the eye and address the maltreatment exhibited toward her.

"Why did you abandon me?" Phoebe's voice cracked. She curled her lip at herself, casting her gaze to the floor.

"I didn't…" Asteria's voice trailed off as she reached for Phoebe again, but she slapped her hand away. "I didn't abandon you, Phoebe. The further along students get in their time at the Academy, the deeper they fall into their designation. You went the Diplomat route, the only path I don't interact with."

"Don't try to bullshit me." Phoebe snorted despite the sound being unbecoming of a queen. She glared up at Asteria through her lashes. "Odo also took that route, but you seemed to have a fine time taking him under your wing as your apprentice."

Once again, Asteria flinched, and her face dropped into stunned silence. Those vibrant eyes fluttered as she appeared to mull that over.

Phoebe always knew Odo was the reason Asteria had stopped paying her any mind. Even if the attention she gave her before that was like a disgruntled aunt more than a sister.

"Now you have nothing to say?" Phoebe frowned, throwing her arms up between them. "The benevolent, loving Goddess of Sirians has nothing to say to her bastard sister."

"It's because you're my *bastard* sister that I couldn't choose you—"

The crack of skin meeting skin echoed like thunder in the space between them.

Phoebe's hand dropped as quickly as it had risen, her chest rising in short breaths. The anger she'd felt the entire time she looked upon Asteria snuffed out in an instant, replaced by a cold weight in her stomach.

She hadn't really meant to strike her, but the word—*bastard*—uttered by someone she yearned to accept her rang in her head, raw and jagged and true.

Phoebe stepped back, distancing herself as she clasped her hands before her. She redirected their conversation back to the alliance. "You must understand I don't wish to put a target on my back. Yes, I'm worried for this world, but also for my people and kingdom. They are, first and foremost, my priority. I can't save everyone else's kingdoms."

Asteria closed her eyes, dipping her head. "At least talk more with Wells and Piers—"

"I'll listen to what the Carraphims have to say." Phoebe sighed, averting her gaze. "I understand you believe you can offer me protection, but I must tell you other Lemurians and Andromedans are offering protection alongside Gallus so long as I stay neutral. I know Etherea joining this war will only even the chances of winning, not entirely tip the scale. You still need Celestia, which you insinuated you don't have. You can't guarantee that my losses would be worth it in the end.

"The people who requested I stand down have made good on their promises." Phoebe drew her gaze to the window as she waved toward it. "There have been no attacks on my villages. There is no more Obsidian Decay. Even Endora was able to deliver on an elixir I asked of her long before I knew she was on the theoretically wrong side—"

"What elixir?" There was an undercurrent of bright blue animosity at the mention of the Andromedan.

Rightfully so, considering what Phoebe knew of Sybil's attack.

"It's nothing dangerous," Phoebe assured, shaking her head. "I asked her to create an elixir that would make me mortal, and she delivered."

CHAPTER 53

ASTERIA

"I t did what?" The blood roared in Asteria's head. It took every ounce of control in her body to keep her emotions in check and maintain patience with her sister.

Losing her shit on Phoebe would do nothing to repair the deep wounds of their relationship, especially considering she was coiled like a caged animal ready to pounce.

The sting of the slap may have faded as quickly as it had come, but Asteria could still feel it in her soul.

Phoebe's eyes started glowing that warm light of her god-power again, blinking at Asteria before biting out, "I don't believe your judgment is warranted—"

"No!" Asteria held her palms up, but instantly brought them back down in case she saw it as a threat. "I don't mean it as judgment. I'm just... You're telling me Endora has created an elixir that stripped you of your immortality, but you still have your powers?"

Phoebe frowned, but there was something calculating swirling deep in her brown eyes. She tilted her head momentarily before her expression smoothed out. "It seemed to take away anything linked to the enhanced body that makes one immortal, at least for an Andromedan. I didn't have access to any of my powers—the Aether or the god-power—for about a day. I saw Endora a few weeks later, and when she cut me with a letter opener, it healed slower than it normally would have. Marin read my blood and confirmed my body is mortal."

Asteria's heart thundered in her chest. Her mind raced as she considered what this meant, the first question immediately being…

If it worked for an Andromedan, would it work for a Lyran?

She'd longed her entire life to be separated from the Lyrans, to be closer to those she found camaraderie with. If this elixir worked for a Lyran, she would no longer be a Lyran.

Not in the ways it mattered to them.

"Why?" Asteria kept her voice even. She didn't want to come off as disapproving. It must have worked because Phoebe visibly relaxed. "Why did you do it?"

Phoebe warred with something, her jaw working as she rubbed the back of her neck, eyes narrowed on Asteria. After a moment, her shoulders hunched as she sighed. "You, Gallus, and the Andromedans never accepted me. The circumstances of my birth forced me and anyone who knows the truth to suppress it, which meant I couldn't acknowledge my status as an Andromedan or my familial relations.

"My life found meaning when I met Dustin." Phoebe's lips twitched into a smile that Asteria recognized. It looked just like her own and Gallus's. "He loved me for who I was. His family took me in as their own and have been better parents than any of mine. The knowledge that I could outlive Dustin by *centuries* made me ill. The thought I would outlive my children nearly took me down. I could never survive that type of burden."

Asteria's heart clenched because of how parallel her and Phoebe's existences were.

Never feeling like they belonged with one designation over another, yearning for acceptance and understanding amongst their family and peers.

It was Phoebe's truth that slapped Asteria in the face this time.

Immortality had always felt like a gift forged into a cage. The games, the alliances, the weight of eons with the same people breathing down her neck, pressing down on her chest—she'd bided her time, worn the masks, danced the same tired steps year after year, century after century.

Asteria's throat tightened. Maybe immortality wasn't a pinnacle of the Lyrans' existence. Maybe it was a trap, and she didn't know she wanted out until there *was* an out.

It's not that she wanted to die, not tomorrow anyway. No, she wanted to live, to taste fleeting joy. To choose every day with each breath who she was without the weight of eternity telling her otherwise.

And just as Phoebe had found what she was looking for her entire life in Dustin, Asteria may have found that with Wells.

She abruptly gathered her skirt in her hand. "I know you don't want to listen to me. I'm possibly your least favorite person in the world, but I advise you to speak with Piers and hear him out. You will have a better conversation with him than with Wells. The youngest prince tends to be... charming. You may think I don't know much about you, but I know you're not one to fall for political charm.

"You want facts and blunt honesty, and Piers will give that to you." Asteria turned on her heel and headed for the door.

"Asteria!" Phoebe scoffed, but the sound nearly broke her heart. It was coated in disbelief, and she felt the undercurrent of hurt.

Asteria couldn't turn her back on Phoebe again, but she couldn't think past the elixir. She paused as she opened the door, throwing her head back over her shoulder to meet Phoebe's gaze.

She might barely share any resemblance with Gallus, but Asteria saw so much of her younger self in her sister. A version that existed before Rod and Danica tried to force her into a box.

"I know you may hate me and think I hate you, but I want you to know that's not true." Asteria had never hated Phoebe. She loved her sister—it was all just too complicated to get into at the moment. "I could sit here and make excuses for the past, but that's unfair to you. Just know I'm sorry for how I've treated you, and I'm proud of who you are, if that means anything. Your words at your coronation were beautiful, and I knew you would be a great queen."

"Wait—" Asteria stopped at the threshold, looking back again. Phoebe's eyes were wide, her skin gaunt. Her voice was soft and timid as she asked, "You were at my coronation?"

Asteria frowned, her lip curling unintentionally. Out of the entire apology, *that* was what Phoebe took from it? "Well, of course. I've attended all my siblings' coronations."

She wanted to speak more with Phoebe, especially as her sister's mouth dropped open, but this elixir was heavy in her thoughts, swelling and taking up every last inch of space. Asteria left the study and reentered the receiving room, heart hammering in her chest.

Wells, Piers, Gavril, and Dustin all stood from their seats, gazes bouncing between Asteria and the open door of the connected room. Her entourage looked at her expectantly, but Dustin was rather perturbed.

Asteria waved a hand behind her. "She's well, although something I said before exiting may have very well broken her."

Dustin's frown deepened, but he quietly excused himself as he slipped past Asteria.

Gavril smirked, shoving his hands into his pockets. "I'm going to guess that if you broke your own sister, the chat didn't go as you planned."

Asteria snarled at him before walking toward Piers and Wells. She stretched her hand toward the latter, and he raised his eyebrows, but immediately accepted. She felt Gavril's intense gaze locked onto the connection.

"Phoebe wants to speak with you at some point," Asteria explained to Piers, her grip tightening on Wells as anxiousness buzzed beneath her skin. "She's someone who won't be convinced with flowery words. She's strategic, and I feel you may be better suited for the conversation than

Wells."

Gavril snorted, and Piers shot him a wary glance before nodding once. "If that's what you think is best."

"I know it is." She opened a portal beside Wells, and he frowned at it, pursing his lips.

"And where are you taking my brother?" Piers raised an amused eyebrow.

"I need to check on something, and I would appreciate backup if it goes awry." She shrugged, waving her free hand toward where Dustin and Phoebe still hadn't emerged. "I'm sure they'll show you back to our rooms."

Without another look at Piers or Gavril, she briefly met Wells's curious gaze, her heart picking up its pace again at the unyielding trust she found there.

He didn't question where they were going. He simply said, "Lead the way, Blue."

She was about to learn just how much Wells trusted her as they stepped through the portal into Endora's private room.

CHAPTER 54

ASTERIA

Asteria didn't give Endora a chance to register who'd stepped into her study.

With a flick of her wrist, Aether sailed across the room, yanking Endora's hands wide and wrapping around her torso. With another flick, Endora flew back against the shelves on the far wall of her dim study, jars and books crashing to the ground.

"Fucking Gods, Asteria," Wells muttered, the Aether swirling in his hands. "What are you doing?"

"She's come for retribution." Endora chuckled darkly, wincing. "She's angry with me for what I did to Sybil."

"Actually, I came here to talk about something entirely unrelated." Asteria sneered, scooping her other hand up. Knives rose from a worktable, glowing gold with Energy. "But thank you for the reminder."

Asteria splintered the shelves on the wall with a ball of Energy, then threw two knives at Endora's open palms. The other two sliced through her shoulders, pinning her to the now-empty wall behind her. Endora cried out as Asteria removed the Aether from her body, the four knives the only thing suspending her.

"Asteria…" Wells's voice was even, but there was an undertone there she had yet to hear from him.

It wasn't the anger she anticipated. It was something gentle, caressing her without a touch.

"That's—" Endora clenched her teeth, head lolling back against the wall. "That's more like what I anticipated with a visit from the Goddess of Sirians."

Asteria hummed as she crossed her arms behind her back. She slowly walked around the cauldron in the middle of the room until she stood before Endora. "You acknowledge me as your Goddess, yet you entice my wrath by attacking someone I consider a sister."

Endora laughed, shaking her head, but tensed at the tendon movement it elicited in her shoulders. "The irony of that entire sentence is fascinating, Asteria. You wish to acknowledge your status as a Goddess when you want to invoke your wrath, so what does it matter what I try to *entice*? You then refer to my sister as your own, while I think I have developed a familial relationship with your sister."

Asteria narrowed her eyes, a strange growl rumbling in the back of her throat. "My blood sister is why I'm truly here."

Endora rolled her black eyes. Blood soaked through her tunic, making her appear haunted. "You expect me to believe you're irked by my relationship with Phoebe?"

"I could care less about who Phoebe associates herself with," Asteria chided, crossing her arms over her chest. "Phoebe told me about the mortal elixir."

Endora startled, her body stiffening, which only caused more blood to gush from her wounds as she cried out—a sharp bark. She recovered quickly, lifting her chin with defiance.

"What of it?" she rasped.

Asteria squinted. "She said it took her immortality."

Endora hacked a dry cough. "And you'll have me believe you suddenly care how long Phoebe lives?"

"Wait, what?" Wells asked from behind her. Asteria finally glanced over her shoulder, studying his face. His brows were furrowed, but those bright eyes glittered with curiosity. "Did Phoebe willingly give up her immortality?"

Asteria nodded as Endora said, "Of course she did. She loves her human so much she refuses to outlive him."

"She said she maintained her powers, save for the first day after taking it, but she lost her enhanced physical abilities like healing." Asteria narrowed her eyes at Endora, studying her and feeling for any change of the Aether within her. "You're telling me that you were successful, and there are no dramatic or dangerous side effects?"

"The only side effect we have identified thus far is it nullified her ability to have more children," Endora drawled, eyes flickering over her face. "There have been no others. Why are you asking?"

Suspicion seeped from Endora with the slowing flow of her blood. Asteria took satisfaction in the way the Andromedan's wounds mended around the steel knives, the enhanced healing they spoke of kicking in.

"Would it work on a Lyran?"

Asteria swore she sensed Wells stiffen behind her, his intake of breath quick but quiet.

Endora's frown deepened, then her face slackened. Her gaze flicked behind Asteria, and the corner of her lip twitched ever so slightly as she stared intently at Wells.

Fuck me.

Endora's voice turned oily. "Now why would a good *Little Lyran* want to be mortal?"

"Answer me," Asteria snapped, blue veins flashing once.

She didn't flinch as she said, "I am answering. I don't know. I've never tested it on a Lyran. But"—her eyes flicked to Wells again—"if you're volunteering samples, I'll have an answer once I've run my tests. Assuming I feel inclined to."

"I'm losing my patience, Endora." Asteria lit the knives with Energy

461

again, twisting them in a single rotation, and Endora yelped.

"*Bitch*," Endora hissed, blinking rapidly as she pressed her lips together. She inhaled slowly through her nose. "Im telling you—"

"How would you test it?" Asteria kept her face even, resisting the urge to look back at Wells. She didn't want to give Endora even more of a reason to report this back to Gallus and the others.

"Just as I did before having Phoebe ingest it." Endora's eyes bounced from Wells to Asteria. She prayed he wasn't staring at her like he usually was. "I would need a vial or two of blood to test it on. It allows me to watch how it reacts or changes when in contact with the elixir."

Asteria scanned the room, her eyes snagging on a few empty vials on the counter.

She gently wrapped the Aether around two, bringing them toward her. She summoned another knife from the table, guiding it to her hand. Asteria quickly sliced her palm and filled the first vial before corking it. The wound was already sealed by the time she was through, so she sliced again to fill the second one.

"Good enough?" Asteria wiggled them as she raised an eyebrow at Endora, gently laying them back on the counter as the necromancer nodded.

"That should be fine—" Endora's words cut off in a cry as Asteria yanked all the knives from her body. She went crashing to the floor at Asteria's feet. "*Fuck*, Asteria."

Asteria crouched before Endora, snatching her chin between her index finger and thumb, digging her nails in as she jerked her head up. Endora groaned at the awkward angle, glaring at Asteria as she breathed in and out through her nose.

"You know damn well I could do far worse to you," she whispered harshly, her breath brushing loose strands of hair from Endora's face. "I *dream* of the moment I can burn you with my starfire, only until you are a moment from death. Then, I would let your body heal only so I could repeat the process over and over until I was bored.

"But you have something I may want." Asteria wanted it more than anything and couldn't deny what—or who—drove the desire into a manic need. "You won't tell *anyone* about what I've asked you to research, do you understand? I *will* know because the moment any Lyran finds out I want to rid myself of my immortality, I'll hear of it."

"Why would I do anything for you?" Endora snarled through clenched teeth.

"Because of what you did to Sybil," Asteria said, bringing their faces closer together. "You either do this for me, or I take you back to Eonia and do exactly what I dream of doing."

Endora's black eyes flared momentarily with a milky glow, then narrowed. "You want this badly. I can see it. You're practically humming with hunger. Threats of torture don't woo me, Asteria, so if I do this for you… I want something in return."

Asteria mimicked Endora's expression in an almighty staredown. "You're in no position to bargain. You forget who I am."

"Yet here we are," Endora spat, followed up by a deep, crazed chuckle. "I do this on *my* terms, Lyran. Call off Eldamain's spies trailing me. Otherwise, you'll never get your precious mortality, and I'll go straight to your father with this tidbit of information."

Asteria slowly twisted her head over her shoulder at Wells, raising an eyebrow. Her heart hammered in her chest at the empty shock on his face, his mouth propped open. He blinked and shook his head to clear his expression, but he nodded once as he held Asteria's gaze.

"Consider it done." Asteria laid a hand flat against the side of Endora's face and shoved her away as she rose, staring down with starfire flickering at her fingertips. "When you have an answer, you know how to call for me. I would advise against an ambush. If you attempt to trap me, I will burn everyone to the ground, consequences be damned."

"Oh, I will," Endora whispered, sneering up from her hunch on the ground. "And you'll come, because you are no different than any other Lyran despite the pedestal you sit upon."

Asteria hesitated, bile burning at the back of her throat at the insult.

Endora appeared pleased as a sly grin crawled up her cheeks. "Don't forget it was I who nearly killed your precious drakon. *You* crossed the line in the sand to bargain with the enemy for something you want, damning all those around you for your selfish desires."

She wasn't about to fall for the bait.

Asteria flung herself around, marching toward Wells as she threw open a portal. Her heart hammered for a multitude of reasons as she stepped through into the room she was granted at Rigel's Keep in Etherea.

CHAPTER 55

ASTERIA

The fireplace was already at a dull glow when they entered the room at Rigel's Keep, casting haunting shadows along the deep burgundy wallpaper and reflecting off the gold frame of the bed.

Asteria couldn't care less about a fire, though. Not when her body buzzed with anticipation, hope, excitement, and something she'd believed she never felt before.

Fear.

Fear of an unknown future, but one that guaranteed an ending. Sure, war could kill her if properly done, but this potion?

It granted her mortality—something she thought entirely unattainable.

Something that guaranteed an ending in death.

"Asteria," Wells said quietly, the tenderness in his voice snapping her out of her trance. She continued to stare at the fading fire. "What the hell was that?"

"Hope," she whispered, barely perceptible. She hadn't realized how close Wells was until he appeared beside her in her peripheral.

"How was that hope?" he asked, not unkindly.

Asteria gnawed on her lower lip, contemplating whether or not this was something she was ready to admit to Wells. In the end, there was no reason to. He didn't dictate her life or what she should do with it. He didn't understand what it was to be immortal, the burden on their shoulders.

Wells was different, though. She knew how special he was, not only as a man but as a mortal. There would be no judgment from him; there had yet to be thus far in their relationship, whatever it was. He wouldn't try to force her into a decision or outcome she didn't want.

He always saw her for *her*.

Meeting him and experiencing the passion she had with him was what ultimately had her seriously considering a mortal existence. He deserved to know why she'd dragged him to Endora's.

"I've lived a long time," Asteria whispered. His fingers tucked under her chin, gently urging her gaze to his. She met those beautiful beige eyes, freckles peeking out against his skin. "I don't wish to live longer. Look what it's done to the other Lyrans. I have no desire to turn into"—she waved her hand around them as he slowly dropped his finger—"that."

"You wish to be mortal?" he asked, as simply as if he wanted to know whether she wanted honey in her tea.

"This immortal life has only brought me responsibilities I didn't ask for," she explained, walking toward the bed and running a hand through her hair. "I've always found myself far too much like mortal Beings, and I want to keep that quality about myself. I would rather have a shortened life and honorable death over an extended, dishonorable life. I want to be remembered rather than despised for my survival.

"Phoebe knew she would live an excessively extended lifespan as an Andromedan." Asteria sat on the edge of the bed, staring at her palms. "She didn't want to outlive Dustin. She wanted a mortal existence with him."

Emotions burned the back of her throat. Too many words were left unsaid, an insinuation she wasn't sure she wanted him to catch.

Wells's boots clicked against the stone floor as he approached. She looked up through her lashes, apprehension bubbling in her chest.

"Part of me feels this is you asking for death," Wells explained. "But I've seen you fight for life. You *yearn* for life—to exist without conditions. If the positions were flipped, I can't say I would deny the opportunity to live just a little longer than the average Sirian."

He stared at Asteria with far more wisdom than someone his mortal age should have, and it had tears burning the backs of her eyes.

She didn't know how a simple meeting by chance led to him being someone she cherished far too dearly for her liking.

"Well..." Asteria cleared her throat, throwing herself backward on the bed. She stared up at the elaborate canopy, sighing heavily. "As an immortal, things also become predictable. You lose the element of surprise and excitement. Mortals only know this one life, and you get to experience the different things one life offers. *Everything* is unpredictable to you."

The mattress dipped as Wells sat beside her, leaning back on his hands and gazing down at her with a raised eyebrow. She wanted to reach up and brush the stray curl from his forehead, but she folded her hands over her stomach instead.

"Would you say any events unfolding around us were predictable?" he inquired, tilting his head.

She pursed her lips, averting her gaze to the ceiling again. "I can't say it was predictable, but I would argue it was inevitable. It just happened far sooner than I originally thought."

His hand slipped over hers, slowly peeling her fingers away from her other hand. She held her breath as he raised it, his thumb pressing into the middle of her palm. He studied it like he reigned from the House of Echidna, reading her future within the lines.

"And me?" He hauled his gaze to hers, his smirk barely contained. He inched closer, grabbing her other hand and slowly pinning both on either side of her head. Heat ignited within her. "Was I predictable?"

Stars, no. From their first meeting, everything about Wells had been unpredictable. She was content with being alone until he appeared behind Odo in his office.

I think Destiny has given him to you…

He could be temporary, or he could be everything.

She'd accepted him the moment he broke down the first of her forged barriers.

"Are you pondering *that* deeply, or are you stubborn enough not to answer?" Wells leaned closer. She locked onto his lips. "Or do you believe you can counter what I've said with your wit?"

She tightened at his proximity, an invisible magnet urging her to close the distance between them. She longed for those lips, loved how she fell into him, and he utterly consumed her.

"I'll concede," she whispered, lifting her head to brush her lips against his. He followed, only the words she spoke separating them. "Only because I've come to enjoy being excited by you."

"I excite you?" She felt his smile as his hand roamed down her arm and gently swiped the side of her breast, leaving fire in its wake. "Or is it my hands that excite you?"

He slowly inched the fabric of her dress up her leg, gathering it to the side as he exposed her calf, her knee, her thigh, higher—

Then she remembered he'd asked her a question.

"Everything about you," she gasped as his fingers tickled the sensitive skin on the inside of her thigh. She arched into the movement, coaxing him closer. "Your words, your hands, your eyes…"

He moaned with satisfaction as he lowered his lips to hers, lazily tracing them as his hand came to the apex of her thighs, skimming over her undergarments. He climbed higher as he deepened the kiss with a tilt of his head, devouring her while skimming a path back and forth.

Wells's lips moved across her cheek, featherlight, at the same time his fingers slid beneath the fabric and straight to her center. He dipped into the slickness gathering there, a low, guttural groan rumbling in his chest.

"Excited indeed."

Then slowly and deliberately, he slipped two fingers inside her. Her breath hitched, but it turned into a moan as he pressed against that tender place that made stars burst behind her eyes. His fingers curled just right, rubbing in a torturous rhythm that dragged fire up her spine. Her hands fisted the blankets, but then climbed—grasping his solid biceps, sliding up the curve of his shoulders, his neck, until she tangled her fingers in the soft waves of his hair.

Wells curled his fingers again in response, coaxing another cry from her lips as his mouth found the curve of her throat. He nipped gently at the sensitive skin between her neck and collarbone, the sharp tease sending a jolt straight to where he worked her.

"Wells," she muttered softly, unable to keep herself from grinding against his palm in desperation.

"Use your words, Blue," he demanded, pressing his thumb against her swollen clit as he moved his fingers. "You have to tell me what you want."

"Anything." It was all she could think of outside of how he knew exactly where to touch to send the heat pooling in her lower stomach throughout her body. "Please."

"I appreciate your manners," he murmured against her throat. She almost whimpered when he removed his fingers until she felt him tugging at her underwear and sliding them down her legs.

Her stomach knotted, but when he sucked his glistening fingers, her skin flashed blue with feral need.

The look on his face was something she would engrave in her mind for the rest of her days.

Awe, lust, wonder, pride—all captured in his smirk.

"You've truly earned your nickname," Wells said, lowering to his knees on the floor beside the bed. She frowned, but he pushed her dress up further and added, "Now, be a good girl and spread your legs."

Asteria willingly opened her legs wider, biting her lower lip. His hands slid up both her thighs, his gaze following his path until he came back to her knees. Suddenly, he gripped them tightly and yanked the curve of her ass to the edge of the bed. He draped her legs over his shoulders, then proceeded to place delicate kisses up her thigh as he kept his eyes on hers.

He stopped just before he reached her core, then repeated the path on the other side as his two fingers spread her open. When he kissed the space between her clit and thigh, there was a devilish glint in his eye.

He winked, then lowered his mouth again, flattening his tongue against her in a single stroke, curling as he climbed.

Asteria gasped, her spine arching as her entire body locked up. Every sense narrowed to the soft claiming in that motion, the way he dragged it back down with sinful patience. She cried out when he dipped into her, the sound coated in pure ecstasy.

Wells pulled back just enough to replace his tongue with two fingers, sinking them deep. His lips returned to her clit, the slide of his tongue stroking in tandem with the thrust of his fingers. She whimpered helplessly as her hands scrambled to find something to hold. The sheet twisted in one hand, his hair tangled in the other, but nothing grounded her against the overwhelming wave building in her core. She climbed higher and higher with the pace of his fingers, her thighs trembling on either side of his head.

On the next thrust, he hitched his fingers at just the right angle, and she clenched around him. Her vision blurred, hips jolting in an effort to chase him.

The next curl shattered her.

Pleasure splintered her into a thousand fragments.

She rode the wave of it, hips grinding against his hand with broken cries. He didn't stop, not even as she shuddered around his fingers. He gradually slowed, drawing out every aftershock while his lips pressed soft kisses along the inside of her thigh.

"Watching you come undone has become my most passionate

hobby," Wells muttered, kissing a trail up her hip and stomach, between her breasts before resting his chin there. "Does that make me a deviant?"

She wanted to answer his question, except if previous moments together were any indication, she knew he was aroused just as much as she was. The act of sex still had her chest thudding uncomfortably, but she knew of another way she could repay him.

One she'd never done before.

"What if I wanted to watch you come undone?" she whispered, slowly rising. His eyes darkened as he moved onto the bed until they kneeled before one another on the mattress. "To touch you." She trailed her fingertips down the middle of his chest and abdomen, then stopped at the waistband of his pants. "To taste you."

"Whatever it is you wish to do to me…" Wells hauled her lips to his, then dragged her on top of him as he fell backward on the bed. Asteria yelped, but she smiled against his lips and giggled, her heart warming from his playfulness. "Just know your giggles unravel me as much as your mouth does."

Asteria adored how sweet he was to her, so much so it hurt. It only made her want to do this more. She slowly shimmied down his body but stopped at the hem of his shirt, pinching it between her fingers.

"I need you to take this off," she said, looking up at him.

He laughed at that, pinching her chin before they both worked to lift his shirt up and over his head. Asteria's breath caught in her throat as she straddled his legs, wondering if she would ever not be impressed by him.

Her fingers brushed over that scar on his ribs. He stiffened, nervous tension rolling off him. Her fingers moved to the ties of his waistband, painstakingly pulling them undone as his eyes increasingly darkened. He propped himself back on his forearms to watch her, even as her hands trembled.

She was a Goddess, for Heaven's sake. Why was she so damned nervous?

Unfortunately, he caught it and tilted his head. "Blue…"

"I've never..." She tucked her fingers into his waistband, only one tug away from revealing what she felt straining through his slacks. "I've never used my *mouth*—"

"It's okay." Wells chuckled lightly, gripping her chin and raising her gaze to his. "You don't have to do anything you are uncomfortable with."

"I want to." She swallowed, her stomach swirling. She wanted to do this for him, but she also wanted to do this *with* him. "Will you... teach me?"

Teach me, Blue.

A low rumble vibrated through him. "Trust me, there are very few things you can do wrong."

She glared at him.

"Gods, you are..." He shook his head, but then helped her pull his slacks down to mid-thigh.

Once again, she was breathless.

In truth, she hadn't seen many cocks. She'd recently conjured an expectation in her mind that there was no possible way she could compare a mortal body to that of a Lyran.

But looking at Wells...

She was pleasantly surprised to stand corrected.

Asteria ran her hands up his thighs, every shift of muscle beneath her touch sending a shiver through her. When her fingers tentatively wrapped around him, Wells jerked at the contact. His eyes fluttered shut, and he drew in a deep breath that sounded more like a plea than a grounding effort.

His skin was soft over the hard tension, and her thumb slid along the thick vein on the underside of his cock, the tip already beading with liquid.

Wells moaned, throwing his head back as he clenched his jaw. That sound, throaty and raw, sent a bolt of need through her.

Asteria's lips curved in a slow, wicked smile. Making him come undone wasn't going to be difficult.

"You can lick"—his voice caught as she stroked once—"wrap your lips around it." She repeated the motion, drawing another shudder from him. "Or you could very well keep doing that, too, if you please."

"I'll start," she whispered, her voice hoarse. His eyes pulsed black with the Aether. "You guide me."

"I'll try my damnedest, but the minute you—*fuck me.*"

Asteria dipped her head and dragged her tongue along the base, tasting him fully for the first time. He twitched in her hand, so she climbed up slowly, tracing every inch before flicking her tongue over the bead of liquid gathered at the head. His sharp inhale spurred her on. When she circled her tongue around the tip, his entire body reacted.

"Asteria," he moaned breathlessly, chest rising in steady pants.

The way he said her name—not a title or nickname, but her full name—emboldened her.

She pumped him twice, blinking as she asked, "Like this?"

She parted her lips and wrapped them around him, sinking down. She wasn't sure what to do with her tongue, so she pressed it against the underside and drew back with gentle pressure, gauging his reaction.

"You don't—" His voice cracked into a breathy grunt as she curled her tongue along both sides on the next pass. "I don't think you need my help."

She did her best not to smile at the praise, even though his blissful sounds were more than enough to drive her forward. She took him deeper, moving with a little more confidence, wringing more of those gravelly moans from him.

As she picked up the pace, Wells's hand brushed her hair to one shoulder before slipping his fingers into the strands. His grip slowly tightened, firm but gentle, as if asking permission for something. She wasn't sure what he planned to do with her like this, but she wanted it—whatever it was.

She lifted her mouth from him, peering up. "Show me."

"I don't want to hurt or scare you," he whispered, the sound so quiet it nearly broke her heart.

"You can't." Her voice was certain, eyes burning as she met his. "I trust you."

His eyes flashed again, but he nodded. "Just relax your jaw and do what you've been doing."

She took him back into her mouth, doing as he asked. Her stomach coiled when his hand hesitantly wrapped around the hair at the back of her head. When she bobbed, he gave the faintest tug, syncing his movements with her pace.

Then, he thrust.

Just once, careful and shallow, the surprise of it making her gasp around him. She didn't stop, though. She actually liked it far more than she expected. The second time, his grip firmed on her hair, his hips rolling forward with a deeper rhythm.

Her body responded instinctively, thighs pressing together as her own arousal returned from the simple power of bringing him to the edge. The pace built between them, his guidance growing firmer as her confidence surged. She experimented with her tongue, with how deep she could take him, until he swore under his breath.

Wells stopped moving, his fingers slipping from her hair and gripping the sheets.

"Asteria," he warned, rich and sultry. "I can't—I will...Gods above."

She understood.

Her fingers tightened around his base, and she drew her mouth along him once, twice, and on the third time, she looked up, eyes locked onto his.

That was all it took.

Wells shuddered beneath her, and she felt the tremor of his release pulse through every muscle as he spilled onto her tongue. She took every last drop, never breaking eye contact, relishing the taste of him—salty and somehow uniquely *him*.

His hand returned to her hair, but it wasn't to pull or guide, but to bring her back to him. He urged her up the length of his body, pulling her into his arms.

"Come here," he grumbled, grabbing her face between his hands and bringing their lips together.

He rolled them to their sides, his kiss slow, steady, and yet just as consuming as the fiery ones. She liquified in his embrace, one hand pinned beneath her, the other resting on the scar on his side.

They were both panting when they finally pulled away, and she was so close to his face she could count the freckles across his nose. His thumb traced her cheekbone as he searched her eyes.

"What're you looking for?" she asked quietly, her thumb drawing along the scar.

He sighed contentedly, encasing her in his arms and tucking his face between her cheek and the pillow. His smell engulfed her, his chest and throat vibrating as he spoke. "If it's any consolation, you excite me, too." He buried his nose beneath her jaw, planting kisses between his words. "You do far more than excite me."

She frowned, but then the conversation before they lost themselves in each other came back. "You're quite late to that conversation."

He chuckled, and she dipped her head to place a featherlight kiss to his throat. "Oh, Blue. What have you done to me?"

"If you're unaware of what just transpired, I'm certain I did something wrong," she mumbled into his throat. "That or you and I have very different definitions of a—"

Wells burst into laughter, the sound bringing a wide smile across her face as she chortled at her own humor. He pulled back to look at her again, grinning in awe. "I feel very privileged to see this side of you. Your laugh and smile are something I want to keep bottled away for when I need it most."

Tears burned behind her eyes, and she hid her face in his shoulder to keep him from seeing. "You bring this side out in me. I've come to enjoy it."

He kissed the top of her head, his arm stroking her back.

Her heart swelled, the safety of his arms something she'd never had before. Not just safe from threats, but her heart was safe with him. She knew with absolute certainty he would never hurt her. Asteria didn't think she could trust another so profoundly, but he repeatedly proved to her why she could.

He agreed to stay again, and as they settled in for the night, she knew what she would do if Endora told her the elixir would work.

CHAPTER 56

PHOEBE

Phoebe slowly sank into the chair behind her desk while Piers sat in one on the opposite side. She stretched her hands out in front of her, resting her palms flat on top of the cluttered parchment.

Piers was far too patient for a Lieutenant General. His elbows rested on the arms of the chair, his hands folded together, dangling above his lap. He blinked those green-hazel eyes, his sun-kissed skin a mask of indifference.

From what she remembered, all the Carraphim brothers looked alike, except Piers and Quintin were far more similar than Orwell was to either of them. They had angled, strong jaws and broader builds with wide shoulders. Quintin and Piers also had harsher brows, whereas Orwell had a softness to his eyes—not to mention his were a different hazel than his brothers, more beige than green or brown.

Piers didn't look like a Lieutenant General, and maybe that's what really threw Phoebe off.

He looked like a prince, which of course he was.

He would make a good king, and Phoebe wondered how much of

Quintin competing in her marriage games was an attempt to put him on Etherea's throne with her so Piers could be on Eldamain's.

If that were true, the spare heir was truly Orwell.

Phoebe inhaled through her nose, pausing before speaking calmly. "You can't understand the impossible position I've been put in."

"Help me understand, then," Piers said, shrugging. "I'm a man of strategy, and there isn't a puzzle I can't solve."

"Sure." Phoebe snorted, earning a raised eyebrow. "Gallus and a few other Andromedans threatened my husband. My *human* husband, as well as every other human within my borders. Etherea arguably has one of the highest human populations of all the countries. You can see why a parlay of sorts was enticing."

"What were the terms of your *parlay*?" Piers seemed to be a master at keeping a neutral, firm facial expression. Not a single muscle twitched, even as he emphasized the term.

She expected a sneer at the least.

"Etherea stands down on both accounts," Phoebe explained, drumming her fingers over a tome. "We remain neutral during this war, keeping to ourselves within our borders. In exchange for that decision, Gallus promised my country and humans will remain untouched, even after the war has ended."

"Should his side win." Piers blinked expectantly.

Phoebe tilted her head back and forth. "I would venture it happens despite who wins. Would you and your allies punish a kingdom for remaining neutral in an effort of self-preservation?"

"I can't speak on behalf of those sitting on thrones or wearing crowns." Piers crossed his arms over his chest, relaxing against the back of the chair. "Alas, I don't foresee my brother punishing you and your kingdom for making the best decision for Etherea. As for the other countries..."

Piers shrugged, pursing his lips. "Eventually, you must interact with them, form relationships, and strike trade agreements. Remaining neutral will make it quite difficult for them to trust your intentions."

"I disagree." Phoebe smirked and wiggled her hand over the desk. "My decision—as far as the public is concerned—isn't driven by ambition or blood lust. It's genuinely thoughtful. My kingdom's best interests are in mind."

"That's another way to look at it." Piers sighed, averting his gaze to one of the shelves of books on her wall. He squinted as if trying to read something. "Do you even wish to hear what an alliance with us would look like?"

"I respect you and your brothers too much not to." Phoebe straightened in her seat, resting her forearms on the desk. "It would be a disservice if I sent you away without at least hearing your terms."

"It would be *disrespectful* to waste my time if you have no intention of considering the proposal." Piers jerked his head back to her, eyes glowing subtly with Energy. "Should I continue?"

Dustin's words echoed in her mind as she considered turning Piers away. Her initial instinct was to say no regardless, but something deep within her gut urged her to listen and absorb what they had to offer.

What they could do for her people.

"Should you accept, there's a treaty that offers various benefits for each kingdom involved," Piers began, crossing an ankle over his knee. "There are prettier words Wells will be far more useful for. I know that's not necessarily what you care for at this moment, so I'll elaborate on what you do care about.

"I tell you this in good faith that you truly are neutral and won't side with Gallus and the others." He raised an expectant eyebrow.

Phoebe nodded once. "You have my word."

He scrutinized her but seemed to accept her promise. "The plan is to send military aid in waves. Once allies are sealed and confirmed, the first wave of soldiers from The Northern Pizi will come to Eldamain, and the first wave of Riddling will come to Etherea. This will be enough between our armies and theirs to protect our borders should any skirmishes break out.

"The second wave will follow, and that will be to bolster the military further. Our forces initiate the first offensive attack on the north side of Sylvan while yours and Riddling's attack from the south. You have a sizable, skilled army, so we also want your naval forces to bolster Riddling's to defend at sea. Based on Sylvan's reaction to our push, we assess the third wave."

It wasn't a bad start; she had to credit them for that. Riddling coming to her borders offered additional protection to her people.

There were holes, though, and she planned on poking at them.

"If I agreed, what happens when the Lyrans discover I've turned on them?" She twisted in her seat and gestured toward the map on the wall. "I have enemies on either border: Sylvan and Teslin. There's a measly forest separating us from Teslin, who is ripe with Caine's drakon spawn."

"We would hope to conceal your agreement until you received the help you needed from Riddling," Piers explained, adjusting in his seat.

"And will you be too late again?"

Piers startled at the question, a deep line forming between his brows. "I'm not sure—"

"Quintin sent me a letter, which I now believe was a warning about Endora." Phoebe retrieved the letter from her drawer with a flick of her hand, releasing it into the air and passing it over her desk to Piers's outstretched hand. She continued as he read it over. "Unfortunately, the letter got to me the day Gallus appeared in my study with my beaten and bloodied husband in the arms of the *Darkness coiling too near to my throne.*"

Phoebe rose, slowly walking toward the map. Piers tracked her movements with the parchment hanging limp in his hand. She tapped the map, directly in the middle of the ocean between Riddling and Etherea.

"This expanse takes too much time." Phoebe traced her fingers from the empty ocean to where Thalassa lay. "If Riddling sends forces from Sitara, they'll have no choice but to travel in Thalassa's view. That island is full of nereids and keteas, not to forget this ocean here"—she tapped the middle of the triangle of water between Riddling, Celestia, and Sylvan—"is Sylvan's."

"Phoebe—"

"Yes, my navy could support, but not before our generals have the chance to convene. If they were to meet Riddling tomorrow without any communication, we risk counteracting one another's strategies."

"We could always—"

"Nen would see this. Once word travels to the other Lyrans, they'll attack Etherea, and you'll be too late." Phoebe walked back to her desk but didn't sit in her chair. She leaned against it, wrapping her arms around her midsection. "I want you to know, I wish I could accept the alliance. I don't deny it lightly. You know I stand by humans just as much as you and your family, but I have to think about *my* humans before trying to save the rest of the world."

Piers rubbed at the stubbled mustache and beard hugging his lips. "Gallus and his league may vow to protect your people, but they're unstable. Every last one of them. Don't forget the threats they've promised alongside their protection."

Phoebe narrowed her eyes, clenching her fists where they were tucked into her ribs.

Piers rolled his head on his neck before rising. He approached Phoebe, standing toe-to-toe with her. She had to crane her neck a few inches to meet his gaze. "Asteria offers protection—no bargain or request for payment. Protection is her only motivation."

Phoebe swallowed down the emotions conjured by her sister's name. The revelation that Asteria attended had her coronation and Gallus hadn't...

Phoebe shoved it down.

"Do you truly believe they won't harm your people and leave your country alone?" Piers frowned, studying her face as if it might hold the answer he was looking for. "Without you, we'll lose. They want to eradicate humans, Phoebe. They'll come for Etherea and its humans eventually. Maybe not right away, but there will be more threats dressed as promises once again."

Piers grabbed his military coat off the back of the chair, draping it over his arm as he strolled toward the door.

"For now, my decision stands," Phoebe said softly, tears stinging her eyes. He stopped with his hand poised on the knob. "I won't get involved."

"I think it should be you who tells Asteria." Piers nodded, peeking over his shoulder at her. She tried to bury the burn in her chest at the thought of confronting her sister again. "There's no expiration date, Phoebe. The offer to ally will stand until we don't."

He swung the door open and moved under the threshold, pausing one final time as he turned, bracing his hand on the wooden frame. "I'm sorry things have appeared strained between our countries since your marriage games, but you should know Quin never held any resentment toward you for rejecting him. He isn't that type of person."

Phoebe's shoulders slumped once Piers was out of sight, her head hanging. The letter from Quintin sat on the chair, his handwriting blurring the longer she stared.

The Carraphims owed her *nothing*.

Piers was right in that it was she who rejected Quintin in her marriage games when she rigged them for Dustin. Asteria and the Carraphims knew she'd claimed neutrality because of Gallus when they came here today, yet they granted her the opportunity to change her mind.

Despite her words and decision, they *still* left her with the invitation.

Phoebe sat alone with that for some time, all the while Piers's words chanted like a curse in her head.

They'll come for Etherea and its humans eventually.

CHAPTER 57

ASTERIA

A steria stood beneath the murals adorning the arched ceilings within the chapel in Rigel's Keep, a scowl straining against her cheeks.

The art was well done and absolutely beautiful, but it irked her to no end at how it portrayed what appeared to be the creation story of the Sirians.

The scene on her right was undoubtedly Gallus painted in his god-form in the center, his black form nearly indistinguishable against the deep indigo background. Naked mortal forms surrounded him, each with a six-pointed Mark standing stark against their skin. The Marks were outlined in black, tendrils flowing from them to Gallus's outstretched fingers.

The other scene was Danica, also depicted in her god–form, a female figure of bright gold glistening against the light blue day painted in her illustration. Similar to Gallus, humanoid forms stood entirely nude around her except their Marks were outlined in what could very well be pure gold paint, strings of it traveling from the center of their foreheads to her open palms.

Directly in front of Asteria, though, before the endless rows of pews, was *her* mural.

Except in hers, she was depicted as an infant, resembling her mortal form rather than her god-form.

Not to mention she was also nude.

She sighed heavily as her eyes scanned the various nude figures around her infantile form, those with black Marks on her right, the others with golden Marks to the left. The aura around her was starfire blue, with specks of black and gold spattered within.

"I've always thought it was rather disturbing they depicted you as a baby," Phoebe said from behind Asteria, her voice echoing through the empty chapel.

She shot a wary gaze over her shoulder to find Phoebe a few feet away, hands clasped behind her back. Asteria scoffed before resuming her criticism, eyes latched onto those black and gold spots. "I found out about this chapel at your coronation. It took all my willpower that day to remind myself I couldn't burn this place down."

"Because you didn't want to massacre the hundreds of people in this room?" Phoebe stepped up beside her, eyes studying Asteria's face.

Asteria couldn't help the coy grin gracing her lips. She peered at Phoebe from the corner of her eyes and shrugged. "I didn't want to ruin your day by making it about me."

She thought maybe Phoebe would find entertainment in that sentiment since they both seemed to be rather hostile individuals unless it came to those they cared for.

Instead, Phoebe just stared at her with an empty expression, eyes flicking wildly over Asteria's face. The longer they stood there, the tension transcended the usual, more of a permanent uneasiness.

"You said no," Asteria concluded, turning to face Phoebe, arms slack at her sides. "You'll remain neutral."

Phoebe swallowed audibly, so contrasting to the woman who fought with her in the study yesterday. Asteria frowned, unsure what changed in her sentiment toward her. "I told Piers I don't make this decision lightly, but unfortunately, I have to think about my people and the options before me right now. I can't bet on maybe, and as of right now, Gallus has only given me truth. He's left my people alone."

Asteria nodded slowly as she lowered onto the bench behind her. She rested her back against it, tipping her head up to the ceiling with a heavy sigh, the weight on her shoulders pressing down. She shut her eyes to avoid seeing either Danica or Gallus in their murals, trying to quell the anxiousness swirling in her chest.

"I know this is an inappropriate time to be hashing out our relationship," Phoebe began, her voice wrapping around Asteria. She sensed her lowering onto a bench nearby, the wood creaking with the shuffling of her gown. "But I would be lying if I didn't admit… I didn't know you were at my coronation."

"What about that is so startling to you?" Asteria snapped her head up and over, squinting as she shook it. "You're truly hung up on that."

"You have to be joking." Phoebe deadpanned, but a harsh laugh broke the stern expression. "Asteria, I don't know how you have viewed our relationship thus far, but you coming to support me at my coronation is quite out of character for you."

"Why do you think that?" Asteria frowned, unable to wrap her head around Phoebe's perspective. As she told her sister, she'd attended all her siblings' coronations. Heavens, she'd attended the coronation of *every* new Sirian king or queen.

Why would Phoebe be any different?

"You have been nothing but bitter and coarse to me since the moment I stepped into the Asterian Academy!" Phoebe flung her arms out as she rose from the bench. She pointed toward the mural, maybe in hopes that was the direction of Celestia. "I know for a *fact* you were the one who took on Dionne and Taranis's Warrior studies because of their god-powers. Sure, Dionne helped with Taranis's, but you could barely be bothered to take me under your wing to teach me. Dionne shouldered that responsibility."

"I would come to your lessons—"

"To bully me!" Phoebe's voice cracked, startling Asteria. She blinked rapidly, her mouth propping open.

She'd never considered that she bullied Phoebe. She knew her resentment toward Gallus at the time may have reflected in her ill treatment of Phoebe, but to consider being a bully to her own sister?

"Phoebe..." Asteria opened and closed her mouth a few times, but words failed her. She had no idea what to say or how to move forward. She studied her sister's face, and that's when she finally saw the sorrow buried deep in those brown eyes. "You truly think I hate you?"

"How am I supposed to know otherwise?" Phoebe's hard exterior cracked enough that a nearby sconce reflected off a single sheen of dampness on her eyelid. She shook her head, and the dampness vanished. "I haven't seen you in ten years. You were nothing but brash with me when I did see you... It's not like we have tea, Asteria."

Asteria winced, the words striking harder than she expected. They were so simple, but they broke her away from herself and her selfishness because all she could think of was Dionne sitting at a table in his room having tea and the ease with which she could tease him.

She couldn't do that with Phoebe, and the fault of her actions slammed into her.

Asteria had been cold to her sister because it was easier. The distance helped her cling to an ideal that Gallus used to piece her back together after Rod cheated on her. All he preached was how awful the cheating was, and that nothing good could come from such an act.

But as she looked at Phoebe's face—into eyes so achingly familiar in shape—Asteria saw something she hadn't allowed herself to see.

Hurt.

And not just any hurt.

Hurt she had caused.

"I didn't mean to be cruel," Asteria murmured, her voice brittle. "But I was."

Phoebe gave a short, sharp laugh. "That's your grand admission? You *didn't mean to be cruel*? Could've fooled me."

"I know." Asteria swallowed hard. "I know…"

Because she *had* known.

Of course she'd known, even back then. Every time Phoebe had looked at her, wide-eyed and hesitant, like a student hoping for a scrap of praise from her teacher instead of a sister reaching for kinship.

Asteria had seen it. She'd felt it, and she had turned away.

Because it was easier to make Phoebe a symbol rather than a person. Easier to cast her as the consequence of a betrayal than as the girl who wanted to belong. It was easier to protect herself with coldness than admit the man who raised her had shattered the ideals he'd rebuilt her with.

Phoebe had never broken anything; she'd just been born.

"You didn't deserve any of it."

Phoebe only crossed her arms.

"I—" Asteria started, then paused again. Her gaze fell to the stone floor between them, hoping to the Heavens the answers for how to repair this may be carved there. "When Gallus told me what he'd done to bring you into this world… I felt like everything I'd been taught was a lie. He told me loyalty mattered above all else, and that honor was sacred. Then he—he destroyed that. Why? I still don't know. But you were the proof."

Phoebe's face darkened, but Asteria rushed on. "That's not your fault. I know that now. I think… I think I knew it then, too, but I didn't want to. It was easier to put all my anger on you, when you only ever wanted to belong."

The last words left her lips in a near whisper.

Phoebe blinked, mouth parting in quiet surprise. "You made me feel like a mistake."

Asteria finally met her eyes. "And that was a failing of mine, not yours. I punished you for a sin that wasn't yours to bear. I've spent a decade pretending how I treated you at the Academy was normal, when it was actually cowardice."

Phoebe stepped forward, arms still crossed but her posture softened. "Are you only saying this now because I've confronted you? Have you known all of this for the last ten years, or are you truly coming to this conclusion before me?"

"I've had a new perspective on life as of late," Asteria grumbled under her breath, and she thought she caught the corner of Phoebe's lips tick up. "You said a lot of things yesterday that made me realize I've spent ten years pushing away one of the few people who might've understood me best. I've been learning to keep those types of people closer to me because I don't want to be alone anymore—"

Asteria choked on the abruptness of that admission.

She blamed this entirely on Wells.

Phoebe didn't answer right away. She studied Asteria with the same scrutiny Asteria had used on her earlier.

Then said, "I don't forgive you. Not yet. But…"

Asteria nodded, something cracking her chest at the words. "Just that alone is more than I deserve."

She had wielded her disappointment and confusion like a blade, cutting Phoebe out of her life. Punished Phoebe more than she ever deserved, all because she was too afraid to admit how deeply wounded she'd really been by Gallus.

How she treated Phoebe had been *exactly* something Danica would've asked of her. Something a Goddess would've done.

And Asteria never wanted to be a Goddess, not how the Lyrans viewed the title.

She wanted to be the Goddess her people thought she was.

CHAPTER 58

MORANA

Morana sat between Danica and Asteria, occasionally glancing at Rod to ensure he didn't make a poor decision. Every muscle in his mortal form clenched tighter the longer he stared at Orwell across from them, his gold aura pulsing.

She hoped the two-chair space between Asteria and Rod was enough.

"Would you stop *simmering*?" Asteria snapped, curling her body around Morana and Danica to glare at Rod. "You harm a single hair on his head and—"

"You'll set him on fire," Gavril drawled, slinging his arm around the back of Piers's chair. "Honestly, darling, we must find a new threat for you."

Asteria whipped her gaze to the male, a playful smirk twitching her lips. "Do you have suggestions? Maybe we can test them on Rod. Wells had a fascinating idea the other day—"

Orwell choked on the chalice he was sipping from, droplets falling from his lips. He raised glittering eyes to Asteria, dabbing his mouth with the back of his sleeve as he suppressed a coy grin. Morana peeked at

Asteria to find a similar smile on her face.

The sight both warmed her heart and chilled to her bones.

She didn't recognize the warmth in Asteria's eyes whenever she looked at Orwell. Before they took their seats, the draw to one another was evident. It was like their bodies and minds were in tune, responding with small glimpses and featherlight touches.

She knew Asteria far too well.

This was what falling in love should've always looked like for her little spitfire.

"Thank you all for coming," Quintin began, taking his seat at the head of his Council table. "I appreciate everyone meeting in Eldamain. I want to thank Lady Morana, Lady Danica, and Lord Rod for bringing anyone who didn't have faster means of travel."

There was an assortment of grunts and huffs in acknowledgment. The same individuals who were in Eonia had gathered once again, and this time Savaric wished to attend with Dionne.

Morana only hoped it would be less hostile. Unfortunately, the bickering between Rod and Asteria had already begun, and the meeting was just starting.

It also didn't bode well that Phoebe wasn't present.

"As you can see, Phoebe isn't here," Asteria echoed Morana's thoughts, her hands pressing into the wooden table. Those beautiful blue eyes swirled, a light occasionally flickering in their depths. "So that means, for now, Etherea isn't joining the cause. In fact, they're not joining either side. They chose to remain neutral."

"What does *for now* mean?" Taranis asked, tilting his head at his sister. "You believe there's still hope?"

Asteria leveled him with a glare. "I won't give up on her. We told her the offer still stands should she change her mind."

"I disagree," Savaric interjected with a frown. He looked to Quintin. "I don't believe it's fair Etherea will be allowed to participate in the treaty regardless of when they join."

"So you wish to leave them in the dust should things turn south?" Dionne narrowed his eyes at Savaric.

"That's not what I suggest," he amended, shooting him a glare. "I just mean they shouldn't be involved in the treaty. We'll come to their aid and fight in arms beside them, but they shouldn't benefit from the treaty."

"Hear, hear!" Taranis shouted, slamming his hand on the table in quick rhythm.

"Would you stop?" Asteria snarled at him, her eyes flashing entirely blue. "Just because you're my brother—"

"Blue," Orwell whispered, and the entire room fell silent.

Everyone caught the nickname this time.

"Fuck," Sybil muttered, hiding her face in her hands and sliding lower in her seat. Piers chuckled beside her, bumping her shoulder with his.

Morana suppressed the burn of anger in her throat.

She still needed to talk to her daughter about *that* piece of information.

"What did you call her?" Surprisingly, it wasn't Rod who spoke, but Danica.

Heavens save him, Orwell didn't back down. He crossed his arms and shrugged. "It's a nickname. Mine is Wells, Quintin is Quin, Sybil is Syb... We give nicknames to those we care for around here."

Danica and Rod bristled in their seats, but Morana only paid attention to Asteria. There was irritation in the tight lines of her face, but overall, she'd calmed down after the prince spoke to her.

A single word, and Asteria folded.

Oh, Heavens...

"We should continue with the assessment," Quintin said, clearing his throat. "As you all know, we're ready to provide every last resource to this war regarding the bodies and funds necessary."

"You have Riddling at your disposal," Savaric vowed with a nod in Quintin's direction.

"As do you have The Northern Pizi." Taranis kicked his boots up, balancing them on the table as he rocked on the chair's back legs. "So where does that leave us?"

"Not in a good place," Rod said, slowly rising from his seat. He rested his fingertips on the table, shaking his head. "Celestia and Etherea still claim neutrality."

"Where *exactly* does that leave us, though?" Asteria asked, slumping into her chair and rubbing her face.

"To start, we're three countries against four," Rod began, his voice steady—a rarity between him and Asteria. Morana prayed to the stars that lasted the rest of the meeting. "The military numbers alone are outmatched."

"Not to mention the amount of Lemurians and Andromedans in Sylvan and Allanis compared to any of our countries," Quintin said, his face paling slightly. "Granted, we may have Sirians, but so do they."

"I thought Riddling was a rather large country," Morana asked, frowning at Dionne and Savaric. "Don't you have a military to rival Teslin and Sylvan combined?"

"Unfortunately, not where it matters." Dionne rubbed the back of his neck as he shook his head. "Teslin is renowned for their navy, as is Thalassa, not to mention their oceanic presence. We may have a strong navy, but not enough to counter both of theirs and an attack by ketea within the waters."

"We needed Etherea's naval support," Piers agreed, his gaze bouncing between Asteria and Orwell. "Please don't threaten me... Is there any chance we could speak to Odo again? Possibly just us?" Piers gestured to himself, his brothers, and Gavril.

"I don't think he'll be swayed," Orwell said, his eyes on Asteria. "He's still quite firm in their neutrality until the Elders can take it to a vote."

"I still think you should—"

Morana jabbed her elbow into Danica, her words strangled with a grunt. Danica glared, but she set her jaw as Morana stared right back.

She refused to set Asteria off any further with commentary about forcing her Sirians into something they disagreed with. It wasn't going to happen, no matter how much Danica pushed.

The Lyran was incapable of grasping that.

"I can't believe Phoebe won't join the cause." Dionne frowned, looking like Phoebe's decision may have wounded him.

Morana didn't know the history between the siblings of Asteria, but especially the boys with Phoebe. Her and Taranis were both presently on the throne, so there was a potential overlap, but she came up empty as to why Dionne took it so personally.

"You're not the only one baffled by the decision," Gavril grumbled, sitting up straighter. "She claims to be an ally for humans."

"She's scared for them," Asteria said softly, fingers twisting in her lap. "She's trying to protect her people as best she can with what she was given."

"It's not your fault," Morana assured, wrapping her hand around Asteria's. Her guilt was on display for all. "Your relationship shouldn't dictate a wartime decision, and I don't believe it swayed her agreement to be neutral."

Asteria relaxed, hands going limp in her lap.

"So what do we do?" Quintin looked at Rod, shaking his head. "How are you all involved in this?"

"Excuse me?" Danica screeched, her form flickering. "How dare you—"

"It's a valid question, Danica," Rod interrupted, holding a hand up to her as he answered Quintin. "Lyrans must be wary of how involved we get on either side. When we're in these mortal forms, our powers are muted by the confines of them, so we can't access our full abilities."

"I'm not sure if that's good or bad," Gavril drawled, his gaze shifting between Morana and the others, including Asteria. "I've seen Asteria in her god-form. She fought the thirío as if he were nothing but a rag."

"While that is fine on *occasion*"—Rod paused to level Asteria with a stern look, but she rolled her eyes and waved him away—"that can't

493

happen frequently. It's why I created a weapon for each Lyran to help siphon their powers in a more manageable manner that doesn't threaten the stability of Aveesh. Asteria just refuses to use hers, despite the consequences for using that much power on this plane."

"Consequences?" Orwell asked, dragging his gaze from Rod to Asteria. He pinned her with a frown. "What consequences?"

"Too much use of our power within a short time can lead to Fracturing," Morana elaborated gently. She immediately recognized Orwell's genuine concern. The last thing he needed was Rod or Danica jumping down his throat. "It's when our minds fall prey to our powers. The more power you have, the more susceptible you are to becoming Fractured.

"There's also the matter that if multiple Lyrans battle in their god-forms on this plane, it'll permanently alter it. It can cause tremors, floods, avalanches... It could very well sink an entire land mass."

"Sweet fuck," Gavril whispered, slowly hauling his attention to Asteria. "You could've brought down the Black Avalanches."

"That's not what she's saying," Asteria grumbled, rubbing her temples. "They mean when Lyrans fight each other—"

"Or when a Lyran is lost to their power," Rod interjected, and she shot him a sneer. Morana rested a hand on Asteria's shoulder. "I'm sure when you fought the thirío, you were entirely calm and collected. You said so yourself you were trying to get him to stand down, not brawl with him."

Asteria huffed dramatically, throwing herself back into her chair, but there wasn't the usual passion behind it. Morana narrowed her eyes at that, filling it away for later.

She had to give Asteria credit, though. She was doing rather well with Rod, all things considered. Morana was unsure whether that was because of the matter at hand or the male watching Asteria from across the table.

"So you will fight beside us?" Taranis dropped his feet from the table, reaching for his chalice. "I've always wanted an excuse to fight beside my sister rather than with her."

Dionne mumbled an agreement from where he sat with a hand cupped over his mouth.

"We all will," Rod confirmed, tilting his head back and forth. "Primarily in our mortal forms. We'll only use god-forms if the situation becomes dire. Unfortunately, that still may not be enough."

"Godsdamnit—" Gavril grunted as Sybil whipped her arm across Piers and scratched him, just as she had in the last meeting.

"The Gods are right there, buffoon," Sybil scolded.

Morana didn't understand those three. Sybil and Gavril seemed to bicker as though they were siblings, and Morana now realized the admiration Sybil typically showed for the Carraphims differed with Piers. When she'd found them kissing in Celestia, she thought maybe Sybil had found someone for herself, if only temporarily.

When she realized Gavril and Piers were partners, she'd never felt more resounding disappointment in her daughter.

Morana inhaled slowly to quell her displeasure, earning a brief glance from Asteria.

"The Lyrans are evenly matched," Danica explained to the group, flourishing a hand from herself to Rod, Morana, and Asteria. "Morana can portal and enhance basic commands—locking doors, lighting things up, giving swords a little extra strength and assertion. Rod can do the same and manipulate the land, but we fear playing with terrain will only compromise its integrity. I have the Energy, and Asteria is arguably the most powerful of us all."

"When you say *us all...*" Piers painstakingly hauled his gaze to Asteria.

"She's the most powerful Lyran," Rod muttered, his gaze softening on Asteria.

Another silence descended over the table, Dionne and Taranis blinking through their confusion.

"I didn't know that..." Dionne trailed off as he gazed at his sister.

"You never said—"

"It's not something I *willingly* share," Asteria said, staring at a point on the table.

There was a gentle tap from Orwell, and he threw her a wink. Morana's heart fluttered when Asteria's tension lessened.

"And the others?" Quintin asked, watching Danica expectantly.

"Zephyr can take on the form of *any* Lemurian. He receives the same gifts but amplified in power and size." Danica listed on her fingers. "Gallus controls the Aether and both starfires, which puts him and Asteria quite close to one another in terms of power and strength. Valeria can infect you—"

"And she will." Morana set her shoulders back, startling at Asteria's featherlight touch on her leg. Sybil offered her a small smile. "She's Fractured, so she'll be relentless."

"Don't say that, Morana," Rod almost pleaded. "We don't know—"

"She is." Morana swallowed back her tears. Admitting it out loud was like experiencing the loss anew. "I mean, look at her, Rod. Her god-form no longer looks the same as it once was, and it hasn't been the same since Sybil. On top of that, she tried to have Sybil killed to hurt me. That's not the Valeria we came here with."

The silence was deafening as she and Rod stared at one another. It was the gravity of the situation finally hitting them.

They were going against their friends and family—the only connection to their old home.

"Nen will be at a great advantage for any naval attempts," Asteria finished for them, clenching her jaw. "He can very well make it impossible for any of us to win."

Rod shook his head, clearing his throat. "Which is why we believe it would be best to portal your armies to one another instead of relying on ships."

"Won't that expend you all?" Orwell pursed his lips, waving a hand at them. "I've seen what multiple portals in a day does to Asteria. It happened numerous times. Can you create and hold portals long enough to transport *two* armies?"

"We'll have to go in waves as you suggested," Rod explained, and Morana wanted to hug him for how thoughtful and calm he was with the male who clearly held affection for Asteria. "The four of us forming a portal together will be large and strong enough to hold without too much loss of strength, but it will have to be one country per day to account for creating that portal and each of us portaling back to our residence to rest."

The room settled, but Morana sensed the hovering unease radiating from each mortal and Andromedan. Shockingly, it was Piers who spoke first.

"We have to tell Phoebe," he said, looking at Asteria. "The sea was part of her argument against joining. Frankly, it was her only argument."

Asteria bristled beside Morana, nodding once.

"That doesn't truly answer Quintin's question," Savaric said, his face stern. "According to all, we're still at a disadvantage. So what will happen? You've left out Lady Dola and Lady Irena, the latter of which is the Goddess of War and Peace. So what of them?"

"Yes, what of us?"

Asteria and Morana jumped in their seats as Quintin swore under his breath. Morana looked to the corner of the room where Irena stood with her arms crossed, leaning against the wall.

She wore her usual gold armor that hugged her ample curves and matched the tattoos glistening against her bronze skin. She lowered her pointed chin at Morana with a raised eyebrow, her curly, chocolate brown hair swept back from her face with a gold band.

"Where the fuck did she come from?" Gavril blurted, his face gaunt. "And might I say, I don't think I've met Lady Irena. You are absolutely *stunning*—"

"Gavril!" The shout came from Sybil, Asteria, Wells, and Piers simultaneously.

"What are you doing here, Irena?" Danica sighed, and Rod rubbed at his forehead, muttering to himself. Whatever he was saying actually earned a snicker from Asteria.

"I wanted to see you lot strategizing for war." Irena shrugged as she shoved away from the wall, strutting up beside Dionne. She ruffled his hair, and he snarled at her. "You know, since I'm the Goddess of War."

"The exact reason you refuse to interfere," Rod argued, glaring at her. "Although I don't understand your reasoning since this seems to be something you should be involved in."

"I'm also the Goddess of Peace." Irena wagged a finger at Rod, and the corner of Asteria's lips curled. "Don't be ignorant."

"I tell him this all the time," Asteria drawled, and Rod shot her a burning glare.

"You asked about Dola and me," Irena said gently to Savaric, tilting her head. "She can't be involved because Fate forbids it. She's incapable of interfering, so she must sit it out. Much like Sybil *should* be sitting all of this out."

With the accusation, Irena jerked her head toward Sybil, who rolled her eyes.

"I can understand that." Dionne nodded with Savaric. "But you?"

"Other than the Peace of my title, someone has to stay with Dola." Irena strutted toward Morana, resting her hands on her shoulders. "If you truly need me—if there seems to be no end to this war, or you are at risk of ruining this world—I will step in."

Asteria scoffed, tapping her fingers against her lips.

"To finally answer your first question about what will happen if we are at a disadvantage," Danica interjected, her attention bouncing from Savaric to Morana. "I may have found a fail-safe should all hope be entirely lost. I came across it in some of our ancient tomes."

Irena stiffened behind Morana at the same time Piers did from across the table. Danica caught it, narrowing her eyes at the prince.

"If you're not a Lyran"—Danica flicked that menacing gaze to Orwell—"leave the room."

CHAPTER 59

SYBIL

Sybil walked out of the Council room behind Gavril and Piers, slipping between them as Gavril jogged to catch up with Quin, Taranis, Dionne, and Savaric. She curved down the hall, following the sconces glistening off tan walls, but then quick footsteps echoed behind her.

"Syb!" The footsteps grew louder as Piers's voice carried. A hand wrapped around her forearm, trying to slow her pace. "Sybil, please stop."

"I'm not in the mood to speak with you right now," she grumbled, ripping her arm from his rough grasp. She glared at him as he walked beside her, but she didn't slow. "There are far bigger things—"

"Oh, I'm well aware," Piers said, snorting. "I wanted to speak about Celestia."

"We don't need to speak about it." She shook her head, the vision of Morana's disappointment seared into her brain. "It happened, and we are where we are."

"That's not all it is." Piers skipped forward and slid before her, gripping her shoulders. "You can't tell me that entire conversation *just happened*."

She snarled as she jerked back, but he only dug his fingers into her skin, leveling her with a glare. She grunted as she fought back, shoving his chest away. "Piers, just let me go!"

"Absolutely not," he muttered, quickly switching his grip to her hand, dragging her behind him.

"What's wrong with you?" Sybil shot her claws from her free hand.

She swiped at him, but he quickly turned them down a narrow hall into a shadowed alcove. He trapped her against the wall between his arms, caging her head. She flattened her palms against the cool stone behind her, blinking.

"What in the Heavens has gotten into you?" she whispered hoarsely through clenched teeth. "We're in the middle of the castle where anyone can stumble upon us, and this isn't the most friendly position to be in."

"Don't dismiss me as though I'm one of your temporary passions," he snapped, searching her face. "We mean far more to one another than that."

"This isn't one of your puzzles to solve, Piers," she muttered, narrowing her eyes. "You don't owe me anything."

"I don't regret kissing you." His breath fanned across her cheeks, skimming her ear. "Do you regret it?"

She opened and closed her mouth a few times before answering, "It doesn't matter whether I do or don't. You're in a relationship with Gavril and claim to love us both, yet I haven't heard from his lips if he's aware."

"Syb…" Piers groaned, throwing his head up. "I nearly watched you die. I've yet to wrap my head around what I went through and what that means for me now. Too much has happened since then."

"You need to think about it, then." She scoffed, frowning in disbelief. "You can't sit there and use me in the meantime."

"I don't use you, Sybil." Piers grinned, but there was a dark glint in his eyes. "If I wanted someone to use, I would have no problems finding a volunteer. I *crave* you—nothing can compare to your taste beneath me."

Sybil whimpered as he pressed his hips into her, his chest pinning

500

her between him and the wall. She turned her head to resist the desire swelling within her. He dipped his and nipped at her skin, coaxing a gasp from her.

"You seek to torture me as my penance," she whispered breathlessly.

"Penance?" Piers's head snapped back. "Whatever for?"

"For all the times I teased and taunted you," she admitted, swallowing against his fierce gaze. "You said as much in Ghita."

Piers snarled, the noise calling to the primal part of her, and he captured her lips. She squeaked at the sudden movement, but his soft lips drew hers into a deeper kiss, his tongue sliding along her bottom lip. She moaned, lost in the moment, until his callused hand gripped the side of her face.

Sybil planted both of her hands on his chest and used her strength to shove him away. He stumbled back in slight shock, but it gave her enough room and time to sneak back out of the shadowed hallway to continue her journey.

Tears gathered in the corners of her eyes as her fingers trembled against her lips. Her heart struggled to beat, banging against her chest. It was angry with her for walking away and equally as angry for kissing him back yet again.

She'd never stopped loving him. While his admission in Celestia of still loving her warmed every facet of her being, the fact remained he and Gavril were partners, and she was unaware if Piers had spoken to him about what happened.

Sybil was near the corridor leading to the stables when a sharp pain shot from the back of her head through her eyes, her vision vanishing altogether. She cried out, her hands and knees connecting with the rough ground. That sensation vanished along with any semblance of reality.

Screams echoed endlessly, drowning in bloody humidity. It clogged the air, pressing in until it bled from wounded limbs.

Aether spun like a web through the bodies piling on either side, lightning streaking across the sky with a violent crash that summoned a rumbling roar.

"Now you will watch as I destroy the only thing you ever loved."

The world rattled, the chorus of screams rising again as blue fire chased flashes of white and gold, disembodied voices uttering words too garbled to understand.

The middle of a barren field rose, green-hazel eyes dulling as blood dripped from the corner of his mouth. The drakon's call wailed, its anguish blinding, breath ripped away as it plummeted to the ground—

Sybil came to with a start, gasping for the air that had been ripped from her lungs.

"You're okay," Piers whispered against her head, holding her in his lap. He hushed her, pressing a kiss to her temple. "I'm here. You're safe."

Sybil scrambled frantically from his lap, panting as the images in her head slowly faded. She whipped her head back and forth, studying her surroundings because she was no longer in the hallway.

This was Piers's quarters, that much she knew, although she didn't know how she'd gotten here. He sat on the sofa in the middle of the room, staring at her like she may shift into the drakon in his room.

"Breathe," he said gently, rising from the cushion at a painstaking pace. "Stay with me."

She swallowed, wincing at the dryness at the back of her throat. "What happened?"

"You fell in the hall and began to have a vision," he said, taking one step forward. "I brought you up here because you were gasping for air. Right before you woke up, you started to scream."

She shook her head as she willed her breaths to calm, shutting her eyes. They immediately flew open when the back of her lids replayed the vision.

She met Piers's eyes.

His *green-hazel* eyes.

A sob unexpectedly rose in her chest, and she tried to stifle it with a hand to her lips as he neared.

Sybil knew it was Piers in her vision. The truth hummed in her like a bell, ringing through her chest.

And she couldn't tell him what she'd seen.

"Hey." He gently lowered her hand from her lips, his other laying against her cheek. "You're trembling. Can you speak about it at all?"

She shook her head wildly, and it released a tear down her cheek. Piers caught it with his thumb, a slight pout to his lips.

"How can I help?" His hand slid down her bicep as the other lifted to the other side. "What do you need?"

You.

She needed *him*.

She needed to go back in time and stop herself from ending things between them. Whatever she saw wasn't far away, which meant she would lose him from this world.

Sybil thought she would lose him with old age, decades from now. She felt utterly foolish for wasting the last few years as his friend, keeping her distance when she could've spent the rest of his life with him.

Separating them did nothing to lessen what this loss would do to her.

Sybil launched into Piers's arms, clasping his neck as she yanked his mouth to hers. His hands immediately clung to her waist, anchoring her as he pulled her flush, their bodies colliding with desperation. She consumed him, her kiss frantic and feral, driven by the panic still nestled in her chest.

This wasn't soft or measured; this kiss was feverish and frenzied. Their hands scrambled for purchase—her nails scraping through his hair, his fingers tugging at the fabric of her kirtle, both needing contact.

Every second that passed filled her with warmth. She wanted to touch every inch of him, to remind herself he was alive—here with her. That

Fate hadn't taken him from her yet.

She broke the kiss long enough to breathe, her forehead resting against his as her voice came out hoarse. "Please." She brushed her nose against his as he wrapped his arms around her tightly. "Don't leave."

The small plea was all she could manage. She didn't know if she was pleading with him, or Fate, or the Heavens, or whatever conversed with her. She wanted him to have something different—a different future—because that's what he deserved.

Maybe there was still time to change it.

"I'm right here," he murmured as he cupped her neck, his face pinched with emotion. "Until you ask me to go."

"I won't again." Sybil toyed with the strings on the collar of his tunic, a foreign heat swirling deep in her stomach, one she couldn't name but felt with every breath she took.

It wasn't desire, but something sharper and heavier. It heightened the arousal building within her, her movements driven by the primal instinct to claim Piers back.

She looked at him through her lashes, meeting those depthless eyes. Her hands trembled as she dragged them down his chest, slipping beneath his tunic to rest her palms against the firm muscles of his stomach. They flexed under her touch, and she remembered just how easy it was to send this Lieutenant General to his knees.

Piers let her lift his tunic over his head, flinging it aside. Then he was on her, his lips at her neck, his fingers working the ties of her kirtle. His kisses were softer, but every so often he added a bite, searing tiny shocks through her. His trimmed beard tickled the sensitive skin between her neck and collarbone, a contrast of rough and tender that tore a breathy moan from her throat.

His eyes lifted to hers, the faint white-gold glow of his Mark shimmering on his brow as he shoved the kirtle from her shoulders to the floor. "Gods, I missed that sound."

Sybil clung to the adrenaline coursing through her, every nerve alive, urging her forward. She painstakingly curled the hem of her chemise in her hands, drawing it inch by inch, her heart stuttering at the way his gaze followed the movement. She dragged the fabric over her head and tossed it aside, her bare skin kissed by the cool air.

The moment her hair tumbled free, he lunged with a low groan that rumbled around them. His lips crashed to hers, his grip iron-clad at her waist as he pushed her backward. The stonewall slammed into her back, nearly knocking the wind from her, but she didn't care. She drove her hands into his hair, tongues tangling as he shoved his pants down around his ankles.

Sybil drew back to admire him, her eyes devouring the sight, breathtakingly beautiful beneath his layers. Of the three Carraphim boys, he was the most honed, every muscle carved by the Heavens above. She traced a finger down the ridges of his abdomen until she reached the edge of his hips, those sinful lines guiding her straight to what she wanted.

Piers didn't give her time to hesitate. She swallowed a breath when he hauled her into his arms, her legs instinctively wrapping around his waist. He braced her against the wall, her body arching into his. She swept his hair back from his face, dazed by the weight pooling low in her stomach, too intoxicated by him to think about it for too long.

Piers reached between them, guiding his cock to her entrance. He peered up at her, his pupils wide, breath ragged.

She didn't think—didn't pause. She hurtled herself with all her force into this moment.

Sybil nodded once, and that was all the permission he needed.

Piers twitched his hips, the head slipping into her, and they groaned together. He plunged deeper with each slow thrust, and when he finally seated himself fully, her head thunked back against the wall. She moaned, tightening her grip on his hair. He readjusted his hold, one arm wrapping around her waist as he braced his other hand flat on the wall beside her head.

"Fuck," Piers whispered, the word barely audible as he looked down at where he was buried inside her. "I forgot how unbelievable you feel."

Sybil released a breathy chuckle. "Then get moving, Prince."

He jerked his head up, his gaze dark and hungry with a smirk ticking at the corner of his lips. He drew back and lifted her slightly, then thrust in with a snap of his hips that ripped a cry from her throat. The rhythm built with each movement, the muscles in his arms flexing, heat racing through her. With every stroke, the ache inside her climbed, her breath catching on moans she couldn't suppress.

"Piers," Sybil gasped, yanking his head closer. He pressed his forehead to hers, their breath mingling as he angled his hips and thrust deeper, harder. "Stars above—"

Piers chuckled, the sound thick with lust. "So wet... and warm... and tight..." He nipped at her ear before dragging his teeth down her neck. He wrapped his mouth around her shoulder and bit.

The drakon within her roared to life at the primal claim, forcing her over the edge. Her climax tore through her like fire, blinding and consuming. She may have said his name repeatedly—may have cried out—but she was lost in the haze of her release. The only thing that pulled her out was her name whispered on his lips as Piers found release.

For a moment, they stayed locked together, her head on his shoulder, her fingers stroking the back of his neck.

When Piers tenderly pulled out, it was with care. He lowered her back to her feet, hands lingering on her hips. She swayed slightly, but he steadied her.

The haze began to lift and clarity rushed in like a plunge into the frigid waters of Orion's Lake. Sybil realized what the heavy weight in her stomach had been, the one that twirled with every damning step. The rush of adrenaline drowned it out, driven by the bodily need to seek pleasure.

It was shame.

And it was reflected in Piers's eyes as the extent of what they'd done barreled into them.

CHAPTER 60

MORANA

Danica rose from her chair, walking toward the lone window while Orwell filed out of the Council room with an encouraging nod to Asteria.

"What have you found?" Rod asked hesitantly, angling his body toward where Morana and Asteria still sat at the table, but his eyes lingered on the door.

Danica stared out the window as Irena took her spot, and Morana couldn't decipher what she was thinking. Her face was emotionless, her mortal form steady despite the uncertainty pulsing through the room.

"Back home, things are very different than the worlds we journey to," Danica began, and Morana knew she was talking to Asteria. "There's knowledge that doesn't exist beyond it. When we journeyed away, we could only take a few tomes. The rest of what we have within our residences in Eonia are recorded from memory."

"I'm guessing you found something that could help in one of those tomes?" Asteria perked up, her gaze bouncing between Rod, Irena, and Morana. "Why is this just now being brought up?"

"To be fair, I forgot it existed," Danica replied, a small laugh of disbelief fluttering from her lips. "I have been scouring my collection, Morana's, and what Gallus left in our former home."

"So you've been in my home?" Asteria said dryly, but Rod immediately countered with, "*Our* home."

Morana tensed, preparing herself for Asteria to mutter something uncivil, but she only sighed heavily.

"I came across one of Gallus's journals he left behind, one in which he recorded what he remembered." Danica reached within her cloak, pulling out a pristine leather journal. She gently laid it on the table before Irena, waving her hand.

Irena opened the page marked with a ribbon, and Morana's lungs deflated. "It's in the old language."

It had been centuries since Morana picked up a tome written in the old language. Seeing the markings, memories flooded her of their home world, images she wasn't sure she could remember.

Galaxies painted the skies, where clusters of stars created clouds of various colors, two moons orbit the world. The land was vibrant and lush, the dullness of Aveesh no match for the bright hues of their former world. In the city sectors, towers and temples stretched like fingertips into the skies, buildings replicating for miles.

Morana frowned, settling back against the chair as Irena and Rod perused the book, her stomach curdling.

She no longer remembered the name of their home world.

"Danica, I don't remember anything by the name of Achlys Lock," Rod said, shaking his head as he drew his gaze back to her. "Do you think this is even real? Not something of Gallus's making?"

"Gallus may be controversial, but he doesn't lie," Asteria muttered, staring blankly at the journal in front of Rod.

"Asteria is right," Irena said, flipping a page back and forth. "He wouldn't write something down if it weren't possible or true. That would be a waste of his time."

Rod drummed his fingers on the table, but the name he spoke rang bells in Morana's head.

"Let me see," Morana said softly, carefully slipping her fingers beneath Irena's to haul the journal across the table.

Reading their old language brought tears to her eyes. She swallowed them back so none escaped and smeared the ink, her fingertips running over the intricate lettering.

"What's the Achlys Lock?" Asteria asked, but Morana felt her gaze. "You know what it is?"

"I believe I've heard it before," Morana replied, briefly reading over the lines. "Before I was granted my gifts, there were a few Aeons related to my sector who spoke of a Realm once lost to them by their brothers and sisters because of this Lock."

"Aeons?" Asteria drew her gaze from Morana to Irena.

"Lyrans who journeyed to other Realms but eventually came back home," Irena explained, leaning back against the chair with her hands on the table. "Each sector had less than a handful of them. Mine only had one"

"Mine, too," Rod grumbled, his gaze distant.

Danica nodded, turning to face them, hands clasped behind her back. "The Achlys Lock is a Lyran-made mechanism that creates a ward around a Realm, sealing it off from any other Realms or Beings who wish to enter. It also works the other way, where those within that Realm can't leave it."

"How would we use it in this case?" Morana stopped reading to look up at Danica.

She wanted to see her face when she explained her thought process, because something wasn't sitting right.

As far as Morana knew, Danica and Gallus were the oldest of them. Morana couldn't pinpoint exactly how old—or how much older than herself—because she couldn't even remember how old she or Valeria were.

If her memory served her correctly, Nen was the next oldest after Danica and Gallus. From there, it was Morana, Valeria, Rod, Zephyr, and obviously Asteria.

Morana had no idea where Irena or Dola fell within that sequence. They were the last two Lyrans Danica and Gallus recruited for their expedition across the Universe. Morana didn't know either female before they traveled together.

That said, Gallus knew about the Lock, and Danica did, too. There was a likely chance Danica was not aimlessly searching their tomes. Danica was looking *specifically* for the instructions for the Achlys Lock.

So why lie?

Morana slid the notebook back to Rod as she and Irena listened to Danica elaborate on this supposed plan. "There are a few ways we could approach using the Lock."

Danica created two balls of Energy, throwing them above the table, one smaller than the other.

"Asteria, form a thin cocoon of Aether around the smaller Energy orb." Danica tipped her head toward them. Asteria hesitantly obliged, the Aether creating a webbing around the small one. "We could lure the others into Eonia, feigning an agreement of sorts. Once they are there, we forge the Lock within Eonia, sealing it from the rest of the Universe."

"Also sealing it off from Aveesh," Morana blurted, shaking her head. "Do we have a choice if we wish to be trapped within Eonia for all of eternity?"

"Or until we kill one another off one by one *within* Eonia," Irena grumbled, pinching the bridge of her nose.

"I won't be trapped with Nen and Zephyr," Rod announced, shoving the book away haphazardly. "I would rather stay here on Aveesh."

"Fuck you." Asteria scoffed, swiping her hand, the Aether net disappearing. "I'll stay on Aveesh. I don't even like Eonia."

"You would have no choice, Asteria." For once, Danica spoke without her words dripping with scorn. Even Asteria startled at the contrast, her head jerking. "The Lock is created from Aether, Energy, and starfire, which means only myself, Gallus, and you could even forge it."

"Any starfire?" Rod scanned the lines in the book, his finger leading his eyes. "You know there are two different ones."

"You can find the line and read it yourself, but it says starfire must be used to weld a Lock." Danica shrugged, waiting for Rod to find it. "As Asteria said, Gallus is intelligent. He would be precise in what he writes."

"No." Asteria shook her head fiercely, eyes flashing. "I won't be trapped in Eonia. What is the other option? You said there were two."

Danica nodded, gesturing to the still-floating orbs. "Replicate the net again, but only around the larger one representing Aveesh."

Asteria repeated what she did before, waiting.

"The other option would be to forge the Lock within Aveesh." Danica pointed at the smaller orb. "Eonia is a pocket *of* Aveesh, which means—"

"Creating the Lock within Aveesh would still create one that encompasses Eonia," Asteria finished, spreading her hand across the space so the net encompassed both Aveesh and Eonia.

"Yes and no," Danica corrected, wagging her finger. "What creates a pocket is a disturbance of the Aether within the Realm.

"The Aether is used to mold the Lock, the Energy is used to charge it, and the starfire welds the two together. If there is an existing disturbance within the Aether, it will warp the net and create a separate blanket over Eonia alongside the one over Aveesh."

Asteria tilted her head and twisted her wrist, and the nets around the orbs split into two so that Eonia was within one and Aveesh within the other, separate from each other.

"In theory, Eonia would be sealed off from the Universe and Aveesh, and Aveesh would be sealed off from Eonia and the Universe." Irena raised an eyebrow, peering at Danica. "Right?"

Danica nodded, but Rod scoffed, throwing a hand toward the

demonstration. "That still doesn't solve the problem of being trapped within Eonia. Someone must be responsible for luring the others out of Aveesh. The only way to do that is to call them to Eonia. Whoever does that will be trapped with them in Eonia."

"Could I make the Lock myself?" Asteria asked, her gaze bouncing between Rod and Danica.

"You would need at least two Lyrans to make it," Irena muttered, squinting at the journal. "I know you have all three powers needed, but the amount you would have to give would kill you."

"Then as someone required to participate in the Lock-making *and* using two of their powers, which I am sure will inch me closer to Fracturing…" Asteria crossed her arms, leaning on the edge of the table. "I won't make the Lock in Eonia. I'm sorry, Mother, but that means you will also be trapped within Aveesh."

"Again, I refuse to be trapped in Eonia." Rod rolled his eyes. "I'll be staying in Aveesh, too."

"Sybil is here," Morana said quietly, her shoulders hunching. She gazed up at Danica through her lashes. "Please don't make me abandon her."

"This is only a last resort if we start to drastically lose this war," Danica explained as she snapped the orbs of Energy out of existence. Asteria dissolved the Aether nets. "We do have some time to consider it."

"We have to face the truth, Danica," Rod exclaimed, boosting himself from his chair. His mortal skin thinned, giving it a glittering, gilded effect. "We *will* lose as we stand right now. Our advantages are not enough against them."

"Irena will step in—"

"I have to say, Danica…" Irena slowly shook her head, shrugging sheepishly. "Now that I know this exists, I would suggest this as your second plan of action. If you anticipate me trying to use my hypnosis to control the Lyrans, you risk Fracturing me. Those are powerful minds to manipulate in the midst of war."

"I agree with Danica—as shocking as that may sound—but to an extent." Asteria slowly rose from her chair, walking between it and Morana's. She cautiously approached Danica and Rod. "This is only a backup plan, not the plan we're moving forward with presently. There's still time for Phoebe to change her mind, and we must give this world and ourselves a chance. Besides, the other Lyrans will find an early meeting amongst us suspicious."

"Things must become dire before you call a meeting," Irena explained, rising from her chair. "You'll trick them into thinking you're giving up and waving your flag of surrender."

Asteria ran both hands through her hair as she released a quivering breath. "We should still come to an agreement on the bare minimum requirements for this Lock scenario."

Morana's heart ached for her because Asteria was right. There was a high chance she could Fracture from the amount of power it would take for her to make the Lock with the Aether and starfire.

The thought curdled Morana's stomach.

"Well, you and Danica have seemingly agreed to forge the Lock." Rod sighed, hitching his hands on his hips. "Morana and I refuse to be trapped in Eonia with the others. How will we lure them in?"

"This is where I would be willing to participate," Irena drawled, her eyes dragging to Rod. "I could request a meeting as the Goddess of War and Peace. I don't foresee the Lyrans putting up a fight with me since Dola and I claim neutrality, not to mention we never leave Eonia. Once they're there, I can use hypnosis midway through a conversation long enough for you to forge the Lock."

"That could work," Morana agreed, nodding slowly.

Rod and Asteria stared at one another momentarily, his eyes flicking across her face. He sighed, his shoulders slumping as he nodded. "Alright. We move forward with the plan of working alongside Eldamain and their allies. If things turn grim, we switch to the Lock and work on the official details when that time comes."

Morana thought Asteria would have relaxed, but her shoulders were still tense. Asteria must've felt Morana looking at her because she slowly drew her gaze to Morana's.

She gave Asteria a questioning look, one eyebrow raised.

Asteria nostrils flared, her lips pressing together in a firm line, and shook her head once.

They would need to speak later.

CHAPTER 61

ASTERIA

Asteria portaled directly to Wells's room in Aggelos Palace, hoping he was present. The fireplace was lit since the spring air of Eldamain was still far too cold at night to go without, warming the space beyond the heat emanating from it. Everything about this room screamed Wells, from the cherry wood furniture to the navy blue silk sheets draped over the bed.

When he emerged from the bathing chamber, his curls damp and chest bare, her body instantly loosened from the discussion with the Lyrans.

"How was the meeting?" Wells asked, crossing his arms and leaning against the doorway. A sly grin spread across his cheeks. "Did you actually reach any conclusion, or have you left in a fit again?"

She would've rolled her eyes and humored him if she were in different spirits.

Her thoughts were scattered, though. She wanted nothing more than to talk with him about what had transpired—what could lay ahead. That was all she could think about the further in the discussion she and the Lyrans went. She wanted to talk to him.

She *needed* to talk to him.

"Blue?" Wells pushed off the wall, slowly walking toward her. He slipped his hands into hers, pulling her body against him. "What happened?"

"Without Celestia and Etherea, we have one final option left to defeat the other Lyrans should things go awry." She frowned, shaking her head. "It's... I don't know how to feel about it."

"Come," Wells said, backing toward his bed. He lowered to the mattress, grasping her waist and pulling her into his toweled lap as he perched on the edge. "Talk to me."

"There is this..." She considered what it was, unsure how to explain it to him. "Where the Lyrans come from, there is something called an Achlys Lock. It's used to conceal a Realm. They want to convince the other Lyrans to meet in Eonia and then deploy the Lock around Aveesh to keep them out."

"Why was this not an option to start with?" Wells straightened his back, eyes flickering across her face. "This sounds preferable to war, to be fair."

"There are a few things about it that require thought," she explained, her hands running up and down his bare forearms. "Eonia is a pocket within this Realm. There is a chance when we seal Aveesh, it will also seal Eonia off from the Universe. It doesn't just keep things out, but it keeps things in."

Wells nodded slowly, pressing his lips together, hands flexing on her waist.

"There would need to be some Lyrans who stay in Eonia with the others to lure them in, which means they would be trapped for eternity in Eonia with one another." Asteria's heart thundered in her chest as she recalled the conversation. "Some would need to stay here to forge the Lock within Aveesh for it to work."

"They can't forge it around Eonia?" He tilted his head, frowning. "Is there a chance they could only seal Eonia off instead of both?"

"It could be done..." She swallowed as her hands trembled. "The thing is, the Lock must be forged from within the plane you wish to conceal. It means the Lock would need to be forged *within* Eonia, and whoever forges the Lock would then be trapped in Eonia with no way out."

"One way or another, Lyrans would be trapped within Eonia," Wells said, rubbing her back. "You are tense, Asteria. What's wrong?"

"To forge the Lock, you need the Energy, Aether, and starfire." The words were so soft she was unsure if he heard until his arms went rigid around her. She raised her gaze to find his eyes frantic. "The amount of power required must come from two Lyrans. Danica, Gallus, and I are the only ones who can make the Lock. We both know Gallus is on the opposing side of things, which means—"

"You and Danica have to make the Lock." He clenched his jaw, but then relaxed. "You don't want to leave Aveesh, and Danica would rather be in Eonia?"

"As it stands, Rod and Morana would rather stay here than be trapped in Eonia. Danica doesn't seem to care." Asteria shrugged, avoiding his gaze. "Irena believes she could be useful in luring the others to Eonia."

"So you're anxious to be trapped here with Danica and Rod," he concluded, fighting a smile. "What has made you so nervous about that prospect?"

"I don't want them to know about my desire to lose my immortality," she whispered, tears pricking her eyes. "But that's not what frightens me."

"You can tell me." He drew her hair back from her face, his thumb brushing her temple. "Maybe I can help quell your concerns."

She swallowed the lump in her throat. She thought the first taste of a promised death was fear.

But this...

This was true, bone-chilling fear.

"There is a chance that using two of my powers to the extent it requires to forge the Lock will Fracture me."

Wells frowned at first, but it vanished as his face went slack with suppressed horror. His eyes frantically searched her face, and he whispered, "What does that mean for you? *Exactly* what could happen to you if you Fracture? I know Morana and Rod spoke of it in the meeting."

Asteria's chest tightened the longer he stared at her. She busied her hands with the freckles along his shoulders, running her hands over them.

"Just as it's rare to have a child between two Lyrans to maintain balance in the Universe, the use of our gifts must also be balanced." His knuckles brushed her jawline as she continued. "As they mentioned, too much use of our powers can cause a Lyran to Fracture. It's a term from their world that means falling prey to the strength of our gifts.

"Dola can converse with Fate, and they have a specific term for Lyrans who Fracture when conversing with Time, Fate, and Destiny—the Madness. Their minds are lost between past, present, and future, unable to decipher where they are, who they truly are, and what is real in the moment."

"How has Valeria Fractured?" His eyes glistened as he kept his attention on her.

"She's the Goddess of Healing and Disease," Asteria explained with a shrug. "According to Morana, Valeria is nothing like she used to be. We've discussed Valeria falling prey to her powers is the equivalent of a disease infecting her mind. It's burrowing into her, making her own lies truth and other's truth lies. She doesn't think before she acts, and she's unable to actually care for or love anything. It's only what she and her powers want, damn the consequences."

"So if you Fractured…" His voice was so tender, a tear nearly slipped from the corner of her eye.

"Sometimes I wonder if suppressing my god-form for so long has tested the line of Fracturing," Asteria explained, remembering the most recent switch into it when she battled the thirío. "I'm not entirely sure what will happen, but I believe the starfire and Aether are stronger than the call of the Energy. It just wants everything to burn… It feels as though my mind is swelling with this mess of darkness that wants to swallow everything in its path."

Wells's face was void of emotion or any sign of what he was thinking. "We'll take it all one day at a time—"

"How can you be so calm about this?" Asteria launched from his lap, wrapping her arms around her midsection as she suppressed a sob. "This isn't a simple ailment that can be healed, Wells. This is something that could completely alter who I am. It could destroy the very person you've come to know."

"You've said so yourself this isn't the current plan." Wells rose slowly, adjusting the towel he still wore. He didn't approach her, though. "We're going to give ourselves and Phoebe a chance. There are still so many things we can do to keep this from happening."

"But what if it *has* to happen?" She stopped pacing to face him, keeping a few feet between them. "Wells, you've already lost someone important to you in a horrific way. I can't burden you with the possibility of another tragic loss of someone you care about."

For the first time, Asteria witnessed Wells clench his jaw, a muscle twitching in his neck. She bit back the burn of disappointment in herself for causing this emotion from him—whether it be anger, agitation, or a form of hurt.

"So, let me understand correctly…" Wells crossed his arm, balancing his elbow as he scratched the stubble along his jaw. A breath of disbelief left him before he added, "You have the desire to create distance now"—Wells gestured at the current space between them—"because you fear the outcome of an act we're not even certain we have to commit?"

"It shouldn't be your responsibility to stay and fix this should it come to fruition." Asteria's lips quivered, and she cast her head to the side. "I can't burden you with this—I can't burden you with me."

"For fucks sake, Asteria!" Wells's pained laugh echoed around them in the silent room. "You're not a burden. I want to help. I want *you*. I choose *you*."

Asteria snapped her head to him, her mouth parted as shock and something like hope left her rooted to the floor.

Wells stepped forward, swallowing against something he warred with. He opened and closed his mouth a few times, his hand poised between them. His bright eyes met hers, and his hand fell to his side, every muscle within him relaxing.

Not only was she stunned by his words, but it appeared Wells had left himself speechless.

She would've laughed if this were a different conversation.

He reached out, gripping her shoulders to keep her grounded. "If we must choose this plan, I will be with you when you create the Lock."

Asteria opened her mouth to protest because that was far too dangerous, but he shook his head to silence her. "I'll remind you of who you are—that you're not the Aether or the starfire. You wield them, but they don't wield you. I will talk to you the entire time. I will remind you that life is far better if you stay with me. I will remind you of all those who love you and how much they love you. How much I love you."

"You—" Asteria's breath caught in her throat, her power pulsing. "You love me?"

"Of course I do." His voice was low and steady but wrapped in so much tenderness. "Gods, do I love you."

He loved her.

Without condition. Without compromise.

Many overwhelming emotions surged through her veins at the admission. There was anxiousness, awe, excitement, lust.

But something stronger than all of that—something Asteria realized maybe she'd never had with Rod.

Asteria had spent so long feeling like love was about obligation. About enduring, not choosing. With Rod, love had felt like a tether, being chained to something expected rather than something desired. It'd been carved out of necessity and performance, a mold they tried to fit her into.

And Heavens, how lonely that had been.

She'd grown used to hiding the parts of her that didn't fit, learned to smile through the hollow ache of being loved for who they wanted her to be instead of who she truly was.

She wondered how she could've mistaken what was between her and Rod for love when what she felt for Wells was endless—*unfathomable*.

"I don't know if what I had was ever love," she admitted to him, fighting to hold back her tears. "But this, with you… I choose this love. I choose *you*, too, Wells. I love you. There is no *suppose* about it. I love you *deeply*."

Wells relaxed against her as he released a heavy breath. "Gods, I didn't… I didn't plan for this."

Asteria huffed in disbelief as she whispered, "And you believe I did?"

He grinned, his hands framing her face, thumbs caressing her cheeks. "I thought I wouldn't find love again, but this is so very different."

Asteria's heart ached for them both and their losses. The loss of his first love and her loss of time experiencing less than the love she deserved. She wanted to handle Wells with so much care because his love for her was a gift, and he *chose* her.

No love from obligation or requirement, but for the sheer simplicity of falling for who she was.

"Lyrans converse with many forces of the Universe," she murmured, brushing a curl from his forehead. "Fate and Destiny are similar, and yet not. I think Fate led us to one another, but it was Destiny that let us decide if we wanted love again or at all. *You* made me want that. I didn't know love until you, Wells."

He sighed, the sound like a whimper, before yanking her against him, their lips crashing together as he wrapped his fingers through the hair at the base of her neck. His tongue swept in as he tugged, angling her head to deepen their kiss. Asteria's core tightened as his other hand snaked behind her waist.

This was what would save her from Fracturing.

This was what she lived for now.

She lived for the warmth and kindheartedness of Wells, the safety she felt in his arms, the freedom he gave her to be herself, and the way her heart sang at the sound of his laugh.

Too soon, he pulled away, but Asteria knew what she wanted. She knew what she'd wanted for quite some time now. Even her body—maybe her soul—knew long before she did.

"Wells," she breathed, both panting as he held her. She toyed with the hair curling at the nape of his neck, smiling as he shut his eyes against her touch. "Wells, I want—"

"Anything," he urged, holding her back to look into her eyes. "I'm utterly and entirely yours."

"I want you to show me..." She paused, gnawing on her bottom lip. "Show me true love."

She swore she saw something glistening in his eyes as he smiled at her. "I would be more than honored, Blue."

His hand slowly drifted to the top of her dress, pulling at each string as their eyes lowered to watch his movements. Her heart hammered, anticipation setting her aflame from within.

Something warm tickled her ankles beneath the hem of her dress. She snapped her head to him at the familiar call of the Aether. It climbed higher as he peered up at her, his Mark darkened, eyes black. Her head reeled with a spark of arousal when the Aether brushed along the sensitive skin of her inner thigh.

Too many beautiful ideas filled her mind.

Asteria removed the kirtle, letting it fall from her shoulders. She only wore a frail slip beneath, and a glance down revealed the deep pink of her nipples peeking through the sheerness.

Lifting her eyes to Wells, his darkened further, pupils already overtaking his irises. Wells's hands shot out to grab a handful of fabric and help her lift it over her head. Standing utterly bare before him, she trembled for a new reason as his eyes slowly trailed from the top of her head, down her body, and back up again, the beautiful beige of his eyes returning.

He dragged the back of his hand down the side of her body, caressing her breast, waist, and hips. Her eyes fluttered shut at the fiery sensation that followed.

"There has been no other who occupies my mind like you," Wells whispered, and she couldn't stand the space between them. "I'm wholly yours. I belonged to you from the moment we met."

She pulled the towel from his waist and pressed him back until he sat at the edge of the bed. She climbed onto his lap, straddling him as his growing erection brushed her core. She dragged her fingertips down his abdomen, relishing in the flutter of them under her touch.

"You…" Tears pricked her eyes, and she pressed her lips fiercely to his. She pulled back enough to whisper, "I believe you are half my soul."

He clung to her waist and crashed back into her, moving his lips with purpose and tenderness. In one fluid motion, he gently flipped them on the bed, his body cradling hers. Asteria gasped at the journey of his hand up her body, and his mouth curled into a smirk against hers, a breath of warmth between kisses as he carefully cupped her breast. He gently kneaded his palm, then rubbed his thumb over her peaked nipple, sending a jolt of sharp, aching pleasure straight to her core.

She whimpered, pressing her hips into his, and Wells hummed in satisfaction.

"I believe you said my hands excite you," he murmured, kissing the curve of her jaw, then the slope of her neck.

His hips shifted, his cock grinding along the heat of her. His palm continued to coax quiet moans from her with each pass of his thumb, each drag of his lips.

"Wells," she breathed, digging her fingers into his bicep and ribcage. Her knees quivered as he nipped her ear.

"Yes, my love?" he asked, a smile heard within the question.

She glanced down between them, her attention instantly finding his hard length. Asteria marveled at every glorious inch of him, remembering his taste and the control she wielded when she'd took him in her mouth.

She went molten at the thought of him inside her, and her skin illuminated a faint blue.

"I love it when you glow for me," Wells growled as she cupped his cheek.

He returned the gesture, and she leaned into that touch. The next roll of his hips had the head of his cock pressing against her entrance, and everything felt slightly intimidating.

Wells's smile morphed into a tender frown. "I know it's been a while for you, so I'm unsure if I will hurt you. I promise I'm here with you. I'm always here with you."

"I trust you," she assured, those three words so familiar now, just as his voice, his smile, his touch were. "I'm yours."

He gently kissed her forehead where her own Mark sat, identical to his. Looking down at her body, she watched him grip his cock, lining up with her entrance. Her heart rate picked up with her breathing, and her nerves suddenly sneaked in.

Wells instantly noticed, and he stopped moving as he searched her face. "Relax, Blue." He kissed both cheeks before pressing his lips back to hers, her mind distracted and her body relaxing.

As Wells's body shifted above her, he slowly slid inside, inch by inch, his breath shaky against her cheek. Asteria gasped against his mouth, her hands gripping his shoulders as the sudden, forgotten sting spread through her. Her body stretched around him as he sank deeper, muscles trembling with the effort to control himself. The fact that he was even fighting that war between restraint and desire unraveled something deep in her chest.

"Asteria," Wells whispered, voice hoarse as he buried his face in the curve of her neck. His warm breath caressed her skin, her mind absorbed in the whole feeling within her. "Gods above, you are…"

She closed her eyes, absorbing him. The way he filled her, the way he held still as her body adjusted, the way her walls throbbed gently around him.

"You can't pray to me while buried inside me," she managed around her reeling mind. He twitched within her in response to her clenching, a groan rumbling low in his throat.

"I don't pray, Blue," Wells rasped, leaning back just enough to meet her eyes. He pulled his hips back, dragging himself through her, pausing with just the head of his cock within her. "But I'll happily worship you."

Wells sunk back into her steadily, and the breath tore from her throat. Not from pain, but from the sudden surge of pleasure lighting up her veins. Energy tickled her arms, tingling at her fingertips and igniting her skin with every drag.

Now this…

She could definitely live for this.

He repeated the motion, and this time, he adjusted his angle, hitting somewhere deep inside her that flashed lightning through her body. She cried out, arching her back.

"Look at you," Wells groaned, curling over and rolling her earlobe between his teeth. "Look at how well you take me."

She forced her eyes open, dizzy with sensation, and peered down at where they were connected. The visual of him disappearing into her, slick with arousal, made her clench again.

"Tell me what you want."

She knew this was her end. The way he spoke to her and the curve of his hips as he moved within her was too much, yet not enough.

"More," was all Asteria could say as she dug her nails into his shoulders, eliciting a hiss between his teeth.

"How much more?" he goaded, leaving a trail of fire down her neck.

"All of you." She turned her head, lips resting against his cheek. "I want all of you."

Wells's eyes flashed with heat, something molten blooming behind them. He adjusted his grip, one hand sliding to the headboard, the other wrapping tight around her hip. Muscles flexing, he ground into her, weaving his hips like a wave as he picked up his pace, following a rhythm that only managed to push her higher and higher with addicting ecstasy.

She gasped his name as he lifted her leg and hitched it around his waist, thrusting deeper, quicker. Her breathing became ragged, her body locking up.

"I can feel that pretty cunt tightening around me." Wells grunted, and she could only whimper in response. "Come for me, Blue."

With his next thrust, that coil snapped within her, walls pulsing around his cock as he continued to move within her. She called his name into the chambers as she gripped his biceps, pleasure seeping into her being as he let her have as much of him as she wanted.

"Asteria," Wells moaned, and she felt his movements slow to a languid pace, his hips jerking as he finished with her. His head dropped to the crook of her neck as he sighed.

He slowly removed himself from her, tumbling onto the bed beside her. He grabbed her wrist, tugging her into him. "So how does love feel, Blue?"

She smiled softly as she nestled into his side, curling her leg over his. "*Your* love is everything I've been searching for my entire life."

He chuckled blissfully, kissed the top of her head, and he laid his cheek against it. She shut her eyes against the feel of him beside her.

This wasn't something she would give up.

She would burn the world to keep him by her side.

CHAPTER 62

ASTERIA

Asteria woke before Wells and carefully adjusted to study his relaxed face. He was so calm and vulnerable in his sleep, bringing a gentle smile to her lips. She lifted a hand and rested it against his cheek, brushing her thumb over the freckles.

Wells hummed as he curled toward her. They faced one another on the bed, his eyes peeling open. The position gave her a better view of the freckles trailing across his nose and down the other cheek, her fingers following.

"What are you fascinated by?" Wells asked quietly, his fingertips skimming her shoulder.

"Your freckles," she admitted, stopping. He peered down his nose with a raised eyebrow. "I think they're beautiful."

"Beautiful?" He peeled her fingers from his skin, kissing each pad before folding her hand between them. "That's a first, I have to admit."

"Lyrans don't have blemishes," Asteria explained, chuckling. "I don't even believe Andromedans do. Yours are so perfectly positioned across your nose and shoulders. It's like the stars have fallen on your skin."

Wells brought her hand back to his mouth, placing a kiss on her palm, then to her wrist without breaking eye contact. Asteria's stomach twirled with the each touch of his lips. "How have we managed to get ourselves into this?"

Asteria laughed, tucking herself closer to him, lacing their legs together. Her thigh graced his rather hard member, and she stilled.

"I think I have an idea of how we got ourselves here," she mumbled, yelping as he yanked her closer, their chests pressed against each other.

"I believe I may know as well." He tucked a finger under her chin. "Is it disgraceful of me to want to do it again first thing this morning?"

"Thank the Heavens," Asteria grumbled as she shoved him onto his back and straddled him.

Her thighs braced on either side of his hips, hair falling over one shoulder as she looked down at him. He stared up at her with a half-grin, a devious glint in his eyes.

"My turn," she purred.

"Oh?" was all he got out.

She rolled her hips back, her already slick warmth rubbing along his thick length, the low rumble in his chest reverberating through her. She wrapped her fingers around him and aligned him with her entrance. She held him there, teasing as she bit back her smirk.

"You're absolutely wicked for that," he rasped, firmly gripping her hips. He quickly twitched his hips and thrust upward, dragging her down in one swift, brutal motion. She gasped and threw her head back, his thumbs caressing her skin. "Unfortunately, I've gotten a taste of you, and now I'm ravenous."

She moaned as he lifted her again, setting the rhythm with deep, dragging thrusts that hit a new depth, her eyes rolling to the back of her head. "Wells…"

He sat upright, his hands sliding up her spine as he stayed seated within her. His mouth found the valley between her breasts, then one peaked nipple where he flicked his tongue and bit gently. The sharp sting sent a bolt of lightning to her core.

He replaced his mouth with his fingers. "Ride me."

She didn't hesitate. She wanted him to unravel because of her.

She lifted herself and plunged her hands into his hair, yanking his head back. She sank back down, her lips skimming his. She hovered just out of reach as she rode his cock, his hand roaming up and down her back. When his hand wrapped around the ends of her hair and gave a rough tug, her inner muscles clenched around him with her ragged whimper.

"Oh, if you like that," he muttered against her throat, placing a kiss there, "I have so many incredibly filthy things I want to do to you."

Asteria widened her straddle, lowering further until he filled her to the hilt. A husky moan rumbled from his chest and sank into her bones. His head tipped back as she rocked against him, her lashes low, mouth parted in a silent gasp.

Then his legs shifted, and he braced one hand behind him, the other wrapping tighter around her back. It was the only warning she had before he met her movements, thrusting up as she came down, ripping his name from her lips.

"Fucking Gods, Blue," Wells groaned, dragging his lips over the swell of her breast as he chased her movements. "I may never get enough of you."

"I have no complaints." She panted, her head lolling back as he flicked his tongue over her nipple. "I have all the time in the world."

Wells laughed at that and buried his head in her chest. "Of course you do."

There was no warning this time.

He pulled her off him with infuriating ease, her body throbbing around nothing, already mourning the loss of him. She'd barely caught her breath before he tenderly flipped her onto her stomach.

Her knees dug into the mattress as he hauled her hips up with one hand, tilting her pelvis. The other traced the length of her spine, the lightest of touches making her shiver as he pressed her chest into the pillows.

"This—" Wells used his knee to nudge her legs wider. She whimpered, her back arching with need. "This is something I fantasized about far too frequently."

He didn't give her time to respond. He sank into her again, deeper than before, both of his hands tucked in the bend of her hips as he pulled her back into each thrust. Her eyes rolled as he hit a place inside her that made her entire body tremble, her hands fisting the sheets.

Each stroke ground her, pleasure rippling outward from her core as he thrust into her. The sound of skin on skin filled the room, punctuated by his groans and her broken cries. Her arms trembled as she braced herself, the pleasure growing overwhelming in the best way.

Wells drove her to a place that left no room for thought.

"You feel like fucking Heaven," Wells whispered into her ear, his breath warm on her neck. "I wonder how many times I can make you come—"

A knock on the door startled them both. All movements ceased entirely.

"Come in," Wells announced, and Asteria squealed in horror as she scrambled away from him and slid under the covers. She turned with the sheet clutched to her chest in time to meet Gavril's lavender gaze.

"You know, I would also be curious to know how many times you can make her come." Gavril leaned against the doorframe, his hands in his pockets. "Shall we take bets?"

Wells rolled his eyes as he fell back on the bed beside Asteria. She threw the blanket over his still-hard cock with a scowl, but he only winked before turning back to Gavril. "What are your bets? It better not be offensive."

"As much as I want to participate, I *come* with a purpose."

"You're unbelievable," Asteria muttered, rolling her eyes.

"You may want to get on with it," Wells said matter-of-factly, propping himself up on his forearms. "I was busy with matters I would enjoy getting back to—"

Asteria slapped her hand across his chest, gawking at him, although she was fighting the grin working its way up her cheeks.

"Your matters will need to wait." Gavril's face suddenly turned serious as he directed his attention to Asteria.

Her back stiffened as she blinked at him. "What is it?"

"Some of our Lemurian spies delivered a new report." He paused, gnawing on his lip as his gaze slid from Wells back to her. Her heart hammered, and she reached for Well's hand beside her. "There's talk of an attack on Chimbridge in Etherea."

"By who?" Wells asked as her hand tightened in his. Gavril just stared. "By *them*? I thought Gallus promised he would leave their humans untouched?"

"How do you know this?" The blood roared in her ears. "Where are your spies? I thought you stopped them from trailing Endora."

"We did," Wells answered, shaking his head. "These ones were amongst Lemurians following Zephyr."

"Chimbridge is where Dustin's family is from," Asteria whispered, but she maintained Gavril's stare. "I believe they still live there—it's an entirely human village. We must warn Phoebe."

At the same time she uttered those words, the Aether swirled within her chest, carrying a desperate plea, a single word.

Please.

"It's Phoebe," Asteria blurted, hand clenched over her chest. "She's calling me."

"We might be too late." Gavril's face went gaunt, something dark flashing through his eyes.

"Get Piers and wait outside the door while we dress," Wells said, flinging the covers off. "We'll all answer her call."

Gavril nodded sternly, chancing one last glance at Asteria before shutting the door behind him. She sat there as Wells moved about the room, the belt for his sword clattering.

If Chimbridge had already been attacked, and that was why Phoebe was calling her…

The only thing Asteria could think about was how Gallus knew.

He *knew* where Phoebe's family was—where the love of Phoebe's life was from—and he let them plan an attack.

How could he? Who was this man? Because there was no way this was the father she knew—

"Blue." Wells appeared in her vision, grabbing her face in his hands. She wrapped her hands around his wrists, suppressing the angry, hot tears of another betrayal by her father. "We have to go. Can you do this?"

"If this is true…" Asteria scrunched her face as she shook her head in Wells's grasp. "She'll never forgive him. I'll never—"

"I know," Wells said, catching a rogue tear. "I also know you'll want to hurt every last one of them, but this is her fight. You only move on her mark, okay?"

Asteria nodded firmly, melting beneath the kiss Wells placed on her lips. When he pulled away, a resolute determination settled into her bones, and she whispered, "There's something I have to get."

Asteria took a deep breath as she strolled behind Wells outside the bedroom, her shoulders tensing at the sight of Piers and Gavril. She made eye contact with the former, who offered her a grim smile before catching the weapon in her hand.

His eyes blew wide, but Gavril sputtered, "What the *fuck* is that?"

Asteria peered down at the labrys in her hand, testing its otherworldly, lightweight material.

She had to give it to Rod; he made beautiful weapons.

The two blades on either side of the labrys glistened gold at their tips, a gold cross securing them to the shaft, another gold piece at the pommel. The majority of the blades and shaft were made of an opaque, foreign glass material she could ignite with starfire to make the weapon even deadlier.

Not that she'd ever had a real need for it, but she definitely hadn't touched it since they'd separated. This war felt like the proper opportunity to bring it into her arsenal.

"You don't see me questioning your swords," Asteria said with a shrug, waving the end of the labrys toward Gavril's belt. He took two steps back.

"Because that is my *only* means of protection." Gavril laid a hand on his chest. "Unlike some, I can't set my entire body in blue flames to wield as I please."

"Pity." Asteria smirked, and he shook his head. She cleared her throat, which settled the jovial mood to a somber one again. She repeated what Wells had said to her, "We let her lead. This is her kingdom, and we're her allies."

"Agreed," Piers said sternly, nodding once. "Let's go."

Asteria opened the portal directly into Phoebe's study in Etherea, and all three men followed on her heels as she stepped through. Her heart fluttered erratically in her chest, even more so when she found Phoebe staring out the window behind her desk, eerily still.

"Phoebe," Asteria said gently as the men filed into the room. "Phoebe, I don't know—"

Phoebe grunted, holding a hand up. Asteria's eyes pulsed once at the frantic Aether swirling within Phoebe. For the first time, she finally felt the imprint of the god-power within her.

Where Taranis resembled a brewing storm and Dionne felt like molten fire in her chest, Phoebe's signature reminded her starkly of Gallus.

It was an innate pull, a humming—similar to how her powers hummed when nature stilled.

Oh, Heavens.

"What do you wish to do…" Asteria trailed off as she caught what Phoebe was looking at out the window.

In the direction of Chimbridge, black plumes of smoke swirled into the sky.

Gavril swore under his breath, and Wells stiffened beside her.

Asteria didn't know what was happening out there, but she knew exactly what was going through Phoebe's head, her words ringing from the other day.

His family took me in like their own and have been better parents than any of mine.

"Phoebe, where are Dustin and the kids?" Asteria blurted, rushing around the desk to stand beside her sister. Not a single muscle twitched on Phoebe's face. Her eyes glowed the warm light of her god-power. "Phoebe—"

"They're here," she said quietly, her voice hoarse. Speaking seemed to flip something within her. She painstakingly twisted her head to stare at Asteria, her voice barely audible. "Was I truly that foolish to believe?"

"No." Asteria shook her head, heart aching. She hesitantly reached out and tucked a strand of hair behind Phoebe's ear. "It's him who's foolish. He could've kept one of his daughters. Now, he's lost both."

A muscle in Phoebe's jaw ticked, the first sign of emotion. She blinked, but the glow didn't clear. "Take me there."

Asteria offered a tight-lipped grin, opening a portal to Chimbridge. Piers and Wells exchanged a wary glance, but they conjured the Aether and Energy as Gavril unsheathed a sword from his belt.

"If there are too many forces for us, we leave," Piers demanded, gauging Phoebe's reaction to his demand.

She ignored him, throwing her shoulders back and marching toward the portal. There was a single bob of her head at each male before stepping through.

"Follow her lead," Asteria reminded sternly, her grip tightening on the labrys. "If she gets out of control, let me handle her."

With that, they followed Phoebe into Chimbridge. The air left her lungs once they stepped through the veil.

There was nothing left.

CHAPTER 63

PHOEBE

Piles of rubble surrounded Phoebe, smoke billowing as far as she could see. It stung her eyes and clogged her throat, clinging to her gown. She waved her hands, her god-power blowing the smoke in different directions to grant her a better view of the village.

With a bone-chilling horror that ripped any sense of self from her mind, Phoebe realized there was nothing left to look at.

Other than some larger stone and marble columns that once held up grand buildings, not a single home remained. Her mouth dropped open, face morphing as she slowly spun to take in the wreckage around her, heart pounding in her throat.

"This is…" Phoebe shook her head, trying to blink the burn of tears away. A few escaped and slid down her cheeks. "I don't understand."

I don't understand.

A scream built its way up her chest, lodging behind her collarbone and building with the cramp in her stomach.

They promised her.

He promised me.

They promised not to touch a single hair on a mortal's head within her country.

Why the fuck would they level an entire village of innocent people?

"I would venture it has something to do with the mortal population—" Gavril grunted, rocks skidding.

The answer from Gavril made her realize she'd shouted the question out loud.

Her chest heaved with frantic, shallow breaths. Her fists clenched and unclenched at her sides, over and over, as her body fought to make sense of the growing numbness in her limbs. Her fingers tingled before going cold.

Not only had they destroyed this village, but she wasn't sure where Dustin's family was. His parents, his sisters and their children, his cousins...

They all lived here.

They were the first to welcome her without question—not as a Sirian, not an Andromedan, not a bastard daughter, and not even as a queen. They showed her what love was supposed to be without thrones or manipulation.

They were the family she never thought she'd have.

A sick, sharp certainty bloomed like frost across her skin as she wrestled with the knowledge that there would be no survivors.

Phoebe splayed her hands in front of her, fingers spread wide, and rubble rolled across the cobblestone street. She made her way toward the first block where Dustin's family lived.

She wasn't sure what she would find, but she needed to see it.

"Phoebe!"

Asteria's voice chased her, but Phoebe shut it out. Her hearing tunneled as the roaring in her ears grew louder, her power surging in response as a dull hum vibrated under her skin.

The moon called to her, a rhythmic thudding in synchronization with her heart. When she looked down, white light threaded through her veins, her aura spilling out around her in waves.

This village shouldn't be silent.

It should've been full of life, laughter echoing through narrow streets, the sound of music drifting from the tavern square, children shouting as they ran between houses, dogs barking, blacksmiths pounding iron.

Instead, the only sound was the brittle crunch of debris beneath their feet.

Phoebe growled, erupting from her chest in raw, aimless rage that had no outlet as reality crashed into her anew.

Thousands of mortals lived in this city. Sure, there were some Lemurians and Sirians, but it was a small percentage, not enough to protect the entire village from decimation. Chimbridge was also the second largest village in Etherea outside of Eryphus, where Rigel's Keep resided.

And they leveled the entire thing.

A choked scream clawed from her throat, somewhere between a sob and another growl. She threw her arms wide and lifted from the ground, soaring over the ruin.

But Phoebe knew.

She didn't need confirmation, but she deserved to see it with her own eyes.

After all, it was her decision that led to this outcome.

It was her fault.

Phoebe chose to ally with an untrustworthy father out of desperation and fear instead of accepting the help of her sister and her allies, even after Asteria bared her soul to her.

Her family had paid the price.

Phoebe dropped from the air and hit the ground hard, stumbling to her knees in the dirt and gravel. She crumpled in front of what remained of two houses: one that belonged to Dustin's parents, the other to his youngest sister and her family.

Both were reduced to nothing more than charred stone and splinters.

Her breath caught, and a sob ripped free before she could swallow it. Her hand flew to her mouth to suppress more.

She crawled toward the shattered wooden fence in front of his sister's small yard, debris cutting through her skin. Blood smeared the fence where she gripped a shattered beam.

To hell with no enhanced healing.

Phoebe needed to feel her mistake.

She needed the pain to etch itself into her memory so she could never forget what her choices had cost.

"You're no longer immortal," Asteria said gently, squatting beside Phoebe. She rested her weapon on the ground beside them and laid her warm hands on Phoebe's trembling shoulders. "The integrity of these homes is unstable. I'm not sure…"

"Open and honest." Phoebe's voice didn't sound like her own. It was cold and hollow, except for something menacing promising retribution beneath.

Asteria sighed heavily. "Even Sirians and Lemurians couldn't survive something like this." Her eyes swept over the wreckage. "I'm so sorry, Phoebe."

Phoebe hung her head, shoulders shaking. A harsh, broken sob heaved from her chest, threatening to split her in two. She squeezed her eyes shut, but it didn't stop the flood. Grief poured from her in a steady trickle.

Stones scattered to her left, and Phoebe froze. Asteria rose in a heartbeat, hand snapping toward her weapon.

"I would advise you to stop where you are," Asteria snarled in warning, the labrys glowing blue out of Phoebe's peripheral.

Phoebe slowly turned her head toward the intruders. There were a handful of Lemurians she didn't recognize standing a few piles down, but even from this distance, Phoebe knew they were drakons from those signature, jewel-toned eyes.

Her heart stopped in her chest at the person with them.

K.M. DAVIDSON

The Andromedan stood poised as ever, her hands tucked into the billowing sleeves of her gown. Her gray and black hair was rolled into a bun high on her head, her black eyes matching the dark Mark on her forehead. Aether leaked from a small gap in her sleeves.

"I come here with good news," Endora said calmly, in contrast to how Phoebe felt. She rose from her crouch, facing the small group head-on. Endora directed her attention to Asteria. "Something told me you may be here, so I decided to make an appearance just in case."

Asteria stiffened beside her, but the starfire within the labrys and her other hand didn't waver.

"Go on," Asteria ground out, her eyes now engulfed in a glowing blue light.

Phoebe wondered if she would get the chance to finally see her sister's god-form.

"It will work," Endora answered vaguely.

That must have meant something to Asteria because she let out a heavy breath of disbelief.

Phoebe's patience snapped.

"Why?" Phoebe shouted, her power returning tenfold. The ground rumbled beneath them, and Endora's eyes flashed wide. "What was the point of this?"

"I don't know what you mean, my *Queen*," Endora drawled, frowning in mock innocence.

"Oh, don't play coy with me, you stupid bitch." Phoebe chuckled, the sound laced with a hint of hysteria. She gestured around her, arms spread wide. Small chunks of brick rose with the movement. "Why would you attack my village? We had a deal—"

"I can't begin to guess the inner workings of the Lyrans—what they wish to do, what pieces they wish to play next." Endora shrugged, the Aether fading from her eyes and Mark. "Despite Gallus and I being rather close as of late, he doesn't disclose all his plans with me."

"What do you mean by *close*?" Asteria asked, uttering the word as though it were foreign.

"Just as you have decided to warm your bed with a mortal Sirian, we all have desires, Asteria." Endora winked.

"Oh, you have got to be *fucking* kidding me." Asteria transformed then. The labrys clattered to the ground and Asteria's clothes burned to ash as her entire body morphed into the depth of night.

Stars swirled and flashed within her silhouette, blue flames dancing around her body except for those closest to the edge. Those flames bled from purple to blue, waving wildly with the ones that were now her hair. Her eyes glowed like blue orbs, and there weren't enough definable features to determine what sort of expression she gave Endora.

Phoebe wished she could take another moment to admire how beautiful she was in this form.

"If it's a fight you wish to have, know I'm amply prepared with an army," Endora explained, her hand lazily gesturing at the houses that used to be Phoebe's family's. "What happens when you try to kill that which is already dead?"

Oh, fuck no.

She meant to raise the dead—Dustin's *family*—to do her bidding.

Phoebe burned with rage so all-consuming she worried she'd never return.

It was grief incarnate, and it poured through her.

Before Endora had a chance to conjure the necromancer power that allowed her to resurrect the dead, Phoebe lifted her body.

Only to slam it back down into the cobblestone ground.

Phoebe didn't understand what the Lemurians accompanying her were shouting, nor did she care.

She spread her fingers wide, holding each one in place, restricting their movements. She twirled the Aether up their legs, arms, chests, and necks with her other hand.

"They say the Obsidian Decay is only for humans," Phoebe said, tilting her head. "I beg to differ."

She flicked her wrist, spearing a sharp prong of Aether into the Lemurians' ears. Her fingers wiggled as the Aether burrowed into their minds. She sprawled them out to dispel it, shattering their brains.

Their mouths opened, and maybe they screamed, but the veins in their foreheads turned black, blood dripping from their noses and eyes. Phoebe released them, and they crumpled lifelessly on the ground.

Phoebe caught Endora struggling to rise from her peripheral, her arm bent at an improper angle. "Where do you think you're going?"

Phoebe elevated Endora from the ground again, and the Andromedan screamed as Phoebe brought her closer. She wished she still had her enhanced strength because she would've loved nothing more than to hold Endora up by the throat.

What she did have planned would require a bit of her strength, though.

"I told you that if you used a *single* human for nefarious purposes, I would tear your heart from your chest and feed it to my hounds." Phoebe found it a miracle she spoke at all anymore. "Unfortunately, my hounds aren't here…"

Endora's eyes blew wide, her face paling as her mouth opened in a silent scream. With one hand, Phoebe held Endora up. She laid the other hand against Endora's chest and called up as much power as she could.

"I can still honor the first part of that promise, though."

With numbness washing over her, Phoebe *pulled* against Endora's chest. The wet, splintering sound of ribs cracking filled the air.

One. Two. Three.

She counted the snaps as they came, each one echoing inside her like the tolling of a bell.

Four. Five. Six. Until Endora's sternum gave way with a sickening crunch.

Her ribcage split open. Bone tore upward, jagged white shards punching through skin and flesh in uneven angles. She shoved any sharp points out of the way with a flick of her finger to avoid cutting herself and plunged her hand into Endora's warm chest. There was a slick give of tissue that throbbed with the thrum of a heartbeat against her palm. Endora's chest convulsed.

Phoebe looked up and met her dimming black irises. Her lashes fluttered, mouth twitching as if to speak, but no words came.

There was only a depthless terror in her void-like eyes.

She squeezed her fingers around the tender organ, contractions pulsing in protest against her grip.

Then, she tore Endora's heart from her chest in one brutal yank.

She released her hold, and Endora's body crumpled to the ground with the snap of more bones.

"Holy fuck," someone said behind her, although it felt miles away.

She stared at the heart, wishing it held any significance to her. Blood pooled in her palm, warm and thick, spilling between her fingertips as it dripped at her feet.

Something warm twisted up her leg, pulling her out of her trance. She silently dropped the heart with a wet thunk. Phoebe glanced down to find the Aether retreating.

She spun around quickly, immediately meeting her sister's illuminated eyes.

Asteria was still in her god-form, hovering a few inches from the ground above the dull labrys. Phoebe swallowed, relieved she couldn't read what Asteria was thinking of her as the weight of what she'd done crashed into her.

"What was Endora talking about?" Phoebe asked, startling herself with the absurd question.

"It doesn't matter—"

"Tell me."

Asteria was right. It didn't matter in the slightest, but Phoebe needed something other than devastation and grief and guilt and death to grab onto.

She sighed, her bloody hand finally falling limp at her side. "Please," she whispered.

Asteria held her form steady, blinking. Another beat of silence passed, then her ethereal voice answered, "I asked her to test if the elixir she gave you would work on Lyrans."

Phoebe maintained a stoic face, but she released a huff of air.

She knew immediately that was where Asteria had gone after their heated discussion in the study, and she understood why. Phoebe witnessed the looks she and Wells exchanged, the proximity between them that they only diminished reluctantly.

Asteria had fallen for a mortal Being. Maybe he'd given her the taste of a mortal life, and she didn't want to live without him.

If the roles were reversed and Phoebe had only just learned about the elixir, she would've done the same—enemy sides or not.

"If we go to her residence, I can show you where she keeps her formulas—at least for this one." Phoebe nodded firmly, aimlessly swiping a hand over the skirt of her gown.

Her cream-colored gown.

"Phoebe," Asteria said, but she ignored it.

It made no sense to her.

Gallus either decided they no longer needed her neutrality, or this was punishment for speaking to Asteria and the Carraphims. Maybe he and the others thought this would teach her a lesson, scare her into complete submission, that she would join their cause in hopes the Lyrans wouldn't punish her again.

That might have been the case for other kingdoms.

Unfortunately, they fucked with the wrong queen.

They would regret stepping foot in her study that day.

"Phoebe!" Asteria shouted again. This time, her voice no longer carried the ethereal tone of her god-form.

Phoebe drew her attention away from the rubble. While she was lost in thought, Asteria had returned to her mortal form. She held the labrys once again and wore a tunic that barely covered her. A quick look at

Wells revealed he no longer had a shirt.

"What do you need from me?" There was no judgment or disgust in Asteria's face. If anything, there may have been a glisten of pride in her gaze.

It was identical to the expression Gallus had given her when she'd bargained with him.

Phoebe took an unsteady, shuddering breath. She directed her gaze to Piers and Wells. "Etherea will ally with Eldamain."

CHAPTER 64

GALLUS

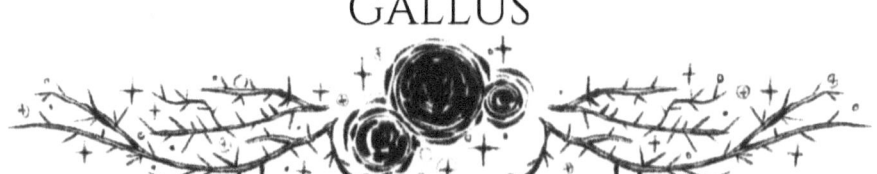

G allus stepped through the portal into Etherea where he knew he would find her. He didn't know exactly which room she occupied, so he called the blue starfire to his outstretched palm.

She would come to him.

He floated through the halls in silence, the blue flame dancing in his hand as he waited patiently for her to emerge.

Instead of using her portal, Asteria quietly snuck out one of the rooms, softly closing the door behind her. She stepped into the middle of the hall at Rigel's Keep, her jaw set as she glared at him through narrowed eyes.

The corner of his lips twitched as her powers radiated from her, the anger beneath her mortal skin peeking out in the similar night of his own god-form.

"Come," Asteria demanded, storming off toward another room farther down the hall without waiting to see if he would follow. Once she closed the door behind her, he portaled inside.

"Are you out of your mind?" Asteria hissed in a hushed tone, whirling on him. "You can't just show up here. You forget a war has begun—one by the likes this world has never seen—and you're on the opposite side of

Etherea, now."

Gallus stared at his daughter, his Brightest Star. He'd always loved every part of her—the kind, the wild, the untethered, the ferociousness, the softness for those she cared for. She was his greatest accomplishment, and he could never be more proud of the woman who now stood before him.

There was a light within her that was never there before, though. The ghost of the scowl that normally shadowed her face was gone, replaced by glittering eyes, even as she looked at him with a mix of resentment and grief.

"You've found a purpose," Gallus said, his voice even as tilted his head. "I see it in the way you hold yourself."

"I wouldn't call it a purpose," she explained, shoulders tense as her guard remained up. Quieter, she muttered, "More like passion."

He waited for her to elaborate, but she only continued to stare at him. He supposed this was the risk he took in moving forward with his intentions.

After all the talks of Asteria not wanting to be a Goddess, always keeping neutral ground, he underestimated how much she cared for the humans in the end.

"You *can't* be here," Asteria said, forcing the words out. "I won't ask again. Why are you here?"

"To see the truth for myself." Gallus took a step forward, gauging her reaction. She rolled her eyes but let him inch closer. He circled her, observing the way she held herself. Asteria was the same, and yet different. "My daughters allied against me."

"For Heaven's sake, Gallus." She spun, roughly grabbing his shoulder to keep him still. "Why the fuck are we in this position?"

He raised a black eyebrow at her.

"More importantly, why did you attack Chimbridge?" Asteria scoffed, shoving him back. She paced across the small space. "You practically had Phoebe eating out of your palm with this neutrality. She openly denied allying with Eldamain, and it's like you punished her regardless. I don't know what game this is you're playing. You're far more strategic than this."

Gallus clasped his hands behind his back, remaining silent. He'd already told Asteria and Phoebe his objective.

Danica and Gallus had originally set out with their fellow Lyrans to create their own world. They were both less than pleased when they happened upon a world that already contained humans, but everyone wanted to listen to the damned Talons of Fate. He and Danica pretended to go along with what the others wanted, content with watching the world evolve.

When they finally created the Sirians, it was exactly what they wanted. Things were better when Morana and Valeria acted out of desperation to save Sybil, ultimately leading to the creation of the Lemurians.

He and his Morning Star never wanted a world with weakness. They wanted Beings who thrived.

Gallus just gave the world a shove in the right direction to finally rid itself of its feeble links.

Asteria stopped pacing, staring at him through a narrowed gaze. "You gave me this whole dialogue on slower change being safer than abrupt change, that too large of a move would cause unrest. That is why I don't understand what you had to gain from not just Chimbridge, but the attack on Heridy, too."

Gallus's jaw clenched briefly at the reminder of what had occurred in Heridy.

It wasn't because he was angry with Asteria for killing the spare heir of Allanis. Quite the contrary, because it only verified the point he wished to prove.

The powerful would prevail, and Asteria was the most powerful.

He realized his mistake when Asteria's scrunched expression went slack. The corner of his lips twitched just a fraction.

She truly was her father's daughter.

"They went against you." Asteria's swirling blue eyes twinkled from the stars within as she studied his face. "You don't have any control over them, do you?"

"I can't control Lyrans." Gallus sighed heavily, waving his hand in the air. "They will do what they please, no matter how much I reason. Nen always tries to undermine anyone who appears more than him or challenges his perceived notion of authority. Zephyr navigates to the one he finds most powerful in the room and doesn't have a single thought of his own.

"Valeria is Fractured." He chuckled low, but it was pained. "She's a true wild card—"

"Fuck, Gallus." Asteria ran both hands through her hair, gawking at him. "Not only have you created a division amongst the Lyrans—and the world—but you have a divide within your own party."

She was correct, which was why Gallus had nothing to say. All he could focus on was what he planned on doing. He supposed the outcome of his entire experiment was not entirely controllable, and yet...

The powerful *would* write the laws of life on Aveesh, would they not?

"It's not too late," she whispered, tears welling in her eyes. His throat burned, but he kept a neutral expression. "Come to us. Be on our side of things. Don't be on Nen's, because that's what you're doing now. It's not your campaign anymore."

She rushed upon him, staring up into his eyes as a tear tracked down her face. His daughter looked so young again, and he saw the child she'd been, always running to him to protect her from her mother and the others.

How awful it was to see he was the reason for her pain, now. She had run *from* him.

"I don't wish to lose you because of this." She threw her hands and gaze up before dropping them both back down, another tear with it.

Gallus cupped her cheeks, swiping the tears as he balanced her jaw in his hands. "It's not you who will lose me. My heart belonged to you the day you were born. It always has and always will, even when you and I are nothing but memories. You're my greatest love and my greatest weakness. In the end, it is I who will lose you in this."

Her lower lip quivered, her eyes flashing starfire blue in anger, or maybe it was hurt. She ripped her face away from him, and he knew then.

He'd lost his daughter.

"Danica wants to use the Lock." She twirled back to look at him, desperation enhancing the dampness in her eyes. He frowned, though, and not because of her but rather what she said. "You know of it?"

"I'm well aware of the Achlys Lock."

It'd been quite some time since someone spoke of the Lock to seal a Realm. He and Danica were required to learn of it since he not only wielded the Aether, but also inherited both starfires, and she the Energy.

"How do they plan to do that?" He wanted to see how much Danica remembered.

"Danica needs me for the Lock." Asteria's eyes latched onto Gallus's frown. "I would create the Lock with her using the Aether and starfire."

Danica never was the smart one. She exuded this grand confidence and superiority, even when it wasn't warranted. That sort of mindset resulted in some of her more distasteful qualities, like her lack of empathy and accountability and sense of entitlement.

Leave it to her arrogance and competitiveness to goad about a contraption she didn't remember how to forge.

Gallus chuckled low, averting his gaze to the window outside. "You realize using two of your powers to forge a Lock around a Realm will Fracture you."

"You could help us." Asteria reached for his hands, clutching them close to her. "Father, you could fill in with us as starfire or Aether, it doesn't matter to me. None of us will sacrifice anything to build it."

"When it comes to your mother, there is always something to be sacrificed." Gallus yanked his hands out of hers, sneering. "You've done well thus far not to fall for your mother's manipulation, Asteria. While we may be on opposing sides, don't succumb to her now. You're still your own person. You have your own mind and your own choice. Don't risk yourself for a fragile plan."

Asteria's eyes hardened as she took two steps back. "The Lock is a final resort. Make better choices and control your Lyrans, then maybe I won't have to risk my sanity."

"Ah…" Gallus nodded, locking his arms behind his back. "This is supposed to serve as a threat."

"I don't make threats." Asteria's sinister grin reminded him how proud he was of her. "I make promises."

"As I hope you do." He smiled then, but it held no malice. He threw all his affection and love into it. "But you meant to threaten me with *you* and your sanity in hopes of swaying me away from my plans, not because of what the Lock could do. For that, I've never been prouder, except you've made one grave error.

"If you've found your passion and purpose, I know you. You won't forfeit that so easily to form a silly Lock for your mother."

Asteria swallowed, blinking rapidly as she dropped her gaze to the floor. Gallus retraced their steps from one another, gripping her chin and lifting her eyes back to his.

"I don't care about anything as much as I care about you," he admitted softly, and he thought he saw her heart shatter in her eyes. "No matter what happens, just know if I were to see you on a battlefield, forced to face you…"

Asteria stopped breathing, her eyes flaring and swirling wildly.

"You. Are. My. Weakness." He bent down and placed a soft kiss on the top of her head, whispering, "I would die by your hands before I harm a single hair on your head."

With that, Gallus opened a portal behind him and stepped back without allowing himself to look at her face again.

He would've done anything to heal the heartbreak he'd caused if he had.

END OF BOOK I
The story continues in book II of the Andromedans Duology

SHROUDED REALMS

AUTHOR'S NOTE

Thank you so much for reading *Sundered Heavens*! I hope that you enjoyed it and fell in love with the characters just as much as I have.

This book was different for me compared to my debut series—and honestly, any other book I've written in my life. It was the first time I *didn't* write in first person, and this was by far the most POVs I had in a single story. It was also where I finally got to take all I'd learned thus far and turn it into an absolute epic fantasy tale.

On top of that, the struggles the FMCs faced in this book spoke to me on so many intimate levels that I found myself healing little bits and pieces of me. Asteria's desire to just be accepted and loved for who she is and not what people hope for her to be, Phoebe's quick-to-flip emotions and her fierce protection of those she loves, Sybil's blasé exterior while secretly screaming on the inside, and Morana's loss of the person she loved while they're still right in front of her.

You all don't know how excited and yet absolutely terrified I am to dive into this second book.

If you enjoyed this book, I would be so touched if you left a review on your retailer website, social platform, or Goodreads.

If you'd like to be among the first to know about new releases, new art, and all other kinds of fun stuff, consider signing up for my newsletter at kmdavidson.com, joining my Patreon and/or Discord (invite at beacons.ai/kmdavidsonbooks).

Thank you again for joining this ride and I hope you'll stick around for the next ones.

ACKNOWLEDGEMENTS

Everything about this book challenged me in some of the best ways, and I had a tribe of people behind me that helped make this book possible. I'm going to do my best to put things as eloquently as I can, but I make no promises. So, without further adieu:

First, I want to thank all the fans of The Sirians Series. You all are absolutely amazing, and this expansion would not be possible without you. Your passion fueled my creative well for this world, and I just wanted to thank you all from the bottom of my heart for following me this far.

To my Alpha readers: Ashley, Kelsey, Andie, TJ, Kayla, and Brittany. For those of you who read The Sirians Series before this, thank you for being the first to read this new installment in my universe and all the incredibly valuable feedback. For those who were introduced to my writing with this book, thank you for taking the chance on me and helping in this process.

To my Beta readers: Daph, Joanna, Sarah, Sarah B, Ally, and Sabrina. You got to read 20,000 more words than the Alphas and gave me the confidence that these additions were the right move. A majority of you were sending me live updates if you weren't commenting in a document, and to see you all going crazy was just the highlight of this experience. Thank you for those who have been with me and to the new folk, thank you for being willing to read SH before it was perfected.

Now, it's time to get a little more personal…

To my editor, Hannah: I think we were meant to find one another for this story. Your feedback was absolutely invaluable, from your kind words to your constructive comments, this book would truly not be where it is today without you. I can't wait for the next one!

To my girly-pop, Alyse: You have become my personal hype-girl, and I am so glad we met through the Bookstagram world. You always have the kindest words to pull me out of my ruts and my imposter syndrome, and I want you to know how many times your words *really* saved my confidence in this story. I'm so happy to have you in my corner, and just know I will always be in yours.

To one of my best friends and fellow authors, CA Blooming: Courtney, I swear to the Gods—and I don't mean this lightly—this book *would not be possible* without your friendship. Little do you know, but the idea to create this multiverse came to me the morning before the first day of LTUE 2024, so when I met you and heard you *also* wanted to create a multiverse, I knew it was divine intervention that we crossed paths. Since then, you have been not just a sound board, but a problem solver. There were so many plot points I was stuck on or needed help working out, and you were always there to just validate what I was feeling or encourage me to take the damn challenge. I love you to death, and you know I gotchu.

To my husband, Jake: I will never forget the day I plotted this entire duology. I knew I needed to write the true mythology of the Gods of Aveesh, and I looked you dead in the eye in our living room and said out loud, "If there used to be more Gods, where did they go?" You shrugged and said, "Who said they went anywhere?" From there, I proceeded to research quantum physics for 2 whole hours at our dining room table. I showed you my notebook and my doodles and scribbles and you said with so much love that my mind was a scary place. I love you, and thank you for your support. I have never had anyone in my life encourage me to the extent you do and support me in the ways you have. *I believe you are half my soul.*

ABOUT THE AUTHOR

K.M. "Katie" Davidson is a fantasy romance author. Her authorial journey began as a young writer creating YA fantasy novels in composition notebooks and publishing them on Wattpad. After getting her Bachelor's in Creative Writing and Master's in English Literature—and abandoning 20+ book ideas—she finally sat down in 2023 and finished her debut novel, *Darkness Comes Again,* Book 1 of the Sirians Series.

Outside of writing and reading, Katie is a Content Marketer and pilates instructor. She loves dance parties with her husband and dog, hiking, traveling, entertaining conspiracy theories (none more than aliens), collecting more rocks, and buying old copies of books published over 100 years ago.

Follow K.M. Davidson on all social platforms @kmdavidsonbooks.